DOOMED

DOOMED

TRACY DEEBS

WALKER BOOKS
AN IMPRINT OF BLOOMSBURY
NEW YORK   LONDON   NEW DELHI   SYDNEY

First published in the United States of America in January 2013
by Walker Books for Young Readers, an imprint of Bloomsbury Publishing, Inc.
www.bloomsbury.com

For information about permission to reproduce selections from this book, write to
Permissions, Walker BFYR, 175 Fifth Avenue, New York, New York 10010

Library of Congress Cataloging-in-Publication Data
Deebs, Tracy.
Doomed / Tracy Deebs.
p.   cm.
Summary: Pandora Walker unwittingly unleashes cyber Armageddon on her seventeenth
birthday and must play a virtual reality game in order to save the world.
ISBN 978-0-8027-2373-4
[1. Virtual reality—Fiction. 2. Computer games—Fiction. 3. Science fiction.] I. Title.
PZ7.D358695Do 2012   [Fic]—dc23   2011050974

Book design by Amy Manzo Toth
Typeset by Westchester Book Composition
Printed in the U.S.A. by Thomson-Shore, Dexter, Michigan
2 4 6 8 10 9 7 5 3 1

All papers used by Bloomsbury Publishing, Inc., are natural, recyclable products
made from wood grown in well-managed forests. The manufacturing processes
conform to the environmental regulations of the country of origin.

Manufactured by Thomson-Shore, Dexter, MI (USA); RMA586LS790, November, 2012

To Noor, the light of my life

DOOMED

My seventeenth birthday starts with betrayal.
Lies.
Mayhem.
Fear.
It ends the same way,
but that's a different part of the story.
At least for now.

1

DAY ONE

MY ALARM GOES OFF AT SEVEN, just like always, and I spend a few minutes staring at the ceiling, blinking at the cool early-morning shadows and trying to get my tired brain to work. I was up late last night—insomnia strikes again—so it takes a little while, but eventually I remember what day it is.

November sixth.

When it registers, I drag myself out of bed and grab my laptop. After logging in, I skim through my e-mails. There's a happy-birthday message from Origins and another from my dentist, but the one I'm looking for—the one I've been hoping for—isn't there.

Big surprise.

I shove the computer away, tell myself it doesn't matter. But it does. I grab my cell phone before I can talk myself out of it, check the texts. Nothing there, either.

It's early, I remind myself. Only five in Alaska. But even

as I lie to myself, as I make excuses for her, I know what I'm doing. Of course she's awake. She hasn't slept past 4:00 a.m. in years.

It doesn't matter. She'll call. Or e-mail. Or text. Something. She always does . . . except when she doesn't.

Except when she forgets all about me.

The thought has me staring at the phone before I decide, what the hell? There's no law that says I can't call her first. I dial her number. Wait, breath held, as it rings. There's nothing wrong with jogging her memory, after all. She'll hear my voice, see my name on her caller ID and—

"Pandora."

"Hi, Mom."

"Is something wrong?" Her voice is cool, collected. Not unwelcoming by any means, but she could be talking to anyone.

"Everything's fine. Why?"

"I can't think why you're calling me this early. Don't you have school?"

"Yeah. In a few minutes." I hate how stilted I sound, how I can't relax. "I just—I wanted to say hi."

"Oh." Her annoyance crackles down the line. "Well, then, hello, Pandora."

Silence stretches between us, and as I sit there, waiting for her to remember, waiting for her to *hear* me, I wonder when I'm going to accept that I just don't register on her radar.

"If that's all you wanted, I need to go. I was dialing into a meeting when you called."

"Oh, right. Sorry." I clear my throat. "I guess I'll talk to you tonight?"

She sighs and I can almost see her shake her head. "Call me if you need me, but when you do, please have something to say."

And then she hangs up, leaving me alone. Again.

I try to shake it off. It's not like I expected things to be any different. So what if I'm not as important as her job? At least I get to do whatever I want while she's off defending Big Oil as they do their best to destroy the planet. She's a corporate lawyer for one of the largest oil companies in the world, and right now she's in Alaska, negotiating drilling rights that will strip away more of our natural wilderness.

Last month she was in South America; the month before that, Dubai. And the month before that . . . I don't even remember. I have trouble keeping up.

It doesn't matter, I tell myself again. I'll go to school, hang out with Emily and Jules. Maybe after class we'll hit Barton Creek Mall and shop till we drop. I'll buy something fabulous . . . on my mom's card, of course. Not that she'll care, or even notice.

In fact, there's this great new body scrub I've been wanting to try out . . . I open my computer again to print out my birthday coupon from Origins. Except this time when I pull up my e-mail account, there's another message there. One that reads *Happy Birthday* in the subject line. Only it's not from my mom or any of my friends.

It's from Mitchell Walker.

From my *father*.

For long seconds, I don't move. Don't breathe. Which is ridiculous, I know, but I can't help it. My dad's been the bogeyman my mom has used to scare me for too long. There's no way I can be blasé about an e-mail from him, even if it is just birthday wishes.

A few minutes pass as I stare at it, wondering what I'm supposed to do now. Should I open it? Delete it? Just ignore it until my mother gets home at the end of next week?

I roll the mouse over it, once, twice, but every time I get ready to click on this first piece of correspondence I've received from my father in a decade, my mom's voice from long ago echoes in my head: "Your father is a very bad man, and I don't want you to have anything to do with him. If he calls you, hang up on him. If he comes to the door, don't answer it. If he sends you a letter, don't read it. Promise me, Pandora."

I'd promised her—what else could I do when she sounded so distraught? I'd only been about seven at the time, and a letter from my father had set her off. She's made me renew that same promise numerous times in the last ten years, and I always have, because doing anything else would make the glazed, frazzled look in her eyes turn downright nuts.

And now here he is, in my e-mail, with birthday greetings. The very same greetings that she forgot.

She doesn't have to know, a voice whispers in the back of my head. I won't have to tell her if all it's going to do is upset her. I wouldn't even have to lie—it's not like she bothers to ask what's up with me these days. I could just read the e-mail and then delete it, and she'd never have to find out. Besides, shouldn't I get to have at least one of my parents acknowledge my birthday?

I tell myself not to do it as all of my mother's warnings coalesce in my head at once. But it doesn't matter—it's already too late. My name isn't Pandora for nothing, and this, this is a letter from my father, from the man I've been curious about for as long as I can remember. There's no way I'm *not* going to see what he has to say.

I open the e-mail, skim the letter I find there. It's relatively short considering it's the only e-mail he's ever sent me, but it has excitement thrumming through me anyway. I settle back and read it again, this time paying close attention to the details:

Dear Pandora,

I know it must seem strange to hear from me after all this time, but I wanted to wish you a happy seventeenth birthday. I've tried on numerous occasions through the years to get in touch with you—have sent cards, presents, letters on your birthdays—but they've all come back unopened. I suppose I should take the hint, but I couldn't give up without trying at least once more to contact you.

I want you to know that not a day goes by that I don't think about you and wonder how you're doing. What you're learning. What your friends are like. What instrument you play or if you prefer sports to music. It's not much to go on after ten years of absence, but please know that you've always been in my heart and on my mind.

I hope that you're doing well and that you're happy. I like to think of you the way you were the last time I saw you—hanging upside down from your jungle gym, swinging back and forth, laughing the whole time. I didn't want to leave that night, but your mother insisted. And she was right, though it pains me to admit it even now.

I know I have no right to ask this of you, and if you don't want to know, delete this e-mail and you'll never hear from me again. But for years I've hoped to tell you my side of the story. To fill you in on everything you don't know about me. So I've typed up all the letters I've sent on your birthdays over the years, including for this one, your seventeenth.

In these letters are the answers to any question I could imagine you asking. About me. About yourself. About your mother and her relationship with me. About why we've chosen to live our lives so far apart. If you want to know these things, click on the link I've included. If you don't, ignore it and I promise I'll never contact you again.

Take care, sweetheart, and know that no matter what route you take, I will understand. And love you anyway.

Your father,
Mitchell

I sit on my bed for a long time, trying to absorb everything he's said. And everything he hasn't.

All the answers to my questions—and I have hundreds of them—are at the end of this link. All I have to do is click on it and I'll know, finally, why he walked away from me and my mother. And why he's never come back.

Even as I tell myself that the reason doesn't matter, that

it's too late and I don't care anymore, my hand hovers over the mouse. Because the truth is, I *do* care, even after all this time. I couldn't hold off on opening my birthday greetings from Origins—is there any way I can hold off on opening *this*?

Without giving myself time to think about it, afraid if I do I'll change my mind, I click on the link. And wait for the words that could change my life forever.

2

THE WORDS DON'T APPEAR. At least not at first. Instead, the link takes me to a blog, one that reads, *Happy Birthday, Pandora,* in the header. The home page is divided into three columns, two narrow ones along the sides and a wide one in the center. The center one contains the same letter as the e-mail, while the side columns contain pictures of the two of us.

Pictures I never even knew existed.

Pictures I've asked my mother about numerous times, only to be told that there were none. That my dad didn't like cameras.

Yet here they are, twelve of them. More proof that my mom has been lying to me all along.

I look back at the message, kind of awed that my dad— whom I haven't seen in ten years—did something like this. I mean, I know it's not a big deal to set up a blog these days, anyone can do it, but still. It takes time and I'm amazed he made the effort.

The pictures are small, so I click on the first one, and it explodes onto the screen. I'm a toddler, two or so, and my dad is holding me. We're standing in front of a statue of Sam Houston, grinning wildly. I download the picture, save it. There's another link below the photo, and when I click on it, it leads me to another letter, one that was written by him when I was a baby. He talks about what it felt like to hold me in his arms for the first time, what it felt like the first time I smiled at him. It's a little corny, sure, but I don't care.

It's too nice to hear that I was wanted. That *someone* loved me. It's been years since my mom has done or said anything that made me think that might once have been the case.

I click on the second picture, save it, then follow the link. Do the same for the third and the fourth. I don't know how to describe what I'm feeling as I look at each of the photos and read the words my father has posted for me. It's a strange numbness mixed with exhilaration—sort of what it feels like to be on a Tilt-A-Whirl just as the ride begins to spin.

My cell phone rings and I almost ignore it—what I'm doing is so much more interesting than anything a caller might have to say. But it's Jules's ring, and I know she'll be mad if I ignore her. I've been picking her up for the past two weeks, ever since her car got totaled.

I dive for the phone. "Jules?"

"How far away are you? We're going to be late. You don't want a detention on your birthday!"

Shit, shit, shit. I glance at the clock. That can't be right—how is it eight thirty already?

"I know, I know. I'm on the way out the door," I tell her, fingers mentally crossed.

"You mean you're not even in the car yet?" she screeches.

"I am. I swear, I am." I hang up the phone, then dive for the jeans I left discarded on the floor last night. I yank them on before running into the bathroom and doing the world's fastest teeth brush and face wash. And then I'm heading for the bedroom door—finger-combing my hair as I go.

Except, as I'm walking out, my eyes fall on my computer. I can't help it, even if it's going to make me later than I already am. I run over and upload all the photos to my local Walgreens account superfast, so I can pick them up after school. It may sound lame, but I want something tangible to prove that these photos exist. To prove that my father really does care about me.

I want to hold them in my hand.

Those five minutes cost me, though, and Jules and I end up being tardy. We split off at the school's front door, Jules running to her government class and me heading at a more sedate pace to AP English. Which was my big mistake, because while Mr. March isn't a crazy man about punctuality—at least not like some of the teachers at Westlake High—he is big on accepting the consequences of your actions.

And in this case those consequences are painful, because when I hit the door about five minutes late, he's already formed groups to analyze scenes. And instead of letting me go to my regular group, made up of a bunch of my drama and Amnesty International friends, I get stuck with the other students who've had the misfortune of cruising in after the bell today.

My new group consists of me; head cheerleader Tara

McKinney (who wears about an inch of makeup every day and drives a Barbie-pink Hummer—Barbie pink!—need I say more?); Zane Connolly (the biggest nerd in the school, which is fine, except he has a crush on Tara and it's painful to watch him try to get her attention); and the two new guys, Theo Jamison and Eli Sanders, who have been here about two weeks. I don't know much more about them than what the school gossip mill says: they're stepbrothers, they seem to hate each other, and they're seriously hot, though in totally different ways.

Theo is all dark and broody and gorgeous, despite dressing like a total prep. Piercing blue eyes partially covered by his shaggy black hair, superbroad shoulders beneath a navy-striped button-down dress shirt, and a really good face complete with strong jaw, full lips, and razor-sharp cheekbones. Plus he's smart enough to be in all AP classes. Too bad I've never once seen him smile.

Eli, on the other hand, is a total charmer. Bright green eyes, carefully styled blond hair, his own set of broad shoulders, and a killer smile that he uses to great advantage. Not to mention that he has awesome taste in music, if the band T-shirts he usually wears are to be believed.

In the time they've been here, they've all but revolutionized Westlake's social scene. Eli's slid right into the spot of star basketball player and top dog to the popular crowd (big surprise), and though Theo has so far resisted the Dark Side, it hasn't kept him from developing his own very large bunch of groupies. Watching girls trail them down the halls would be funny if it weren't so embarrassing. I've kept my distance on purpose—who wants to be confused with one of the adoring horde—and I don't appreciate having to change that now.

Especially when I look around and realize that every girl in the classroom is shooting hostile looks toward Tara and me. Which is ridiculous, since I didn't ask to be put in this group. Plus, I look like hell—it's not like any of them could consider me a threat. Yesterday's jeans, the vintage but wrinkled Hendrix tank top I slept in last night, and hair that looks as if I stuck my finger in an electric socket. To say that I'm not at my best today would be woefully understating the problem.

Still, as we slide our desks together I realize Eli's looking straight at me. He smiles, and I melt a little at the sight of the dimple in his right cheek, even as I tell myself to get a grip. But it's hard. I'm a sucker for a dimple and always have been.

Being with them makes reading Shakespeare a million times more difficult, especially when I end up playing Desdemona. I'm totally the wrong person to cast as Desdemona. I don't have an innocent bone in my body. Nor do I exactly look like your typical, wide-eyed ingenue.

Instead of the long blond hair and big blue eyes of most Desdemona actresses—which Tara possesses, incidentally— I've got short, spiky red hair with violet streaks in the front. Plus, I've got muddy brown eyes and I'm also close to six feet tall, a height that doesn't exactly scream cute, cuddly, and in need of protection. Thank God.

But I can't argue, especially when everyone else seems okay with their parts.

"So you're good with playing Iago then?" I finally ask Eli, hoping he'll disagree so I can, too.

He grins cockily. "I'd rather play Othello." I'm not sure if his enthusiasm is good or bad, seeing as how Othello's main role in this scene is to *kill* me. But I'll take it, at least until he says, "Then again, that does seem like a role for Theo. Since Othello is completely nuts by the time this scene rolls around."

Theo looks up, and the air around us crackles with hostility. An awkward silence descends, one that no one—especially not Theo or Eli—seems inclined to break. Which is a problem, since Mr. March is already making the rounds and we're directly in his sights.

"Are we going to spend the whole class talking, or are we going to do this thing?" Theo finally demands. His book hits the desk with an annoyed *thump*, and when I look at him, his scowl is blacker than ever.

Talk about typecasting.

No one else says anything—either not brave or not stupid enough to push Theo—so the next few minutes pass in silence as we read the scene to ourselves. And after I read for a while, I realize I'm not nearly as icked out by the story—or the thought of playing Desdemona—as I expected I'd be. After all, I might not have finished the play, but I already know how it ends: with my murder, my friend's untimely demise, a bunch of innocent people's deaths, Othello's suicide, and Iago's torture. Shakespeare definitely knew how to make a statement.

But when I get to the part where Othello accuses Desdemona of infidelity—because he believes his lying-sack-of-shit best friend—it's my turn to slam my book down on the desk. "What's wrong with Desdemona, anyway? Why doesn't she run away from Othello toward the end? She can't miss the fact that he's losing it."

"She loves him, Pandora," Mr. March says as he walks by. "She doesn't want to leave him."

"Even though it's obvious the man is completely out of his mind? I mean, seriously, I don't care how hot the guy is. He's got 'crazy stalker husband with a gun' written all over him." In my mind, sociopathic behavior trumps love and attraction any day. Or at least it *should*.

"It's a sword, actually, and he doesn't use it on her," Theo tells me as Mr. March heads on to the next group, who are already standing up, rehearsing.

"So what does he do? How does he kill her?" I turn to Theo impatiently, though the truth is, I'm a little embarrassed that he now knows I haven't finished the play. But since the test on *Othello* isn't until next week, finishing it hasn't been high on my priority list.

Theo shifts a little, until he's so close to me that I can smell the mintiness of his mouthwash and a warm, fresh scent that is curiously inviting. It's a combination of the forest near my old house—all piney and delicious—and the lemon tree in my backyard.

His midnight-blue eyes are laser focused as he watches me, and I squirm despite myself. But I still take his hand, let him pull me to my feet. He's even taller than I thought, and now that I'm standing next to him I feel completely overshadowed. Completely overwhelmed.

"He's tormented, Pandora. Nearly insane with his love for her and the idea that she's betrayed him. That he isn't enough for her. That she wants another man."

His hands come up to cup my face, and my heart starts beating so fast that I can barely hear Eli over the thunder of it when he says, "Knock it off, Theo."

We both ignore him.

"Why does . . ." My voice breaks. "Why does Othello ask her if he won't believe what she says?"

"He has to ask. He wants to believe her. But then he can't, when his most trusted friend's words are in his head, telling him that she's been with Cassio." He slides his palms down until they're ringing my throat. They're a little rough as they scrape against my collarbone. Shivers slide up my spine. "She's crying and pleading with him, and she looks so beautiful, sounds so innocent, that it makes him even crazier. Because in the back of his head is Iago, convincing him that she betrayed him. Providing proof that she gave his gift to another man as a token of her affection."

I can't breathe, fear and panic and fascination welling up inside me as I stare at this guy who suddenly looks as intense as I imagine the real Othello would. The thought flashes through my head that Eli might be right, that Theo might be a few cards short of a full deck. But even as every instinct I have tells me to get away, I don't move. It's insane, but I'm trapped by the promise in his eyes as much as by his hands around my throat.

Maybe I *was* too hard on poor Desdemona.

And then he begins to squeeze and my too-fast heart nearly explodes.

"Stop it." I shove him away from me, stumble backward, and though his fingers had barely tightened on my neck—just enough to be felt but certainly nowhere near hard enough to hurt—I can feel the imprint of each one.

"What's *wrong* with you?" I demand.

"No, that's perfect!" Mr. March exclaims from his spot across the room. "That's exactly the right vibe for the scene. Othello is desperate. He's crazed, furious, a wounded animal, and Desdemona knows it, but she loves him so much that she can't believe he'd ever hurt her. Even as he strangles her, she can't believe it. She thinks he'll stop."

The bell rings, thank God, and I shove my stuff into my backpack and head for the door, not even bothering to turn my desk around. I can't remember the last time I felt this idiotic and have no idea how I'm going to face Theo later today in AP Government.

Behind me I hear Eli call my name, but I don't turn around. I can't. I'm afraid Theo will be standing there, watching me, and I can't get the sensation of his hands around my neck out of my head, off my skin. I swear I can still feel them there, warm and slightly calloused.

It's only ten o'clock, but already nothing about this birthday is turning out like I thought it would. Perhaps I should take that as a warning . . .

3

THE REST OF THE DAY passes in kind of a blur . . . and
with no more close-to-homicidal incidents, thank God.
Class, friends, Amnesty International meeting at lunch, more
class, an Eco Club meeting after school, and then sweet,
sweet freedom. Jules gets a ride home from her boyfriend,
so Emily and I hit the parking lot five minutes after the
meeting ends.

"I can't believe you want to stay home on your birthday,"
she complains as we climb into the gas-guzzling behemoth
that is my car. My mother bought it for me after I crashed
my first car and nearly died. It completely wasn't my fault—
some idiot ran a red light and plowed straight into me—but
I think the fact that she had to come home from DC early to
take care of me stressed her out enough that she bought me
a car that puts about a thousand tons of steel all around me.
Either that or she gets a bonus at work for actually owning
a car with the worst gas mileage on the planet.

"So, what *do* you want to do for your birthday tonight?" Emily asks as we head out of the parking lot.

"Sit on the couch and gorge on ice cream?"

"Well, obviously." I can almost hear the eye-roll. "I mean, besides that."

"Not much." I start to tell her about the e-mail from my dad, and the blog he's set up for me, but I stop at the last second. It's still too new, too personal, to share with anyone, even my best friend. Especially since I'm not even sure how I feel about the whole thing yet. "Maybe go out to dinner, if you want."

"Of course I want. But I'm talking about more than pizza at Little Nicky's. You only turn seventeen once. We should go out, party!"

"I like Little Nicky's."

"So not the point."

I bite back a grin—even after all these years, she's just too easy. "I thought we were planning on doing plenty of partying with Jules, Chase, and Steven tomorrow."

That distracts her, as I knew it would. You don't spend most of your life being someone's best friend without knowing what buttons to push, or not push, as the case might be.

"The Black Keys concert is going to be awesome. I can't wait." She pauses. "Did you ask Theo and Eli if they want the extra tickets, like we talked about yesterday?"

"What? No!" I can feel heat crawling up my cheeks at just the mention of their names. "*You* talked about that, not me. Why would I *do* that, anyway?"

"Because I don't have any classes with them, so I can't

ask? I've been trying to figure out a way to meet them for two weeks. I mean, they're gorgeous and smart and way taller than you—which, you have to admit, is rare. Add in the fact that you guys are doing a scene together, inviting them to go out in a group of friends seems pretty normal to me."

I glance at her incredulously. "Yeah, well, obviously you missed the part of our lunch conversation where I told you Theo tried to *kill* me in English today. That's not the kind of friend I want or need."

"Give me a break. You don't even have a mark." She pulls on my necklace to make the point.

"Are you listening to yourself? You act like it's normal for a guy I barely know to wrap his hands around my throat. And squeeze."

"It is normal if he was *acting*."

I crumple up a napkin from the front console and throw it at her. "Your definition of normal is highly suspect. Besides, I'm not so crazy that I'd ask out possibly *the* hottest and most homicidal guy in school. Besides, have you seen the way he dresses? So not my type."

"Hey, he's rocking the Harvard vibe. Nothing wrong with that."

"Yeah, well, my mom rocked that same Harvard vibe, and see how well she turned out."

"Hmm, good point. So maybe you should go for Eli and I'll go for Theo."

"Do you seriously have nothing better to do than sit around plotting out my love life?" I demand.

"Someone has to." Emily reaches over to hug me as we

stop in front of her house. "Someday you're going to regret all the things you didn't do," she says as she pulls something out of her bag and thrusts it at me.

I glance down at it. It's wrapped in newspaper and has a kick-ass black-and-red bow across the top that's nearly as big as the gift itself. "Open it later," she says as she climbs out of the car.

"Why?"

"I don't know." She shrugs. "Because presents go better with cake? I'll see you tonight at seven, okay?"

"I'll be there." I wave as she turns to walk away.

And then I'm pulling into traffic, cruising down the winding, hilly road that surrounds Austin's Lake Travis and leads to Walgreens and my house. Every minute or so, I glance at the package Emily gave me, and I decide that it's later, even if there's not a chocolate crumb in sight.

I can't help it. From the time I was a toddler, I've never been able to stand not knowing the answer to something. Whether it's a question at school or how something works or what was in the presents my dad used to hide for me—it doesn't matter. My curiosity drives me crazy until I feel like I'll die if I don't find the answer.

For a second it flits through my mind that that's the reason my dad sent me the e-mail. Because he remembers my Christmas-present scavenger hunts as a kid and knew I wouldn't be able to resist opening the link. Not that it matters, I guess. But still, I wonder if he knows me that well. If he still cares enough to remember. He was the one who insisted on naming me Pandora, after all.

The second I pull into the parking lot at Walgreens, I'm

ripping into Emily's present. I grin when I see what she got me, and I can't stop the little bubble of excitement that works its way through me. A first-issue copy of Stone Temple Pilots CD *Core*, autographed by the entire band. Could she have picked a more perfect gift? I've been collecting first-issue CDs for years, and the fact that it's signed makes it even better.

I grab my phone, text her a thank-you. It takes a minute or so to go through, which is odd, but when she texts me right back, I forget all about it. I smile when I see her message:

> I knew u couldn't wt. It's a sickness, Pandora. Srsly.
> Get help now. LOL.

I run into Walgreens and pay for the photos I ordered this morning, then take them out and look at them right there in the store. There are only twelve, but in that moment they feel more precious to me than anything else I own—even my new CD.

I drive home slowly, thinking about them. Thinking about my dad and the website he set up for me. Anxious to check it again, I head up to my room as soon as I get home. I didn't have a chance to read all of my dad's messages this morning, and I want to see what the others say. Except when I type in the address of the blog, nothing comes up. I try again—still nothing—and then finally go searching for the e-mail my dad sent me. I must be remembering the address wrong.

But the e-mail is gone, too. Which isn't possible. I mean, I was in a hurry this morning, but I would know if I'd deleted it, wouldn't I? Still, I check the trash folder, just in case. Nothing's there. Then I check the spam folder, but the only things there are ads for cheap prescription medicine and cheaper mortgages.

I'm totally bummed now, and if I didn't have the twelve pictures I might have thought I imagined the whole thing. But I *do* have them, so I know I'm not crazy. It happened.

I just don't know what occurred afterward. Was I really in such a big hurry that I trashed the only e-mail I've ever gotten from my dad? What a moron.

Frustrated and pissed off at myself, I insert the *Core* CD into my laptop and lie across the bed. My stomach growls and I think about going back down to the kitchen and grabbing something to eat, but I'm too annoyed. Instead, I stare at the ceiling, studying the hundreds of CD covers I have tacked up there and contemplating my father's letters to me while "Wicked Garden" plays in the background.

If I hadn't been stupid enough to erase the e-mail, and if the website hadn't disappeared off the face of the earth, would I have written back to him? And if I did, what would I say?

The thing is, I don't know the answer to either of those questions. His letters were nice and so are the pictures. But they're not much to hang a relationship on, especially since I haven't seen him in ten years.

Eventually my hunger gets the best of me, so I grab my laptop and cruise down to the kitchen. On the way, I flick on the television and start streaming the first season of *Supernatural*, right where I left off, at episode 4, "Phantom Traveler." Then I head to the pantry and pour myself a bowl of cereal. Crunch Berries, of course. Between mouthfuls, I open my laptop and boot it up.

I play around for a while—Facebook stuff, checking out the Cliffs Notes for *Othello*, looking for a new pair of boots because my old ones are pretty much trashed. By then it's after five thirty and my mom still hasn't called. I check my phone to see if I missed a text from her—sometimes reception can be spotty in the house—but there's nothing.

I start my calculus homework, but it's not due until Friday, so eventually I give up on it. Being productive is highly overrated. Besides, I *so* shouldn't have to do advanced math on my birthday.

Finally, I do what I've wanted to do for the last forty-five minutes. I log on to Pandora's Box. Usually I play it on my iPad, but I'm too lazy to go up to my room and get it right now. Besides, it works fine on my laptop, even if the colors aren't quite as cool.

I'm kind of excited about playing again—when I left off yesterday, I had just hit level twenty-seven. I want to get through it quickly and find the alternate-reality, or AR, gate that will transport me to the next level, because Jules says twenty-eight is the best so far.

Except instead of dropping me off in the middle of the barren wasteland that was once New York City, the game flashes a new message across the screen:

Happy Seventeenth Birthday, Pandora!

What the . . . ?
I stare at the screen, confused. How is it possible that

the game knows my birthday—and my name? My user name is totally unconnected to my real name. And yet, there it is, staring at me in a very distinct yellow font. *My* name.

I think back to when I first jumped on the Pandora's Box bandwagon, months ago. I'd resisted for a long time—because of the name thing—but when I finally gave in I remember having to register, just like with any MMO. Had they asked for my birthdate? I vaguely remember that they had, and it calms me down a little. Still, I make a mental note to ask Jules if she got the same greeting four weeks ago on *her* birthday. The last thing I need is some weird pervert guy hacking my account . . .

I click to get to the new screen and the birthday message slowly fades, only to be replaced by the words:

You've reached the point of no return.
Welcome to the real Pandora's Box.

Underneath is a giant, flashing number 10 in bright red, just to make sure you don't miss it. I try to click on it but nothing happens. Try to click on the message, but no luck there, either. Then the letters dissolve only to re-form with a new message:

Total annihilation in 10, 9, 8, 7, 6, 5, 4, 3, 2, 1 days.

The 1 is huge, takes over the entire screen for a brief second before morphing into a graphic of the earth. Seconds later, the world blows up, little pieces streaming across the screen like fireworks. Then everything fades to black. Nothing.

I click on the screen, hit Return, Escape, all those things they teach you to do when your computer does something weird. But nothing happens, and I have to admit I'm a little freaked out. It's stupid, I know. Pandora's Box is just a game. And yet . . . and yet, I can't help viewing this new bizarre message as some kind of threat.

A weird feeling hits me, and I reach for my cell phone, dial Jules. Wait impatiently, but it never starts to ring. I pull it away from my ear, check the reception. No bars. Of course not. Why is it so difficult to get decent coverage out here? I live near the lake, not in the middle of the wilds of frickin' Africa.

Tossing my cell down on the table, I cross the kitchen. Reach for the cordless phone I almost never use anymore, and dial Jules's number: 555-3782.

Nothing happens.

What. The. Hell?

I hang up and try again: 5-5-5-3-7-8-2. Put the phone to my ear and wait even more impatiently. Still nothing. I click the Off button again, then hit Talk. Hold the stupid thing to my ear. There's no dial tone. Nothing. Just the strange, eerie silence of a dead line.

4

THE EERIE FEELING IS BACK, along with an increasing uneasiness that has me glancing across the room at my computer and the words that have just started scrawling across it again. "Total annihilation in 10 days." The 10 flashes.

I wait for the countdown, for the earth to blow up again, but nothing happens and I shake myself out of it. I can't believe I'm letting a video game weird me out. Talk about ridiculous. Especially since the loss of service isn't all that unusual out here.

Like I said before, I live by the lake, which has a lot of advantages—including the dock and boat right at the bottom of our property. But one of the disadvantages is that a lot of the time, coverage out here leaves something to be desired. If there's a storm, or even just a really windy day, we lose the phone and sometimes even electricity.

I glance outside. The sky is growing dark, but without a cloud in sight. And the trees are barely moving. Still, that doesn't mean anything. I'll give whoever's in charge of this kind of thing at the phone company a few minutes to figure it out and then try again. No big deal.

But just then, the fan on my laptop starts running full speed. The screen blinks off and on. It whirrs some more and then does the same thing again and again. I rush over, try to shut it down, but it won't do anything. Won't budge from Pandora's Box. I try to force the game closed, but it doesn't work. Nothing does, and I'm starting to get a little nervous.

What is going *on?*

I head for the stairs, for my mom's office, with some half-formed plan of checking out her computer, making sure it's okay. I'm halfway up before I register the unnatural silence in the house. Waste of energy or not, I always have something going, always have some noise around me. It helps me feel less alone. In this case, I know I turned on the TV as soon as I got downstairs, started streaming *Supernatural.*

But the TV isn't streaming anything—instead, there's just the bright blue AT&T U-Verse screen that usually comes up whenever I first turn on the TV.

Are you kidding me? Totally frustrated, I go back down the stairs. I push a few buttons, but nothing happens. No streaming. No regular TV channels. Nothing. The TV signal's out, too. Terrific. Emily's going to love that when she comes here tonight.

At that moment, the light over the stairs flickers off, on, off, on, off, on again.

I hate the dark and I panic, am out the front door before my brain even registers leaving as an option. Either the utility companies are having the mother of all bad days or the house is suddenly possessed. Whichever it is, I'm done trying to figure it out.

I pause at the end of my driveway, try to decide what to do. I'm being stupid, I know I am, yet I can't bring myself to go back inside. Maybe I should check with the neighbors, see if they're having the same problems I am. If they are, then it's no big deal. I can go back home and get ready for the birthday dinner that suddenly feels like it's a million miles off.

And if they're not having the same problems? a little voice whispers in the back of my head. *What then?*

I ignore it, shove it back down where it came from. So *not* going to deal with that eventuality right now.

Instead, I try to figure out which neighbors to crash in on. To my right are the Hensons, but they're both doctors and usually aren't home until eight or nine. To my left are the new neighbors, the ones who moved in a couple of weeks ago. I haven't even met them yet.

After a quick mental debate, I turn left, praying the new people are home and that they don't mind answering the door to strangers. Especially strangers who are having a really, really weird day and look a little crazed because of it.

By the time I get to their front door, about five minutes have passed even though I came close to running the whole way. That's because out here houses are a lot farther apart than in your regular suburban neighborhood. Most of the homeowners—especially the celebrities looking for a retreat from Hollywood and the crazed paparazzi that stalk them—are *very* big on privacy.

I ring the doorbell, and when no one answers in the first five seconds, I start pounding on the door. Please, God, let someone be home. I don't want to go back to my house alone right now.

After another minute, the door flies open, and I look up, up, up . . . and straight into Theo's eyes. I'm not sure which one of us is more surprised. *He's* my new neighbor? But how has he lived here two weeks without me seeing him? Or Eli? We go to the same school, have the same schedule. Surely I would have noticed.

But I didn't, and neither did he, it seems, as he looks as shocked as I feel. "Pandora?" he asks incredulously. "What are *you* doing here?"

He doesn't exactly sound happy to see me, a feeling that I assure myself is totally mutual. Still, when I try to tell him why I'm banging on his door like a crazy woman, nothing comes out. It's like the connection between my brain and my tongue has suddenly stopped working, and all I can do is stutter. "I—I—"

"Are you here for Eli?" His face changes as he asks the question, settles back into the cold, emotionless lines I'm used to seeing.

"No. I'm . . . I . . . It's just . . ." I cough a little, rub my neck as I can't help remembering what it felt like to have his hands wrapped around my throat. The memory irritates me even as it jump-starts my brain and I blurt out, "Is your phone working?"

"My phone?" Blankness changes to puzzlement, then concern. "Are you okay? Did you have an accident?" This time, when he looks me over, I can tell he's checking me for damage, looking to see if my bizarre behavior is the result of hitting my head too hard.

"No, no, I'm fine." I point back toward my house. "I live next door and I'm having some weird problems with my phone and utilities. I was wondering if you were having the same issues over here."

"Next door?" he asks.

"Yeah. Small world, right?"

"Come on in." He opens the door a little wider, waves me inside.

I cross the threshold but do my best to keep out of reach. No use tempting fate or anything. A smirk flits across Theo's face, as if he can tell what I'm thinking. Then, almost before I can register it, it's gone.

"So, what kind of problems are you having?"

The question jerks me back to attention and I tell him.

He frowns. "No, I think everything's good here." He walks into the kitchen, gesturing for me to follow him. Picks up his landline, listens. "We've got a dial tone."

"Oh."

"You don't have to sound so disappointed."

"I'm not." I turn all my attention to the phone in his hand, try to ignore how nervous I am around him. "I was just hoping the whole area had been hit by something. Then people would be trying to fix it, and I wouldn't have to . . ." Wouldn't have to what? Worry that my house has been taken over by demons? It sounds so stupid in my head, I can't imagine saying it out loud.

"Wait around for a repairman?" He finishes my sentence.

And since his interpretation sounds so much better—so much saner—than mine, I go with it.

"Exactly. A repairman."

"You can call from here if you want." He sits down in front of the computer resting on a small desk in the corner of the kitchen. "Do you need a number?"

"Um, yeah. AT&T."

He nods, types the info into Google. I glance at the bulletin board above the computer and blink a little at the pictures there. Each one shows a small airplane in a different stage of construction, from beginning to end. Theo's smiling in all of them, his face lit up with so much joy and satisfaction that I almost don't recognize him. In each he's standing next to a very tall man who bears a striking resemblance to him. His father?

I start to ask what it was like to actually build an airplane, but when I glance down at him—and the screen he's scrolling through looking for the customer service line— the computer blinks off. Then on. Then off again. I freeze, because it's almost the exact same thing my laptop did when everything in my house went nuts. From upstairs, someone calls, "Hey, is the Internet down?" And that's when it hits me. If Theo's home, Eli probably is, too.

I run a self-conscious hand through my hair, glance down at my shirt and jeans to make sure I'm presentable. When I look up again, I realize Theo is staring at me. He saw my whole little primping routine, subtle as it was. And even worse, he knows who it was for.

Ugh. I glance at the ceiling, wonder what the hell I've

done to piss off the universe so completely. Because I have to say, this is the Worst. Birthday. Ever.

I brace myself for a snide comment or twelve, but he doesn't say anything about my idiot behavior. Instead he starts to reboot the computer, and I spring into action.

"Wait! Don't do that!"

"What's wrong?" he asks impatiently, and I'm not sure what to say. How to explain what I'm thinking—particularly when I'm not even sure what's going through my head. I only know that this whole thing is strange. Really, really strange.

Is it possible that some kind of virus attacked my house and is now spreading to my neighbors'? Maybe it's working its way down the block, one house at a time . . . Just thinking it sounds insane, but what other explanation can there be? Laptop? TV? Phone? Internet? Electricity? Everything acting funky at once. I mean, I'm no computer expert, but everything I've ever heard says that isn't possible—at least not without a major storm or disaster.

My gut, however, says that's exactly what's happening. I just don't know how, especially since I have a Mac and I've always been told they don't get viruses.

"I logged on to Pandora's Box and everything went to hell," Eli yells down.

At first Theo doesn't answer, just scowls as he restarts the computer despite my warning. Only then does he call up the stairs, "Hey, come down here. Your little friend just showed up."

I bristle at the words and the tone he says them in. Like I'm some kid and he's the grown-up I'm bugging. It's annoying and I start to snap at him, but I glance at the stairs just in time to see a pair of faded jeans and huge bare feet take the last few stairs in one giant step.

Eli has arrived. Big and strong and a lot more rumpled than he was during class this morning. The large kitchen suddenly feels stifling with both of them in such close proximity. I back up, try to get a little more breathing room. I mean, seriously, has the world been invaded by giants and I just didn't get the memo?

Eli spots me before I move more than a few inches. "Oh, hey, Pandora. What are you doing here?"

"I didn't know you guys moved in," I blurt out, wanting to make sure he knows I'm not stalking him.

"Yeah. We moved in a couple of weeks ago, the same time Theo and I started school."

Now they're both looking at me, which makes me realize that I need to say something else. I clear my throat, try not to choke on my own spit—which, incidentally, is not as easy as it sounds.

I turn to Theo. "No Internet?" It's not brilliant, but it's the best I can manage.

"I don't know. The computer won't even restart." He frowns at Eli. "What did you do this time?"

"Nothing." Eli's face is closed, his response surprisingly defensive. But there's that whole undercurrent again, the one from earlier in class. It doesn't feel any better this time around. "I told you, I logged on to Pandora's Box and the whole thing just wigged out—the TV, my PlayStation. Everything."

"Pandora's Box?" I ask. "I logged on to Pandora's Box a little while ago."

"Oh." Eli looks a little puzzled. "That's cool, I guess."

Theo gets the connection right away. "You think there's some kind of virus in the game?"

"I don't know. I mean, nothing else makes sense." I nod to the blank computer screen. "I got some weird message I'd never seen before and then everything went nuts."

"What was the message?"

"You've reached the point of no return. Welcome to the real Pandora's Box." It's Eli who answers, and I glance at him, startled. He smiles at me, dimple flashing, and I duck my head.

"What the hell does that mean?" Theo demands, yanking me back to our present dilemma.

"I don't know. Then it just started with this strange countdown," I tell him.

"To what?"

"Total annihilation." Eli and I answer at the same time.

"Total annihilation?" Now it's Theo who sounds like a parrot.

"Yep."

He stares at me blankly for a moment, before rubbing his hands over his face and then up through his hair—the universal gesture for stressed out and a little pissed off. I know, because I was doing the same thing not very long ago.

"Okay," he says after a minute. "Let's think about this rationally. Did you have landline phone service before you logged on to Pandora's Box?"

"I don't know. I mean, I didn't check it or anything until after my cell phone stopped working, too."

"Your cell phone isn't working, either?" Now he's completely incredulous. But still, he and Eli reach into their pockets at the same time, check their own phones. From the looks on their faces, I'm guessing their luck is about as good as mine is today. "That's not possible." Theo turns his phone off and then back on again, frustration stamped into every line of his body.

"That's what I said, but it's happening—"

"No, I mean, really. It's not possible. They run on totally different networks. There's no way your landline and cell phone can be infected from the same virus—at least not this quickly. And not if it started from an MMO you were playing online."

I don't say anything, but then I don't have to. Because it's glaringly obvious that, whether or not it makes sense, it appears that's exactly what has happened.

The million-dollar question is, what do we do now?

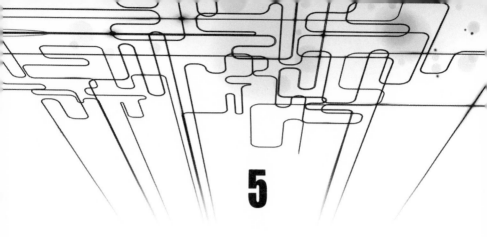

5

AT THAT EXACT MOMENT—as if in answer to my silent query—the computer on the desk blinks back to life. We all watch, mouths open and eyes wide, as a series of bright red words scroll across the screen:

You've reached the point of no return.
Welcome to the real Pandora's Box.

"What. The. Hell?" This time it's Eli who asks what all three of us are thinking.

Theo reaches for the mouse, tries to exit the game. It won't let him close, however, won't let him do anything, no matter that he tries to force shutdown using about five different ways I never even knew existed.

Instead, the same numbers I saw at my house—the countdown from 10 to 1—flash one after the other. It's even creepier watching it over here, when I know that Theo never logged on to Pandora's Box from this computer to begin with. Plus, the fact that it's not just me, that it's happening to them, too, makes it all seem more real. Less about the demon possession I originally feared and more about some kind of technological meltdown.

I think I'd almost prefer the demons.

Finally, Theo reaches over and unplugs the computer from the wall. The screen goes blank, of course, and we all breathe huge sighs of relief. I know it sounds stupid, but for a minute I was really beginning to believe that there was no way to turn the thing off. That somehow Pandora's Box had done what its namesake had and seized control of our whole lives with whatever evil was inside it.

Theo waits about a minute or so, maybe a little longer. The silence is heavy around us, but nobody breaks it. Eventually what Theo deems is enough time passes, and he reaches down and plugs the computer back in. Then he turns it on and we wait for it to start up.

Now, like I said before, I'm a Mac girl, and this is a PC, but even I know within a few seconds that something's not right. It doesn't ask for a password, but it doesn't load the desktop, either. Instead, it just sits there grinding away for a few seconds, and then the same words scroll across the screen:

You've reached the point of no return.
Welcome to the real Pandora's Box.

Theo still doesn't say anything, just shoves back from the desk and takes the stairs behind us three at a time.

That snaps Eli into action. "Hey, where you going, man?" he demands, starting up the steps after his stepbrother.

"To get my laptop. Get yours, too, okay?"

The next few minutes are oddly surreal as I follow them, watching as Theo systematically checks every computer in the house. Then he checks his iPad, and Eli's—all with the same results. We can't access anything but that stupid message. He flips on the TV in the media room and we all stare as the blue AT&T screen quickly flashes to the Pandora's Box message. I wonder if it's the same at my house now.

Eli tries to change the channel, but nothing happens. He unplugs the TV while Theo heads to the hall closet and resets the whole box. When the television comes back online, nothing's changed. The same black background is there, the same words slowly scrolling across it as the numbers count down.

"*What* the *hell*?" Eli says again.

Theo ignores him, focusing on me instead. "Is this what happened to you?" he asks.

"I don't know. I didn't check everything in the house, just my laptop. And my TV didn't have any message. It was blank."

"So what are we supposed to do about this?" Eli asks again. "Dad and Gayle won't be back from their honeymoon until next week . . ."

Theo turns to me, and his eyes are such a deep, piercing blue that it feels like he can see right through me. Or worse, into me. "This all started at your house with Pandora's Box, too?"

"I think so. I mean, nothing was weird before that." I remember my cell phone suddenly, and how all day today it took a lot longer to text than normal.

"What?" Theo demands.

I tell him and he doesn't say anything. I'm about to add more, but Eli leans over to me and whispers, "Don't interrupt. Boy genius at work."

I start to laugh, but he's serious, despite his sarcastic tone. "Early acceptance to Harvard," he tells me. And when I glance back at Theo, I swear I can see his brain working, the wheels turning behind those unfocused eyes. I mean, I'm straight-A, full-load-of-AP-classes smart, and I know Theo is the same. But looking at him now, I can't help thinking that Eli is right. He's in a whole different class.

Plus it feels weird to just stand here, watching him, waiting for I don't know what. Maybe for him to snap and try to kill me again? Fun as that was, I'm going to have to pass. I start to inch away. Better to fall apart at home than here in front of the two hottest (and possibly craziest) guys in school.

Theo snaps out of it before I make it to the top of the stairs. "We need to go to your house."

"My—" I stop talking because he's already halfway down the steps, his iPad clutched in one hand, his laptop in the other.

"Is he always like this?" I ask Eli as we follow at a more reasonable pace.

"As long as I've known him," he answers cryptically.

"Lucky you."

"You have no idea." He rolls his eyes even as he holds the front door open for me with a gallant flourish.

"Thanks." I step through, and before I can say anything else, Theo shouts, "Come on, move it! We need to figure out what this is before it's too late."

Too late for what? I wonder. But I don't argue, just pick up the pace. Beside me, Eli does the same, though he mutters something under his breath I can't quite catch. Not that I blame him. Theo in full-out hunt mode is a bit overwhelming. Scary, even.

"So, what is this?" I ask as we trudge back to my house.

"Some virus," Eli tells me with a reassuring smile. "We'll get it figured out."

Theo snorts.

"You don't think so?" I ask.

He still doesn't answer, and I grab his arm, try to get him to look at me. "Something—I don't know what yet—is taking over the Internet piece by piece, Pandora." His voice crackles with impatience. "So no, I don't think we're going to be able to figure it out on our own."

"What do you mean?" I demand as a chill works its way up my spine. "It's just infecting our hardware, right?"

He pulls away, starts walking again. "It's infecting the whole Internet."

"That's not possible," Eli blurts out, though I can see a little of the concern he's trying hard to hide. "There's no way someone could do that."

"Yeah. No one thought they could take an entire country off the Internet, either, but Egypt managed to do it. Anything's possible, Eli."

The uneasiness that's been riding me since this thing began explodes into full-blown panic. If Theo's right . . . if Theo's right, then it's only a matter of time before everyone's infected. Before the entire Internet goes down. Right now, Pandora's Box is the most popular game in America, and I'm pretty sure the world, too. How many more people have to log on to play before they manage to bring down the whole Net?

"We need to call someone," I say before I realize how stupid that sounds. Who would we call even if we had that option? And what would we say?

"Trust me, they've already figured out there's a problem," Theo says without slowing down his brutal pace. "I guarantee you, alarms are sounding somewhere while a bunch of government techies scramble around, trying to figure out how hundreds, thousands, of Internet connections simply vanished."

"Maybe it's just our neighborhood," Eli ventures. But I can tell he doesn't believe it. Neither do I.

Whoever did this put a lot of time into it. Like thousands of hours for it to take everything down so smoothly. There's no way that was just to bring down a neighborhood.

We let ourselves into my house, and I go straight to the kitchen to get my laptop for Theo. I'm not sure what he thinks he's going to get from it, but I'm more than okay with letting him try. When I get back into the family room, he and Eli are parked on the couch, staring at my TV screen. It now has the same message on it that everything else does.

But when Theo opens my laptop, I realize that's not

exactly true. Because scrolling across my screen is a new message, one none of us has seen before:

Beat the game. Save the world.

It comes letter by letter, and once it's complete it hangs out for a second so that we can read it. Then it flashes three times and disappears, only to start all over again, one letter at a time:

B.E.A.T. T.H.E. G.A.M.E. S.A.V.E. T.H.E. W.O.R.L.D.

It does this four times, and when it fades the last time, it doesn't start again. Instead, a tiny little speck appears in the middle of the screen. As I watch, fascinated and horrified at the same time, the speck grows larger and larger until it takes up the entire screen.

"It's a present," I say dumbly, staring at the gift-wrapped box.

"No shit, Sherlock," responds Theo, even as he opens Eli's laptop and then his own. Theirs haven't changed at all—the same point-of-no-return message is still scrawled across both their screens.

"So, why is mine different?" I demand, now more freaked out than ever.

"Maybe it's because you've been infected longer," Eli suggests. "The gift thing just evolved on yours, right?"

I nod, certain that it hadn't been there when I'd gone running next door.

"If we give ours a little longer, maybe it will look the same." He glances at Theo.

"I don't think so. Pandora was only at our house a few minutes before you logged on. If we were going to get that message, we would have by now."

"So, again, *what* is going *on?*" Eli demands. "This doesn't make any sense. I thought most computer viruses worked the same way: infect a computer and use its address book to spread to other computers. But what they do to each computer is the same, right? As they replicate? They can't change."

"Usually," Theo agrees. "But this isn't a virus. I think it's a worm."

"What's the difference?" I start to pace behind the couch. It's a nervous habit that drives my mother nuts, but she's not here and I'm too worried to sit still.

"A virus usually piggybacks on some kind of program and replicates itself," Eli tells me. "A worm can use whole computer networks to replicate at a much higher rate."

"So this is inside a network we both use? Anyone who accesses it—"

"Gets the worm." Theo completes my sentence. "But the thing about a worm is it has different components that allow it to move from one network to the next. In the time since you first got the message, this thing could have gone around the world several times."

"That still doesn't account for the separate messages." I'm trying to keep up, but it's hard.

"No, it doesn't." Theo turns away from the computer for

the first time. "Unless you're the point of origin. Then it makes perfect sense."

"The point of . . ." My voice fails me, and I just stare at him, horror wrapping itself around me until I can't breathe, can't think. "That's not possible."

"You sure about that?" He taps the graphic of the present on the screen, the present that isn't on his or Eli's computers. Suddenly, I remember the message that scrolled across my screen first, the one that preceded even the Pandora's Box message:

Happy Seventeenth Birthday, Pandora!

My stomach twists and churns, and for a moment I'm afraid I'm going to be sick. *Is this possible?* I wonder frantically. *Could all this have somehow started with me?*

It's a ridiculous idea, moronic. I don't know much about technology beyond the basics of how to use things. There's no way I could set off something this sophisticated, even if I wanted to. Which I totally didn't. Don't. Whatever.

And yet, when I look at Theo, he seems so sure. So calm. As if he's already got everything all figured out.

"I didn't do this." I turn to Eli, urging him to believe me. But he's too busy trying to get into his laptop to even notice that I'm looking at him.

Nothing he does works, though, and finally Theo says, "You're just wasting your time. You're completely locked out until the system decides to let us in. We all are. Except Pandora."

"That doesn't make any sense! How am I supposed to

know anything more than anyone else does?" I demand. "What am I supposed to do?"

Theo, who's stayed completely calm during my tantrum, finally raises one dark eyebrow at my last question, and it makes him look less cerebral, more dangerous. Reminds me of those moments in English class. I take a couple of steps back even as he says, "The only thing *you* can do."

"What does that *mean*?"

He taps the screen once more. "Open the box, *Pandora*."

6

I'VE ALWAYS HAD a love-hate relationship with my name (I'm convinced my parents were drunk when they named me), but as Theo and Eli stare at me and I stare at the box in the middle of the computer screen, I have never hated it more.

Open the box, Pandora. Theo's words echo in my head, make me tremble.

Make me sick.

Make me wish I was anywhere but right here, in my house, feeling like the harbinger of total and complete destruction.

The words set a fire inside me—a burning, destructive blaze that does a lot of things. But the one thing it doesn't do, the one thing Theo can't *make* me do, is walk any closer to that computer and the mouse he is even now holding out.

"Why me?" I ask the question that has been circling my

brain since Theo first said he thought I was the point of origin. "What did I do to make someone target *me* for this?"

"Who knows?" He shrugs, looking so carelessly unconcerned with the question that is tormenting me that I want to punch him. "Maybe nothing. It could be your profile, your user name, something about your account that set it off. Maybe it's your name that did it."

"Or my birthday?" I whisper.

"Today's your birthday?" Eli demands.

"Yes."

The three of us look at my computer, at the virtual present in the middle of the screen. "Well, maybe it's that simple, then," Theo says. "Maybe it looked for users with today's birth date and launched from there. In that case, you won't be the only one this is happening to." He waves the mouse around. "So let's get started already."

"Wait a minute!" Eli says. "What's to say that she won't make it worse if she opens the box? Maybe we should just wait it out, let them fix the phones and the TV."

Theo looks at him then. "What are you even doing here?"

"Screw you. You think I'm going to stay at home while you hang out with Pandora and save the day?"

Theo reaches behind him to the phone resting on the table that runs the length of the couch. Clicks on speakerphone. There's nothing there. "They're not going to be able to fix the phones, Eli. Whoever did this has seized control of the whole grid, and he or she isn't letting it go until the game gets launched. Otherwise, things would be back to normal already. And even if it does get worse, there's no way to fix it until Pandora unlocks the game."

"How do you know that?" I ask, my voice almost manic. "If what you're saying is even possible, then won't it go away if we just don't play? If we refuse to do anything?"

Theo's laugh is anything but happy as he turns his computer to face me. "Worms don't work that way. They sit there, gathering info and doing what they're supposed to do, until someone blasts them apart.

"Besides, did you even read what the game said? 'The real Pandora's Box'? 'Total annihilation in ten days'?" Then he points to my computer. " 'Beat the game. Save the world.' "

"You can't actually be taking that seriously, can you? It can't *actually* annihilate the entire world."

I've barely finished speaking when the lights go out, plunging the room into shades of purple that echo the inky twilight slowly falling outside. I swallow the scream building in my throat—I already look like a big enough idiot without turning phobic because of the dark—and look around. The only light in the room is coming from the three laptops spread out on the coffee table.

"Time's up," says Eli, who's looking around the room like he expects the bogeyman to jump out at him at any second. I'm right there with him.

"No." Theo ignores his brother and answers me. "I don't actually think the guy who did this can take out the whole world. But I think he can make life pretty damn uncomfortable for our little corner of it until you decide to go along with him."

I look at the screen and I'm tempted. I can't say that I'm

not. My curiosity is fully piqued, and there's a part of me that wants to know what's waiting for me, waiting for *us*, inside that box. Will everything go back to normal if I just click it? Or will everything get worse?

Theo holds the mouse out to me and I reach for it. But at the last minute, I summon up a little bit of self-control and turn away. "I don't care. I'm not doing it."

I walk into the kitchen, grab a bottle of water from the fridge, and guzzle it down. My stomach is killing me, and even though I'm in another room, all I can see is that present. That box. Waiting for me to open it.

But I've learned from my namesake's mistakes. I won't be the Pandora Theo wants me to be. There's enough evil in the world already.

"Damn it, Pandora! We don't have time for this." Theo's standing in the doorway, my laptop in his hands. "Open the damn thing or I will!"

"Why? Why can't I just refuse to play?"

He looks around the darkened kitchen. "Because this is happening whether you want it to or not. It's stupid of you to keep out everyone who can help just because you're scared."

"I'm not scared!" It's a total lie, but I feel honor bound to say it.

The look he gives me calls me a liar, but he doesn't say anything. Just waits. Patiently. Which is somehow much worse than when he was pushing me.

"You really think you can help?" I finally venture after a long silence.

"This is what I do," he answers.

"Play video games?"

He lifts an eyebrow. "Hack systems."

I look at him, standing there in his button-down shirt and khaki pants and can't imagine him as anything but a rule follower of the highest order. I mean, even his shoes are perfectly polished. But then I make the mistake of meeting his eyes, and they're not cold anymore. Instead, they're totally bad ass. Filled with confidence and the thrill of the chase. There's no sign of the sickness that's churning inside me.

Again . . . "You really think you can do this?"

"Damn straight."

Eli comes up to us then, and he looks a little excited—as if he, too, is actually looking forward to getting inside and playing with this monstrosity some crazed hacker has created. "Come on, Pandora. How could they get worse? Besides, what if they get better?"

It's an enticing thought. I look at my laptop, think about doing what they ask. I don't want to. For the first time, ever, I'm refusing to let my curiosity control me.

Sure, it seems like things are bad now. They *are* bad, but a little voice in the back of my head tells me that we don't have a clue what bad is. Not yet. And I just couldn't stand it if *I* somehow made things worse.

I think of my mom, of how annoyed she'll be in Alaska tonight if she tries to reach me and can't get through. How worried she'll be, how worried Theo and Eli's parents will be on their honeymoon, if this thing continues to spiral out of control.

And that's when I know—I'm going to click on the box.

I'm going to play the game.

Because when it comes right down to it, Theo's right. I don't have a choice. Some madman has seen to that.

I take another deep breath, hold it in my lungs, then bring my laptop back to the family room. I don't look at it, don't look at anything, until I'm once more settled on the couch. And then I move the cursor over the box and double-click before I can change my mind.

7

FOR A FEW SECONDS, nothing happens. Then everything does, all at the same time. The lights come back on, Theo's and Eli's laptops beep from the other room, and mine—mine starts to play music—a full-orchestra version of "Happy Birthday" that is totally inappropriate, considering the circumstances.

"Told you," Eli says, looking at the lights. "We've got electricity back."

Theo doesn't seem as happy with that development as Eli does, but when I start to ask, he shushes me. Points to my laptop, which has begun talking to us.

"Welcome to Pandora's Box, the most real game you'll ever play." The voice that comes out is female and so overly sweet it makes me want to gag. It's also completely unexpected and as I listen to it, I wonder what other surprises Pandora's Box has in store for me. The thought weirds me out even more, and somehow Eli knows, because suddenly he's behind me, his big hand rubbing the tension from between my shoulder blades.

"Evil is everywhere. Your only hope is to fix what's broken. Complete the given tasks to level up. Beat the game and find the key to a brave new world. Lose the game and life as you know it will come to an end forever. But be warned: this world is modeled after the real one. No matter how many points you amass or levels you conquer, you can only die once. There are no second chances."

"What does she mean, 'fix what's broken'?" I ask. "What do we need to fix?"

Theo shrugs. "We'll just have to play for a while and see." He's leaning back against the family room wall now, his hands shoved into his pockets. He appears totally calm, totally relaxed, but there's a hypervigilance about him, an alertness in his eyes as he watches me, that negates the casual way he's holding himself.

The graphics on the screen suddenly blur, and as I watch, it feels like I'm being pulled superfast into the box. The game is sucking me through a virtual black hole, with stars and planets rushing by me at alarming speeds. *Pandora's Box?* I wonder hazily as I try not to get dizzy. *Or* Star Trek?

"Wicked graphics," Eli says, and he's leaning forward, his hands on either side of my shoulders, as if he can't get close enough to the game. Which is strange, because I want nothing more than to get away from it.

Theo sits down on the couch next to me, scooting so close in his effort to get a better look at my computer that his leg is plastered to mine.

For one second, I go into sensory overload. Between

looking at the game, feeling Theo against me and Eli behind and around me, it's all too much. I feel trapped.

I shove at Eli's arms with all my strength, desperate to get away before my brain short-circuits altogether.

"Hey, what are you doing?" he asks, and the question hits me hard.

What *am* I doing? Where *am* I going? I want to run away, to bury my head, to make it all just disappear.

But it won't. I can't go back, can't go forward, can't do anything but stay right here and see this through. I helped start it; now I need to finish it.

Theo's hand comes up and holds my elbow, not hard, but enough to let me know that he's there. Normally, I'd be pissed off that he thought he had the right to put his hands on me after what happened this morning, but Theo's grip isn't demanding. I could break it easily if I wanted to.

But I don't want to. It's keeping me grounded, keeping me sane, this small connection to another person who is right here in the present—in this world—with me. He doesn't say anything, but somehow I know that this is exactly what he intends me to feel.

I beat back the panic, the fear, the knowledge that the imaginary has just become my reality, and focus on his hand on my elbow. Focus on the game. The second I let myself be drawn back to it, it yanks me in completely.

I fall straight through the blackness and into a wide blue sky, plummeting, plummeting, plummeting. I plunge through one cloud, then another and another. And then I'm skidding and shuddering to a stop, bumping along hard ground as everything drops away but the world I've suddenly been thrust into.

On the sidewalk, dressed in jeans and a black Jimi Hendrix tank top, is an avatar with short, choppy red hair and brown eyes. She's tall and lean, with multipierced ears, a small star-shaped nose ring, and purple streaks in her hair.

I freeze as I look at her, choke up, and hear Theo inhale sharply next to me.

"Is that what your avatar usually looks like?" he asks.

"No." My voice is shaking and I realize my computer is as well. No, not my computer—just the hands that are holding it.

I put it down on the coffee table, fight the urge to bury my hands in my lap. I don't know why it matters, but I don't want the guys to know how upset I am. Maybe because they're so calm, taking all of this in stride when I'm one small step away from screaming my head off.

"It's the camera," Theo tells me, tapping the top of my computer. "The game sees you."

"Wicked," Eli says again.

"So, where is she?" Theo asks, and I force my fingers back to the keyboard. At the moment, my character is sitting in the middle of an empty street with buildings in every direction. Cars are all over the place—some are stopped in the middle of the street while others are parked at the curb. But no one is in them. They're empty, abandoned, which is nothing like the Pandora's Box I'm used to, usually teeming with other players and NPCs, Non-Playing Characters.

I hit the Up arrow and I stand on-screen.

Even with everything that's happened, I expect to be where I left off—in the middle of postapocalyptic Manhattan. But as I look both ways, and even cross the street to peer into the window of an empty shop, I realize that nothing looks familiar. It's impossible to tell where I am, and there's no one around to ask.

I am completely alone in this new world. It isn't a pleasant thought.

"Look up," Eli instructs, and I follow his directions, looking straight up to the very pointy, very recognizable top of the Frost Bank Tower.

"I'm in Austin?" I ask incredulously.

"It seems that way," Eli answers.

"I didn't even know Austin was an option in Pandora's Box. When I started, the game plopped me down in Boston and I made my way to New York."

"Pandora's Box covers just the big cities," Theo says matter-of-factly. "Or at least the original one does. I guess we'll have to see what this version covers."

"It looks exactly like downtown."

"Not exactly like it," Eli points out, his finger sweeping across the screen. "When have you ever seen North Congress this empty?"

"I don't like it," I say. "What am I supposed to do? How do I beat a level when I'm the only one in it?"

"You don't know that yet," Theo tells me.

"Look around. Do you see another avatar anywhere? Or even an NPC?" asks Eli.

Again, I remember all the NPCs from the original version of Pandora's Box, characters I never paid much attention to as I was working my way through the initial levels. But judging by the look on Eli's face, it's not a good thing that this version doesn't have them.

Not that I'm surprised. Not good is par for the course at this point, right?

"Do you think you're overreacting a little?" Theo says, and at first I think he's somehow found a way to read my thoughts. But then I realize he's talking to Eli. "She hasn't even gone five feet yet."

He's right, I haven't. Maybe all this gloom and doom and poor-me stuff is a little premature. I press the left arrow key and take off running up the street.

"Hey, where are you going?" Eli asks.

I don't answer, because I don't have a clue. I just keep my finger on the button, until I'm running faster and faster. I pass a bunch of side streets, including Austin's famous Sixth Street, where I can hear music coming out of the bars but can't see anyone on the sidewalks. It's eerie to see the most popular street in Austin so empty, and I wouldn't recognize it if not for all the familiar bar signs.

On and on I run until I'm standing, strangely enough, in front of the Texas State Capitol building. It's in the middle of Congress Street downtown, and when the Texas legislature built it, they had one goal in mind: to make sure it was bigger and grander than the national Capitol in Washington.

They succeeded by about fourteen feet, and it's the fanciest, tallest capitol in the fifty states. Beautiful and ostentatious, it towers over everything around it and is a monument to all things Texas. I know this because nearly every year in elementary school and junior high we were forced to take a field trip down here, as if the first five trips hadn't provided enough opportunity to ogle the red granite and pink marble.

I'm not sure why I chose to run here, but as I walk up the long path leading to the stairs in the front, a strange feeling washes over me. I start to turn back, but something keeps my finger on the arrow key all the way to the front door. I go inside, and as I look up at the huge rotunda a memory assails me, one I didn't even know I had.

I'm almost three years old and dressed in a pretty pink party dress—I remember the dress because my mother had it specially made for me. It had layers of frilly petticoats, and I liked nothing more than to stand in the middle of the living room and twirl in circles, again and again, so that my skirts flew up around me.

I used to be such a girly-girl, it's hard to imagine now. Anyway, I'm all dressed up, including little lace tights and black patent-leather shoes, and I'm looking around me in awe (it must have been my first visit to the state Capitol). My mom is standing to my left and to my right—I close my eyes, not sure if I'm trying to banish the memory or capture it. To my right, his large, calloused hand clasped around mine, is my father.

I flash back to the pictures in my backpack, the ones my father sent me this morning. I'm wearing this dress in the one where we're posing in front of a statue of Sam Houston. Was that picture taken here, in the rotunda, I wonder, or somewhere else?

Either way, it's a weird coincidence. One that has me backing out the door and down the stairs. Slowly at first, but then faster and faster. I can't get away soon enough. And even though I have a feeling that there is something for me to do at the Capitol, there is no way I'm going back in there.

"What's wrong?" Eli asks, but I shake my head. I'm back on Congress and have no idea where to go from here. I start up the street at a dead run.

"This is stupid," I say. "There are no directions, nothing to tell me where I'm supposed to go or what I'm supposed to do. I could wander here all day."

But even as I'm speaking, the roads are narrowing, more and more streets are becoming blocked off to me as the game herds me in the direction it wants me to go. I know I should be hypervigilant—I'm supposed to be saving the world, after all—but I have to admit this is pretty boring. Nothing but running and occasionally jumping over something that's in my way.

If this is the best this maniac has, he's not nearly as smart or creative as he thinks he is. Surely someone will be able to beat the game quickly, and then everything can go back to normal.

"I think he's sending you to Zilker Park," Theo says, and as I look at the streets around me, at the big Whole Foods Market and Town Lake, I realize he's right. But since I'm not in the mood for a paddleboat ride or a kite-flying competition, I'm not exactly sure what I'm supposed to be doing here. Unless the guy's programmed the game to happen during the Austin City Limits music festival.

He hasn't, and I slow down as I reach the wooded area near the nature center. I turn in a circle, looking for some clue as to what I'm supposed to do now. Nothing comes to me, and I start walking up the huge rock stairs to the center, getting a little more annoyed with each second that passes.

I turn to Theo with a frown. "I'm beginning to think that the whole 'beat the game, save the world' thing is nothing but a bunch of bull—"

I break off midword as two things happen simultaneously. First, Eli's computer makes a loud beeping noise and he is dropped straight into the game. And second, a huge black monster jumps out from behind a tree and tackles my avatar, sending me flying.

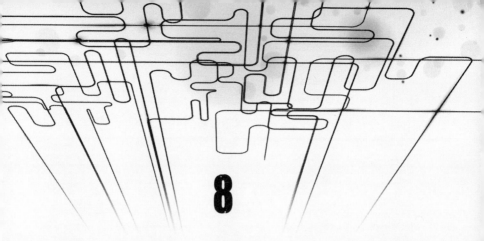

8

ADRENALINE SURGES THROUGH MY SYSTEM, making my heart pound heavily as blood thrums in my ears. "What do I do?" I yell. "What do I do?" In my head is the original warning, about having only one life. If this thing kills me now, I'm out for good and I'm not sure what that means for the fate of my computer. Or the rest of my little corner of the world.

"Run," Eli says, ripping his eyes off his own avatar long enough to check out my predicament.

"Yeah. That's so not going to happen. In case you haven't noticed, I have a gigantic dragon lady on my chest!" I recoil in horror as I get my first good look at her. She's huge, and while her top half is that of a woman—with snake hair—her bottom half is covered in black scales. She has huge claws, a long barbed tail, and her legs, while stationary, are moving. Undulating, really, and I realize they're made up of snakes, too. Snakes that are all looking at my avatar like they want to take a bite out of her. Me. Whatever.

"That's Campe," Theo says calmly, and I almost hate him for being such a know-it-all. He hits a couple of buttons on my keyboard. I buck and roll on-screen, but the huge, nightmarish beast doesn't move. Big surprise. One of the claws rakes my shoulder, and I swear, I almost feel the pain. I know I'm sweating.

"She's going to kill me!" I screech, just as Theo's computer beeps and he's finally thrust into the game, too. He takes off running in my direction, but I'm too busy thrashing around to pay much attention to what he and Eli are doing.

"Hold on," Eli tells me. "I'm almost there."

"I'm doing my best." I hit the monster in her face, and it surprises her enough that I'm able to shove out from under her, but once she recovers, she's enraged. She kicks me, the vipers that make up her legs hissing as they try to take a chunk out of me.

I kick back, catching the beast in her scaly stomach. She screams as she goes down on top of me.

My breath whooshes out, and I try to stay conscious as I shove at the thing. But I'm in bad shape. I'm bleeding from my left leg and right shoulder, and from the way my avatar is struggling to draw in air, I'm afraid I might have a broken rib or three. So much for boring—the game has gone from mundane to terrifying in the blink of an eye.

I look up just as she flexes her long, horrifying claws. They're mostly black, but they're tipped in deep red, and I'm praying that's her normal look, not my blood. She leans over me and her teeth elongate, growing until they're huge and so close to me that I imagine the feel of her hot, stinky breath on my face. I turn my head, close my eyes, and prepare to die before I ever had a chance to live.

But the death blow—or bite, in this case—never comes. Instead, Eli's avatar rushes onto the scene and grabs Campe by the shoulders. His avatar is as tall and well built as Eli is in real life, and with a mighty heave, he yanks the nightmarish monster off me and sends her spinning across the grass, where she lies dazed.

He reaches down and grabs my hand—the one attached to my uninjured arm—and helps me to my feet. "Are you all right?" Eli asks me.

"Just peachy," I answer. "But you might want to look out."

Campe is back on her feet, and she looks a million times angrier than she did before. And this time, all of that anger is directed straight at Eli. She pulls out two glistening knives, and I take a few steps to the right, feeling like a total coward as I do so. But that thing looks like it's going to take Eli apart in a couple of well-placed slices, and I really don't want to have any part of that.

Suddenly, Theo is there, shoving me behind him as he and Eli hold their ground. Campe crashes into them, and they stumble a little but manage to hang on. I guess there's something to be said for being built like Greek Titans, especially in this game.

Campe comes at them again, and this time I know she's going to take a few chunks off them. They're both still a little unsteady on their feet, and the dragon is determined to tear them apart.

I look around, desperate for something to use as a weapon as the game maker hasn't gifted me with anything yet. There's nothing close to me except for some huge rocks, so I grab one, staggering under the weight of it.

As I work my way toward Theo, Eli, and the Mistress of Hell, I try to figure out where the best place to hit her is. Normally, I'd go for the head, but hers is about ten feet off the ground, and I'm pretty positive I can't throw this thing that high. Besides, if I miss, all it's going to do is piss her off more, and I've already learned from bitter experience what a bad idea *that* is.

But what else can I hit that would do any damage? Her body is huge, her skin like armor, and as I stand there, looking at her, I understand a little of what David must have felt when he took on Goliath. But unlike David, I'm fresh out of slingshots.

Theo catches sight of me and the giant rock in my hand. He shakes his head and shoots Eli a look. If I didn't know better, I'd say he was telling his brother that they need to protect me.

Before I can even imagine what they're going to do, he launches himself at Campe, wrapping his arms around her thick right arm and squeezing until she drops the knife. Eli does the same to her left arm, and she roars in outrage, her long barbed tail swinging around and catching Theo in the back. He lets go, but he doesn't fall, the barbs holding him in place.

I gasp in horror, my fingers tightening on the rock even as Eli scurries up her long arm to her neck. He wraps his hands around her throat and begins to squeeze. The monster bucks, tries to rip him off with her crimson-tipped claws, but Theo's grabbed one arm again and is holding so tightly she can't move it.

She bats at Eli with the other, but he won't let go. For the first time since this nightmare of a game began, I see panic in the crazed monster's eyes and I know that this is my chance—probably my only chance. I step closer, doing my best to avoid the hissing snakes and wildly gyrating tail. Then I heave the rock at her as hard as I can.

By some miracle she bends at just the right moment, and I get her right between the eyes. She freezes for a second, before letting out a long, high-pitched scream that curdles my blood. Her entire body convulses and then she's falling, trapping Eli beneath her.

I rush forward, but Theo's already there, dodging around her barbed tail, which is twitching dangerously. She reaches out with a claw, tries to grab me, and I scramble backward, but even as I do I know that there's no way I can escape her.

She wraps her hand around my ankle and yanks. I'm falling, and I brace myself for impact, my entire body going tense, though I know it's the worst thing I can do. I tell myself it will be okay, that it's just a game, that the person about to be torn apart isn't really me, but I can't help the fear and adrenaline that race through me from all directions.

And then it's too late to think anymore because the snakes are crawling off her legs and toward me, their poisonous mouths yawning wide as they get ready to bite. I kick at a few of them, but it's no use. I close my eyes—this is it—and wait for my avatar to die.

Theo yells at me to move, but I can't. I'm completely

trapped. Then the strangest thing happens—fire shoots from Theo's fingertips straight at the huge, furious monster. It hits her square in the center of her body, and she screams in rage and pain. He follows up the blast with another, more powerful blast to the arm that is holding me down. She screeches, lets go, and I roll away from her—and the snakes—as fast as possible. But Theo tosses a third fireball at the snakes, which writhe on the ground as they are completely engulfed in flames.

"Wicked!" Eli crows, and for a second I'm not sure if it's game Eli or real Eli saying it. Here, in this strange new world, reality and gaming mix until they feel the same. Until they both feel real. "How'd you do that, dude?"

"I don't know." Theo is looking at his hands, puzzled. "It just happened."

"I want to try." Eli holds out his hands in the same gesture that Theo had used, but nothing happens. He tries again, hits nearly every key on the keyboard, but still nothing changes. He starts muttering to himself, determination to figure out what his stepbrother did written into every line of his body.

While he experiments, I check out the damage to my avatar. I'm limping pretty badly, and blood is dripping from the claw marks Campe left in my upper arm and calf, but other than that everything seems to be okay.

Theo comes over and kneels at my feet as he, too, examines my wounds. "If we find a bathroom or someplace with running water, we'll get that cleaned up. You don't want an infection."

"Can avatars even get infections?" I ask.

"They can in MMOs. That's why so many of the resources are medicine or healing herbs—even healing knowledge. Healers are highly prized."

I look down at my leg with new eyes, wishing for the virtual-reality version of Neosporin. It would suck to survive an attack by a crazed dragon lady only to succumb to an infection in a few virtual days.

The thought has me looking at the sky, trying to judge how much time has passed. The sun has sunk behind the trees, and streams of red and orange and purple streak across the sky.

"Come on," I say finally. "We need to keep going."

"Yeah, sure. Of course." But Eli looks totally disappointed as he drops his hands, giving up on bringing forth fireballs, and falls into step beside me. The three of us begin walking toward the huge clump of trees to our right.

We've only gone a few steps when Eli exclaims, "Hey, what did we win?"

"I don't know." And I don't particularly care. If we haven't won a chance to get out of this stupid game once and for all, then I'm just not interested. But when I remember that my real life demands Internet access, a cell phone, and television, I keep my mouth shut.

Barely.

"It's over there," Theo says, and I look to where he's pointing. There's a box sitting on a tree stump, one I know wasn't there when I was frantically scanning for a weapon a few minutes before.

We run to it, and Theo reaches in, coming out with a huge handful of seed packets. Tomatoes, cucumbers, strawberries, blackberries, various types of lettuce—nearly every kind of seed you can imagine.

"We're supposed to plant a garden?" I ask, confused.

"What the hell?" demands Eli, looking annoyed. "How are these supposed to get us to the end of the game?"

I don't answer. I mean, in the real world, I love to plant things—flowers, berries, trees—and watch as they grow. I spend hours in the spring and summer working on the flower beds around my house, as well as the small vegetable garden my mom let me create in the backyard. I have a hella green thumb, and nearly everything I plant flourishes beautifully.

But here? In a video game? What's the point?

"I don't know," Theo says in answer to Eli's question. "But take them, anyway." He throws me a bunch of packets before reaching back into the box for more. "Put these in your pockets."

I follow orders, watch as the two of them do the same. Then say, "Come on, maybe we can find some NPCs and trade them for something."

"Have you seen any?" Eli demands, though he doesn't pause in stuffing his pockets with seeds. "Besides that ugly hag, I mean?"

"No. But that doesn't mean they aren't out there. We'll just have to wait and see."

We start to walk again, and now that we've been playing for a while and Satan's girlfriend is no longer after us, it seems to take forever to get anywhere. We find a place to clean up; then, as we continue on, a few more players join us—real people, not NPCs—following behind as if they expect the three of us to have the answers to all the questions that must be winding through their heads right now. Which I guess proves Theo's theory right. We're not the only ones this is happening to.

Someone IMs me, his message popping up in the bottom right-hand corner of my screen. The user ID tells me he's one of the first people to start following us—the guy who's dressed in jeans and a navy-blue hoodie and looks like he's in his early twenties. Jason47.

What's happening?

I point out the question to Eli and Theo.

"Ask him if he's having the same issues we are," Eli suggests.

So I do, and he comes back with:

This is the only thing working in my whole house.
    Are you from West Lake?
No. Round Rock.

"Shit. That's North Austin," Theo says.

Way north. Like forty minutes from here. How fast is this thing spreading? Theo'd commented earlier that it could have gone around the world several times already, but I don't think I actually believed him before now.

More like I didn't want to believe him.

I type in:

    How long have you been in the game?
About twenty minutes. My computer has been dead for the

longest time, just this weird thing about beating the game and saving the world. Then suddenly it beeped and dropped me in.

I glance at the clock. It's been about twenty-five minutes since I opened the box. He must have been dropped in after, just like Theo and Eli.

Then he asks:

So, what do we do now? This is weird.
    What else? Play the game.

He doesn't answer, so I wait a second before I type:

    I have to go now.

Then I close the messaging, cutting him off. I know it's rude, but I'm losing it and the last thing I need is to deal with someone else who is obviously freaking out. So far, Eli and Theo have managed to keep me calm, but dealing with someone else as weirded out as I am might send me completely over the edge.

"You ready to keep going?" Eli asks, placing a warm, comforting hand on my back.

I stiffen a little at the contact. Sure, things are messed up, but he's still a guy. And his hand is *resting* on the small of my back.

I shrug off my concern, try to keep my eye on the prize as I wonder where this is going to end—or if it is.

"Hey, think positive," Eli says.

"How'd you know—"

"Are you kidding me?" He nods toward Theo. "You and my brother seem hardwired for the whole doom-and-gloom thing."

"It doesn't get much more doom and gloom than this." I gesture to the screen, where we're all just standing around, looking lost.

"Yeah, well, we'll pretend that's not the case." Then he makes some goofball face at me, and I can't help laughing. I'm not sure how Theo does it, because, for me at least, it's pretty hard to stay depressed when Eli's around.

Back in the game, we walk for what seems like hours but is probably only about five minutes—everything with this stupid game feels like it takes forever—until we get to the huge fields where one of Austin's biggest music festivals, Austin City Limits, is held every year. I was just in these fields last month, rocking out to Muse, Sonic Youth, the Flaming Lips, and about two hundred other bands, but the fields of Pandora's Box are as different from the fields in those three fun-and-music-filled days as modern-day America is from ancient Greece.

Lining one edge of the gigantic fields are tents, hundreds of them, six or seven deep. These aren't your typical REI state-of-the-art mobile camping units, either. These are worn-out, worn-down ragtag pieces of canvas that look like the weakest Austin storm could blow them straight to oblivion.

"What is this?" I whisper, as thousands of people pour from the tents into the clearing. They are as dilapidated looking as the tents they've been cowering under—maybe more so—and I feel my breath hitch in my chest. Who are these people and why are they here, in this game?

We walk closer, and as we do, I realize just what bad shape they're in. The little ones are running around in ripped T-shirts, their ribs poking through their skin in stark relief, while many of the adults seem so weak that they can barely stand.

"Are these people real?" I ask, so horrified that it doesn't register that if they don't have food, they probably don't have computers to suck them into this virtual reality.

"I don't think so," Eli answers. "They look like NPCs to me."

"They are NPCs," Theo agrees. "And I think this is our first task." He reaches into his pockets and pulls out the packets of seeds. "My guess is that we're supposed to feed them."

"Are you kidding me?" Eli scoffs. "That's too easy, isn't it?"

"We're at level one. It's supposed to be easy."

"Yeah, because Campe was just a barrel of laughs."

"Either way, I think we need to feed these people to level up," Theo says, holding out some seed packets to one of the girls standing behind us.

She grabs three packets of strawberry seeds.

Theo looks at the players behind us, gestures for them to come closer, which they do, eagerly. I can understand why. Even Theo's avatar looks like someone who's used to being in charge. Though he's young, only a senior in high school, he has that indefinable way about him, and that translates to the game. There's none of the brooding now, and as I watch him get things organized it's easy to forget what happened this morning.

Especially since right here, right now, I'm more than willing to do whatever he tells me, just so long as I don't have to make the decision myself. Fighting Campe as I feared for my digital life took a lot more out of me than I first suspected.

"To beat the game, obviously, we need to advance through the levels. To beat this level, I think the task is to put these seeds in the ground so that all these NPCs can get some food." He walks over to a clear, unmuddy patch of grass and squats down. But when he tries to empty the seed packet into the ground, nothing happens.

"What's going on?" I ask. "Why isn't it working?"

"I don't know. You try," he tells me.

I follow his lead, try to dump out the seeds. Again, nothing happens.

Eli tries, with the same result, as do all of the other players.

"Why won't it work?" I ask again, frustrated. How are we supposed to beat the game if we can't complete the task?

Theo shrugs, presses a few buttons and tries again—to no avail.

"We're missing something," Eli finally says.

"We defeated the monster, got our reward. This is obviously our task, right?" I shove my computer away, stand up, and walk to the sliding glass door that leads to my backyard. Everything out there looks so normal—the grass is green, the trees are swaying lightly in the breeze while a squirrel scampers past a light, a nut clasped in its little paws. So how can everything in here be so screwed up?

"I don't know. But we need to figure it out. Go back over the places we've been and try to see what we missed." Eli retraces our last steps.

I start to tell him I'm out for a while, that I just can't do any more right now. But before I say anything, Emily comes flying through my front door.

"Major change of plans, *chica*."

Now that the action is over, the game lets my avatar drop out. I turn to my best friend, who—despite the beginning of technological Armageddon—looks as fresh as she did when I drove her home from school this afternoon.

"Obviously."

"So you know?" she asked. "I tried to call you, but my phone's out and so are all the ones in my neighborhood."

I can't help it—I start to laugh. It's not funny, but I laugh until tears roll from my eyes. Hysterical much?

Theo, Eli, and Emily are all staring at me like I've lost my mind, although Emily keeps stealing glimpses at the guys, like she can't believe they're sitting in my family room. Of course, if the last two hours hadn't happened, I wouldn't be able to believe it, either.

"I take it that means you already know?" she asks, when my hysteria finally calms down.

"You could say that." I point to Eli and Theo, introduce them to Emily. "They've been helping me try to figure out what's going on."

"Good luck. Someone in the government contacted my dad an hour ago. He's working on it but can't seem to get anywhere yet. Whatever it is, it's a huge mess, some kind of blended threat. He's using words I haven't heard since he helped map out the Stuxnet worm."

I exchange uneasy glances with Eli and Theo. "So this thing is really bad, then?"

"That's the impression I get." She leans back against my couch and blows a bubble with her trademark strawberry gum, looking completely relaxed. Like we're talking about what shade of lipstick she should wear instead of a worm that has shut down nearly every form of communication we've got. "Close to an hour ago the game opened up for everyone, and my dad tried to slip through the matrix to get a handle on it, but he said he couldn't get through. There's something blocking him and all of the other government hackers.

"He says this is unlike any worm or virus he's ever seen, that it's some weird amalgamation of both that's taking over everything it comes into contact with."

"How many people are infected at this point?" Theo asks. "Are there any estimates?"

"I have no idea. I just know it's a lot." She looks at him curiously. "Are you coming to dinner with us?"

"Dinner?" Eli asks, just as his stomach rumbles.

"To celebrate Pandora's birthday. We're going for pizza. You should come."

"I thought you said there was a change of plans?" I ask, suddenly not so crazy about the way Emily is looking at Eli and Theo. I feel stupid for letting it bug me, especially since I barely know either one of them, but I can't help it. I've spent the last couple of hours with them, and even with all the Pandora's Box stuff, it's been kind of nice to have them on my side. Paying attention to me. Which makes me selfish as well as moronic and the cause of all things Armageddon. Fantastic.

"My dad says I can't stay over if there's no phone. Plus, he doesn't want you here on your own, either. He didn't say anything else—my mom started losing it—but I think this is going to end up being a pretty big deal. So pack a bag for a couple of days, and after we have dinner, we can head to my place."

I don't bother arguing, largely because I'm so relieved that I don't have to stay here alone with no phone and spotty electricity.

Emily waits for a beat, but once she realizes I'm on board with the new plan, she turns to Theo. "So, Othello, do you two want to come or not?"

I blush wildly at her reference to what happened in my English class, but Theo takes it in stride.

Eli laughs. "I do." Then he winks at her, and I'm struck, not for the first time, by what a charmer he is. And even more, despite his fan club of legions, how he's really just a nice, sweet guy at the heart of it all.

I can't help liking that about him.

Which is so not what I should be thinking about right now. To keep myself distracted, I shove off the couch and head for the kitchen. "Do you guys want something to drink? The fridge is pretty much empty of food but I've got soda, water, and iced tea."

Right on schedule, Eli's stomach growls again, and he smiles in good-natured embarrassment. "I don't think a soda's going to hold me for long," he admits.

"I guess we can leave the game for a little while." Theo stands up reluctantly, as if he expects the world to end while we're at dinner, and heads for the door. "Just let me run next door and get my wallet and the car."

"I'll go with you."

Emily and I watch as the guys head out. She smiles sweetly when they give us small waves, but the second the door closes behind them, she's on me. "Oh my God! They are even hotter up close." She fake swoons. "And they both seem pretty cool."

"They are."

"So have you decided which one you want? Eli, right? Because of the whole . . ."—she mimes strangling herself—"Othello thing with Theo? Oh, please say Eli. He's hot, but Theo is *gorgeous*. And I totally felt a connection between us . . ."

"They're not candy, you know. We can't just divvy them up."

"Sure we can—one for you and one for me! We don't want to crush on the same guy, after all. And if they were candy, I'd bet Theo would be the kind with the hard chocolate shell and melted caramel center. Yummy."

"I think you mean *nutty* center, don't you?"

She sighs heavily. "Could you be a little more of a wet blanket?"

"Sorry, but the world is falling apart, in case you haven't noticed. Now's not exactly the time to be worrying about hot guys."

"My dad will fix it—he's the best at this stuff. Besides, there's *always* time to worry about hot guys. Speaking of which . . ." She sends me her wide-eyed, pleading look.

"Don't worry. I'm *so* not crushing on Theo."

"I knew it. He's a little too much for you. Plus, Eli's got that dimple, and I know how you are—"

"What is that supposed to mean?" I interrupt, insulted. "Theo's not too *much* for me!"

"He's a little intense, Pandora."

"I can do intense."

"So you *do* want Theo?" Emily says with a grin and an eyebrow wiggle, both of which I ignore.

"I don't want either of them! You're the one who brought up the whole ridiculous subject."

Rolling her eyes, she grabs my hand and starts dragging me upstairs. "Come on, girl. You look like hell, and that just won't do for your first date with Eli."

"It's not a date. It's *pizza.*"

"Trust me, the way he was looking at you? It's definitely a date."

Emily bulldozes around any and all of my objections, even going so far as to insist that I change my clothes. I start to argue, but there's no winning when she gets like this. And besides, it's nice to spend a few minutes doing something normal—or, at least, normal for her—instead of freaking out about that stupid game.

About what's going to happen next.

By the time Emily's satisfied with my appearance, the shell-shocked-survivor look is gone. My choppy haircut has been ruthlessly tamed into submission, and even I have to admit that the shimmery purple tank top Emily found at the back of the closet looks great on me.

"So, are you still determined to go to Little Nicky's for your birthday?" she asks as we head downstairs, my backpack filled with extra clothes slung over my shoulder. "Or can we try somewhere a little more sophisticated?"

"I want pizza."

"Of course you do."

We start to settle on the couch to talk—it's not like there's anything else to do right now—but then the doorbell rings. It's Eli, and he's changed as well. His wild hair is tamed a little, and he's pulled on a cool South By Southwest T-shirt. It makes me smile, because I have the same one upstairs in my room.

He grins when he sees me. "Hey, you look great!"

"Uh, thanks." I'm not sure what else to say, because the way he's looking at me is so flirtatious that my breath catches in my rib cage. Which is stupid. And all Emily's fault. If she hadn't gone on and on about him, everything would be like it was earlier instead of my practically swallowing my tongue while trying to make conversation with him.

"Theo's in the car. Are you ready to go?"

"Sure." I slide my laptop into my backpack with the rest of the stuff I packed, and then sling it over my shoulder, ready to go straight to Emily's house once dinner is finished and the guys drop us off. My own feels kind of strange now. Haunted, almost.

I lock up, then we climb into Theo's fully loaded Range Rover (could he get a little more yuppie-in-training?)—Eli and me in the back, Emily in the front—and head toward the shopping and restaurant area where Little Nicky's makes its home. The three of them talk about Pandora's Box and school and a bunch of other stuff, but I don't participate. Though it's my birthday, I'm tired and my head hurts and I just don't have it in me to try to keep up.

I kind of drift along for the fifteen-minute ride, letting their voices soothe me in a way their words never could. In the back of my head is the worry about where this game will end. About how bad things are going to get before they get better. I try to comfort myself with the knowledge that Emily's dad is working on Pandora's Box. Like she said, he's one of the best there is—surely he'll figure out a way to fix everything.

I rouse myself when Theo pulls into the Little Nicky's parking lot. It's packed, as usual, but he manages to snag a spot in the very back. We walk, paired up, toward the pizza place, and for a minute I can almost forget everything else that's going on.

It's a beautiful night, not too warm, not too cold. The leaves are finally beginning to change color and fall off the trees. We crunch some beneath our boots and I shiver at the sound. It's crazy, I know, but I love the crisp noise they make and always have.

Eli's hand brushes against mine, and though I stiffen in surprise, I don't move away. A few seconds later, his fingers tangle with mine, and I relax. Let him hold my hand. In those moments—despite the game, the lack of communications, my absentee mother, the lost e-mail from my father, and everything else—I'm calm, forgetting to freak out.

Which lasts until we hit the back door of Little Nicky's, and find, inside, chaos reigning in all directions. It's eight o'clock, and the place is still packed as usual. But instead of the regular semiorganized disorder that comes from people jockeying for tables as their friends or family members wait in line, there's an air of palpable panic that is turning the place into a madhouse.

"What's going on?" I ask, absurdly grateful that Eli is still holding my hand.

"I don't know." Theo shoulders his way through the seething crowd and we follow, Emily, me, and then Eli in back. We get close to the counter, and I realize that the three people working there aren't entering the orders into the registers like they usually do. They're handwriting them, then trying to total the items up on pieces of scratch paper.

They don't even have calculators, and from the frustrated looks on their faces, math isn't their strong suit.

We stand there watching. It's kind of like rubbernecking at an accident that's about to happen. You see the two cars about to run into each other, you want to stop them, but you're too far away and the drivers aren't paying attention to you, anyway. You can't do anything but watch as they collide.

Here, at Little Nicky's, that collision is just happening, and the fallout is growing with each passing second. Because even when the cashiers do get everything right the first time, which has only happened once in the nearly ten minutes we've been standing here, the customer can't pay. The credit-card machine is down and she doesn't have any cash on her.

Her shoulders slump as the two children, one on either side of her, start to cry, and it's obvious she's so frazzled by the whole situation that she doesn't know what to do. I think of my debit card nestled in my wallet and how I don't have any cash, either. If I did, I swear I would have given it to that mother with the two hungry kids.

"Let's go," Eli says. "Nothing good's going to come out of this." He starts pulling me back through the crowd, which has grown bigger and more hostile in the time we've been there. People are yelling and demanding service, some are pushing and shoving, and others are berating the people behind the counter for being slow and stupid.

I've never seen anything like this, and it scares me a little. I can tell Emily feels the same way, because as Eli uses his massive build to force our way through the crowd, she clutches on to my other hand so tightly that I fear ending up with a bloody stump when she finally does let go. I look back at her, just to make sure she's doing okay. Over her shoulder, I see Theo pull out his wallet and hand the upset mother some money.

The crowd is spilling onto the sidewalk in front of the pizza place now, their complaints growing louder and louder. Any joy I had in the beauty of the night is gone, and I can see that my friends feel the same way.

"So, do you want to try someplace else?" Eli asks, though he doesn't sound encouraging.

"It's going to be the same anywhere," Theo answers grimly. He isn't looking at us; he's looking across the street and when I follow his gaze, I realize that he's right. I can see through the front windows of the two restaurants across the street—my mom's favorite little French-style bistro and the Greek restaurant Jules swears by—and the situation is just as dire over there.

"Screw it. We have food at my place," Emily says. "Let's go there. My dad has an old radio he's using to keep in touch with his partners. Maybe he knows more about what's going on."

I don't speak until we're back in the car. I'm in front this time, next to Theo, whose hands are clenched on the steering wheel so tightly that it amazes me he can even turn it. "Why are the credit cards failing?" I ask quietly.

"They're not failing. Or at least I don't think they are," Theo says. "But with no phone lines or Internet, they can't make a connection with the banks, so nobody can charge anything."

"And this is happening all over Austin?" I'm horrified.

"I'm pretty sure it's happening all over the country."

"So there's no money?" Emily asks incredulously. "Anywhere?"

"Oh, there's money." Theo shoves a hand into his hair, and this time it doesn't fall back into place. I take it as a marker of how upset he is that he doesn't even notice. "But people can't get to it. At least not without actually going into a bank. And since it's eight thirty on a Wednesday night, that's so not going to happen."

"Oh my God." I slump back against my seat and bury my head in my hands. "Oh my God. Oh my God. Oh my God."

This can't be happening. This just flat out can't be happening.

But as we head through the quaint little shopping

district, I realize it is. People are everywhere—in the stores, on the streets, in loose groups on every corner, and outside every shop. They look angry, confused, panicked, distraught—all of the things I'm feeling but don't know how to express.

Theo flips on the radio. It's tuned to the alternative station, but he quickly presses the scan button. Nobody says anything as the radio plays a few disjointed seconds from each station, but then there's really nothing to say. Nothing good, anyway.

Finally, the radio hits on someone speaking, and Theo presses the button to keep it there. It's a news station, and the commentator is talking about today's communications collapse as if it really is the end of the world.

"The Internet is down in every city and state in America. It's down in Europe and Asia, Africa and South America, and even Australia, crippled to the point of total and complete uselessness by the Pandora's Box worm.

"Phone systems are down. Satellites are failing. The digital networks we use for our cell phones are collapsing in places as far flung as Malaysia and Norway even as I'm saying this. Control systems are also being affected, for everything from assembly lines at the Oreo cookie plant to systems that regulate air traffic control, and they are all grinding to a halt."

Emily starts to cry a little, and I reach back to squeeze her hand even as the announcer's words send me reeling.

"The streets are filling up with preachers screaming that the end of the world is here, while thousands of people are at home playing a game created by the same person who caused all of this, in the hopes of making things return to normal. I don't understand what's happening here. I'm not sure anyone does.

"The Pentagon is calling it cyberwarfare, and Homeland Security promises they have their best agents at work trying to track down the 'evil genius' who created this. In the meantime, they're asking people to refrain from playing the game in case it makes things worse. But no one is listening—the number of players in the game is increasing with every minute that passes, as people buy into the promise, 'Beat the Game. Save the World.'

"Since the government can't stop it, why not give us the chance to fix things? Besides, how much worse can it get, people? All of this seems like too little, too late to me. The Internet is built to withstand nuclear war, but not a worm? Or a 'blended threat,' as Homeland Security is calling it? So what *is* going on, and how on earth are we going to fix something that we never thought could break? That's what I'll be talking about after these messages."

The question hangs in the air for one second, two, before the airwaves are taken over by a commercial for a local oil-change place. I barely hear the cheerful jingle as it plays—I'm too busy straining to comprehend everything the commentator said. But I can't. My brain is on the verge of a total meltdown.

I think of my mother, in Alaska. Wonder what she's thinking—and if she's worried about me. Realize that I'm worried about her—how is she going to get home from Alaska if the worm has taken out air traffic control? It's already started to snow up there. How can she drive in those conditions? And where will she get a car? How will she pay for it?

Just that easily, panic sets back in.

Aren't there fail-safes for this kind of stuff? Government security that stops things from getting this bad? And if even that security has failed, what are we going to do? How are we going to live if there are no communications? No money. The others are talking, but I can't follow what they are saying. I can't think, can't breathe.

My whole body is tense, shaky, like I'm in the middle of a major caffeine rush, and I'm having a difficult time seeing. I blink my eyes a few times and eventually my vision clears. That's when it hits me. I'm crying.

But I never cry. I gave up the habit right after my dad left and my mom told me tears wouldn't change anything. At first, it didn't matter; I couldn't stop. But weeks passed, and once I realized she was right—that no amount of tears were going to bring back my dad—I simply dried up.

I'm not dry now. I lift a trembling hand to my face, feel the water slowly rolling down my cheek.

What are we supposed to do now? I wonder. *What* can *we do?*

The tears continue to spill over as Theo negotiates the streets. I try to be quiet about it, take shallow breaths from my mouth and don't sniff at all, but somehow Theo knows. He reaches over, rubs my knee in a way that I know is meant to be comforting, but it's not. It's just more proof that things are so not what they seem. What they should be. Because in the real world, there's no way brilliant, moody Theo would ever have anything to do with me. Or me with him.

The thought depresses me further, and I pull my leg away. He doesn't say anything, but he moves his hand back to his thigh, where he's tapping out a rhythm only he knows.

It's dark out, and I stare straight ahead at the green light shining like a beacon directly in front of us. The trick is to concentrate on the small stuff, I tell myself. On the things that are right in front of me.

Electricity is still working for the most part. That's good, right? And I'm no longer alone. Homeland Security is on this thing, and so are some of the best computer-security people in the country—people like Emily's dad, who—

A huge delivery truck comes barreling toward us. Theo brakes, but it's too late. It plows straight into us—directly into the right front quarter of the Range Rover.

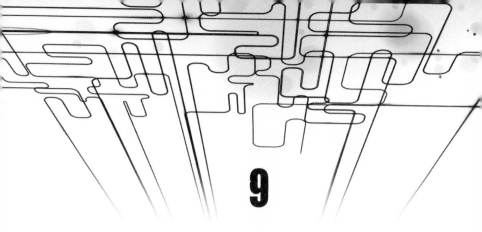

9

EMILY SCREAMS and I try to answer her, but all the air has been knocked out of my lungs at the impact. Then we're spinning, and I can't even think let alone speak as the Range Rover turns in circles again and again.

I reach out and try to grab on to something, to brace myself, but the giant white air bag is in the way. Besides, everything is happening too fast. The world outside is one huge, spiraling blur of lights and colors I can't quite focus on. Like I'm looking at a Kandinsky painting through a lens that has grown foggy with age. Or into the sun after I've been swimming underwater with my eyes open for a long time.

My seat belt cuts into my body as my arms flop uselessly around me. I turn my head, see blood coating Theo's face and the air bag in front of him as we continue to spin. Somehow that's even more surreal than the lights outside the shattered windshield.

I close my eyes. I don't want to see any more.

We rotate for seconds, for hours, for an eternity that feels like it will never end. Except then it does, with a sickening crunch of metal and glass that flips us and sends us skidding across the asphalt on the roof of the car. As we finally come to a stop, the seat belt jerks me hard against the seat back.

We're upside down and pressed hard into another car, the passenger side of the Range Rover squeezed against the driver's side of a small red SUV. My head hurts from where it cracked against the window, a dull ache that blends into all the other aches sweeping over me.

For long seconds, nobody moves or speaks. I swear, we're all holding our breath.

But then Eli coughs, and it breaks the strange spell that has us in its grasp. "Is everybody okay?" Theo demands, a hard edge of command in his voice.

"I think so," Eli replies.

"My leg hurts," Emily moans.

"I think I'm okay," I tell him.

"Good. We need to get out of here." Theo unbuckles his seat belt and falls hard against the windshield, the now-deflated air bag doing little to cushion his fall. He shoves against the driver's-side door, but it's jammed, won't open.

"Can you get your seat belt off?" Theo asks me. He's bleeding from small cuts around his cheek and forehead—*from flying pieces of glass?* I wonder dazedly. *Or something else?*

"Shouldn't we wait for 911?" I ask, craning to look out his window.

A part of me expects an ambulance to materialize from thin air, at least until he says, "There is no 911, remember?" Theo reaches for me, grabs on to my hand. "Are you ready?"

I barely hear his question—I'm too focused on the horror of his first statement. No 911? No police? No ambulances? What are we going to do?

Behind us, Emily starts to sob, and I realize the reality of our situation has finally hit her, too. "It's going to be okay, Em," I tell her, though I'm afraid I'm lying. Right now, I can't imagine how anything is ever going to be okay again.

Theo releases my seat belt right then, and I fall, not nearly as hard as he did, though, as he shifts so that he can catch me. His gallantry costs him. I can tell from his hard exhale, the groan he can't quite bury.

"Sorry."

He shakes his head, lets go of me slowly.

Behind me, Eli has released his seat belt as well and is trying to help Emily out of hers. "I can't," she wails. "It hurts."

"I know it does." He speaks to her soothingly. "But we've got to get you outside, so that we can see what's wrong."

I twist to face her, peer around the side of the seat to get a better look at her. Then I almost wish I hadn't, as she's a mess. She's even bloodier than Theo, her face already bruised and swelling from where she hit something, hard.

"We need to get her out of here," I tell Theo urgently.

"I'm trying," he answers, and then he's pulling back his at-least-size-fifteen foot, slamming it into the windshield as hard as he can manage in his awkward position.

The windshield cracks some more but doesn't shatter, so

I kick with him the second time. The whole car shudders, slides, under the combined power of our blows, but the windshield still doesn't give. A random thought goes through my head—that this looks so much easier in the movies than it is in real life—and then it's gone, as Theo's foot connects squarely with the most broken part of the windshield.

A huge *crack* echoes through the car, and then more small pieces of glass are flying everywhere. Theo struggles a bit, pulls off his shirt, and wraps it around his arm. He's got a gash on his left side, and it's already starting to bruise around it. I know it must hurt to move, but he doesn't even flinch as he knocks out more glass—enough that we can climb through the windshield and onto the ground.

We land in a pile of tangled limbs. "This way," I say, crawling out from under the hood on the left side of the car and scrambling to my feet. Without looking, I know Theo is following me.

"We're coming, Em. Just hold on a little longer!"

"I can't," she sobs, and I hear Eli talking to her quietly. He doesn't make a mad scramble for the front, like I thought he would—like I very well might have in the same circumstances—and I'm grateful he's there with her. Because we have a bigger problem now.

Theo sways a little, and I reach a hand out to brace him. But when I do, I realize it's not him that's unsteady, it's me. I must have hit my head harder than I thought.

Something's crawling on my face and I lift my hand to swat it, but my fingers come away red and sticky. It's not a bug, I realize with a detached kind of horror. It's blood slowly leaking down my face. I wipe at it a little with my arm, but there's no time to do anything else, because once he realizes I can stand on my own, Theo starts walking around to the other side of the car.

"We need to get Emily out," I tell him.

"Hold on a minute. We need to see— Shit, come here!"

There's dismay in his voice, and it galvanizes me like nothing else could have. Adrenaline, already in heavy supply, surges through my bloodstream, and I race to where he's standing as fast as my wobbly legs will carry me.

And that's when I realize what he already has. The car we've slammed up against isn't a parked car as I originally thought. Its engine is running, and there are people in it: a child screaming in the backseat and a man behind the wheel.

I stumble around to the passenger side, yank open the front door. "Are you okay, sir?"

He looks at me, shell-shocked, and I realize I can only see his left arm from the shoulder to right above the elbow. The rest of it must have been resting outside the open window when we hit, because it's crushed between his car and the Range Rover.

"Oh. My. God. Oh my God. Ohmygod, ohmygod, ohmygod!"

"Don't freak out on me, Pandora!" Theo's voice cracks like a whip.

It steadies me a little, has me glancing around wildly for help. But there aren't many cars on the road right now, and the few that are out don't stop.

Their behavior isn't normal. This is a nice area of Austin, where people help each other all the time. So why aren't they stopping? Why aren't they *helping*?

I lift my arms, try to flag someone down, but Theo says, "Don't waste your time. They're too stressed out by everything that's happening. They're in survival mode. We're going to have to do this ourselves."

I'm horrified. Horrified by what he's said, and even more horrified by the actions of the people around us. Across the street is the delivery truck that hit us, the driver passed out over his steering wheel. No one's stopped to help him, either.

"Pandora!" Theo calls my name again and I snap to attention.

"We need to get the cars apart," I say, opening the back door and crawling inside to unbuckle the screaming child. It's a little boy, maybe four or five, with blond hair and blue eyes. He looks pale and frightened in the yellow glow of the streetlights, but he's not hurt—at least, not that I can see. "Come on, sweetie. Let me get you out of here." I reach for him.

"Daddy!" he cries.

"Go with her, Josh," the father tells him, his voice weak and shocked. "I'll be right behind you."

"Daddy!"

"Go, Josh!"

"Come on, Josh," I tell him. "Hold on to me and I'll get you to the sidewalk. Then we can help your dad."

He whimpers the whole time, but he scoots over a little, wraps his arms tightly around my neck. My already-sore body protests his weight, but I ignore the aches and pains and carry him away from the car to a spot about ten feet down the sidewalk.

"Can you wait for me here?"

"I want my daddy," he wails at me around the thumb he's started to suck.

"We're going to get your daddy. I promise. But I need you to stay here so nothing else happens to you. Can you do that for me?"

He nods.

"Okay, good." I start to pull away, but he's hanging on to me with all his strength. "I have to go, Josh."

He starts to cry again, and it's the most pathetic, lonely sound I've ever heard. In a normal world, I'd be able to sit here, comforting him, while others helped his father. But we're a long way from normal, and if I don't work with Theo, no one will. "I'll be back, baby, I promise. But I need to help your dad, okay?"

He lets go reluctantly, and I want nothing more than to hold him on my lap and rock him. But Theo is between the two cars, straining to move the Range Rover away from the red SUV so that he can free Josh's dad.

It isn't working, of course. Theo is huge and strong, but he can't *actually* slide a car across the ground on his own. I run over, lend my strength to his, but that doesn't work, either. I'm nowhere near strong enough to do it.

"We need Eli out of the car for this," Theo says. "He can help."

I rush back around to Eli's side of the Range Rover with Theo on my heels, try to open the door. It's jammed from the roll, just like Theo's, but at least it's moving. Theo and I wedge our shoulders against the car and yank. Metal scrapes against metal but I feel a little give. We pull harder, so hard that there's a sharp pain down my arms and between my shoulder blades.

A little more slide. A little more give.

Theo grunts and pulls harder, and suddenly the door is free. It flies open, sends me careening onto my butt. Eli's out in seconds, and then he and Theo are rushing to the front of the other SUV. I reassure Emily that we'll be right back and then hurry to join them.

By the time I get back to it, Eli and Theo have already taken hold of the front bumper. Under my amazed gaze, they each bend their legs and lift. The front wheels of the car come up, and then I'm rushing forward and we're all pushing.

The car moves a few inches before they drop it again.

We do the same thing again and again—lift, push, drop—until there's enough room for us to squeeze between the cars. But when we get to the driver's side of the SUV, to Josh's dad, I feel the blood drain from my face. His arm is crushed, nearly detached from his body, and now that the pressure of the car is gone, blood is gushing everywhere. He must have severed an artery.

Emily looks over and sees the man. She starts to scream and scream. I want to go to her, but Josh's dad is more important now.

"Eli!" He doesn't look like he's in any better shape than my best friend, so I shove him out of the way, toward Emily. "Go see about getting Emily out of the car. Theo and I will take care of this."

Then I spring into action, terrified that I'm going to do something wrong, but more terrified that this man is going to die right here in front of me. I whip off my sparkly tank top, wrap it around what's left of his arm, and try to apply enough pressure to stop the bleeding with one hand, even as I start to undo my belt buckle with the other.

"Josh," he gasps.

"Josh is fine," I tell him. "He's sitting on the curb. What's *your* name?" My fingers slip on the buckle, and I nearly scream in frustration.

"Anthony."

"Everything will be okay, Anthony," I tell him. "We're going to get you some help."

Theo steps in front of me, bats my fumbling fingers away. "Keep the pressure on," he says as he whips my belt out of my jeans. He loops it around the top of Anthony's biceps, then pulls harder and harder until the gushing blood slows to a trickle. Then he knots the belt so that the pressure will stay on.

I toss aside my saturated shirt, and with Theo on one side and me on the other, we help Anthony over to the curb. To his son. "Someone will stop soon," I tell him, and again hope I'm not lying. "We'll get you to a hospital."

He nods, but he's in bad shape, his face pale and sweaty and his entire body shaking. Still, he wraps his good arm around Josh and pulls him in close.

Unable to do any more for him right now, Theo and I run to the Range Rover, where Eli is back in the car, pounding on Emily's door from the inside. In the crash, it caved inward, wrapping itself around the top of Emily's leg. She's completely wedged in.

Now the only question is, how are we going to get her out?

I look at Theo, but he looks as bewildered as I feel. We need the fire department. The Jaws of Life. Something. But there isn't anything—just us.

"Eli." Theo's voice is calm, but his jaw is clenched so tightly that I have to listen closely to understand what he's saying. He's at the back of the SUV now, trying to open the tailgate, but it won't budge, either. "I need you to crawl into the back. Your dad usually keeps a tool kit there. The red box. Remember?"

Eli starts moving before Theo even finishes his sentence. Emily whimpers as he leaves her. I crouch on the ground, next to her window. "We're going to fix this. We're going to get you out. I promise."

"Found it!" Eli crows, and then a soft-sided red bag flies toward Theo, who is sitting on the ground, next to Eli's open door. He catches it, pulls out a small hammer—the kind you use to break windshields. We glance wryly at each other. Too little, too late. There's also a bigger hammer in the tool kit, a huge screwdriver, a long, heavy flashlight, and some Allen wrenches.

Theo pulls out the screwdriver and hammer, hands them to Eli, who's made it out of the trunk again. "Can you wedge the screwdriver under the caved-in part of the door?"

"I'll try." Eli leans over Emily, and he must have jostled her because she cries out again.

"I'm sorry," I hear him whisper to her.

"That's okay. Just please get me out of here."

"I will." The metal screeches in protest as he pounds at the screwdriver with a hammer, but it moves a little.

Emily starts to cry. I tilt my head so that our eyes can

meet through the car window. "Just a little longer, Emily. I promise. Just a little more."

She nods, puts a hand up to the glass.

I place my hand up so that it meets hers, with only the glass of the car window in between. Palm to palm. It's the way we used to swear promises when we were little girls. We haven't done it in years, but it feels right now, here in the middle of all this chaos. It's a pledge, from both of us, not to give up.

Eli hits the screwdriver again, and Emily screams this time. I don't know if that's a good sign or a bad one, but I smile encouragingly at her. "Come on, Em. We're almost there."

Eli's pounding away in earnest now, and the metal is twisting, shuddering. Emily looks terrified, but I hold her gaze with my own. Will her to be strong, to hold on, not to lose it. Not yet.

"Wiggle your leg a little," Eli tells her, and she does. A smile crosses his lips briefly, and I know it's good news. The door is moving. A little bit at a time, but it is moving.

I glance at Theo, who has run over to the truck that hit us and is trying to rouse the driver. He's not having any luck, and suddenly I'm terrified the driver is dead. That he's been dying this whole time and we didn't even bother to check.

I don't know how this happened. Our light was green, I know it was. I saw it. Did the delivery truck just run a solid red, then? Was he distracted by the radio, by what's going on in the world? I glance up at the traffic lights to make sure I didn't imagine it, to make sure they really are working.

They are. The lights are green. So how . . . And that's when it hits me. From my vantage point I can see a cross section of lights, one that runs north-south and one that runs east-west. Both sides are green. *Both sides are green!*

The worm must have somehow affected the control system that runs the traffic lights, and turned them green in all directions. No wonder we crashed.

And we can't be the only ones. If this has happened at every intersection in the city, in the state, in the country, how many people have gotten hurt? And how many have died?

Horror is a live thing deep within me, twisting and turning, raging and seething, until I can barely think. This can't be happening. It just can't be happening.

I glance down the street, pray for a car to stop. For a policeman to see us. For a miracle—something, anything, but it's no use. Traffic has slowed down even more in the time we've been out here, which is typical of life around here. By nine o'clock things are quiet, and by nine thirty, people are usually tucked into their houses.

Still, we're not completely alone. It just feels like we are.

Minutes tick by as Eli continues to work, and even in the glow of the streetlamps I can see the sweat pouring off him. Josh has stopped crying, so the only sound that splits the silence of the night is Eli's harsh breathing and the hammer striking the screwdriver again and again.

"Hurry," I whisper, even though I know Eli's doing the best he can.

Suddenly Emily screams. I jump, try to peer through the window. Before I can even get a good look, Eli's crawled out of the car, Emily in his arms.

"Oh, thank God!"

"Theo!" he bellows, as he deposits her on the ground

under a streetlamp that's a good thirty feet away from the crash site. "Get your ass over here."

Theo comes running, as if he's just been waiting for Eli's shout.

I crouch next to Emily, check to see how badly she's injured.

"I think I'm okay," she tells me, but I ignore her as I poke and prod at her right leg. Her thigh is black and blue, her knee swollen, but there's no blood, and she can move everything fairly well. I think she's probably right, that nothing's broken, but then, what do I know?

"Just sit there," I tell her when she tries to stand, and after a couple of false starts, she listens to me. Which is surefire proof that she's feeling worse than she's letting on.

Just then a car pulls up to the crash site, its headlights focused directly on the two SUVs. I blink, try to get my eyes to adjust to the sudden brightness. Two men jump out of the car and run around to our side.

"How can we help?" one asks.

I'm a little shocked that someone has finally stopped to help, but I finally point at Anthony, who is listing to the side, his face completely white. He doesn't look good, and I know if he doesn't get treated soon, he'll die.

"Can you take him to the hospital?" I ask. "There are no ambulances—"

"Of course. Let's get the two of them into the back of my car."

It takes a few minutes of maneuvering, but we finally manage to get Anthony stretched out in the back, his head in Josh's lap. Then the two men slide into the car and drive off a lot faster than the forty-five miles an hour the area calls for. Seconds later, the truck that hit us roars to life and careens unsteadily down the street, barely missing Theo where he's standing on the side of the road.

Emily hobbles over to me, and the four of us stare after the truck for long seconds. I'm sure my mouth is open, but I can't summon the will or the control to close it. But then, neither can any of my friends.

A car drives by—a BMW—and the driver honks at us, not even bothering to slow down. He tosses us the bird, yelling out the window at us for blocking the road.

As one, we scoot back. Seconds later, lightning flashes across the sky and it begins to rain.

That's when Eli starts to laugh.

Emily and Theo look at him like he's crazy, and maybe he is, but I understand the emotions ripping through him.

The surreal shock of our present situation.

The horrified amazement at the utter callousness of other human beings.

And, most of all, the sheer relief that the four of us are alive and relatively unharmed, despite the scrapes and bruises that currently decorate every inch of us.

Though now that the adrenaline has stopped pumping quite so fast, the aches and pains I felt before have grown a hundred times worse. Judging from the way the others are moving, the same thing is happening to them. I reach up, gingerly feel the cut at my hairline. There's a bump there, but at least it's stopped bleeding.

"So," Emily says, turning to me once Eli finally quiets down. "What do we do now?"

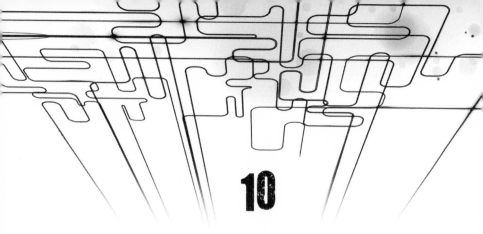

10

TIME TICKS BY, and I don't answer her question, largely because I don't have a clue what to say. Eli does, though.

He strides over to where what's left of the Range Rover sits, lopsided and destroyed, on the pavement. Then he reaches in through the windshield and grabs my backpack and Emily's purse, along with the massive flashlight from the tool kit. After tossing me a shirt from the front pocket of my backpack he slings both bags over his massive shoulder and says, simply, "We walk."

So that's what we do, heading north along Heatherwilde toward my house, which is closer than Emily's. We're a bedraggled group—bloodstained and injured, tattered and weary—walking in pairs, side by side. A song I haven't heard since childhood starts to beat fragile wings against the corners of my bruised and battered mind.

The ants go marching two by two, hurrah, hurrah
The ants go marching two by two,
The little one stops to tie his shoe
And they all go marching down to the ground
To get out of the rain.

I wonder if that's what we look like, and more, if that's what we are to the person who designed this nightmare, who did this to all of us. Just ants scuttling along the earth, annoying and unimportant, as we try to save our useless little existence.

I think we must be, because how else could he do this? How else could he ruin so many lives so easily?

Does he know? Wherever he is, does he see what he's done to us? Is this what he planned all along, or has it taken on a life of its own? Are things worse than even *he* imagined?

A car drives by too quickly for the conditions, and its tires kick up water from the puddles forming near the curb. It sprays all over us, and Emily curses, slips. Theo's right there to grab her, his hand on her elbow, lending support. But the near fall hurts her already-damaged knee, and when she tries to walk again, her limp is much more pronounced.

"I need to rest for a second," she says, and I can hear the pain in her voice. I want to tell her it's okay, that we can stay here as long as she wants, but the storm is getting worse. And what was a fifteen-minute drive is going to be closer to a three-hour walk, especially at the rate she's able to move.

In the end, I don't say anything at all, just start to help her over to the retaining wall that edges the sidewalk. Before we get there, though, Theo and Eli stop us. "Grab on to my shoulders and wrap your legs around my waist," Theo tells her. When she can't pull herself up, Eli gives her a boost onto Theo's back.

"You can't—"

"Just do it," I say. "We need to get going."

She finally does, reluctantly, but asks, "When did you turn into a Nike commercial?"

"Right around the time the world went insane. You got a problem with that?"

"No." She grins at me. "Just checking."

Now that he doesn't have to worry about Emily's leg, Theo sets a brutal pace that has me scrambling to keep up. Which amazes me, considering he's got Emily on his back plus his own injuries from the car accident. She doesn't weigh much more than a hundred pounds, but still. Sometimes he and Eli seem almost superhuman.

We walk for miles in the dark, for hours that seem to stretch on forever even with the steady beam of Eli's flashlight to lead the way. Though the storm finally lets up when we're about halfway home, by the time we make the turn onto my street, I'm ready to weep with joy, and from exhaustion. It's after midnight, and while I'm a night owl, I swear this has been the longest day of my life. I want nothing more than to take a hot shower, crawl into bed. And wake up tomorrow with everything back to normal.

Not that that's going to happen, but a girl can hope.

Suddenly, Emily starts struggling against Theo's hold. "Let me down," she says.

He casts a surprised look over his shoulder. "Just let me get you to Pandora's—"

"No, it's fine. My mom's probably waiting at Pandora's house ready to rip me a new one. We were supposed to be back at my place hours ago."

"And that has *what* to do with my carrying you?"

Emily doesn't answer, but then she doesn't have to. I've known Emily's mom for more than a decade, and while she's great, and everything my mom isn't, she also tends to overreact. If she sees her youngest child being carried home by a half-naked giant, there will be a scene like no other. And Emily will end up spending the night in the emergency room, whether she needs to or not.

"Just let her down," I tell him. "It'll make everything easier."

He starts to argue, but something changes his mind. I'm not sure what it is, though he casts a wary glance down the street to my house. The look is gone almost as soon as it appears—before I can decipher it—and after a second he squats down so I can help Emily off his massive back. When he stands, the streetlight catches his face just right and I realize the other reason Emily is making such a fuss.

Theo looks tired, weary, all the way to his bones. It seems strange to see him like this—all night, he's been so strong, and now, suddenly, he looks amazingly, vulnerably human. But then, he did perform miracles at the crash site before carrying Emily ten miles, all while injured himself.

She must sense that it's caught up with him.

The last little bit seems to take forever. Emily's knee is a lot better and she's barely limping, but the rest of us aren't doing so well. My feet are on fire, and I have blisters on both of my heels.

We finally get to Theo and Eli's house, and I raise my hand in an exhausted good-bye, but Eli says, "You're not getting rid of us that easily. We'll walk you to your front door." If possible, he looks even more tired than Theo, like putting one foot in front of the other requires a gigantic effort.

"I'm not going to my front door," I tell him. "We're going around that curve up there and getting into Emily's car. Everything else will have to wait until tomorrow. I'm done."

"Okay. Then we'll walk you to the car," Eli says stubbornly.

"Seriously?" I roll my eyes, give him a little shove toward his driveway. "Go get some sleep."

"Yeah." Theo puts a hand on Eli's shoulder, steers him toward their house. "We'll see you tomorrow." The gesture, and the words, are totally out of character for him, but I'm too tired to examine his motives.

Eli looks like he's going to protest as Emily reaches into her purse, pulls out paper and a pen, scribbles something on it, and holds it out to them. "That's my address. I live behind the huge H-E-B on Market. Come over whenever you wake up, and maybe my dad can help with the whole accident thing."

Theo takes the paper, nods. "Thanks." Then he turns to Eli. "Come on." His voice is hard, determined.

We leave them there, watching us, though it seems strange. This morning I'd been worried by Theo and disdainful of Eli, and now I don't want to leave them. I know it's stupid, but every instinct I have is screaming that I am safe with them in a way I'm not anywhere else right now.

Still, I let them go—what else can I do? But the moment

we walk around the second bend separating my house and Eli's, I know I should have followed those instincts.

Something is wrong. Really wrong.

Pandora's Box wrong.

The whole back section of the street, which is normally dark and quiet by eight o'clock every night, is lit up like Rockefeller Center two days before Christmas.

My stomach tightens and I freeze. *Please don't let it be for me, please don't let it be for me.* The words run through my head—my own personal mantra against this strange hell my life has turned into.

Emily grabs my hand, whispers, "Let's go back and get the guys. They probably have another car—they can drive us to my house."

"What if your mom's here?"

"She's not," Emily tells me. "Let's go."

"I can't just run away from this."

We move a little closer, scan the front of my house and the cars parked in my driveway. Besides Emily's, there are two white cars with red and blue flashing lights. A black car with ominously shaded windows. And perhaps most frightening is the huge SUV with gun racks visible in the back. For the first time in a very long time, I wish for my mother in more than the abstract. She's a lawyer, and it sucks, just completely sucks, that she is thousands of miles away when I need her most.

"Going for help isn't running away. My dad knows FBI people, works with them. He can help us."

That sounds good. I need all the help I can get.

"I just don't understand why the government is here," she

continues. "They can't be going to every house that plays Pandora's Box. Otherwise we would have seen them when we passed Theo and Eli's, right?"

I don't answer. There's a sick feeling in my stomach as I think back to the birthday present on my laptop screen, the one I hadn't wanted to open. Was I the only one to get that message? The only one in the world picked to unleash this disaster? It doesn't make sense.

I take a deep breath, try to calm down. But the one thought that manages to get through the haze only makes it harder to function. *Did I do this? Did I somehow do* all *of* this?

I think of the chaos at Little Nicky's, of Josh screaming for his daddy, of his father so badly injured. I think of all the panicked people on the street outside the restaurants.

Is all of that somehow my fault?

How can that be possible? The Internet failed before I ever touched that gift. So did the phones and the TV. Pandora's Box might have caused this, but it isn't my fault. *It isn't my fault.*

I repeat it again and again, trying to convince myself.

But then why are the police and God only knows who else in my driveway? In my house? It's not like they have nothing better to do tonight—the accident we were involved in proves that they do.

Emily and I hold on to each other tightly as we take a few steps backward. I don't have much of a plan, short of getting around the bend before they stop us and then running like hell back to Eli and Theo. Everything inside me screams that Theo will know what to do.

But we've only taken a few steps when someone in the driveway points a flashlight at where we'd been standing a few seconds before. "Hey!" a deep male voice shouts. "Who's there?" The light moves as he begins to run toward us, looking anything but friendly.

I want to flee, to race back in the other direction. Except Emily's knee couldn't take it, and where would we go, anyway? Now that they've spotted us, it's not like we can just disappear. And the last thing I want is to bring this to Eli and Theo's doorstep—they don't deserve it.

"Go," I whisper fiercely to Emily even as I step toward the pool of light under the streetlamp. Maybe I can distract their attention, give her a chance to get away. "Get out of here!"

"And let you face this alone?" she answers indignantly. "As if."

"Damn it, Emily, hurry. He's almost here."

I try to shake her off, but her grip on my hand tightens. "I'm not going anywhere."

"You don't have to do this."

"Yes, I do. I'm not leaving you. Besides, they could just be here to help."

"Does he look like he wants to help? And why me? Go, Emily!" I rip my hand from hers and take off running, straight toward the police officer. "Hey, who are you?" I shout, trying to get his attention.

Get away, I tell her fiercely in my head. *Get away, get away, get away.*

But Emily isn't my oldest and most loyal friend for nothing. She hustles after me, calling my name, loud and clear enough for everyone in a two-mile radius to hear.

The policeman stops in front of me, shines his light in my face, and I blink, try to focus. "Are you Pandora Walker?" he asks, his voice deep and serious. He's young, and a little frightened looking despite the no-nonsense voice. His blue eyes are wild in the eerie glow cast by the lights, and his hair is standing on end, like he's been running his fingers through it all night.

"Yes." It takes every ounce of control I have to stop my voice from shaking.

"You need to come with me." He turns the flashlight on Emily, who has stopped right behind me. "Emily Scott?"

"Yes?"

"How did you know her—"

"Is that your car?" he asks, talking over me and pointing at Emily's cute little Prius, sitting at the top of my driveway. The front passenger window is smashed, where they must have broken in to get her information. With no Internet, they couldn't just run her license plate.

She nods, swallows audibly. I can tell she's terrified, and I'm furious she didn't try to get away when I gave her the chance. I'm even more furious that we're in this position at all. It's ridiculous. I didn't do *anything* but play a stupid video game.

"What are you doing here?" I demand.

"Let's go in the house and talk." He sweeps his arm in a mockery of gallantry as he motions for Emily and me to precede him up the driveway.

"What if I don't want to go in the house?"

His flashlight, and eyes, run over me. The rain has washed away most of the blood—and my careful hairstyle—but his gaze lingers on my nose piercing, Social D tank top, and ripped jeans. He's already decided I'm a troublemaker.

"Then you can sit in the back of my police car while I go inside and let the various agents in there fight over where they want to take you."

"The house it is," Emily says brightly, her eyes pleading with me to keep my mouth shut. Which I do, but it bothers me. I don't like being threatened, especially when I haven't done anything illegal.

I start walking.

Behind me, the cop pulls out a walkie-talkie and mutters a couple of codes I don't understand. But the next thing I know, all hell breaks loose.

People flood out of my front door. Men and women in uniform, in suits, in jeans and polo shirts. I don't know who to look at, don't know what to do, and I feel myself shrinking back, curling in on myself. Suddenly bravery and self-sacrifice seem completely overrated and I know—with total certainty—that the only thing stopping me from running, from probably being shot in the back, is Emily's arm linked through mine.

Three people—two men and a woman—break away from the pack. They aren't running, but they are moving quickly and with an authority that tells me they're in charge here. Which seems strange. This is my house, my mother's house, and the idea that all these people have been in there for God only knows how long, pawing through my stuff and finding out every secret we have—which admittedly isn't many—makes my stomach hurt.

"Pandora Walker?" asks the woman, who gets to me first.

She's dressed in a gray pantsuit, and she looks pissed. Her mouth is pinched, her blond hair scraped back into a bun so tight it pulls at the corners of her eyes.

I nod, not knowing what else to do.

"Come inside. We need to ask you a few questions."

"Excuse me, but can I see some identification? Who are you people? And do you have a search warrant?" Emily asks, and I'm grateful all over again that she is with me, though the last thing I want to do is get her in trouble. My brain has all but shut down, so that questions about what is going on are foreign to me. As are thoughts about my rights.

One of the men steps forward, and unlike the other two, he isn't dressed in a suit. Instead, he's wearing threadbare jeans and a black T-shirt—much like Eli was. The lack of formality should put me at ease, but it doesn't. How can it, when his face looks carved from granite, his eyes so dark and intense that it seems like he can see straight through to my soul?

The look he gives me says he's not happy with what he sees.

"I'm Tom Mackaray, with Homeland Security. This is Frances Lessing of the FBI,"—he gestures to the woman—"and this is Michael Lundstrom from the NSA."

Jesus. Is there a domestic law enforcement acronym that isn't represented here? I sway and Emily reaches out, steadies me.

"Where are you two coming from, Pandora?"

"We went out for pizza." Emily again.

He frowns at her, and I'm shocked to see that his face

really does move, after all. "When I want to hear from you, Ms. Scott, I'll address you."

"Yes, sir." Emily quiets quickly under his scrutiny, not that I blame her. Despite his casual appearance, this man looks like he wants to throw us in a deep, dark hole and toss away the key. Which is a bad thing for so many, many reasons, not the least of which is the phobia I've done my best to ignore all night. I'd never last in a cell like that because I'm terrified of the dark.

"So, now that we've all been introduced, let's go inside." It's Lundstrom talking, and he's all but bristling with impatience.

"You still haven't shown us the search warrant." I speak up this time.

"No, I haven't." Mackaray tries to stare me down, but I'm not budging. Not on this. Maybe it's a dumb move, but I don't want to go into the house with these people. Looking into their faces, I'm suddenly aware of just how distant a document the Constitution really is.

Lundstrom grumbles, takes a threatening step toward us. At any second I expect him to grab us and shove us into the house—or to pull a gun and force us in that way. But as long seconds pass, he just stands there, glowering.

Finally, Lessing reaches into her pocket and pulls out a document. As she hands it to me, her eyes go to a spot behind us, and I realize the reason they're playing so nicely is because we have an audience. My neighbors across the street are watching. And though the world seems to have gone to hell in one evening, I guess it's still not a good idea to man-handle kids. At least not if there are other options.

I open the envelope and stare at the words on the page. They don't make much sense to me, but even I know enough to realize that I'm holding the real deal. I skim through until I get to the scary words:

Seize and examine, by persons qualified to do so, and in a laboratory setting, any and all electronic data processing and media devices that may have been used while engaging in cyberterrorism as defined in the Annotated Code of Texas, amended and revised.

Cyberterrorism.

My knees buckle, and I swear I would have fallen if Emily wasn't there, holding me up.

This is happening. Oh my God, this is really happening. Reading those words makes this real. The FBI and Homeland Security are in my house, accusing me of cyberterrorism and searching for— I find the spot on the warrant that details what they want, which feels like everything. My laptop, my cell phone, my digital TV box, my iPod, my PlayStation, my iPad, and any other electronic equipment they can find.

"Cyberterrorism." I can't get the word—and its implications—out of my head.

They think I did this. They think I brought down the Internet and everything else that's started to fail. Traffic lights. ATMs. Telephone networks all over the world.

It's ridiculous, completely absurd. Or it would be if three federal agents weren't currently studying me like I'm a particularly disgusting specimen of bug under a microscope.

Suddenly, I hear Theo's voice in my head. *Unless you're the point of origin. Then it makes perfect sense.*

Point of origin. Oh God.

My blood turns cold at the idea of being alone with Mackaray and his pale, furious gaze. I glance at Emily, who is reading over my shoulder, and realize that our last—our only—objection has just disappeared. "Now, are you willing to come inside with us and talk, or should I let Agent Mackaray escort you to his office?" Lessing asks, her mouth even tighter than her bun. "He *is* claiming jurisdiction."

"No. We'll come inside." I step forward, still skimming the search warrant. They have all of my stuff, everything. I left it out in the open before we left, never thinking for a second that my house—my life—was about to be invaded.

I just don't know what they expect to find. Electronic blueprints for a worm I have almost no knowledge of? It doesn't make sense. Especially since I barely knew what one was before Theo explained it to me earlier.

The three agents sweep us up the driveway and into my house. The second we hit the front door I'm overwhelmed—and strangely it's not because of the three people at my side or the two policemen waiting in my driveway.

It's because my mother's normally pristine house has been torn apart, piece by piece. Every drawer is open, every cabinet emptied. I glance back down at the search warrant. If what they wanted is in plain sight, why are they looking everywhere else?

The answer hits me as I pick my way through the family room, which has been turned inside out. They're doing this, ripping my whole world apart, because they can.

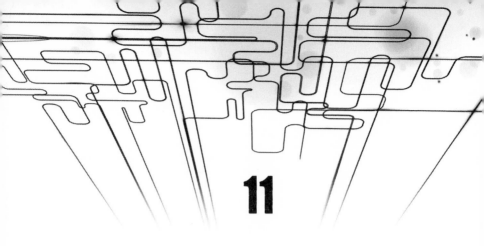

11

I'M SHAKING WHEN I SIT DOWN at the kitchen table, in the chair Lessing points to. A quick look at Emily says she is, too, although from the color in her cheeks as she surveys the damage, I think she might be rallying. Which scares me even worse. I try to catch her eye, to warn her not to say anything else, but she deliberately turns away.

"We want a lawyer. And we're underage. We need to talk to our parents."

"Once we realized you had come back with Pandora, I sent someone to get your father, Ms. Scott. He should be here shortly." Lundstrom eyes her impatiently.

"Good. Because this is ridiculous. You know that, right? He's spent his whole life fighting these kinds of crimes for you guys, and he's going to be pissed that you're accusing me—"

"We're not accusing you of anything."

"Oh. Okay." Emily subsides, the wind knocked out of

her sails just that easily. It's hard to fight someone if they won't engage.

"What about me?" I force out the words. "What are you accusing *me* of?"

"Nothing." This time it's Mackaray who answers. "We just want to talk to you." As his eyes sweep over me, lingering on my wet shirt and scraped-up hands, I decide that I hate him. That I won't tell him anything. Not that there's anything *to* tell, but still.

"What happened to you?" he asks.

"We fell in the dark," Emily says when I don't speak up.

"Are you okay?" Lessing asks.

"They're obviously fine," Mackaray answers for us.

"Tom, go take a walk," Lessing says. She's leaning against the cabinets, ankles and arms crossed, a bored expression on her face.

Mackaray bristles—it's clear he's not used to having his authority questioned—but in the end he backs down. I assume because they think I'll respond better to a woman. Guess that means they haven't figured out everything about me yet.

Lessing crosses to the table slowly, hitches a hip up on the corner. Then she leans down so that we're face-to-face, and I see that she's wearing a sympathetic expression. I don't believe it for a second, but I give her props for trying.

"So, Pandora, are you really okay?" she asks.

Do I look okay? I want to ask. But I don't, just nod sullenly.

"Good." She pauses. "Is there anything you want to talk about?"

I glance around my demolished house. "Are you kidding me?"

"Why don't you tell us what you've gotten yourself into. Maybe we can help."

Yes, because so far they've been sooooo helpful. I decide to brazen it out. "I don't know what you're talking about. It's my seventeenth birthday. Emily came over and we went out for pizza. I don't see what the big deal is."

"Really? You don't have *any* idea what I'm talking about?"

I don't want to answer, but she won't move on. "No, ma'am," I finally say.

"Hmm. Okay. So where did you go tonight?"

"To Little Nicky's. On Red Bud Trail."

"Did you? And what kind of pizza did you order?"

"We didn't. Things were so crazy there that we left without ordering." Lessing is staring at me like she thinks I'm lying, but I'm being very careful to stick to the truth. Just not the whole truth. I don't mention Eli or Theo, because I don't want to bring them into this when all they did was try to help me. Emily's already stuck firmly in the middle—I don't want to do that to anyone else.

For once, the best-friend ESP seems to be working, because Emily doesn't say anything about the guys, either. Just nods along with my story. Her stomach even growls, right on cue.

"What do you mean by crazy?"

I shoot Lessing a disbelieving look. "Surely you've seen it. Whatever's going on with the phones is totally messing up the credit-card machines."

"Whatever's going on with the phones," she repeats, her

eyes gleaming, and I get the impression that I have some-how walked right into a trap. But for the life of me, I can't figure out what it is. "And what *is* going on, Pandora?"

"I have no idea."

"Why don't you give me your best guess?"

"I don't know! I swear, I don't. I just know that every-thing is messed up—cell phones, Internet, landlines, because of the Pandora's Box worm."

"And what do you know about Pandora's Box?" She pounces, like she's just been waiting for me to say the words.

I start to tell her that I heard about it on the car radio, but we walked home. If I admit to listening, to being in a car, she's going to want to know who, what, when, where, how, and why. Any chance I have of keeping Theo and Eli away from this will go right out the window.

"I just know what everybody else knows," I finally say. "I got the total-annihilation message today and then my phones went wonky. Same thing that's happened to a lot of people. Right?"

I wait, breath held, for her response. So far, she's been asking me all the questions, and I admit I like being able to turn the tables on her.

Of course, she's a lot better at this than I am, and all she does is raise one perfectly arched eyebrow at me. "No. You're not. But I am curious. We've been through all the equipment in the house. Nothing shows that you've played at all."

"I'm sorry. I'm not sure what you're asking."

"I'm asking on what device did you play Pandora's Box today? Because nothing in this house registers it."

"Of course it does. My—" I break off right before I

mention my laptop, because I suddenly remember where it is. In my backpack, which, the last time I saw it, was draped over Eli's shoulder.

"Your?" A second eyebrow joins the first.

"My cell phone. I played on my cell phone." I reach into my pocket, pull out my phone, and hand it to her. It's completely dead right now, and when they charge it they'll see that I actually have logged on to Pandora's Box from there before. Will that be enough for them to believe me?

She slips a glove out of her pocket and puts it on before taking the phone and sliding it into a small plastic bag. I love that phone, use it constantly, and now it's evidence. Against me. I watch it disappear into her pocket and wonder if I'll ever see it again. Which is a stupid worry considering how much trouble I'm in, and considering that the phone is basically worthless now. Who knows how long this communications blackout is going to last. Ten days? But what happens when the countdown runs out? What is the Pandora's Box madman's idea of total annihilation?

I'm afraid to find out. We all are. Even the federal agents in front of me. I remind myself of that when Lessing stands up and begins to circle me like a hungry predator playing with its prey. That she's doing all this because she's afraid. And because it's her job.

It doesn't make me like her more, though, or make me want to cooperate. Fearful or not, she takes way too much pleasure in her job.

She's staring at me now, and I force myself not to squirm, not to react at all. For a long time she doesn't say anything and neither do I. She's waiting me out and I can't afford to break. Not now. But the silence is grating—and not just on me. Out of the corner of my eye, I can see Emily's leg bouncing up and down like a metronome on high.

She's also shivering and I realize, with surprise, that I am, too. It's November, so the weather is still warm here in Austin, but the rainstorm cooled things off—especially me. My clothes are clammy against my skin, and they feel gross. I want to take them off, but there's no way I'm asking this woman for a favor. I don't want her to know how miserable I am—or how close I am to caving.

So I wait quietly, without moving, and eventually Lessing cracks. Score one for me. "I have one last question for you."

"Okay." I say it more to fill up the dead air between us than because I think she cares how I feel about things.

"If you don't know anything about the Pandora's Box worm, if you don't have anything to do with the present communications crisis in this country, then please explain to me why we managed to trace the worm's point of origin to this house."

And score one hundred for her. "That's not possible." I try to be firm, but my voice breaks.

"Isn't it?" She reaches into the pocket of her suit jacket, pulls out a notebook, and flips through it. "According to the men who work in the FBI cybercrimes lab—who, incidentally, know more about this stuff than just about anyone—the worm was activated this afternoon. From your IP address. So, unless someone else was here today . . ."

I shake my head mutely.

"No one was here at all?"

"Just the cleaning service this morning."

She pauses for a moment, like I managed to knock the wind out of her. "What time?"

I shrug, feeling guilty about the shit storm I'm about to bring down on the poor cleaning ladies. "I don't know. I was gone most of the day. I just know they were here, because the house was clean when I got home from school. But they never touch my computer or anything," I feel honor bound to add.

"What time did you get home from school today?" she finally asks.

I shrug. "I don't know. Five or so."

"The worm wasn't released until five twenty-three this evening. So, I ask again, was anyone here with you then?"

I don't move, because that sounds about right for the time I logged on to Pandora's Box. "Pandora?" she prompts.

"No."

"But that's not the really puzzling part," she continues. "Especially if you insist on your innocence in this matter, how is it that starting at eight fifteen this morning, someone from this IP address opened the twelve different sections of code that make up this worm and uploaded them onto the Internet, one by one?"

Emily gasps and I want to protest. I want to tell Lessing she's crazy. That I have no idea what she's talking about. But the truth of the matter is that suddenly I do. I know exactly what I was doing at 8:00 this morning.

The tentative fairy tale I've been building in my head all day—the one I wasn't even aware of until right now—collapses. I swear I feel it shatter, and my stomach, though close to empty, chooses that moment to revolt.

I spring up from my chair.

"Hey, you can't go anywhere. Sit back down!" Lessing tells me firmly, reaching into her jacket and pulling out her gun.

12

I DON'T STOP. I can't. Even so, I barely make it to the trash can in time. I don't know how long I sit there, puking my guts up, but by the time I finish, Lessing has put away her gun. Emily is looking at me in dismay, while Mackaray and Lundstrom—who rushed in at Lessing's alarmed shout—are wearing identical expressions of smug triumph. Even Lessing seems satisfied, and I know it's because I've blown it big-time.

It's pretty hard to protest your innocence when you get so upset by what they're telling you that you hurl.

I don't get up right away. Instead, I stay on the floor, my head resting against the cool wood of a cabinet. I think about my laptop, stuffed in my backpack, with all the incriminating evidence on it. I think about what else is in the bag—namely the pictures from my father that I shoved in there at the last minute. All twelve of them. Not that I can prove where I got them, not when all the evidence against my father—the e-mail, blog, letters—has been removed.

I've been racking my brain, trying to figure out why me, and the answer has been there all along. The psychopath who did this, the one who chose me as his harbinger of destruction, is my *father*.

He did this to me. Used my curiosity against me—and the world—and turned me into a modern-day Pandora. Like my namesake before me, I've brought a new kind of evil into the world and there's no going back. Maybe Emily's dad and the others can fix it. Maybe they can't. But either way, I have a feeling that the deep, dark hole they want to throw me in just got a lot deeper and darker.

Every writing campaign I've ever participated in for Amnesty International flashes through my head. Letter after letter about Guantánamo Bay. Sierra Leone. Somalia. Story after story of Americans taken to foreign countries and tortured because they're suspected of terrorism.

Even as I tell myself I'm being silly, I hear the president saying the United States doesn't tolerate terrorists. That's what I am, what my father has turned me into with a few strokes of my keyboard, a few picture downloads that I thought were to celebrate my seventeenth birthday.

A cyberterrorist.

I reach for the trash can again as dry heaves shake my entire body.

What am I going to do?

What am I going to do?

What. Am. I. Going. To. Do?

Behind me, I hear movement and I brace myself to be yanked to my feet. But that doesn't happen. Instead, Emily settles on the floor next to me and hands me a bottle of water. I rinse my mouth out, drink a few sips. Then she's hugging me, stroking my hair. "It's going to be okay, Pandora," she whispers to me. "I promise. It's going to be okay."

I open my mouth, planning on telling them everything and begging for mercy. Instead, only four words come out. Four words I never thought I'd say. "I want a lawyer."

"A lawyer?" Mackaray's eyes gleam with triumph as he crouches down next to me. "Pandora, where you're going, lawyers rank right up there with fairies and unicorns as mythical creatures."

"You can't do that!" Emily protests. "She didn't do anything wrong! My father—"

"Your father is one of an elite few who could pull off something of this magnitude, Ms. Scott." Lundstrom speaks up for the first time in a long while. "So I suggest you close your mouth unless you want to bring a lot of trouble down on him as well."

Emily shuts up, her eyes wide and frightened as she presses her back against the cabinet, almost like she wants to shrink inside. The arms wrapped around me start to tremble, but I barely notice, since I'm shaking just as hard.

"She didn't do anything," I tell them, wondering again if I should just tell them everything.

If I should send them next door to retrieve my laptop from Eli and Theo and get them involved in this.

Do I admit that my father is behind this and let them arrest him, lock him up and throw away the key like they're threatening to do to me?

But if I admit I had only an unwitting part in this, are they going to believe me? The looks on their faces say no, that they've already made up their minds about my guilt. My best bet, then, is to wait for Mr. Scott. He's one of the best computer-security guys in the country. He'll know what to do.

I shut down then, refuse to say anything else. They keep demanding answers, but I ignore them. Even when Mackaray grabs on to my arms and lifts me into a standing position, I don't protest. I'll wait for Mr. Scott, I tell myself. He'll be able to fix this.

As we wait, the house grows quiet around us. The front door opens and closes numerous times, and I hear the slam of car doors outside. The rev of engines that marks the end of the search. The others have done their jobs, and now I'm left alone with these three.

Mr. Scott finally arrives, with a police escort. He's all outrage and concern as he wraps his arms around us, but it becomes clear very quickly that he won't be able to help me. He's not my parent or guardian, and no matter how much he argues with the agents—he knows two of them personally— they aren't budging. But at least Emily seems safe, and that's something.

"I have to go to the bathroom," I say, after Mr. Scott's been here about an hour. They've told him both he and Emily are free to go, but he hasn't budged. I know it's because he doesn't want to leave me alone with them.

"Tough," Lundstrom tells me. "You're not going anywhere."

"Jesus, Mike, she's just a kid!" Mr. Scott exclaims.

"She unleashed cyber-Armageddon—'genius computer hacker' trumps 'kid' every day of the week."

"She's not a hacker!"

"And I know this how?" Lundstrom stares him down. "The worm launched from here. She was the only one here. Ergo . . ."

I can't stand it, can't sit here listening to this for one second more. "Please," I say. "I really need to use the restroom." Even though I don't. I just want a couple of minutes alone to think, a couple of minutes where they aren't staring at me like I'm a monster.

"I'll take her," Mackaray finally says, and I almost change my mind. I don't want to be alone with him, even for as long as it takes to walk to my bathroom. But it's not like I have a choice now, not after I made such a big deal of having to go.

We leave the kitchen together, and when I try to head upstairs to my bathroom, he grabs my elbow and directs me to the half bath down the hall. The one without any windows. I shake my head in disbelief. They already think I'm some kind of genius hacker—now they think I can mastermind an escape from federal custody as well? Who the hell do these people think I am?

"Leave the door open," Mackaray tells me when we get there.

"What?" I stare at him incredulously.

"You heard me." The face staring back at me is implacable.

"Where am I going to go? There's no other way out of the bathroom!"

"Take it or leave it." Something moves in his eyes, and I know he's waiting for me to leave it. But I won't give him the satisfaction.

"Does your wife know you get your kicks by listening to teenage girls pee?"

The hand on my elbow gets tighter, his fingers digging into my flesh until I start to see stars. He pulls me toward him and whispers, "You don't want to play games with me, little girl. I win every time."

I'm straining so hard in the other direction that when he finally lets me go, I stumble, crack my funny bone hard against the door frame.

I go into the bathroom, leaving the door partially open. I turn on the faucet, splash water on my face, blink back the tears.

"Hurry up!" he says after a minute. "We don't have all night."

Before I can respond, the lights blink once, twice, then go out completely. My entire house is plunged into an inky blackness.

"What the hell!" Mackaray says, slamming the bathroom door open all the way. "Either get it done or not, kid. You've got one minute, and then I'm taking you back to the kitchen."

I barely hear him over the pounding of my own heart and the panic clawing through me, overpowering everything else. Even my fear of going to jail. I hate the dark, hate it, hate it, hate it. Ever since I was five and got trapped in my uncle's storage shed, under a pile of heavy boxes that fell when I was looking for my Christmas presents. There'd been no lights or windows, and I'd lain there in the dark for hours, crying, convinced that no one was ever going to find me.

Curiosity had been my downfall then as well.

"Tom?" Lessing's voice drifts through the hall.

"Yeah?"

"Just checking. It looks like the whole grid just went down."

"I can see that."

Lessing must catch the sarcasm in his voice because she shuts up quickly. I hear her walk back down the hall to the kitchen, her heels clicking on the wood floor.

"Pandora—" In his voice is a warning, and I know my time is up. But he stops abruptly, and there's a muffled *thump*, followed by a slithering sound that has me imagining a bunch of snakes sliding down my hallway. I press myself back against the wall and try not to scream.

Something large moves in front of the doorway. "Pandora?"

"Theo?" I whisper, shocked.

He leans forward until his face is only inches from mine. "Let's go." His voice is pitched so low that I have to strain to hear it even this close.

"Go where?"

"Out of here. Come on, we've only got a couple of minutes before they come looking for you."

"Looking for— You want me to break out of federal custody?"

"Would you rather I leave you here?"

"I don't know. I . . ." My head is spinning. Of all the ways I envisioned tonight ending, this wasn't even in the top thousand. "Where's Mackaray?"

"I hit him. He's out, but I don't know for how long. Now, are you coming or not?"

Am I? I look back toward the kitchen, where Emily and her father wait with the other agents. I can't leave her—

It's like Theo can read my thoughts, because he says, "Emily will be fine. She's not the one in trouble here."

He's right; I know he is. But still. Can I do this? Bad enough to be a federal suspect—but to be a fugitive? How is it even possible? They'll find us in minutes.

Except the electricity just went out. Communications are gone. No cameras to catch us running away. No way to get out word of a widespread manhunt (or, in this case, womanhunt). No way for them to track me when they're basically blind, deaf, and dumb. It could work.

But still, do I really want to do this? Do I really want to go down this road?

Hell, yes, I do.

I slip my hand into Theo's, not bothering to ask how he knew I was in trouble, and we glide as silently as possible through the hallway into the living room. He seems to know exactly where he's going, and I wonder how long he's been here, prowling around the house, without anyone knowing.

He slides open the glass door that leads to the deck just enough that we can slip out. As he silently closes the door behind us, I realize this is it.

I really have reached the point of no return.

13

WE HIT THE GROUND RUNNING. Literally.

After sneaking across the deck, we scale the iron railing that keeps people from falling off and then—because the stairs are in perfect view of the windows, thanks to the solar lights I insisted my mom install—we jump the five feet to the ground. I twist my ankle when we land, and bite my lip to keep from crying out. I try to stop to check for damage, but Theo grabs my wrist and yanks.

And then we're running straight into the black.

Theo cuts across the yard—away from more solar lights that illuminate the ground and might catch our movements—to the fence line. We run in close-to-total darkness, the light of the half-moon above us our only guide. I try not to panic, tell myself this is the only way even as my brain tries to turn itself inside out. I stumble a few times, nearly go down, but Theo's there every time to catch me and pull me along.

Fear is a living, breathing nightmare inside me, scraping at me with every step I take away from the house. I block it out, block everything out, including the pain from the car accident and my fear of the dark, and I just run.

I concentrate on the rhythm, on the act itself of putting one foot in front of the other. I don't know where we're going or how we can escape, but Theo seems to have a plan, so I go with it. Go with him.

Our property is huge, over two acres, and there are woods toward the bottom half of it. As soon as we reach them, Theo darts away from the fence and into the middle of the trees. We use them for cover as we keep running.

As we flee, everything around us takes on a surreal quality. A little bit out of focus, just a little bit unreal.

When I woke up this morning, when I rolled out of bed, I didn't have a clue I was going to end up here. When I read that message from my father, rejoiced in the words he wrote and the pictures he sent, I never once imagined where they would lead. How things would end.

Not that this is really an ending. It's more of a beginning.

The beginning of my life as a fugitive.

The beginning of my quest to figure this thing out.

The beginning of the end of my world, and maybe the *whole* world, if the warning from Pandora's Box comes true.

I can't let it come true.

Theo stops abruptly. I know why, just as I now know how he's planning to escape. "They'll figure it out," I tell him, keeping my voice low.

"It's a big lake. They won't know where we're coming out."

"Helicopters—"

"Everything is a mess because of the worm. It'll take a little while for them to get one here. And by then we'll be gone."

He takes my hand, leads me through the darkness and down to the dock. There's a two-seater kayak resting at the very end, one that wasn't there before. "Is it yours?" I ask, pointing.

"Yeah."

We don't talk as we get the boat into the water. Theo climbs in first, then holds on to the dock to steady the boat as I climb in behind him. When I'm settled, he hands me a two-bladed paddle, then picks up a second one for himself.

"You ready?" he asks.

Not even close. But I nod, and he shoves off from the dock.

We start to paddle, straight out toward the middle of the lake. I don't say anything for a while, just concentrate on the side-to-side motion of paddling.

It's been a few years since I've done this, but when I was younger I spent every available second on the lake. The rhythm comes back to me quickly, my body remembering the familiar motion without much help from my brain.

Paddle on the left.

Roll and shift.

Paddle on the right.

Roll and shift.

Paddle on the left.

The world around us is dark and very nearly silent, except for the excited vibrations of the cicadas in the trees.

But as we go farther, even that sound fades until there's nothing but the splash of the paddles hitting the water and coming back out.

It's a lonely sound, a lonely feeling, moving straight out into the black, and I know that I would never have been brave enough to attempt it alone. I owe Theo, huge, and I don't have a clue how to begin to repay him.

Back on shore, I see the flash of police lights from my driveway. Figure it means they've discovered I'm missing. I don't say anything and neither does Theo, but he starts to paddle even faster. Again, I'm left scrambling to keep up.

"Do you know where we're going?" I ask breathlessly after a few more minutes.

"Yes."

I wait for him to elaborate, but he doesn't. Still, the boat is subtly shifting, angling to the left. We're heading toward shore, though I don't know how he knows when to turn. I don't say anything though. When I took Theo's hand back at the house, I put my trust in him. I'm not going to second-guess him now.

We paddle for another thirty minutes or so, until my arms feel like they're going to fall off and I'm completely exhausted. I haven't eaten anything since the Crunch Berries nearly ten hours ago, and it's not like those are exactly the fuel of champions. Had I known what the future had in store I would have gobbled down an entire jar of peanut butter instead.

"We're almost there," Theo says. Again, I don't know how he can tell—I'm just thrilled that he can. A couple of minutes later, he says, "Stop paddling."

I do as he instructs, and we coast up to what I think must be a dock. Theo reaches for it, then curses softly.

"What's wrong?"

"Nothing. Just climb out."

I start to scramble up but someone else is there, grabbing my arm and pulling me forward. I screech, a startled, high-pitched sound that echoes through the night.

"Shhh!" A hand clamps over my mouth as the stranger pulls me against his body. "It's me, Pandora," a familiar voice whispers in my ear.

Eli. My body goes limp as the fight rushes out of me.

"Don't mind me," Theo comments drily as he vaults onto the deck, keeping one hand on the kayak the whole time so it doesn't float away. Then he reaches down to pull the small boat out of the water. Eli lets go of me to help him and I'm immediately bereft. He scared the hell out of me, but he was also something—someone—to hold on to in the middle of this hell.

Instead of putting the kayak on the dock, the two of them start walking with it.

"Come on, Pandora." Theo's voice is low but harsh. "We need to keep moving."

Now that Eli's back in the picture, I guess Theo feels like he doesn't have to be nice to me anymore. After all, if I have a nervous breakdown, there's someone else around to clean up the mess.

"Moving where?" I look around, try to get my bearings. But there's nothing here—just a bunch of trees. We're in the middle of the wilderness.

"Toward the forest," Eli tells me gently. "We don't want to leave this out here like a beacon. I guarantee the helicopter will be up any minute."

"Any minute?" I swear I can feel the blood drain from my face.

"They're crippled by the worm, not completely incompetent," Theo says, obviously amused by my panic. "What do you think they're going to do? Throw up their hands and say, 'Whoops, we lost her'?"

"No, of course not." Which is true. But I haven't exactly had a chance to think it through, either. There hasn't been time.

"Then let's hustle." He checks his watch. "We have places to be."

"We do?" I sound like an idiot, but it's hard to be anything else, since neither one of them is telling me what's going on.

Eli must sense how disgruntled I am, because he bumps shoulders with me as he mutters, "Trust the plan, Pandora. Trust the plan."

I didn't even realize there *was* a plan besides running like hell. But of course there is. This *is* Theo, after all. The guy built an airplane practically single-handedly. Evading Homeland Security must seem like child's play after that.

I snicker a little at the thought as I watch them weave carefully through the trees, kayak in hand. "What's so funny?" Theo asks.

"I don't think you'd get it."

"Too square?" He tosses a glance over his shoulder, and

even though I can't see his features in the dark, I think maybe I've hurt his feelings. Which is *so* not what I intended.

"Of course not. I just . . . I'm shocked at how prepared you guys are."

"Boy Scouts have nothing on us," Eli jokes.

Theo doesn't answer, just gives a little snort that says he doesn't believe me, but his pace never falters. After we've hiked about half a mile into the woods, he says, "I guess this is as good a place as any to lose the kayak."

He and Eli lay it on the ground. Theo reaches into his pocket and pulls out a tiny flashlight, the kind you can hang from your keys, then turns it on and sweeps it around the area quickly, checking to make sure the tree cover is heavy enough. I'm so grateful for the light that I nearly grab it from him, just to prove to myself that it's real.

Theo checks his watch again and I say, "Geez, you're a real stickler for keeping a schedule, aren't you?"

"I'm looking at my compass. So I know how the hell to get us out of here. That okay with you?"

"Yeah, fine." I can feel my cheeks burning. "I wasn't making fun of you."

"Whatever."

"You really have a compass on your watch?" I ask, moving closer.

"I like to hike. Since I don't always follow the beaten path, the watch helps keep me going in the right direction. Which, in this case, is to the left." He pulls a small pack out of the kayak, slips it over his back. For the first time, I notice that Eli's wearing a similar one. "You ready?"

"Yeah, sure. Of course."

We set off again, and while Theo and Eli are still moving fast, they're not setting the brutal pace of earlier. This tells me that Theo's a little more comfortable with our odds of escaping, at least for now.

"So, are you going to let me in on your plan?" I ask him. I don't like not knowing what's going on, especially when it comes to my own safety. While I can totally appreciate everything Theo has risked to get us this far, I'm more than ready to start pulling my own weight.

"There's not much more to it, to be honest," Eli says. "We need to hike to a couple of miles away from where we dropped the kayak, and then we'll pick up Theo's mom's van."

"How'd it get all the way over here?" I ask, but I already know.

"I drove it," Eli confirms, "then hiked to the lake to find you."

"Even though the plan called for you staying in the van," Theo tells him darkly.

"Hey, I wasn't going to let you have all the fun!"

Fun? We must have different definitions of the word because while this middle-of-the-night trek into hell is a lot of things, I wouldn't call it "fun."

"So you guys really planned all this out in the three hours since I saw you last?" I ask Eli.

"Yeah."

He sounds like a little boy, totally pleased with himself, and I can't help laughing. "You know, you're really good at all this fugitive stuff."

He laughs a little. "It's not like this is my first time."

I stumble over a raised tree root, bang into a nearby tree. I scrape my arm on the bark but barely notice. I'm too busy trying to wrap my head around what Eli just said.

But before I can think of anything to say, he laughs and says, "Relax, Pandora. I was just joking."

My breath rushes out in one gigantic sigh. "Well, thank God. I was already imagining the headline for when the police found my dead, rotting corpse."

"Oh yeah? And what would that be?"

Even though he can't see me in the dark, I wave my hand in front of my face like the words are on the world's largest banner. "Modern-Day Pandora Found Naked in Ditch After Unleashing Cyber-Armageddon."

"Huh. That's kind of catchy."

"I thought so."

We walk in silence for a while, and every step I take is an agony. Now that the adrenaline has worn off, I can feel my blisters again and they are killing me. Once this night— once this *nightmare*—is behind me, I swear I'm never wearing these boots again.

"Theo?" I say.

"Yeah?"

"How did you know?" I can't help remembering that moment on the street when he decided to take off, demanding that Eli go with him.

"I'm a good guesser."

I think about that for a second. "You knew they were going to arrest me, and you didn't warn me?"

"I figured they were going to want to talk to you. I just

didn't have a clue that they were going to bring with them the world's biggest pot of alphabet soup when they did."

"Alphabet soup?"

He shakes his head a little. "How many agencies were in your house, anyway?"

I laugh a little as I finally get the joke. "Four, if you count the APD."

"That little birthday present of yours sure pissed off a lot of people."

That gets my back up, but then I remember that he doesn't know. Nobody does, except me. That knowledge makes me want to say it out loud—if for no other reason than to make myself really believe it.

"My father did this."

It's Theo's turn to stumble. "What are you talking about?"

"Just what I said. He's the one who created the worm. He just relied on me to upload it." I tell them the whole story as we walk, about the website and the twelve pictures. About how I haven't seen my father in ten years. Everything.

Neither of them says anything for a long time, then Eli whistles softly. "And I thought my dad was an asshole. Suddenly, living with him doesn't seem so bad."

"Why did he do this?" The question bursts out of me and I try to sound strong, but my voice breaks and I end up just sounding pathetic. But it's been circling my brain since Lessing told me about how the worm was uploaded, and I want an answer. I *need* one.

"Because he's a bastard, Pandora." Theo speaks up for the first time since I started telling the story. "But his choices have nothing to do with you."

"He made them about me. He brought Homeland Security to my door. Shit, it's like he had this in his head all along. Why else would he insist that I be named Pandora when I was born? This game, this worm . . . He created a box of evils and then gave me the only key to open it. And I did. I did."

My breath hitches on a sob and Theo snaps, "Knock it off, Pandora! We don't have time for you to have a breakdown."

"Chill, Theo. Not everyone's a robot like you, you know." Eli wraps an arm around my shoulders and pulls me against his side in a one-armed hug. His warmth feels strange after Theo's deep freeze, and I can't help being a little pissed. Theo makes me sound like a crybaby or a crazy person, when I have every right to be upset. Maybe this isn't the best time for me to lose it, but Theo doesn't have to be so obnoxious about shutting me down. This has been the worst day of my life.

"How much farther?" I ask, my voice stilted by anger and by my determination not to cry.

"Look, Pandora, he didn't mean—" Eli starts, only to be interrupted by Theo.

"I don't need you to interpret for me, Eli!"

"Well, someone needs to. You're acting like a bastard."

"Stop it!" I tell them. "He was right, Eli. I do need to quit whining."

A charged silence hangs over the three of us, and for a second I'm sure that Theo is going to say more, but then he just sighs. Lets it go like I want him to, but for some reason that just makes me angrier. *You're being irrational, Pandora.*

I try to tell myself to chill, but it doesn't work. That part of my brain is on serious overload. So, in the end, I do the only thing I can do. I shut down completely.

Don't think.

Don't feel.

Ignore the pain.

Ignore the fear.

Eye on the prize—isn't that what they say?

We tromp in silence for a little while longer—I've lost total track of time out here, so I can't even hazard a guess at how much more time passes. Ten minutes? Twenty? Exhaustion dogs my every step, and I want nothing more than to be back home, back in my bed. If things had gone as planned, Emily and I would be in the middle of an all-night movie marathon right about now.

And then, abruptly, the forest ends. One second we're in the trees and the next, with no warning whatsoever, we're standing by the side of the road.

Theo curses again, pulls me back into the trees.

"What's wrong?"

"Here, put this on." Using his flashlight to help him see, he reaches into the small bag, pulls out a Dallas Mavericks hat. It's a measure of just how desperate I am to get someplace else that I actually let him put it on my head. Still. "The Mavericks?" I ask, just a little outraged.

"It's Eli's."

"Yeah, well, Eli has crappy taste in basketball."

"Tell me about it."

"Hey, I resent that!"

"Resent it all you like. Facts are facts."

Theo laughs, a startled—and startling—sound out here where everything is still and silent, and the tension from earlier dissolves in the face of this little bit of normal conversation. I can feel it draining out of me, my shoulders and stomach relaxing. We're all on edge. There's no reason for me to hold it against him, especially when he and Eli did all this to save me.

I glance up at the sky. With no lights anywhere, the stars look a million times more brilliant. I study them, neck bent and circling, as I look for it. The North Star.

Except for Venus, it's the brightest light in the sky right now, and it's been my favorite star since I was six. My father had taken me on a camping trip, and I'd wandered off from him when he'd been pitching the tent, and I'd gotten lost. He found me about forty-five minutes later, sitting cross-legged on a log and scratching at a bunch of fire-ant bites that I'd gotten during my adventure. I wasn't crying—I was trying to be brave—and he'd respected that.

He'd pulled me onto his lap and pointed at the North Star. Told me that I could always follow it to find my way back to where I belonged. "The earth," he'd said, "provides everything we need, Pandora. We just have to know where to look."

At the time I didn't know what he meant, but his words stuck with me. Through the years, I've developed a habit of looking for the North Star, not just for physical directions, but for help with decisions when I'm at a crossroads. I know it doesn't actually help, but somehow it makes me feel better.

At least until tonight. Now everything I know about him—everything I remember—feels tainted.

"You ready?" Eli asks after a minute, and though I'm not—I don't think I'll ever be ready for this—I whisper, "Yes."

As one, we step out of the trees, tromp toward the road. When we get there, Theo once again checks his compass. "Which way are we going?" I ask.

"North."

Of course. I look at my star again, then turn to the right, start walking. "This way."

It's all uphill. By now, I'm not even surprised.

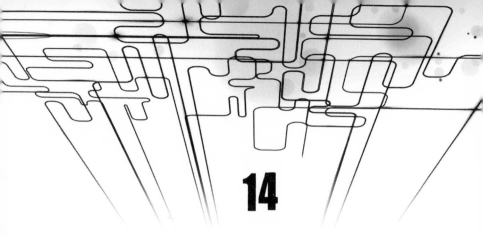

14

WE WALK FOR ABOUT A MILE more—until dawn is just beginning to touch the sky—before we get to a big apartment building. We're at the edge of a large, crowded parking lot, and Theo whips out the tiny flashlight again, tries to scan the cars, but Eli just laughs, shakes his head.

"It's over there." He leads the way to the very back of the lot, stopping next to a silver Odyssey that's half-hidden by a fenced-in Dumpster.

"No comments about the minivan," Eli tells me with a grin as he unlocks the doors. "Theo insisted on taking his mom's ride instead of mine."

"Yours seats two people," Theo responds as he pops the tailgate and sets his backpack inside the cargo hold. "Did you get the gas, like I told you to?"

"The car and both containers are all filled up." Eli slides into the driver's seat.

"Good." Theo opens the door behind Eli, gestures for me

to get in. Then walks around to the front passenger seat and climbs in.

I get my first good look at both of them in the interior light of the car. They've cleaned up since the accident, but Eli has one hell of a black eye while Theo's left cheekbone is swollen. At least the dozen or so cuts on his face and neck have stopped bleeding, started to scab over. I wonder how the one on his side is doing.

"Let's get going," Theo says as he turns out the overhead light.

"I'm already gone." Eli creeps out of the parking lot and then turns left, heading back down the road we just came from.

I put on my seat belt, then slowly ease off my boots and socks, trying not to disturb the blisters. It's still mostly dark, so I can't see anything, but as I touch my heels I feel a telltale wetness, along with shocks of electric pain. The blisters have all popped, and if I'm not careful I'm going to get an infection. When we stop I'll have to go in and get some Band-Aids and Neosporin.

"Where are we going?" I ask as we barrel through the night. Eli's driving fast, but his hands are strong on the wheel, confident.

The guys exchange a look. "That depends," Eli says.

"On what?"

"Namely on what states you have relatives in," Theo answers this time. "I figure with your mom in Alaska, the first place they're going to look for you is a neighboring state where you have family."

His words bring it all back, and suddenly the safety of

this air-conditioned van with its bright, welcoming head-lights, doesn't feel so absolute anymore. "How long do you think they're going to look for me?"

"Until they catch you, or until they fix the damage done from this worm. Even then, I'm sure they'll want to find you."

"Do you think they'll be *able* to fix the damage?" I ask.

"Sure, eventually," he says, but he doesn't sound very confident.

"I was listening to the radio while I waited for you," Eli pipes in. "AM's the only thing working, and it sounds like things are even worse than before. The blackout is spread-ing. It's rolled over most parts of the US, Canada, and Mexico already, and they expect the worm to reach the rest of the world by morning. People are freaking out, and at midnight, central time, that damn Pandora's Box counter hit nine."

My stomach drops. "What does that mean?"

"I'm not sure. But I've got to say, seeing what this worm can do, I'm a lot more concerned with the total-annihilation claim not being a metaphor than I was when this thing first started. Especially since people are screaming that this is the end of the world. Looting's already begun, if you can believe it."

I don't say anything after that pronouncement and neither does Theo. But then, what is there to say? This worm—or blended threat, whatever that means—has done more damage in twelve hours than any other I've ever heard of. I can't even imagine what the world is going to look like in nine days. If there even is a world, I mean. Maybe the religious zealots have it right for once.

"I don't have relatives anywhere. Just my mom. And my dad, but I have no idea where he is right now, so I can't exactly tell you which state to avoid if we don't want to run into him."

"Actually, he's the one relative of yours we do want to run into," Theo says.

"Yeah, right."

"I'm serious. How else are we going to fix this thing?"

"Fix it?" I ask incredulously. "We're on the run from every federal agency there is. We can't even fix our own lives, let alone the mess my dad's created."

My stomach growls before either of them can answer. Embarrassed, I suck it in. Try to get it to stop.

"Sorry, Pandora, I forgot."

Theo crawls into the backseat and leans into the trunk to retrieve a medium-size cooler, which he puts on the floor between us. He opens it up, pulls out a couple of sandwiches, and hands one to me and one to Eli.

At the sight of the food, my stomach growls again—so fiercely this time that it hurts. Theo smirks, but it isn't a mean smile. More like he's sharing the joke with me. Then he hands me a cold bottle of water before helping himself to a sandwich as well.

I devour the food in about three minutes flat, and when it's gone, I'm still hungry. It must be obvious, because Theo hands me another sandwich. I eat this one a lot more sedately, then turn so my forehead rests against the cool glass of the window.

The world outside our car is beautiful. It's started to rain again, and the road gleams, slick and shiny, in the glare of our headlights. If I focus on it, focus on the raindrops falling like whispers onto the back windshield, I can almost pretend that things are normal. That this is any other day.

But if this were any other day, if the end of the world didn't beckon with frighteningly close fingers, I wouldn't be sitting here in this van. Racing the dawn with two boys who have risked everything to be with me.

I wish I knew why they've done it. Why they've chosen helping me over safety. Perhaps they didn't know how much work it would be to rescue me. Maybe they didn't think it would be this difficult.

That explanation doesn't seem to fit, though. Not when they have everything planned down to the last detail.

But why, then? Why help me, why *choose* me, when no one else ever has? My own father used my feelings for him to betray me. My mother simply doesn't have feelings. Or if she does, they're buried so deep that I haven't seen them in years.

"Hey, Theo," Eli says from the front. "I know you want to get out of Texas before we stop for supplies, man, but I think that's a bad idea."

"We need to get past the borders before they set up some kind of roadblock."

"They might have already done that—you don't know how long that kind of thing takes. Remember, they still have radios. But if this thing turns as bad as we think it's going to, we need to get supplies fast. Before things become so out of control that we can't get what we need."

How bad does something have to be before stores stop

being willing to take your money? I wonder. But then I remember the chaos of Little Nicky's, of the employees' general inability to function. And that was when the lights were still on.

"I think he's right." My voice is raw with tiredness and emotion. I need to sleep, but I'm wide awake, my brain racing in too many circles to quiet down. Even now when I'm safe . . . or at least as safe as I can be at the moment. "What supplies do we need?"

"More gas—plus a couple of extra jerricans to hold it. Three pairs of night-vision goggles, just in case. A first-aid kit. Some flashlights." Theo pauses, looks me up and down so slowly that my breath catches in my throat. It's stupid, ridiculous, to be thinking of any boy-girl stuff right now, yet there's something in his eyes that makes me flush. "And we have got to do something with you."

That breaks the spell and I yelp, "Hey! What does that mean?"

He lifts a brow in that way he has. "In case you haven't noticed, it's kind of hard to hide a six-foot redhead with purple streaks in her hair. Not to mention the Social D shirt and Doc Martens. You definitely need a makeover."

My fingers go instinctively to my hair, my first urge to protect it. On the one hand, I know he's right. It's the most distinctive part of me. But on the other hand I can't imagine doing anything to it. I love my haircut, love the violet streaks I've had for more than a year.

Still, it's a small price to pay. One that's next to nothing in comparison to everything else that's happened tonight.

"So where do you propose getting all this stuff?" I ask quietly. "It's barely six in the morning, and it's not like there are a lot of stores around that sell both night-vision goggles and hair dye."

At that moment, Eli hits the brakes hard while turning the wheel wildly to the right as he exits the highway. I grab on to the seat in front of me and start to complain, but then I look through the window and realize where we're headed. There's a Super Walmart less than a quarter mile up the road.

Eli tosses a grin over his shoulder as he parks near the front. There are almost no cars in the lot, although there are very obviously lights on inside the store. "How do they have electricity?" I ask, excited.

"Generator," Eli answers. "A few places have them. But generators won't hold out very long if the electricity doesn't get turned back on soon. Most places only have enough gas to last one or two days. Three if you really push it."

"Do you think it will be three days before this is fixed?" I ask. I hold my breath, waiting for their answer. It feels like my whole life hangs in the balance, and maybe it does.

Eli snorts from the front seat, completely unaware of the panic that has assailed me. "I think it'll be three *months* before they get the electricity back on."

I punch him in the arm, sure that he's joking. "No, really. Tell me the truth."

"That is the truth, Pandora." Theo's face is serious. "There's no easy fix to this. This worm is really destructive. I was listening to the radio while I packed supplies into the van. This worm isn't just shutting things down, it's ripping them apart from the inside. Gutting them, so that the systems can't be put back together. Even if there were power—if the grids weren't being shut down and torn apart—it would take months to fix all the damage that's been done."

"So what are we going to do?" I whisper, the implications of his words resonating inside me with all the power of a shotgun blast.

"We're going to do what we can. We'll get the best supplies we can find and then go from there. We're supposed to beat the game. We need to prepare to do just that."

I nod, reach for my backpack. It's on the floor by my feet, and I realize that I haven't thanked Eli for keeping it safe for me. Haven't thanked them for anything. I start to, but then something occurs to me. Something big. "Supplies cost money, Theo. Especially the ones you're talking about. If I can't use my credit card, I've got nothing. We won't be able to pay for what we need."

"We have money, Pandora." Theo's face is a little stiff, like he can't believe I even suggested that he would do something illegal. Of course, he is the one who clocked a Homeland Security officer and busted one of their prisoners out from under their noses. Next to that, what's a little stealing? "Eli's dad travels overseas on business a lot, often without much warning, so he keeps money in the house."

"He also left extra money for us in case of emergencies, since he and Theo's mom are on their honeymoon," Eli interjects. "This definitely qualifies as an emergency, so we took all that plus what was in his safe."

He opens his door, steps outside. I start to follow, but

Theo stops me. "We'll be quick, Pandora. I promise. Lock the doors and stay in the backseat, where the windows are tinted."

"I really can't go?" I'm pissed, even though a part of me knows he's right. Still, it grates to be left in the car like a little kid.

"You look exactly like you did when you left your house," he says, examining me in the dim overhead light. "It'd be like putting a sign on you that reads, FEDERAL FUGITIVE HERE."

He closes the door, once again plunging the car into shadows, and then walks away without a backward glance. I watch them until they disappear into the store, then reach for the flashlight Theo left on the dash. I turn it on and immediately the churning panic in my stomach subsides a little.

I tell myself to turn off the flashlight, that it will attract attention, but I just can't bring myself to do it. At this point, I think I'd rather get caught than spend one more moment in the dark.

Dropping the flashlight on the floor of the van, where its light will be less conspicuous, I yank out one of the two spare bras I packed and one of the last couple of shirts. I change quickly, then curse myself for being so shortsighted when I packed this thing. Why the hell didn't I pack a second pair of jeans? Or even better, a pair of yoga pants so that I could travel comfortably? Pajamas aren't going to cut it if we have to ditch the van and run.

Probably because, when I packed, I hadn't dreamed I'd be fleeing from the authorities. I'd been going for sleepover necessities at my best friend's house. Next time I'll be sure to do better.

The absurdity of that last thought catches up with me and I start to laugh. Because the truth is, if there ends up being a next time that I have to flee for my life and my freedom, then I'm just going to give up and let them do to me what they will.

Still, I'm grateful that of all the guys in my high school, I managed to team up with two of the smartest and most prepared.

I fiddle with my hair, brush it a little, though there's not much to be done after that rainstorm and the subsequent humidity. Still, it feels good to do something normal. I slick some lip gloss on my mouth. Refresh my deodorant. Then stretch out on the floor of the van, between the two seats, and try not to drive myself insane.

It doesn't work.

Everything that has happened these last few hours catches up with me, and I start to cry. Long, loud, jarring sobs that rack my entire body.

I can't believe this is happening. Simply can't believe that I'm here, in the middle of nowhere North Texas, running for my life. Or what very well feels like it. Agent Mackaray's face appears in front of my closed eyelids, and I cry some more.

I have the feeling I've made—we've made—a powerful enemy in him. He doesn't strike me as the kind of guy who likes losing his prey. And he really doesn't strike me as the kind who can stand being one-upped by a teenager.

I don't know how long I lie there crying, the flashlight clutched in my hands.

Long enough to curse my father with every swear word I've ever heard.

Long enough to release some of the pent-up emotion inside me, so that I no longer feel like I'm going to explode.

More than long enough for night to turn to dawn and dawn to turn to daylight.

It's that early-morning light that finally calms me down, has me wiping my eyes and taking a few deep breaths. I switch off the flashlight—we need to conserve the batteries— then sit up as the thought registers that the guys really should be back by now.

I'm not wearing a watch, but I know that over an hour has passed since they went inside. Concerned for a whole different reason now, I lean forward and peek my head out the window. What could be taking them so long?

I try to tell myself that I'm overreacting, that nothing bad has happened to them. But with each minute that crawls by, my heart beats an uneasy tattoo in my chest. *Should I go in and check on them?* I wonder frantically. *Or will that only make things worse?* If they're in trouble, the last thing they need is to have me show up in the middle of it. I don't know if Mackaray and the others have managed to get out my description—without Internet, faxes, or the phone, that would be difficult. But not impossible.

Is it conceivable he saw what Theo looked like when he came for me? I don't know how he could have, with it being as dark as it was in my house. But maybe he did. Maybe he released Theo's description as well. And while I agree with

Theo that it's hard to hide a six-foot redhead, it's even harder to hide two giants, especially ones who look like Theo and Eli do.

I turn on the van with the keys Eli left for me, check the time. It's 7:19. I'll give them ten more minutes. If they aren't back by then, I'm going in. I don't care if it's a risk. They came for me when I needed it. I can't do less for them.

The thought galvanizes me, has me searching the van for sunglasses. I don't find any, but in the back I do find a ton of supplies already. Nonperishable food like granola bars and cereal, water, portable gasoline cans completely filled. Three sleeping bags. A couple of flashlights. Some blankets. Duffel bags full of extra clothes for Eli and Theo. A wicked-looking knife that has me drawing back in surprise.

I want to pretend it's for nothing more ominous than cutting twigs for a fire, but it isn't a hunting knife. And I'm not that good a liar—even to myself.

I glance back at the clock, silently counting down on the dashboard. It's been eight minutes. I close my eyes, make a wish. Then I reach for the sheathed knife and tuck it into the waistband of my jeans. I don't know what I'm going to do with it, but it's better to be prepared, right? Especially when I don't think that one blow from *my* fist is going to result in anyone falling unconscious.

I'm reaching down to put on my boots—something I really, really don't want to do—when I see them walking out the front door. Theo is pushing a fully loaded cart and Eli is carrying a bunch of extra bags. Did they buy out the whole store?

I want to leap from the van, to rush up and throw my

arms around them, which would be insane, not to mention a hugely unnecessary risk. But the relief rushing through me at the sight of them is so potent, so huge, that it's nearly impossible for me to stay sitting in the car, waiting.

They reach the van soon enough, Theo opening the tailgate and loading in bags, one after another. I scoot to the back, start to help him as he organizes the stuff. At the same time, I surreptitiously drop the knife where I found it. No need for them to know I was ready to take on the Super Walmart to break them out.

"Just throw everything in there for now," Eli suggests to Theo. "Two of us can get it all sorted while the third one drives. We need to move."

"Here, Pandora." Eli hands me the bags he's carrying, and I take them, start pawing through them. In one is some sunscreen, face moisturizer, and brown hair dye. In the others are a couple of pairs of yoga pants (thank God), jeans, a hoodie, and some shirts. Mostly tank tops. And to be more specific, mostly low-cut tank tops.

I pull out a particularly lacy, low-cut, spaghetti-strapped shirt in electric purple. Eyebrows raised, I ask, "Who decided that this was what I needed to blend in?"

Theo just rolls his eyes, holding his hands up in the universal not-me gesture. I turn to Eli, who is grinning wickedly at me, charm all but oozing out of his pores. "It's purple," he says, like that explains everything.

"It's practically nonexistent."

"Hey, it's the end of the world. A guy needs *something* to look forward to."

I laugh, shove the shirt back down in the bag. "Dream on, buddy."

"Oh, I will." Another grin, this one accompanied by a wink that makes my stomach do some kind of odd little flip.

I ignore it. There will be no flipping. None at all. I have more than enough problems as it is.

"Come on, Pandora. Sit in front with me. Eli's going to stretch out and try to sleep." Theo tosses me a plain black hat. "Until we can get you to a motel somewhere so you can dye your hair, that's better than the Mavericks cap."

I nod, slip the baseball cap into place. Then crawl through the car to the front seat.

Theo's there waiting for me, standing in the open passenger-side door. "Let me see your feet."

"My feet?" I look at him uncertainly, but he just raises a brow and holds up a bottle of hydrogen peroxide. He noticed the blisters, bought stuff to take care of them. To take care of me. My stomach does that strange little flip thing again, and this time I'm too dazed to remember to ignore it.

I extend my right foot tentatively. Theo grasps it in strong fingers, then turns my leg so that my knee is facing out and the blister is toward the side. He mutters something when he gets his first good look at all the damage I've done, something low and obscene that I can't quite catch. Then he says, "This is going to hurt."

It's all the warning I get before he liberally douses my heel with peroxide. Razor blades of agony slice along my nerve endings, and I have to bite my lip to keep from screeching.

"I'm sorry," he tells me, as he carefully blots the blisters dry with gauze and then applies some Neosporin and a couple of large Band-Aids. He repeats the process with the second foot, wiping the last of the blood away with a couple of Handi Wipes before pulling a pair of black flip-flops from another bag. He slips them on my feet and then walks to the back of the car, where he stows the first-aid stuff.

Eli is already asleep—I can hear the deep, even rhythm of his breath—as I wait for Theo to come around to the driver's side. And then he's there. Turning on the car, buckling his seat belt, pulling out onto the nearly deserted road.

Within minutes, we're back on the highway, driving fast, going nowhere even faster, into a real-world Pandora's Box.

15

WE'VE BEEN ON THE ROAD half an hour or so when Theo says, "Make yourself useful. Reach behind you and get that bag."

He's smiling when he says it, so I flip him off before turning around to do what he says.

"This is a CB radio," I tell him. "What do you expect me to do with it?"

"Figure out how it works."

"You're the tech genius. Isn't that supposed to be your job?"

He cracks up, and as I watch him, I realize it's the first time I've ever really heard him laugh. It's a good sound—happy, like the opening chords of Third Eye Blind's "Semi-Charmed Life." When he turns to me, his eyes are the brightest blue I've ever seen, clear and laser focused.

"Pandora, a CB radio is about as low-tech as you can get. If the girl who unleashed 'cyber-Armageddon'"—he puts air quotes around the words—"can't figure out how to work that, then I don't know what to tell her."

"Whatever." It's a lame comeback, but the best I can do under the circumstances.

Opening the carton the radio comes in, I fiddle with it for a little while. Nothing happens, so I give up trying to look cool and go straight for the directions. Theo's right. It is pretty low-tech, and it only takes a couple of minutes to get the thing up and running.

Of course, there's nothing out there when I scan the channels. After all, no one uses CB radios anymore, except maybe truckers. And I'm not even sure about that.

I say as much to Theo, but he just shakes his head and says, "Give it a little while. In a few hours, that thing is going to light up. It's pretty much the only means of communication out there right now. We got the second-to-last one on the shelf."

I snort. "Did it ever occur to you there were only two to begin with? It's not like it's a high-demand item, after all."

"The world just changed overnight, Pandora. You haven't got a clue what are high-demand items and what aren't."

I think of the extra first-aid kits I glimpsed in the bags Theo shoveled into the back of the car. The medicine and batteries. The three sets of walkie-talkies. Stuff I never would have thought to buy.

"How did you know what to get?" I finally ask. "You're so prepared, so calm, like you've done this a million times before."

"I watch the History Channel a lot," he says. "You'd be surprised how many shows they have about the end of the world. Though usually it's because of some weird viral pandemic sweeping through and taking over, not something like this. The rest is just common sense. Either way, it's not going to be long before civilization starts breaking down—forty-eight to seventy-two hours. We've already seen some of the cracks."

How long will it be before everything goes to hell? Not nearly as long as it should be, I think. Not nearly as long as I want it to be.

"Why did you come back for me?" The question is out before I know I'm going to ask it. But it's one I've wanted the answer to since the adrenaline wore off and I was able to think clearly again.

"You don't actually think I would leave you in that mess, do you?" he demands, obviously insulted. "When I helped put you in the middle of it?"

"You didn't do anything! I'm the one who was stupid enough to pull down those pictures from the Internet. My father . . ." My voice catches and I stop, swallow. Try not to show how humiliated I am. "My father did this to me, to all of us. You had nothing to do with it."

"I'm the one who told you to open that present. Besides, I thought we were starting to be . . . *friends*." The word comes awkwardly to him. "I couldn't just let Homeland Security get their hands on you."

"How did you know they'd be there?" It's another one of the questions that's been bothering me. "How did you even know that I'd *need* help?"

"From the second I saw how things were going at Little Nicky's, I started to get worried. Then with the car accident, no 911, I don't know. I just knew. If I'd planned this all out and then shown up at your house last night and you'd been fine, I would have felt stupid. But Eli and I figured it was better to be wrong than risk letting something bad happen to you."

My own *mother* doesn't have time to wish me happy birthday. My father turned me into a destroyer, gave me a technological Pandora's box to open. And Theo and Eli didn't want to risk leaving me behind.

It's a lot to wrap my head around. I swallow once, twice, try to get rid of the lump in my throat. It doesn't work, and my voice is husky, barely audible, when I say, "Thank you."

Eli stirs in the backseat, sits up, and when he reaches for my hand I realize he's been listening for a while. "It's going to be okay, Pandora. We're in this together now."

It's a ridiculous line, completely corny, and any other time I would have called him on it. But right now, it's exactly what I need to hear. I glance down to where our hands are joined, his so much bigger and broader that it all but envelopes mine. It makes me feel sheltered, protected, something I've never felt before. And something I never knew I was missing until this moment. I can do things on my own if I have to—I've learned that in the last few years—but it's nice to have a partner.

Two partners, I think, glancing back at Theo. He's staring straight ahead, face once again blank and fingers clamped tightly on the wheel. I want to say something to him that will bring back the camaraderie of the last few minutes, but he's already a million miles away.

Ignoring Theo, Eli scoots forward until he's sitting

cross-legged on the floor of the car, right behind our seats. His green eyes are still a little foggy, the last remnants of his nap not yet gone from them. He looks adorable. "Where are we?"

"Way North Texas."

Eli nods. "Where are we going?"

"I'm thinking Kansas, maybe," Theo answers.

"What's in Kansas?" I demand.

"Not much. Which is exactly the point. It's easier to hide you if we stick to rural areas."

"We're going to need gas soon," Eli says, nodding at the gas gauge.

I hadn't noticed, but it's on empty, the red light already blinking. "I know," Theo says. "We'll stop at the next place we see that's open—or we'll crack into the gallons we have in the back."

We drive past three more gas stations, all closed, before we find one that is operating. Theo coasts into it—we're literally running on fumes at this point—and pulls up to the last open gas pump.

"You should dye your hair here," Eli says, handing the box to me. "We can hang out for a few extra minutes while you do it."

"It takes longer than a few minutes," I answer.

"Still, it needs to be done ASAP," Theo tells me. "If a cop sees you . . ."

I take the box with a nod, and try not to think about what I'm going to do. Becoming upset won't change things—better to just get it done.

I hop out of the van and walk around to Theo, who is

counting out a hundred and eighty dollars in cash. "So much?" I ask, shocked.

"Look at the price of gas," he tells me. I do, and I am astounded that it's three dollars more a gallon than it was when I filled up two days ago. Creepy.

Eli starts to come with us, but Theo says, "Stay here, outside the van. And stand up straight."

"I've got to take a leak," Eli complains.

"When I get back," Theo growls. "Pay attention!"

We do, and it takes only a few seconds for his meaning to sink in. Almost everyone standing around is looking at us, sizing us up. I can practically see the wheels spinning in their heads as they try to figure out what, if anything, we've got in our van.

Forty-eight to seventy-two hours before civilization breaks down, Theo told me, but it's barely been fifteen, and already things are starting to change. These people all look normal, like the same kind of people I would see at a gas station any number of times. Except there's a palpable aura of panic around them now, as if they know that things are only going to get worse and they'll have to protect themselves—their families—any way they can.

My stomach ties itself into knots, and I know Eli must feel the same way. All he says is, "Dude," but then he straightens up until every one of his seventy-eight inches is on full display. He towers over the van, and the blank look on his face as he glances around the station is completely intimidating. More than one man drops his eyes.

Convinced that Eli and the van are safe—or as safe as

they can be, Theo grabs my elbow and starts propelling me toward the front door of the convenience store. "Should we tell him to get the knife out?" I whisper hoarsely. "To protect himself?"

Theo shakes his head as he pulls the door open for me. "If he does that, they'll know there's something in the van we want to hold on to."

"But he's alone out there!"

"And we're alone in here," Theo snarls, stopping dead. I crane my head around his massive body to see a man guarding the inside of the door, a huge shotgun slung over his shoulder. I freeze in place, don't even dare to breathe as he shifts the gun down to rest on the palms of his hands.

"The store is closed, except to paying customers," he says, the twang of his North Texas accent sounding absurdly threatening.

"We have money." Theo reaches into his pocket, pulls out the cash he'd put there a little while before. "I need to buy gas and some water."

The man eyes the money greedily. "How much gas you need?"

"Enough to fill up my van out there, and a few extra containers."

The man nods. "The water's down at the end of the first aisle."

Theo nods back. "Where's your restroom?"

"At the back of the store. It's an extra five bucks if you want to use it."

I gape at him, but Theo doesn't say anything. Just puts

his hand on the small of my back and walks me in the right direction. "Go in there and get it done," he says. "Quickly." He hands me his watch so I can time how long the dye's on my hair.

"It's going to take twenty minutes at least."

"Then get started. I'll be right out here if you need me." There's an underlying urgency in his voice that I've never heard before, not even when we were running toward the dock, the threat of discovery a spark in the very air we breathed.

The future doesn't look good.

I rush into the women's bathroom, which is one of those single-use kinds with no stalls, just a toilet and a sink. At least it's clean, which is more than I had dared hope for. I tear into the box and mix the two containers quickly. Pop on the pair of gloves, rip off my hat, and start squirting the dye onto my hair. Some drops sprinkle onto my T-shirt as I'm rushing like a crazy person, but I barely notice.

My mind is on Theo, who is outside the door with a gun-toting man. And Eli, who's alone at the car. Defenseless.

After I get the dye on, I glance impatiently at Theo's watch. The countdown begins now. I clean up, toss everything in the trash can, then wash my face.

Go to the bathroom.

Wash my hands.

Count the cracks in the ceiling.

Glance at Theo's watch again. Only five minutes have passed and I'm losing my mind. What's going on out there? Is Theo okay? Eli? I feel like I'm going to jump out of my skin.

The next fifteen minutes are probably the worst of my whole life. I imagine Eli being jumped, beaten. Theo getting shot. The two of them having to fight everyone outside the station, and I curse my father again and again.

How could he do this? How could the man I remember, the man from those pictures, voluntarily throw the world into such incredible chaos? What did he hope to gain? And how could he think whatever it was was worth it?

The twenty minutes are finally up, and I bend down into an excruciating position and begin to wash the dye from my hair. There's a lot of it, and the water flow is not great, so it takes a lot longer than I want it to.

I'm almost done when there's a loud banging at the door. "Girl, what are you doing in there? Other people need to use the bathroom, you know."

It's the old man with the gun. "I'm coming!" I shout. "One more minute. Please."

I scrub my head hard, trying to wash out the last of the dye as quickly as possible. It's only after I'm done that I realize I've screwed up again. My hair is soaking wet, dripping all over my face, my shirt, the floor, and I have no towel.

Way to think ahead, Pandora.

The knock comes again, so I grab a few paper towels from the dispenser on the wall and squeeze them over my hair. It's not great, but it will have to do. I jam the cap back on my head and open the door. The old man is there, looking furious, and behind him are three women who seem just as pissed.

"Sorry," I say, and then I run. Eli is waiting for me at the end of the aisle. "Theo's with the car," he says in response to my look of surprise. "Let's go." He wraps an arm around my shoulder as he hustles me to the front of the store.

"You got it done?" he asks as we all but run up the aisles.

"Yeah."

"Good. Now let's get the hell out of here."

I'm in total agreement, as the suspicion I felt leveled at us when we first got out of the car has cemented into crackling resentment in the half hour I've been inside the store. I wonder if my hogging the bathroom is what set them off, and I feel awful. I knew this was a bad idea.

Theo's pulled the van up to the front door, and he's inside, motor running and doors locked. As soon as he sees us, he opens the locks and we literally hop in on the run.

I fasten my seat belt and look around the car. Theo has jammed water bottles everywhere he can find space. Under the seats, in the aisles. Enough to last us a week, maybe more, if we're careful. I have a feeling we're going to be very careful.

Suddenly, Eli shouts, "Holy shit! What happened to you?"

I'm in the backseat, so I can't see anything but the right side of Theo's face, which looks fine to me, bruised cheekbone and cuts from the accident notwithstanding. Scrambling out of my seat belt, I lean forward and finally see what Eli is talking about. There's a jagged wound at Theo's left temple, and blood is dripping from it, all the way down his face.

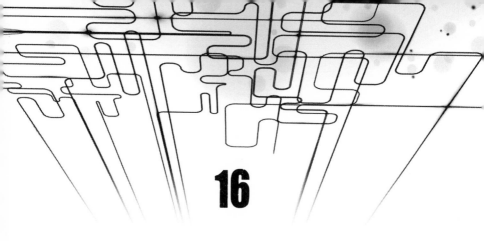

16

THEO SHRUGS, barely bothered by a cut that looks intensely painful. "Nothing big. Just an altercation over the allocation of resources that we paid for."

"What does that mean?" asks Eli.

"They jumped you for the water?" I say at the same time.

"They did."

"Why didn't you call me, man? I would have had your back."

"And leave Pandora on her own? Or the van unattended? I don't think so."

Anger sweeps through me at the condescending answer. "I'm not the one who got his face bashed in," I tell him. "They weren't after me."

"You'd be surprised at everything those guys were after," Theo says, and there's something in his voice. Something that tells me the fight was about more than water. The knots in my stomach twist a little tighter.

Eli must have figured out the same thing because his cheeks flush angrily. "It's like *Lord of the Flies* out there. Any second I expect someone to jump out and scream, 'Kill the pig!'"

"Pull over," I urge Theo. "I want to look at your face."

"In a little while. I want to put some distance between us and them."

"But your cheek—"

"Will be in a lot worse shape if those bastards catch up with us. Keep driving, Theo," Eli snarls. He's furious and I don't blame him. I want to go back to that stupid gas station and beat the hell out of the guys who messed with Theo. For him to look the way he does, there had to be more than one or two of them. He's just too strong and too big for it to have been anything else.

I drop my gaze from his face—I can't look at it anymore—and end up staring at his bruised and skinned knuckles instead. How much worse is this thing going to get?

I scoot to the back, pull some ice out of the cooler, and wrap it in one of the shirts they bought me earlier at Walmart. "Here, put this on your face," I tell Theo.

He starts to argue, but I stare him down in the rearview mirror, and finally he gives in. "Fine. Thanks."

"No problem."

I pull out another shirt—a pale-pink ribbed tank top—along with the second of the two bras I packed in my backpack. I'm soaking wet from my awkward-in-the-extreme hair washing.

"Don't look back here for a minute," I tell them, even

though I know it's ridiculous. They saw me running around at the accident scene in nothing more than a bra, but this is different. More intimate.

I try to climb into the third seat, but the supplies are stacked so deep that it's almost impossible. I give up, settle on facing backward as I shimmy out of my wet clothes and into the new ones.

I turn around just in time to catch Eli watching me from the mirror in his sun visor, and I smack him on the back of the head. "I think we need to establish some ground rules," I growl.

Eli just laughs, his green eyes gleaming mischievously. "I think you have me confused with Theo. I'm not the rule-following kind."

"You need to start. At least when it comes to seeing me naked."

Theo's eyes jump to the rearview mirror. "He saw you naked?"

He sounds so annoyed that I swat him, too, for good measure, before settling back against my seat. I'm exhausted, completely drained. It's been over twenty-four hours since I've slept, and I know I should try to rest now, but I can't. I'm way too hyped-up and nervous.

"Pandora, have you got any gum?" Eli asks about fifteen minutes later.

I toss him my backpack. "I think there's some in the front pocket."

"Thanks." He opens it up, then pulls out an envelope. "Hey, what are these pictures of?"

Too late I remember shoving the pictures I downloaded from my father into my bag—back before I realized that he was the cause of all this.

"They're the pictures my father sent me. The ones that uploaded the worm when I clicked on them."

Theo swivels to face me. "You have copies of the photos?"

"Yeah. Why?"

After glancing in the rearview mirror to make sure that no one is following us, he pulls the van over. "Let me see them."

"Why? They're just stupid pictures of when I was little. Nothing else."

"Still." He all but rips the envelope out of Eli's hands. He doesn't say anything while he goes through the stack, and neither does Eli, who is also looking at them. They flip through all twelve, then start at the beginning again. "What are you looking for?" I demand.

"I don't know. But I have a hard time believing these are just pictures. Your father seems too smart for that," Theo says.

"They aren't just pictures. They were the worm!"

"There's got to be more. Otherwise, why have *you* launch the worm? Why not just do it himself?"

"Hey, isn't that the Capitol building in Austin?" Eli asks, pointing to one of the pictures.

"Yeah, so?"

"So your dad reprogrammed Pandora's Box to start out next to the Capitol. Don't you think that's strange?"

I start to tell him that this whole thing is strange, but

then I remember my weird shock at being dropped into the game in the center of Austin. The strange feeling of déjà vu that overcame me. "What are you trying to say?" I ask, taking the picture from Eli.

"Get out your laptop," Theo tells me. "You need to go back."

"Go back where?"

"To the beginning of the game. There's a clue hidden in the Capitol somewhere."

"That's ridiculous! A clue to what?" I'm totally confused.

"I don't know. But it's there." He glances at Eli, and for once there's no animosity in his voice when he asks, "How much do you want to bet?"

"Nothing else makes sense," Eli agrees. "We knew you were missing something."

"Why would he do that? Why would he go through all the trouble of bringing the world to a crashing halt, only to leave clues as to how to make it okay again?"

"Isn't that what it said? 'Beat the game. Save the world?' "

"Do you really believe that?"

"I think we have to believe it. Or what's the point?" Theo interjects.

"There is no point! He's crazy."

"Look, just try, okay?" Eli says. "What's it going to hurt?"

Me, I think. It's going to hurt me even more than I already have been. I don't want to get my hopes up, don't want to pretend that my father is something more, or better, than he is. It'll just hurt too much when this whole thing ends up being nothing but a wild-goose chase. I want to say all that, but I can't. Not even to them. I don't want anyone to see what's inside me right now.

But they're both looking at me, waiting for me to do what they want or give them a reason why I won't. They've risked everything for me and this is all they've asked. How can I say no?

I take out my laptop and try to turn it on. "The battery's dead."

Theo reaches into the glove compartment, pulls out a charger, and hands it to me. "Did you think of everything?" I ask him, astonished.

"I tried."

I plug one end of the charger into the 12-volt outlet and the other into my laptop.

The screen comes to life and it looks exactly the same as when I last left it. Except Eli's right. The number in the countdown has changed. "Total annihilation in 9 days."

I press a few buttons, but my avatar doesn't appear. The screen doesn't change. Nothing happens at all. "I'm locked out," I tell them. "When the Internet crashed, it must have taken the game with it."

"Let me see." Eli grabs the laptop and messes with it for a few minutes, but I can tell by the frustrated expression on his face that nothing's coming of it. I don't know how I feel about that. Disappointed and worried, sure. But there's also a sense of relief. If I can't get in, can't play the game, then I'm not responsible for fixing things. Which sounds really good right about now, if I'm completely honest. There's something to be said for a father who is not just a psychopath but a screwup as well.

"Here." Eli hands the computer to Theo, who's been impatiently watching his every move. "You're the hacker. You try."

Theo pulls a wireless card out of his wallet and inserts it into my laptop.

"That won't work," I tell him. "It's not that we don't have wireless coverage out here. It's that the Internet is down. Gone."

"It's not gone. It's just that the pathways that let us access it have been shredded." He spends a few seconds getting around my operating system, and after that, I'm not sure what he does. It's all in code that makes no sense to me at all. But after about ten minutes, he hands the laptop back to me. The game is live and ready to play.

"What did you do?" I demand.

"It's complicated."

"I think we can follow along," Eli snarls.

Theo doesn't answer, just stares at him with that blank face he slides into place at will. But when I look at him pleadingly, he relents with a sigh. "After the Egyptian government took their whole country off-line, it got people in Congress and other government agencies here all interested in having that same kind of power in the United States. A bill authorizing a presidential kill-switch started circulating—not for the first time. And while it hasn't gained enough support to be voted on, the idea of it interested me."

"It interested you?" I ask incredulously.

"In a strictly academic and horrifying kind of way," he clarifies. "So I started messing around, researching a bunch of stuff, hacking into other stuff, and I realized our government already has the capability to do that. I mean, it only makes sense, right? If a developing nation can do it, of course we should be able to. Especially since our military is the one that laid the entire Internet foundation anyway."

"You mean the president can just kill the whole Internet?"

"Not legally. At least not yet. But Homeland Security has the ability to do it. They also have the ability to safeguard a small section of the Internet, so that they can communicate with each other even in the middle of a massive disaster like this one."

"How?"

"I would imagine the most hackproof safeguards out there and some massive generators to keep everything going electronically."

"Which means what exactly? They have the Internet even when no one else does?"

"That's my guess."

"So what does that mean? That they do still have Internet and communications access? They actually can spread around pictures of me from city to city?" Panic tears at my throat. If I'm spotted with Eli and Theo, it's not just my life on the line. It's theirs, as well. I've never liked that idea, but at least when I thought the government was blacked out, I didn't worry so much about us getting caught. About them getting arrested for cyberterrorism as well.

Theo shakes his head. "No, because only the highest levels of the government would have access to this. All the regular government agencies are screwed like everyone else."

"So what does this mean in reference to the game?" Eli asks. "How did you get it going again?"

"It was just a theory I've been working on." Theo shrugs. "It seems to me that this worm has to work on several different levels, taking over communications, electricity, et cetera. But to take over the Internet the way it has, I figure your dad has to have access to that kill-switch—and probably the safeguarded government area."

"How?" Eli asks. He looks fascinated, which I don't understand. The more Theo explains, the sicker I feel.

"That, I don't know. I need the game matrix to have any hope of figuring that out."

"So what did you do? Did you get into that area?" I ask, suddenly more afraid for him. For all of us.

"In ten minutes? No way. I just figured that even though he crashed everything else, your dad had to have left a pathway open to the game, one that probably connects to those government controls. I don't know that for sure, though. I'm just guessing. Anyway, why go through the trouble of setting up this elaborate game if no one can access it?"

"You found the pathway?"

"I did. It's disguised, but not so hidden that someone who knows what he's doing can't access it. You probably won't have the average person who knows nothing about computers beyond Facebook and e-mail accessing it and playing the game. But gamers, hackers, programmers— anyone with a little know-how should be able to find it."

"I wouldn't have been able to find it," I tell him.

He raises an eyebrow. "Well, then it's a good thing you've got me, isn't it?"

In more ways than one, it seems. I look at the laptop again, fight the disgust welling up inside me. The little voice that tells me to get as far away from the game as possible. But in the end, I only sigh and give in to the inevitable.

I enter the game right where I left off, in Zilker Park. Except now I'm alone and dressed in a pink tank top that looks remarkably like the one I'm wearing. And my hair is muddy brown.

"Which way is the Capitol?" I ask Theo, my voice a little pissy despite myself. I don't want to do this.

"You have to turn to the right." His voice is as calm as ever, and I find myself wondering if anything frazzles him. Even back at the gas station, when I was scared to death, he took everything in stride.

I do as he says, keeping my finger on the arrow key so that my avatar is running through the streets as fast as she can. More than once, some creature jumps out and I have to fight it while Eli and Theo give me pointers.

I finally make it to the Capitol, but when I get there I'm not sure where I need to go. So I look for a few minutes, checking out the gardens, the hallways, all to no avail.

"See," I tell them, feeling an odd kind of triumph. "There's nothing here."

"Yes, there is. You just have to find it." Eli's voice is firm, resolute, and I'm annoyed all over again. Every step I take is a reminder of what my father did and of how stupidly gullible I am. He hasn't made any effort to see me in ten years, yet the second he e-mails me I jump through his hoops . . . and end up here. It's humiliating.

"Where in the Capitol was that picture taken?" Eli finally asks, as I continue to bumble around.

"The rotunda," I answer with the surety of someone who

has been forced to walk the Capitol many times. "See the statue of Sam Houston?"

He stares at me blankly, and Theo explains, "Eli's from California. He moved to Austin when our parents got married." He says the last word like it tastes bad. It sets off a warning bell in my head, one I want to listen to and explore a little, but there's no time.

I glance behind me, for the first time wondering if we're attracting attention sitting here on the side of the road. Everything looks okay, but right now, that doesn't mean much.

Theo must read my mind, because he throws the van into gear and pulls back onto the highway. "Keep playing the game while I drive."

I turn left, head toward the rotunda that is the very center of the Capitol building. Walk up to the Sam Houston statue, but nothing strikes me as different. There's no task I missed, no creature to battle. It's a total waste of time.

I start to put the computer down, but Eli urges, "Trust me. It's there."

"How do you know?"

He shrugs, grins. "A feeling."

I groan, but keep the computer on my lap. "What's the most important part of the rotunda?" I ask Theo abruptly. "The pictures of the governors? Or the statues of Austin and Houston?"

He shrugs. "I like looking at the ceiling, myself. I've even taken that tiny staircase all the way to the top."

"No way. Seriously?"

"Yeah."

So have I, but in all my time going to the Capitol, I've never met another person who has. Small and white, the staircase shoots up from the top floor in a tight spiral all the way to the top of the dome and intimidates almost everyone. Even I, who have no fear of heights at all, was a little nervous as I climbed the tiny, narrow steps. But it was totally worth it when I got to the top—the view was amazing, and if I reached my arm up, I could touch the ceiling.

I wonder . . .

I move to the staircase, take the first flight of stairs. Then the second, then the third. Up and up my avatar goes until I'm right there, on the bottom step of the last narrow staircase. I start to climb it, too, when I realize I don't have to.

"Look!" I point to the very pinnacle of the rotunda, where, in real life, the star of Texas is painted, with one letter of the word "Texas" in each of the spaces between the star points.

But in the game, it's different. The star is six pointed, not five, and where the letters would normally spell out Texas, there are numbers. I stare at the six numbers—57, 101, 50, 43, 35, 11—and try to break the code. I add them up in my head, divide them, try to think of different things they could be a code for, but nothing seems to work.

"I don't get it," I tell the guys, frustrated. "This has to be it."

"No, you're right," Eli tells me reassuringly. "This is it. Don't worry—we'll figure it out."

"You try." I hand him the computer and settle back into my seat. "I'm so tired my eyes are crossing."

Eli clicks a couple of keys, blows up the numbers so they're a lot bigger than they were, and right away he crows, "I've got it!"

"What? You do?" I spring forward, excited and a little miffed, too, that he figured it out so easily when I couldn't.

"Do you see that?" he asks, pointing to the number 35.

There's a little degree circle next to it at the top, and Theo—who is watching the game as much as he is the road— calls, "Latitude and longitude!"

"Exactly. Here, write this down, Pandora. The coordinates are N 35°11'57" and W 101°50'43"."

My hand is trembling a little as I write, not from fear this time but from excitement. Finally, we have a lead. Finally, we have something to go on. Finally, we have . . . what? What exactly do we have? And why do I even care? Shouldn't I be more worried about saving myself from the tentacles of Homeland Security than I am about this stupid game?

Around the world there are hundreds of thousands, maybe millions, of people playing Pandora's Box. People who are much better at gaming than I'll ever be. I should leave it to them. Besides, who even cares? How can a game save the world? Just because my father—who has proven himself to be a psychopath—says it can, doesn't make it true.

Yet even as I'm thinking these things, even as I'm telling myself I don't care what he's created and what point he wants to make, I'm leaning forward, watching as Eli tries to plug the coordinates into the game.

It doesn't work—big surprise. The game's not set up to take latitude and longitude. Not the original, and not this tweaked, nightmarish version of my father's. In the original, you can hop from city to city through the AR door, but you have to know what city you want to go to. It must be the same in this version as well.

"This doesn't make sense," Eli says. "Why leave us a clue that we can't follow? How the hell are we supposed to know where this point is if the game won't take us there?"

Suddenly, something occurs to me. "Maybe the coordinates aren't meant for our avatars. Maybe they're meant for us."

"You think your dad wants us to just run around the world checking out GPS coordinates?" Eli sounds skeptical.

"I've got a GPS app on my phone. We could—"

Theo laughs, and it takes me a second to figure out what's so funny. And then I remember. No network, no GPS. We're out here in the middle of nowhere with a set of GPS coordinates and no way to figure out what they are. Except . . .

"We need to find a library!"

Eli looks at me like I'm crazy, but Theo gets it right away. Libraries have atlases, and atlases have latitude and longitude.

Of course, there's just one problem. The next town big enough to have a decent library is hundreds of miles away— maybe in the wrong direction. What I wouldn't give for a map right about now . . .

"Hey, what are those coordinates again?" Theo demands as he continues to drive north.

Eli repeats them, and Theo hits the steering wheel excitedly. "That's Amarillo!"

I stare at him, bewildered. Supersmart is one thing, but actually having a bunch of GPS coordinates running around in your head—that's just plain weird.

"How do you know?" Eli demands, and it's obvious he's thinking the same thing I am.

"My dad and I used to geocache—"

"Geocache?" I ask, completely lost.

"It's like a giant scavenger hunt. Someone buries something and then throws the GPS coordinates up for other people to use to find the object. Whoever digs it up logs that they found it and can either replace the thing in the cache with something of their own or leave it exactly as is. Either way, they have to put it back in the same spot for others to find."

"And you did this for fun?" Again Eli asks what I'm thinking.

"It's cooler than it sounds." Theo shrugs and manages to only look a little insulted. "Anyway, my dad grew up in Amarillo, so when we had a free weekend we'd fly up there to check out the caches. We landed at those coordinates enough for me to know them."

"And you're sure these are the right ones?" I ask.

"Positive. Those are the coordinates listed on a map for Amarillo, Texas." He rattles the numbers off again, this time without looking at them.

"Okay. I'll go with you on this," Eli says. "But where in Amarillo?"

"I don't know. Probably downtown?"

"What good are general coordinates going to do us?" I

ask, frustrated. "Amarillo isn't as big as Austin, but it's large enough that we can't just go wandering around, hoping to figure out what my father wants us to do next."

"Why not? We found the clue in Austin."

"Yeah. In the game. And we only found it because of the . . ." I freeze as the truth hits me like a runaway train.

I fumble for my backpack and the stash of photos. As I pull them out, Eli's already made the connection—we're definitely on the same wavelength today.

"What's the next photo?"

"I don't know. They aren't in any order." I rack my brain, try to remember what order the pictures were in on the blog. But I only saw it that once, and a lot of things have happened since then. Maybe the picture of my dad and me near the huge solar array was next? Or was it the one with us close to the silo?

I just don't know—and my age in the photos isn't a good indicator. The pictures were all mixed up on the blog—no order that I could tell, except, obviously, for this one.

"Look for markers," Eli says. "Anything that seems like it could give a clue about where these places are."

"I'm trying!" I snap. "It's not as easy as it looks."

Eli doesn't say anything and neither does Theo. Which makes me feel doubly guilty for jumping at Eli when he was only trying to help.

"Here." I hold a few of the photos out in a pathetic attempt at a peace offering. "Maybe you'll see something I missed."

Our fingers brush as he moves to take the pictures, and a warm tingling works its way down my fingers. He smiles but doesn't say anything, so I try to ignore it.

I shuffle through my pile of photos again, and this time I see something in the corner of one of them. My dad and I are in front of a huge sign that says ENDEAVOR FARMS, but to the left of us is a small road sign. I squint, try to make it out, but it's a ways from us, and the numbers are slightly blurred.

Eli leans toward me to get a closer look. His breath is warm on my cheek and I ignore that, too. "I think the first number is a two," he tells Theo.

"And the last number is a seven!" I trace its lines with my pinkie finger.

"Twenty-seven?" Theo asks, his voice dark and a little disappointed. "I don't think—"

"No. Two eighty-seven," Eli corrects him. "There are three numbers, and I'm almost positive the middle one is an eight."

"But I can't read what state it's in. That part's too blurry." I sink back against my seat in disgust.

"Yeah, well, there's a two eighty-seven that runs into Amarillo, so we're going to take a huge leap of faith and assume this is it," Theo says. "We can pick it up about an hour north of here and follow it all the way in. We're looking for Endeavor Farms, so once we get to Amarillo we can grab a phone book and figure out where it is."

"Do they even still *make* phone books?" Eli asks.

Theo doesn't answer, but his hands tighten a little bit on the steering wheel at the same time as mine clench into fists on my lap. They'd better still make them—and we'd better be able to find one—or we are screwed before this thing even begins.

And so is the rest of the world.

17

WE SWITCH DRIVERS about an hour out of Amarillo, so I'm behind the wheel when we hit the city limits.

"Start looking for a gas station or something like that," Theo says. "Someplace we can find a pay phone."

"You make it sound so easy," Eli mutters, but he turns to stare out the window. "When's the last time you *saw* a pay phone?"

I'm about to ask for a backup plan when Eli shouts, "Hey! There it is!"

I turn, expecting to see a pay phone. Instead, we pass a huge sign that reads, WELCOME TO ENDEAVOR FARMS. It isn't the same color or font as the one in the picture, but I'm not sure that means anything. It's been about thirteen years since the photo was taken, after all.

Looks like our luck is taking a major upswing, though I guess that has more to do with Theo than any goodwill from the universe.

I glance behind me out of habit, make sure no cops are in the vicinity—though to be honest I think they all have better things to do. Then I slow down a little and make a U-turn right in the middle of the highway, bumping and sliding us across the huge patch of grass that separates the two sides of the road.

"Drive much?" Theo asks as I turn right at the farm's entrance. Eli just laughs.

"I thought we were in a hurry." I don't take my eyes off the sharp curves in front of me. The driveway's built like a sidewinding roller coaster.

I keep going for about a half mile into the property, before I have to stop in front of a huge iron fence. The thing is about twelve feet high, with ornamental spikes at the top—not to mention a thick chain and padlock holding the gates closed.

"So much for the welcome," I mutter.

"Got your climbing boots on, Pandora?" Eli asks.

I flex my feet in the flip-flops I've been wearing for hours. "Not hardly." I turn around to look at Theo in the backseat. "I don't suppose you have bolt cutters back there, do you?"

"I left them in the garage." He looks completely chagrined—like he took my question seriously and can't believe he forgot something as *obvious* as bolt cutters.

I crack up. I can't help it. "Then I guess we're doing this the old-fashioned way, huh?" I back the van into a small turn-around area, then pull forward as if I'm preparing to leave.

"Hey. Where are we going?" Eli asks in alarm. "I can climb this thing easy."

"Yeah, but why should you have to?" I back the van up until the rear bumper is almost touching the fence.

"Very smart, Pandora." Eli grins his approval.

"I have my moments."

Slinging my backpack over my shoulder, I scoot out the passenger door just in time to see Theo climb onto the hood of the van. "Need help?" he asks, extending one large hand down for me to grab. I stare at it a second, trying to decide if I want his help. He's been kind of obnoxious for the last few minutes.

That jerkiness doesn't outweigh his having made himself a national fugitive for me. And it's not as if I have much of a choice, anyway. Refusing would look petty.

But I've waited too long, weighing my options, and I watch as Theo shuts down once more. I swear, the boy has more layers than an onion, and I can't seem to get past the skin.

"Theo . . ." I reach a hand out to him, but he doesn't turn around. And then Eli's next to me.

"Hey, Pandora, need a boost?" He squats down, laces his fingers together.

"Yeah," I say, though I don't take my eyes off Theo. He doesn't bother to glance back at me.

I clamber onto the hood and then follow Theo onto the roof. It's a little bit tricky in my flip-flops, but I manage. And then I just have to grab on to the top of the bars, pull myself up and over without impaling myself on an iron stake . . . or three.

Piece of cake, I tell myself, but my palms are slippery as I boost myself over, putting my feet on the horizontal rail that runs along the back of the fence. I start to climb down and my hands slip off the fence. I scramble for purchase, but it's too late. I'm falling. I try to roll so that I won't land flat on my back on the ground, brace myself for an impact that doesn't come. Instead, Theo catches me against his hard chest, his heavily muscled arms like tree trunks around me.

"You okay?" he murmurs in my ear.

"Yeah. Great." Suddenly I can't remember how to swallow. "Thanks."

"No problem."

Eli jumps down beside us. "Does anything hurt, Pandora?"

"I'm fine."

"Good." He glares at Theo. "She can walk, you know."

"Yeah. I got that." He slides me slowly, carefully, to the ground. "You ready?"

He's asking me, his body language shouting that he doesn't give a shit if Eli's ready or not.

Instead of answering, I strike out down the remainder of the long driveway that leads straight toward two huge buildings. One looks like a barn and the other is a massive greenhouse directly behind it. In the distance is a small house, but it's too far away to see if anyone lives there.

We cautiously walk up to the first building—the barn—and I know we're all wondering if there's anyone here. And if there is, are they as afraid of strangers as everyone else we've run across seems to be? We're standing in front of the door, but none of us wants to be the one to open it—just in case there's a guy with a gun on the other side. But it's my dad who created this mess, so after a deep breath for courage, I reach for the door handle.

It's locked.

Of course it is. I knock a few times, wait. Knock again, wait some more. No one comes. Which is probably a good thing, as I have no idea what I'd say to them if they did.

"Now what?" I ask.

Eli reaches into his pocket, pulls out a Swiss army knife. After a second of fiddling with the tools, he slides one into the lock, jiggles it around. A few seconds later, I hear the lock click.

Theo and I both stare at him in shock, but he just shrugs. "Summer camp."

He leads us into the barn, which is actually a huge room without windows. The ceiling is lined with recessed lights that cast an eerie yellow glow, and the room is filled with large rectangular tanks with pipes leading into and coming out of them. There are all kinds of gauges on the tanks and a bunch of machinery clustered at the end of each one.

"What is this place?" Eli asks. "And how do they still have electricity?"

"Generator?" I venture.

"More like solar panels," Theo says, staring at the ceiling.

"Why didn't an alarm go off when we entered?" I ask, completely uneasy. Something about this doesn't feel right. Who leaves a place like this unmanned and unguarded, especially in the middle of a crisis?

Eli points to the wall behind me. There's an alarm panel hanging there. Some of the lights are red, but most are green. "Only a few of the alarms are actually armed," he tells me.

"Which ones?" I step up to the panel. All the lights marked "doors" are green. Only the ones marked "control systems" are armed. I say as much to Eli and Theo.

"The alarms are probably just to ensure everything works right," Theo says. "If we don't mess with any of the equipment we should be fine."

"That shouldn't be a problem." I'm afraid to breathe in here, let alone touch anything. "But I don't understand. The sign says it's a farm, but it looks like a water-treatment plant."

Just then, we hear a splash, followed by another one and another one. For a second, every horror movie I've ever seen flashes through my mind, and I imagine a monster inside the tanks, crawling up the slippery sides in an effort to get out.

"We should go!" I say, starting to back up, but Theo just laughs.

"I know what this is. I've read about places like these."

"A zombie storage unit?" Eli mutters. He obviously has seen the same movies I have.

Theo looks at him like he's an idiot. "It's an aquaculture plant."

I must look as lost as I feel, because Theo shakes his head impatiently. "A self-sustaining fish farm. The greenhouse out back is used to grow organic vegetables using the waste from the tanks." He points to one of them. "See?"

At first I don't know what I'm supposed to be looking at, but then I see a fish jump out of the water and dive back in. It's followed by a second and a third fish.

The source of the splashing sounds we heard. Not zombies. Fish.

I feel like a total moron.

"That's cool," Eli says, climbing up the ladder of the closest tank. "Jesus. There are thousands of them in here."

"Don't touch anything!" Theo barks. "You'll contaminate—"

"I'm not an idiot." Eli stays up there for a little longer. He pretends he's fascinated by the fish, but I know he just doesn't want to look like he's backing down to his stepbrother.

"So what do we do now?" I ask.

"You need to find the password for the game." Theo speaks slowly, like I'm stupid.

"I know that. But how?" I throw my arms out, gesture to the room around us. "This place is huge." I turn and walk away from him, from them, looking over the entire place as I search my brain for memories that I just can't access.

"Why don't we look around," Eli suggests. "See if anything jogs your memory."

It seems like a better idea than standing here, frustrated, so the three of us go exploring. It turns out this aquaculture thing is really cool—a totally self-sustaining farm on only a few acres of land. It's fully automated, with machines that fill automatic timed feeders, an elaborate filtration system, and it's completely climate controlled, independent of weather or drought. It's—

"That's it!" I exclaim, rushing past the last tanks toward the door that separates the fish barn from the greenhouse. "We were supposed to grow crops in the game, right? The clue has to be out here somewhere."

"But where?" Eli demands, following me. "This place is so big I don't even know where to start looking."

It really is. Row after row of crops—on tables, in

planters, some grown directly in the soil beneath our feet. "It's here someplace." I don't know how I know, but I do. The key to the whole level, to moving on, is right here in this greenhouse.

"Am I the only one who thinks we should grab some of this food for the road?" Eli asks suddenly. "If what happened at that gas station is happening everywhere, who knows when we'll have another chance to stock up."

He's right, but I can't help hesitating. When I went to bed two nights ago everything was normal, and now it's like I really have opened a box that I'll never be able to close.

Theo sees my indecision. "We won't take a lot. Just what we need to survive for a few days. We can leave some money."

He's waiting for me to say it's okay. They both are. I look around at the plants, the watering systems. And then, before I can say anything, Eli reaches down and pulls a couple of strawberries off a plant, pops one in his mouth, and offers the other to me.

The line from the game pops into my mind again. *You've reached the point of no return.*

I take the strawberry.

The next few minutes pass in a blur as the guys gather up some berries and vegetables for the road, and I search the greenhouse for some clue into my father's psyche. Some idea of what he wants me to remember.

I find it in a basket of pomegranates resting on the edge of one of the tables, five of the ruby-red fruits just sitting there, ripe for the taking. Beneath the table is a flashlight and an extra pack of batteries. "Don't pomegranates grow on trees?" I call to Theo.

"Yeah, why?"

I reach for one of the fruits, hold it up for him and Eli to see. There are no trees in this greenhouse, at least none big enough to yield pomegranates this size.

Eli takes it from me, turns it over and over in his hands. "Isn't there something in the Demeter myth that talks about pomegranates?"

"It's how Hades bound Persephone to him," I tell Eli. "He got her to eat a pomegranate. Which is how the Greeks explained the seasons. Demeter, the goddess of the harvest, only allowed things to bloom in the spring and summer, when Persephone was with her."

"The harvest," Theo says, but I'm already pulling out my laptop. Waiting impatiently as it asks for my password. Because the myth fits too perfectly into the game to be anything else. And besides, standing here, holding the fruit, reminds me of something. Pomegranates are my father's favorite food.

The game finally flashes on, and there I am, standing in the middle of the Capitol again. I take off, straight for Zilker Park this time, and as I run, I realize something I'd been too frazzled to notice earlier. The Austin I'm running through, the Austin in the game, is drought ravaged, starving for water. We've been in the middle of a drought for a couple of years now, with the lake levels falling and water conservation efforts in effect, but this is the Austin experts warn us to expect in the next eighteen months if we don't get some rain. This is Austin on the brink of dying. Austin with the evil of climate change released from the box.

I finally make it back to a drought-stricken Zilker Park,

where hundreds of NPCs stare at me for help. Even worse, we're not the only ones there. The crowd of players from earlier has grown. There must be seven or eight hundred of them, all looking like they tangled with Campe, standing around or trying to find a way to plant the seeds. There are also dead bodies littering the far reaches of the field.

Every time I take a step, I run into another one. IMs flash across the bottom of my screen from user names I've never heard of. And the invisible wall is still there, the one that prevents me from planting any seeds. From bringing in Demeter's harvest.

I run through the crowds, through the tents, to the AR gate Eli found yesterday when we were playing the game. I plug in the word "pomegranates" and wait, hoping that I've found the right code. For long seconds nothing happens, then I'm knocked off my feet. Blown back about twenty feet from the AR gate. And I still can't plant seeds.

"Wait a minute!" Eli says, dropping the fruit as he crouches down beside me and takes over my computer. "You typed in 'pomegranates,' but in the myth it's only one pome-granate."

"It couldn't be that simple," I whisper as he types in the singular word.

"Why not?" He hits Enter and the whole screen lights up. Then the number 10 flashes across the screen.

"We're back to ten days?" I ask, confused.

"More like ten minutes." Theo taps the screen, where seconds have begun to count down: 9:58. 9:57. 9:56 . . .

"There's a time limit to complete this task?" I screech, horrified, even as I take the computer back and my avatar reaches for her pocketful of seeds. "Don't just stand there. Help me!"

"We can't," Theo tells me grimly. "We left our computers in the van. You're on your own."

I barely keep myself from freaking out as my avatar runs back to the center of Zilker Park. "What do I do?"

They both look at me like I'm crazy. "Plant the seeds!" Eli says, trying once again to take my computer from me.

I shrug him off and, because he's squatting, he loses his balance, slamming against one of the poles that deliver water to the plants. He grabs on to it to steady himself and ends up cracking the bottom half of the pole clean off.

A loud shrieking sound erupts.

18

"IS THAT AN ALARM?" I demand as the lights go out, fighting the urge to cover my ears against the loud shrieking sound that suddenly fills the room.

Theo's too busy hopping to his feet—and pulling me to mine—to answer. "We need to get out of here!"

I know he's right, but I'm paralyzed with fear. The dark. The alarm. The countdown. It's too much. My brain's on overload, and instead of following Theo and Eli down the long center aisle, I just stand there. Quietly freaking out.

I spend my life avoiding the dark and now I'm stuck in it again, for the fourth or fifth time since this nightmare began. I don't want to do this anymore.

I guess Eli suddenly realizes I'm not with them, because he calls to me from halfway across the greenhouse. "Come on, Pandora. Don't lose it now. We need to run."

I still don't move. The blackness is closing in on me from every side, and my heart is pumping like crazy as adrenaline courses through me. I want to move, want to leave this place, this game, far behind, but my feet are glued to the rich soil.

"What's wrong?" Theo asks. "Why aren't you moving?" He sounds impatient and a little vicious. Not that I blame him. I'm being an idiot. I know it—I just can't do anything about it.

The words come out of their own volition. "I don't like the dark."

"Don't like . . ." Eli curses, then I hear him making his way back to me as the plants between us start to rustle.

"It's okay, Pandora. I'm right here." His hand is on my shoulder, stroking down my arm, warm and soft and comforting. It snaps me out of the stranglehold of terror, has me gasping for air as perspiration pours down my spine.

He pulls me against him, into a full-body hug that buries my face against his chest. He smells like coffee and sandalwood and not unpleasantly of sweat. I stand there for a few seconds, just absorbing the strength and comfort he's offering me. It feels good.

"Come on." Theo's voice is a low, insistent throb in the dark. "They'll be here any second."

"Who?" I whisper, but as the blood stops rushing through my ears, I hear the sound that has him so nervous.

Dogs. Barking and growling in the distance. With every second we stand here, it sounds like they're getting closer. The only thing worse than being trapped in the dark is being trapped here in the dark with vicious, snarling dogs.

I pull away from Eli, grab the flashlight that was resting against the table leg. "Let's go."

We have to run back through the huge tank room—if there's another door in the greenhouse we're not going to find it in the dark—and that eats up more precious seconds. The barks are a lot closer now.

Even worse, I get a glimpse of my laptop screen as we run. The timer at the top now reads 6:51.

"The game's still going!" I pant, my lungs nearly bursting with the pace Eli and Theo are setting. "We have less than seven minutes."

Eli curses and so does Theo, vulgar, vile words that only make me feel more desperate. We're at the entrance now, and Theo's hand is on the doorknob. "What should we do?" Eli asks, and for the first time he sounds a little lost.

It steadies me. "Can we stay here for a few minutes, just long enough for me to crack this level?"

At that moment, the door at the opposite end of the room slams open and three snarling dogs burst through it, followed by two men speaking in Spanish.

I'm out the door before I make the conscious decision to move, Eli and Theo at my heels. We're sprinting full out now, trying to make it back to the van before the dogs get us.

Outside is better. It's dark now, but there are solar lights set up all along the driveway that guide us back the way we came.

My flip-flops twist and slide with each step that I take. They slow me down, and I expect Eli and Theo to surge ahead, but they stay steady with me, refusing to budge an inch. "Maybe if we just stop and explain," I gasp, clutching at the stitch in my right side.

"Somehow I don't think those dogs are going to buy our excuses," Eli says.

"I've got to play the game." The level clock now reads 4:32.

"Then play it," Theo snarls, scooping me up and tossing me over his shoulder.

"What are you doing?" It takes every ounce of willpower I have not to scream as we go bumping down the lane.

He doesn't answer, just swerves off the path a ways. Eli follows, sounding as baffled as I am. "Theo, what—"

Theo rips the laptop out of my hands, gives it to Eli. Then lifts me up and away from him. "Grab the branch of that tree and pull yourself up," he orders.

I do what he says, largely because he doesn't give me a choice not to. It's grab the tree branch or go face first over it. As I struggle to pull myself onto it, Theo gives me a final boost. Then he grabs the laptop from Eli and hands it to me.

"This isn't going to work," I tell him furiously. "We're sitting ducks out here." The dogs are much closer now—they sound like they're only a few yards away.

"Just play, Pandora." Theo turns to Eli. "Get behind the tree and watch out for her."

"What are you going to do?" I ask.

He doesn't answer. Just turns away and races back the way we came. Sacrificing himself so that Eli and I will be safe. So that I can play the stupid game.

Which I have to get back to if I have any hope of beating this thing before time runs out in three minutes and eighteen seconds.

In the distance I hear a renewed frenzy of barking, along

with a few shouts from the two dog handlers. The yells are followed by the *thud* of body hitting body, a high-pitched yelp, and more snarls. It's proof that Theo's decoy plan is working. Maybe it should reassure me, but all it does is chill my blood as I think about Theo at their mercy, sacrificing himself to help me and the stepbrother he can barely tolerate.

"Go help him," I snarl at Eli, panic-stricken at the thought of Theo fighting off dogs and humans alike.

"I'm not leaving you," Eli snarls back. "So play the damn game already so we can get back to him."

For the first time since I plugged in the password, I'm paying attention to what's happening on-screen. And it's totally bizarre. On-screen, I'm glowing, my entire body lit up a strange, vibrant red that looks wicked crazy even as it frightens me a little.

What's wrong with my avatar? I wonder as I push buttons randomly. Was Campe radioactive or something? Have I managed to contract some bizarre case of nuclear rabies? I hope not—surely my avatar couldn't survive that. Damn the ancient Greeks and their screwed-up monsters.

Not willing to go down without a fight, especially since everyone—NPC and player alike—is staring at me, I extend my hands out in front of me, the way Theo did when he shot fire. On-screen, I jump and kick, punch and crouch, but nothing else happens. And the glow doesn't disappear, either.

"How's it going?" Eli demands.

"Crappy!" I tell him. "Nothing's happening."

"Hit Control+F. That's how Theo shot fire."

"Already tried that." But I do it again, and this time—I don't know why—rays of light explode from my fingertips. Every character on-screen with me jumps back a good five feet.

In the distance, the dogs growl and snap. A strangled cry of pain drifts through the night air, and I know Theo's been injured. "Eli!" I shove him with the hand that isn't holding the laptop. "We have to help him!"

"After you beat the level," he says grimly, and I can tell that, despite everything, he also feels awful about leaving Theo to fend for himself. "You've got to get past this or everything we've done doesn't mean shit."

He's right, but that doesn't make it any easier to concentrate. I have to, though—the time on the screen reads 2:39. I just wish I knew how to harness this new power. I hit Shift+A, Shift+S, Shift+D, but nothing happens. I keep going along the keyboard unti I hit Shift+P and suddenly the rays blast forward, straight at the ground.

"That's it!" I crow.

"What's it?" asks Eli. In the distance, the snarls and yelps have gotten more furious.

I reach into my avatar's pockets, pull out more seeds. This time they scatter on the ground. The players around me, seeing this, do the same with their packets. We have thousands, as they were rewarded for passing Campe in the same way we were.

I aim the rays at the seeds and blast away. Beneath my feet, strawberry plants begin to poke through the soil.

This is it. I've found a way to complete the task. I keep shooting the rays, and soon the beginnings of blackberry bushes appear, followed by watermelon vines and the tops of corn stalks.

"This is cool," I tell Eli, caught up in the idea that somehow what I love to do in real life—gardening—has translated into this game. I don't stop to think why or how my father knew this about me. I just concentrate on enjoying the fact that I can make plants grow and feed hungry people.

As more and more plants come to life around me, a strange figure starts fading into the screen right behind me. I pray it's not another monster—the countdown now reads :46. I don't have time to grow the last of the plants and fight off a Greek nightmare at the same time. And I can't stand the idea of losing, not when Theo is being injured, right now, just to save me.

I ignore the new NPC as long as I can, concentrate on making sure I hit every seed I can find. With six seconds left to go, I hit the last seed and the figure materializes completely. It's a beautiful woman, wearing a crown made of corn husks and carrying a torch.

Demeter. Goddess of the harvest.

Somehow in coming here, in discovering this self-sustaining, eco-friendly farm, we've managed to harness the power of Demeter and the harvest. Hers is the power I channeled there at the end, the hope Austin needs to survive.

"Get me down!" I shriek, and Eli does, immediately. "I finished the level. Let's get Theo." I start running at a diagonal, back toward the road and the awful sound of snarling dogs.

Eli's right on my heels as I hit the road. I stop, look both ways, listen. The barking sounds close, but the wind makes it impossible to tell which direction it's coming from. "Which way—" I ask, breaking off as Eli's hand clamps around my wrist.

He starts dragging me down the road toward the van. "I need to get you to safety."

"Don't you dare pull that sexist crap on me!" I twist my wrist out of his grasp. "Theo needs—"

"Theo needs to get the hell out of here," Theo says as he runs up on us from behind. "Let's go!"

"You're okay!" I gasp, nearly dizzy with relief.

"Just peachy," he answers, "but they're really close."

We start running toward the van again. Beside me I can tell that Theo is laboring a little. I match my pace to his. Maybe he's just tired, or maybe something really is wrong. I can't tell in the dim glow cast by the ground lights.

We hit the fence a few seconds before Eli does, and I can hear more barking behind us, along with rapid-fire Spanish. They're a lot closer than they should be. I'm not sure we'll make it over the fence . . .

"Go, Pandora." Eli picks me up again, giving me enough of a boost that my hands close around the spindles near the top of the fence. I scramble up and he braces my feet with his chest, giving me the extra support I need. I land on the roof of the van with a loud *thump*. Then he and Theo are climbing the fence. Eli makes it over first, while Theo struggles. That's when I know, no matter what he said, something is really wrong with him.

The men appear on the other side of the fence. One of the dogs with them jumps up, latches on to Theo's boot while its master grabs Theo by the seat of his jeans and starts to pull him down.

I lash out through the bars with my foot, catch the guy right in the balls. He lets go, crumpling to the ground with a groan. His partner makes a lunge for Theo, but this time Theo's ready for him. He hits him in the face with one of his massive fists before clambering to safety.

We fling ourselves into the van. I have the keys, so I settle myself in the driver's seat, not even waiting for the doors to close behind Eli and Theo before I hit the gas.

19

"ARE THEY FOLLOWING US?" I ask, afraid to take my eyes off the road long enough to check my rearview mirror. The driveway is dark and bumpy, and the last thing I want is to get a flat tire or run us off the road at one of the many bends.

"I think we're okay," Theo says, exasperated. "With them being on foot and all."

"They must have a car," I tell him defensively. "They could run back and get it."

"Yeah, well I'm more worried about the fact that they could easily have gotten our license plate. If they find a way to report this to the cops, Homeland Security is going to have a pretty good idea of what we've been up to," Eli remarks as he moves to climb into the seat.

As he does, he brushes against Theo, and Theo sucks in his breath on a hiss of pain. My heart drops. "You're hurt. Where?"

"I'm fine."

He doesn't sound fine. Now that the adrenaline is subsiding, he sounds weak.

I turn onto Highway 287, then glance at Eli. "Go check on him."

"He says he's fine."

"Are you frickin' kidding me? Find out what's wrong with your brother!" I sound like an old-fashioned schoolmarm, but I can't help it. Is he seriously going to let whatever shit they have between them keep him from being a decent human being?

"He's not my brother." They both respond at the same time, and I blow out a breath, completely annoyed by them.

"Then you tell *me* what's wrong." I make it an order and even risk glancing in the mirror so that Theo can see by my eyes that I mean business.

He shrugs. "I got bit a couple of times."

"Shit." I swerve the van to the side of the road. "Take over," I tell Eli, climbing into the back without even turning off the engine.

I hit the overhead light. "Let me see."

"I'm fine, Pandora. Just tired."

"I'm sure. But I still need to see how badly you're hurt."

"Geez. He says he's fine." Eli doesn't even try to hide his annoyance.

I want to hit him. Theo's pale and a little clammy, and now that I'm getting a good look at him I realize there's blood on his palm, on the sleeve of his shirt, on his leg. "*How* many times were you bitten?" I demand, looking at a particularly nasty bite on the side of his hand.

He shrugs, grimacing a little at the movement. That's it. I've had more than enough of the stoic behavior. "Get your shirt off." I climb into the cargo area and fumble through bags until I find the first-aid kit and peroxide.

When I turn back, Theo hasn't so much as moved. I get in his face. "Take the stupid thing off or I'll do it for you." I reach for the hem to prove I'm serious.

Theo does move then, ducking and twisting a little to get his T-shirt off in the close confines of the van.

I gasp when I see him. There are claw marks on his already-injured side, a couple of bites on his left biceps that blend into the cuts from the car accident, another on his right forearm. "When was your last tetanus shot?" I ask, opening up the first-aid kit. I really hope none of the bites are deep enough to need stitches. I'm so not up for that.

"I don't know," he mutters. "About two years ago? I know I was in high school."

"Thank God. And we're going to go with the assumption the dogs weren't rabid, as they're kept as protection for that farm. Which means we just need to clean these thoroughly and hope they don't get infected."

"Fantastic." Theo sounds as grumpy as Eli did, but when he looks at me, his eyes are wary. Aloof.

I start with the bites on his arm, thoroughly dousing them with peroxide and pretending not to notice when Theo swears a blue streak under his breath. After the peroxide dries, I cover them with antibacterial cream before bandaging them up. Then I move on to his hand. This cut is deeper, nastier, will leave a pretty decent-size scar. Which is a shame because Theo has beautiful hands, broad and long fingered, despite the numerous calluses. Or maybe because of them. Unlike his perfectly pressed khakis and polo shirts, those calluses seem to fit the Theo I'm getting to know.

Not that he looks much like a prep now. I think back to what he looked like yesterday in class, compare it to today. His cheek is still bruised from the crash; the huge gash from the gas-station fight has crusted over but I'm afraid it will also scar. And now all these wounds, all this pain. I bet he wishes he'd never answered his door yesterday. God knows, I would in his place.

"I don't think this needs stitches," I tell Theo as I clean his hand, being as gentle as possible. My voice sounds strange, husky, but I can't do anything about the lump in my throat. I suspect it's not going away any time soon.

"Good." This time when our eyes meet, his aren't cold or distant. I smile a little and he smiles back, at least until I pour peroxide down the long, jagged scratches that run the length of his right side.

"Really?" he demands, his voice hoarse from the pain. "Was that actually necessary?"

"Don't be a baby." I want to give him sympathy but know enough not to. Theo isn't the kind who takes well to people feeling bad for him.

"I'll remember this the next time you have an open, bleeding wound."

"Hold on to that thought," I say as I rub gauze along the edge of the widest scratch, making sure it's clean. "At the rate we're going, it'll probably be tomorrow."

"No doubt." He looks less than gleeful at the prospect.

"Are there any more?" I ask, scooting closer to look at his back. His tan, sculpted, beautifully muscled back. As soon as the thought crosses my mind, I have the urge to scrub my brain out with bleach. The last thing I need to be thinking about right now is Theo's muscles.

"There's a scratch on my hip," he says, looking out the window over my shoulder. "And a couple of bites on the back of my thigh. But I can get them."

"Oh, really? I'd like to see that. Drop your pants, buddy." I work hard to sound more nonchalant than I feel.

Theo grins. "If you insist." He fumbles with his belt buckle, the bandage on his right hand making him clumsy where he never has been before. At least I think it's the bandage, as I'm suddenly feeling a little clumsy myself.

Eli swerves off the highway into a secluded rest stop, brings the van to a screeching halt. A second later he appears between the two front seats, his face twisted into a snarl. "Give me the damn peroxide. I'll do it while you drive."

Except I don't drive anywhere. We're about an hour away from Endeavor Farms, and if anyone from there was going to catch us, they probably would have already. Besides, driving around out here wasting gas without knowing where we're going seems like a really crappy idea. So, instead, I sit on the hood of the van, computer on my lap, while Eli takes care of the bites on Theo's leg.

I'm not sure which one of them is more pissed off and miserable about it. Theo, probably, since Eli seems to be going out of his way to be a little rough with the cleaning.

I lean back against the windshield and look up at the stars in the sky. It's a clear night and the sky is filled with the small twinkling lights. I don't usually get to see them this well because most times when I'm outside in the dark, I make sure I'm surrounded by lamps.

But out here too much light would call attention to us. Plus, there's something oddly comforting about listening to Eli and Theo bicker in the back of the van. Usually, it's just exhausting, but tonight the savagery of their relationship has been replaced with a much more mellow vibe. I don't know why, but I'm grateful for the reprieve.

"You look deep in thought," Eli says when he climbs out of the van a few minutes later.

"Just stargazing."

He levers himself onto the hood next to me, settles down to stare up at the sky, too. "What are we looking at?"

"Where's Theo?" I glance into the van, realize the light went out when Eli closed the door. I wait for the familiar alarm to overtake me, but it doesn't. With Eli next to me and Theo close by, these moments in the dark don't seem so bad.

"Taking a much-needed nap. We figured we'd hang here for a while, play the game. Decide what we're supposed to do next."

Exactly what I'd been thinking before I was seduced by the constellations. "See that weird-shaped vee up there?" I tell him, pointing at the very top of the sky and tracing the shape.

"Is that Pandora?"

I laugh. "No. My namesake caused entirely too much destruction to have a constellation named after her. That's Andromeda."

"Ah, the princess who was to be sacrificed to the Cracken."

"You really do know your Greek myths."

"I know *Clash of the Titans*. I must have watched it a million times when I was little."

"Who hasn't? The old one, with the terrible special effects and Harry Hamlin as Perseus, right?"

"Is there another one?"

I start to tell him about the remake before I realize he's joking. "So who was your favorite character in the movie?" I ask instead.

"I don't know. I've never really been a Greek-god kind of person. I was always more about the Titans, which is why my mom gave me the movie to watch in the first place. She didn't realize it was a loose interpretation of the word 'Titan.'"

"How can you like the Titans? Cronus isn't exactly a nice guy."

"Cronus, no. But the rest of them weren't so bad. Especially Gaia."

A gust of wind blows by and I shiver—November in North Texas is a lot colder than it is in Austin. Eli scoots closer, puts an arm around me to warm me up. I think about shifting away but don't. The truth is, I kind of like the way it feels to be held.

"Do you see that constellation up there?" I point to the very bottom of the sky and trace my way up through lots of angles and turns. "That's my favorite. It's Eridanus the River. There's no huge story about it, no major myth, just the belief that the ancient Greeks and Egyptians wouldn't have life without it. We can't actually see the whole thing from where we are—we need to be south of the Equator if we want to see Achernar. It's the brightest star and also the southernmost tip."

I wait for Eli to comment, but he doesn't say anything. When I turn to look at him, I realize it's because he's fallen asleep.

I think about waking him, sending him inside the van. But where's he going to sleep, with Theo already wedged into the only available spaces? The hood of the van is as good as one of the passenger seats, I figure.

Besides, the company's nice. I'm as exhausted as he is, but my brain is going too fast to even contemplate sleep. Snuggling a little deeper into Eli's embrace, I flip open my laptop.

If Theo's Internet bridge has held up, it's time for level two.

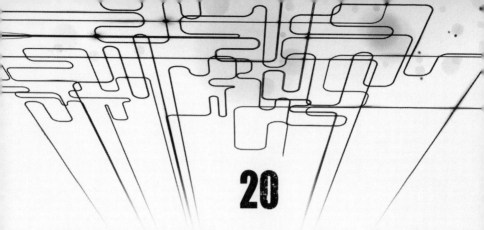

20

THIS TIME, THE GAME DROPS ME in the middle of
nowhere. Which isn't exactly accurate—there are a few gas
stations around, a diner, and a couple of stores—but it
might as well be nowhere, since I have no idea where I am.
I try looking up, like I did back in Austin, but all I see is a
wide black sky dotted with stars. A sky that, now that I
think about it, looks remarkably like the one I've just spent
the last hour staring at in real life.

I must still be in Texas, then, or somewhere close, though
I don't know how I got here. Leveled up to it, I guess. Whatever else he's done, my dad sure has put a lot of time and
thought into his version of Pandora's Box.

I start walking—what else am I supposed to do out
here?—but try to keep an eye out for whatever is going to
attack me. I know something's coming, because it always
does—fight first, task second. It's the way the game has
always been set up.

It doesn't take very long for me to realize that other players have beat me here. I don't know how, since I can't imagine anyone else managed to guess "pomegranate," but as I step over a few dead bodies and weave my way through the crowds that have gathered, I realize I've seen some of these people before: Lilia628, Violet41, Master97. They were with me in the fields, and with me still when I raced against time and a bunch of vicious dogs in an attempt to make it to this level.

Which means, somehow, I leveled them up with me. Which is weird, but kind of cool. At least I'm not alone, trying to figure this out all on my own. Part of me wonders if that's what my father intended all along. He set me on this crazy, destructive mission, but at least he hadn't planned on my going it alone—it's not like he could have known about Eli and Theo in advance.

But, though I like not being alone, I have to admit, I'm not crazy about the way everyone is crowding around me, jockeying for position. Following me like I'm the leader when I really don't have a clue what it is I'm supposed to be doing.

IMs keep popping up at the bottom of my screen, though I ignore them as I continue walking. But then I come across a large group of people gathered around a big rock. One is bleeding heavily, and the others are sharpening sticks. Preparing for battle the best way they can—which is extremely limited in this brave new world.

In the old Pandora's Box I had wealth and weapons and a pretty decent fighting strength. Here, in this version, all I have are the clothes on my back and the people around me.

Though, when I look at my strength in the game, I realize I've outstripped everyone else by nearly fifty thousand points. I'm not sure why, but I'd guess it's because I'm the one who entered the AR gate password.

I decide to IM one of the men sharpening weapons. He's an older guy, dressed in a suit, and he's definitely the leader of their little pack. His user name is Roger919.

> Hey, Roger. What's going on? Who are you
> fighting?

There's silence for a couple of minutes, but then he pings me back.

> There you are, PStar. We've been looking for you.

That makes my stomach hurt.

> Why?
> The AR gate opened a couple of hours ago, and we've all
> moved up. But the giants are here. We've lost sixteen
> people fighting them already.
> And you think I can do better?

I glance around, looking for the huge creatures that are Gaia's children. So far, I don't see anything.

> You can't do worse, that's for sure.

We IM back and forth a little more, him giving me whatever pointers he has—and one of his sharpened sticks. It seems like a pretty pathetic weapon against a couple of giants, but I'll take what I can get. Besides, I'm just trying to get the lay of the land. I won't actually do any fighting until Eli or Theo is with me. The last thing I want to do is die because I decided to take the game on without their help. Now is definitely not the time to be overconfident in my gaming skills.

We start walking again. Past the last gas station and out onto the long, lonely stretch of highway that looks remarkably like the one I'm currently parked along. At least until we get to the desert castle. It comes out of nowhere, a huge, towering citadel lit up in all directions by purplish-red lights. Instead of turrets it has pipes that interconnect in fascinating patterns. It's beautiful and eerie and every instinct I have is screaming that the place is bad news and I need to get the hell away from here.

Of course, that's why I have to go in. If my dad has the giants hidden anywhere out here, this would be the place. It's the only structure I've seen so far that would be big enough.

Besides, now that I'm seeing the whole thing, I understand one of the pictures my father put on the blog. It was the three of us—my mom, my dad, and me—in front of one of the strange purplish-red lights. I'm in a stroller between them, and my mom is smiling in a way I haven't seen from her in far too long. My dad, however, looks miserable.

Which could account for the ominous feeling that blankets the entire place and presses down on me as I walk through it. Whatever it is, my dad doesn't like it.

As I get closer, I see a sign that reads ANDERSON NATU-RAL GAS CORPORATION. Of course. No wonder my mom had been smiling. Working for Anderson was her first big job as a corporate attorney. I can't help wondering what it says about her—and them—that my dad has programmed the place into the game as a source of danger.

Ignoring the dread that wells up in me, I clutch my stick and look around for possible escape routes. If I end up running into the giants in their den—or their factory, as luck might have it—I need to make sure I can get away quickly until my backup arrives.

The factory is four stories high, with outdoor walkways and railings. If bad comes to worse, I guess I can jump—and hope I don't break every bone in my body.

Finally, I say to hell with it and start running. If I'm going to get flattened by a huge woman-eating monster, I might as well get it over with.

I make it through the gates and up the main walk before someone falls in beside me. I don't pay much attention to him at first, but when he bumps against me, I burst out laughing. I'm even less alone than I thought. Theo is with me.

Leaning down to peer in the window of the van, I see him sitting cross-legged, his tablet on his lap as he moves his avatar along with mine. When he catches me looking, he slides open the door.

"I thought you were sleeping."

"Sleep is overrated," he says. "Ready to do this thing?"

"Why not? I'm all about kicking some giant ass."

He laughs, and suddenly I feel a million times better, like I've actually got a shot at this.

"I see you've picked up some friends."

I glance back at Roger, who also appears pretty happy to see Theo. "Looks that way."

A deafening roar rips through the eerie mood music, and we look up to see two giants, complete with bows and arrows, standing on the fourth-story walkway. They're bellowing for all they're worth, and I know that this is it, even if the bottom of my stomach has just dropped down to somewhere in South America.

"Want a boost?" Theo asks.

"I got it," I say, and then I hit Shift+J and jump about ten feet in the air. I catch the edge of the railing, pull myself up, only to find Theo already standing there, waiting for me.

"Show-off," I tell him as we take off running, looking for the staircase that will lead us to the third and then the fourth floor.

My avatar is still injured from my run-in with Campe, so Theo slams up the stairs ahead of me and the others, which means he's the one who gets to the giant first. He's also the one to take the first hit, from an arrow that sinks itself into his arm even as it sends him flying about fifteen feet through the air. He stumbles to his feet, a little disoriented, and the giant that shot him heads for him while the second one takes on a group of attackers from the other side. I jump in front of Theo, determined to protect him until he can protect himself.

Not sure what else to do, I poke the giant with my stick, and he yells even louder. Fantastic. Nothing like enraging the monster to make the game more interesting . . .

The bow comes down again, this time aimed straight at

me. I manage to stumble out of the way, but that just makes the monster more eager to get me. He shoots again and again, and I'm lucky enough to avoid him—at least until he shifts and the arrow comes from a new angle, catching me unaware.

I practically feel my lung puncture under the speed of the shot, and no matter how hard I try to stay on my feet, I can't do it. I sink to my knees, try to crawl away, but I'm afraid this is it. I won't even make it past the second level.

Theo, who finally seems to have come back to himself, shoves me out of the way at the last minute and grabs hold of the bow, refusing to let it go no matter how much the giant swings it. Even when he starts beating it against the ground, Theo hangs on—at least until the very ground beneath my feet begins to tremble.

Theo falls off, goes flying, grabbing me on the way. And then we're doing what I had contemplated all along—jumping, or in Theo's case, soaring—over the railing and down three stories.

I manage to catch one of the pipes as we go down, and Theo follows my lead. We drop to the ground, and I start to ask him what we're supposed to do now, but before I can get the words out, the giant jumps the four stories and lands right in front of us.

A large earthquake rips through the desert, huge cracks and fissures showing up in all directions. Behind us, Roger and two of his group scream as they slip into one of the cracks.

I race over to check if I can see them, but they're gone. The fissure is too deep.

To make matters worse, the giants keep stomping around, trying to crush us with their gigantic feet. We dodge them, but the earthquakes get stronger in magnitude and longer in duration so that it becomes not just about dodging the NPCs, but about missing all the cracks—and the noxious fumes pouring out of them—around us as well. More and more players slip through the new crevices and disappear.

"We've got to do something," Theo mutters. "Or we're going to be the only ones left."

"If we're lucky enough to survive, don't you mean?"

"I was trying to think positive." He jumps over one of the giants' feet but narrowly misses sliding into the largest fracture.

I reach for him, pull him to safety. "Well, don't. At least not until we're out of here."

"Well, then, if we're being pessimistic . . . If this doesn't work, run like hell, okay?"

"If what doesn't work?"

"This!" he says as he launches himself at the giant's legs, using every ounce of speed and power he has—which is considerable.

The giant roars with rage, tries to shake him off even as he struggles to keep his balance. But, as before, Theo hangs on like a leech. He even manages to drive his stick—my stick—straight into the giant's foot. The monster screams and shouts and hops, squishing people by the dozens even while making more cracks with each landing. I'm about to try to drag Theo back and call this whole thing a major failure, when the giant trips over one of the big pipes leading out of the factory and barely catches himself.

This is it. I can feel it. I run straight at him, picking up a discarded stick as I do, and plow it straight into his upper thigh as hard as I can. He screeches like a scalded cat and then falls straight into the biggest fissure in the ground and, hopefully, straight to hell. Or Hades's underworld.

Unfortunately, he takes Theo with him. I scream—in the game and in real life. Eli jumps beside me but doesn't wake, and it turns out Theo isn't quite so easy to kill. Thank God. When I get to the opening, he's holding on for dear life as he dangles over a deep, dark abyss.

I tangle my hands in his shirt and refuse to let go, even as he starts to slide down. With the help of a few other players, I manage to pull him to safety.

By the time he's up, I'm shaking and soaked through with sweat. Theo, however, seems as cool and unaffected as ever. "So, how about that GPS code?" he says.

I want to throttle him. Want to lean into the van and beat the hell out of him for scaring me and for looking so unruffled, but I don't. I can't, because he's right and I know it.

Far behind us, the other giant goes down, and we spread out, start to hunt for the coordinates. Other people try to join in, though they don't know what we're looking for. I don't tell them. Getting help in the game is one thing, but dragging them into the real-world mess is a whole different story.

Theo's the one who finally finds the coordinates, on the sign I saw at the very beginning of the battle. The street number for Anderson Natural Gas is 350639N and its zip code is 10636-36W.

"I don't suppose you have these coordinates memorized, too, do you?" I ask.

He laughs. "Nope. I only remember coordinates for places I've landed."

"You mean in that plane you and your dad built?" I close my laptop, then climb off the hood so that I'm face-to-face with Theo.

"Yeah." He shuts down, his whole face closing up right in front of me. He doesn't say anything else, not that I expect him to, but still. An explanation for his change in attitude would be nice. It's only been a couple of days since I met him, and already I'm sick of the Dr. Jekyll/Mr. Hyde thing.

I open my mouth to tell him so, but something about the way he's holding himself—the way he looks so alone—has me shutting up. Even as I wonder how a guy like him, with his legion of groupies, could possibly know what it's like to be lonely.

The silence stretches between us, taut as a circus high wire, until I think of something to say that has nothing to do with what I actually want to know. "So, I guess we're going to head out in the morning, find somewhere we can pick up an atlas?"

He glances at his watch. "It's close to four a.m. Why don't you get Eli in the car and we'll head out now? You can sleep while I drive."

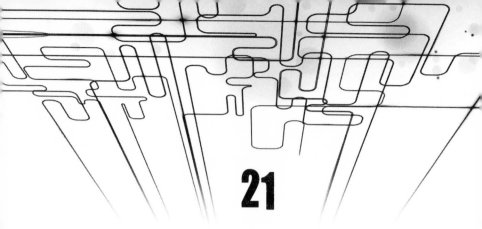

21

DAY THREE

"WE'RE HERE, PANDORA." A warm, rough hand strokes down my arm, and I come awake with a jolt. Sitting up, I nearly bang heads with Eli, who is leaning over me, green eyes gleaming mischievously as he watches me wake up.

"Where's here?" I lie back down. My head is spinning, and, despite my nap, I'm still so exhausted that I'm nauseated with it.

"Hobbs, New Mexico."

We're in New Mexico already. That means I slept about five hours, because the last thing I remember is being about two hours from the Texas–New Mexico border. Wow.

As I lie there, everything that has happened comes crashing in on me, and tears fill my eyes. I close them quickly—I don't want Eli to see—and then spend a minute willing away the pain and the terror.

It's somehow worse, now, after I've slept, because of that one moment—you know the one—when you're just waking up and you forget the new reality. Forget how your life has spontaneously combusted and instead think it was all just a bad dream. That everything's going to be okay.

Until you remember. You jolt up, look around, and realize nothing is ever going to be okay again. That's exactly where I'm at right now.

"You ready, Pandora?" Theo asks me from where he's standing outside the car. He's rocking back and forth on his heels, and I can tell he's impatient to get inside. To move on to the next step of this quest we've found ourselves on. His face doesn't look so bad this morning. The swelling is just about gone, and somehow the cut temple and bruised cheekbone only make him look better. Maybe because they've humanized him a little, made that too-perfect face of his look real.

"Pandora?" he says again.

"Yeah. Sure." I grab my backpack and slide out of the van. My mouth tastes like something crawled into it and died while I was sleeping, and my eyes are gritty, swollen. The librarian is probably going to take one look at me and run screaming in the other direction.

Not that I'd blame her. If I could run away from myself right now, I would do it in a heartbeat. Maybe even faster.

I glance around as we walk, notice that most of the businesses around us have CLOSED signs on the windows. No electricity equals no cash registers, no computer systems, no lights, no stoves, no refrigeration. Nothing that usually makes the world of small business go round.

People are hanging out in the streets in small, desperate knots. Talking fast and casting furtive looks over their shoulders, like kids trying to avoid detention. Whatever they're planning, it doesn't look good.

Theo and Eli must feel the same way, because they move closer to me, flanking me. I don't know whether to be annoyed or relieved by their obvious attempt at protection.

With everything going on, I worry that the library won't be open, but I guess librarians take their jobs seriously, because as we get closer, we realize this might be the only place in town that *is* getting a brisk business. The usually automatic doors are propped open, and as we walk in, I notice that there are more people in here than I've ever seen in a library before. I guess when there's nothing else to do, people remember that books kept whole generations entertained for centuries before TV was even invented.

It's actually kind of cool to see this many people reading, though a lot of them are just sitting around and talking, their wary eyes constantly moving around the room.

The building was designed to maximize the amount of light coming in, so it's not dark at all as we wander up to the information center in the middle of the main room. I can't help being grateful, at least until we get to the banks of computers that hold the catalog to the library's contents. Without them, will trying to find a specific book be like searching for a needle in a haystack? Thank God atlases are all grouped together, at least.

Theo must figure the same thing, because he heads straight to the nearest help desk—and the very frazzled librarian standing there, trying to single-handedly deal with a line of people that has grown exponentially longer in the time we've been here.

"Come on," I tell Eli. "Theo's going to be there forever. Let's see if we can find the maps section on our own."

We wander from one area to the next, and I'm surprised at just how big this building is. I haven't been to a library besides my school's in years, but the ones I remember were small and cramped.

This place is a work of art.

We troll through the different fiction sections, past children's and teen lit, into nonfiction. But there are a million categories of nonfiction to work our way through, and it takes forever. I'm beginning to think Theo had the right idea when I stumble on the reference section. There are a ton of almanacs, encyclopedias, and atlases, along with a bunch of other books that I have no use for.

Eli grabs a US atlas off the shelf—it's a big, heavy book that weighs about twice what my calculus book does, and that's saying something. But after he lays it on a table and opens it, he looks baffled. "How do you work this thing?"

I laugh. "You don't work it—it's not a machine." But to be honest, I'm not sure, either. I remember learning how to do this in third or fourth grade as part of a study-skills unit, but it's been a lot of years since I've had to do more than type a question into Google. Still, it can't be *that* hard.

I sit down and start pawing through the book until I get a feel for it. Then I ask, "Do you have the coordinates?"

Eli doesn't answer, and when I turn to him, he has a

weird look on his face, like I've just caught him doing something he shouldn't. "Are you sniffing me, dude?"

"I'm sorry. Your hair smells weird."

I stiffen at the insult. "That's because I dyed it yesterday, which—if you remember correctly—I did because you and Theo made me. So get over it."

I keep my spine ramrod straight when I turn back to the book, fuming and embarrassed. I take a deep breath and try to concentrate, but now all I can smell are the chemicals from my hair. Eli's right—I do smell weird.

I glance at him out of the corner of my eye, and he's watching me, waiting for me to do just that. He crosses his eyes, makes a face that looks absolutely ridiculous. I laugh—I can't help it—and somebody at the next table shushes me.

It's such a normal thing to do when the last two days have been anything but, that it makes me feel better in a way nothing else could. The world might be going to hell, but there are still some rules. Still some semblances of normalcy.

And then Eli's laughing, too, earning more dirty looks. He grabs the atlas off the table, leads me through the maze of stacks until we're almost at the back of the library. There's no one around and we sink to the ground, lean against one of the bookshelves and spread the atlas out on our laps.

Now that I've remembered how to read an atlas—using the gazetteer at the back to point me in the right direction—it doesn't take us long to figure out what city the coordinates are pointing us to: Albuquerque, New Mexico.

I turn to Eli, confused. "What's in Albuquerque?"

"You mean besides desert?"

I roll my eyes. "Yeah, besides that."

"Resorts? Golf courses?"

"We're supposed to save the world from a *golf course*?"

"Hey, stranger things have happened."

"So, you're a golfer, huh?"

"My dad is. He had me on his course almost before I could stand. By the time I was four, I had my own little set of clubs." His voice is soft, his eyes a little dreamy and faraway. It's an unexpected glimpse into this boy I'm traveling with but barely know. This boy I picked—or who picked me—to help save the world.

The softness doesn't fit his smooth, popular image any more than it does the happy-go-lucky persona I've seen over and over again on this trip. But something, I don't know what, tells me it's more real than any other aspect of him that I've seen.

"You must be really good if you've been golfing all these years," I say, working hard to bring my thoughts back to the subject we'd been discussing.

"I don't do it anymore."

"Why not?" It's obvious from the way he talks about it that he loves it. I can't imagine giving up something that I feel that strongly about.

"My dad and I stopped getting along about a year ago. Golfing's not as much fun when you're doing it with someone you can't stand." He blinks, and the softness is gone, replaced by the cocky grin and I-don't-care attitude that I've grown accustomed to. I recognize it because, God knows, I've done it enough myself through the years. I'm an expert at pretending my relationship with my mom doesn't bother me.

"Yeah, but is it worth giving up something you love just to hurt him?" I put my hand over his, squeeze.

"I'm not trying to hurt him. I just don't want anything to do with him. I mean, he hasn't unleashed a virus on the world or anything, but he's still a bastard."

I rear back at the reminder, feel shame swamp me as I know he wanted it to. Which sucks. I was just trying to help . . .

Eli must realize he's gone too far, because he reaches for my hand and pulls me toward him. I try to yank away, but he holds me steady. "I'm sorry. That was uncalled for."

"Yeah, it was." I turn to look somewhere, anywhere, else. "I was just trying to . . ." What? What had I been hoping to do by talking about his father? It's not like I wear my feelings for my parents on my sleeve for the whole world to see.

"I just—I don't like talking about him. He cheated on my mom with Theo's mother, treated her like crap for months. Then he left her and she couldn't take it. Couldn't be alone, couldn't be without him. So she tried to kill herself a couple of months ago and has been in and out of psych hospitals ever since."

My stomach clenches. No wonder he hates Theo so much. I mean, it's not Theo's fault, but I can see why Eli would have a hard time understanding that.

"Don't look at me like that," he whispers. "That's why I don't tell anyone. I can't stand the pity."

"I don't feel sorry for you." The words are automatic and untrue, but I do my best to sound sincere.

"Good. Because sympathy isn't what I want from you."

"Eli—"

His hand comes up to cup my cheek, and I start to freak out because I think he's going to kiss me, and I'm not sure how I feel about that in the midst of all the rest of this.

I start to tell him so, but he's leaning toward me and—

Someone clears his throat from the end of the stacks. "Good. You found the atlases."

Theo's voice is dry and distant and galvanizes me to action like nothing else could. I all but leap away from Eli, head ducked and fingers pressed against my mouth. My cheeks are burning, and I know I'm the same color as Theo's polo shirt.

Eli pushes to his feet more slowly, and the look he gives his stepbrother would fell a lesser person. I steal a glance at Theo from under my lashes. His back is straight, his jaw tight, his eyes darker than I've ever seen them. And when he looks my way, they are completely shuttered. No life, no expression, no emotion in them at all. I don't know if that's a good thing or a bad one, but I know I'm getting to hate how he can just lock everything inside. How I never know what he's thinking or feeling.

"We need to get to Albuquerque," Eli tells him. Am I imagining the slight challenge in his voice? The wispy edges of triumph?

"Do we?" Theo asks mockingly.

"That's where the coordinates are for, at least according to the atlas." I jump in, try to smooth things over.

"Then we'd better get started." He starts to walk away, then glances back at the book near my feet. "You should bring that. I doubt Albuquerque's going to be the end of this scavenger hunt."

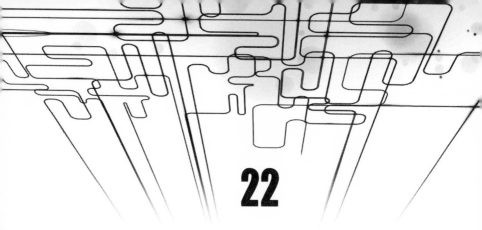

22

ELI AND I END UP STEALING THE ATLAS. As I smuggle it out in my backpack—grateful that the alarms are off-line and can't sound—I tell myself it's okay. That saving the world trumps stealing a book any day, but it still makes my stomach hurt a little. Stupid, I know, but there it is.

The lines between black and white are blurring more with every second we're on the road, on the run, until distinguishing the varying shades of gray has become next to impossible for me. Fleeing the authorities, breaking and entering, stealing. And even worse is the knowledge that there's nowhere to go but down.

When Eli and I get back to the car, Theo's already there. He's sitting in the backseat, legs up, computer in his lap.

"What are you doing?" I ask.

He doesn't even bother to look at me. "Searching for the AR gate in level two, so once we get to Albuquerque we can plug in the password, solve the task, and move on."

"Have you found it?" Eli swings up next to him, grabs a few granola bars from the stash in the back, and tosses one to me. He tries to hand one to Theo, but Theo ignores him.

"I haven't found shit."

I pull out my laptop from where I stashed it under the seat, then climb into the front. We sit there in awkward silence for over an hour, each of us exploring a different section of the level, looking for the AR gate. As we do, I try to figure out what the task is. I know it has something to do with healing the cracks in the earth, but I'm not sure how we're supposed to do that.

I remember talking to my history teacher a couple of years ago about some guy who had purposefully set a huge wildfire in West Texas. It burned half the state, including his ranch, before they got it under control, and in the end he was left with nothing.

I had been struggling with why anyone would do something so deliberately hurtful—especially if they ended up getting hurt themselves—and she'd told me that some people can't see past their obsessions. They set fires just to watch them burn, cause mayhem just because they can. And if they get caught in the cross fire, then they very often consider it an acceptable price to pay.

I'm afraid my father is like that man, only he's set fire to the world. Is he sitting back somewhere, enjoying the show? Watching everything burn, even knowing that he'll end up torched with the rest of us? I think he is, and that frightens me more than anything, because how can anyone reason with a zealot? Or out-think one?

Another fifteen minutes pass with us going nowhere

before Theo slams his laptop shut. "This isn't going to work."

I had just been thinking the same thing, but hearing it from Theo—who has been so unflappable through this whole disaster—alarms me in a way I haven't let myself be scared since I thought I was facing Homeland Security and the FBI on my own.

"Sure it is." Eli doesn't look up from the game. "We just need to find the right spot—"

"There are too many damn variables in this game." Theo climbs into the driver's seat, turns on the ignition. "Shut the door, Pandora. We need to get going."

I do as he asks, then keep playing the game as he drives.

A few minutes later, he turns into a nearly empty gas station. But as we pull up to the pumps, I realize that only two are working—OUT OF ORDER signs decorate the rest. Plus, gas here is almost twice as expensive as what we bought the last time I looked.

"What's going on?" I ask. "Why the huge jump in price again?"

"The control systems for the pumps are failing," Theo says.

I run his words over in my head, but they don't make much more sense the second time than they did the first. "I don't get what that means."

He sighs and I want to punch him. It's the first time he's treated me like I'm a pest since this thing began. "Each pump has a separate controller that regulates it," he tells me. "It has a battery and that battery is somewhere in the pump.

But it doesn't run forever—it needs to be charged. No electricity—"

"No charge," I finish for him.

"Exactly. More and more gas stations are going to start failing in the next couple of days, if they haven't already."

"Which accounts for the price hike," I say.

"That and the general hysteria that's beginning to crop up." He nods toward the small store behind the pumps. Even from here I can see that the shelves are half-empty and that this owner, too, is guarding what's left with a shotgun.

"If he's so scared, why does he even bother coming to work at all?" I ask.

"Probably because this is his business, his livelihood," Eli says. "If he wasn't here, people would just break in and take whatever they want. Better to be here, afraid, and benefit somehow than lose everything and have no way of taking care of your own family."

He's right, but the image he paints is so disturbing that it makes me miss the library, where everything was so civilized, at least on the surface. But then I remember the atlas tucked in my backpack and wonder how many others stole books today when no one was looking.

"You knew this was coming," I tell Theo. "That's why you stocked up on gas."

He shrugs. "What we have in the back isn't enough to do much good, anyway—fill up one tank, maybe, and ensure that we aren't stranded in the middle of the desert. But after that, we're out of luck."

"Do you always have to be such a downer?" Eli demands.

"Can't you just sit back and take things as they come for a little while?"

"If I did that, Pandora would be in jail and you'd be sitting at home sucking your thumb."

"Screw you and your fucking savior complex. There are other people in the world who are just as capable as you are, you know. You're not always right. You almost killed her in that car crash, remember?"

Theo's jaw is so tight that I'm afraid he'll crack a tooth. I don't blame him. Eli's being a jerk, and even knowing the cause doesn't make it easier to swallow.

Besides, I'm grateful for Theo's savior complex, or whatever it is. It's the reason I'm standing here, and I think it sucks for Eli to throw it in his face in such a crappy way.

I start to tell him so, but something holds me back at the last second. I don't like this feeling of being in the middle of two powerful but opposing forces. Especially when I owe them both.

Not knowing what else to do, I jump out of the van and start heading toward the front door of the shop. I don't say a word to either of them, but since they both seem to feel like they have to play the rescuer to the role of damsel in distress that they've cast me in, I figure my disappearance should put a crimp in their fight. Sure enough, it takes only a few seconds before Theo comes jogging over to me.

"Where are you going?" he demands, catching my elbow with his huge hand.

"Away from the two of you, before you make my brain explode," I say as I shrug him off. "And don't grab me like that."

"Sorry." He puts his hands up in mock surrender, backs away a couple of steps, and just looks at me. I fight the urge to squirm. I'm sure I look awful—I haven't done anything with my hair since I dyed it yesterday. And despite the rainstorm two nights ago, and the accident, and everything else, I realize I haven't had a shower since before this whole thing began.

Though I'm studying the beads on my flip-flops, I know we're both conscious of Eli standing by the car, watching us. I can feel his need to come over, to bust up whatever he thinks is going on over here. But the service station is getting busier, and after what happened last time, I know he won't risk leaving the van unprotected.

"You know I appreciate what you and Eli have done for me, right?" I tell Theo. "I never could have gotten away if you hadn't helped me. But that doesn't mean you need to keep protecting me, and it sure as hell doesn't mean you need to fight with Eli over the best way to keep me safe. I know you two think you're total bad asses, but I can hold my own. I need to know that you respect that about me."

"Bad asses?" he asks, an eyebrow raised in disbelief. "Seriously?"

"Would you rather I say you have a superhero complex?"

"Jesus, what is with you people today? Savior, superhero, bad ass. I'm just me."

"And I'm just me. Not a damsel in distress, not a princess waiting for you to slay my dragons. I messed up, big-time. I'm the first to admit that. And you saved me. But you don't need to keep doing that. I'm more than capable of taking care of myself."

"Come on, Pandora. Don't be stupid. We know that."

"Then why all this arguing about what's best for poor little Pandora? Neither of you even thought to ask me what *I* think."

He looks like he wants to argue, but he doesn't. Instead, he swallows whatever objection he has and says, "Fine. I'm asking now."

"Why do you look like it *hurts* you to say that?"

"Because it does." He's exasperated and it shows in his voice and the huge hand he runs roughly through his hair. "I don't want you to go along with Eli just because . . ."

His voice trails off, and I know I could torture him by making him say what's on his mind. But the fact is, we both know what he's worried about, and I don't have it in me to string this whole conversation out.

"I don't make decisions based on anything but what I think is right. If we stand a chance of winning this game, we have to agree that we're all equal. And that we all have the responsibility to speak up when we think something's going wrong. I won't throw my lot in with Eli, but I'm not throwing it in with you, either. Not blindly."

He closes his eyes in obvious relief. "Thank you, Pandora."

"I think you have that backward." I reach for his hand, squeeze it. And there's that strange feeling, that odd little spark again.

The shutters come back down over Theo's eyes, and I know he feels it, too. I start walking toward the store again. "Hey, where are you going?" he asks.

"To pee. Is that okay with you?"

"It's fine." He reaches into his pocket and pulls out some

money, presses it into my hand. "Have him put this on pump number six, okay? And if you're not back out here in five minutes, I'm coming in after you."

It's a big concession, but I'm not stupid enough to think Theo would let me walk into danger alone. Nor would I want to. In this case, he's just assessed the danger and decided things aren't going to get out of hand at this small, out-of-the-way gas station.

Still, I'll take my victories where I can get them, and as I head inside I feel lighter than I have since I saw my father's e-mail in my in-box. It's hard for me to believe that was only a couple of days ago. It seems like a year has passed, at least.

Part of me still wants to go back, to rewind the clock. But it's too late for that, too late to do anything but follow the course set out for us. It looks like it's Albuquerque or bust.

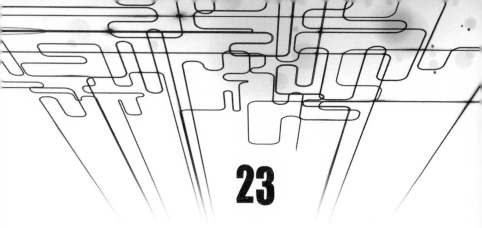

23

IT'S MY TURN TO DRIVE and I do, all three hundred miles to Albuquerque while Eli dozes next to me and Theo wedges himself between the seats in the back. It doesn't look comfortable to me, especially the way he has to twist his body to make all eighty inches of it fit, but I guess it's better than being stuck in the seat.

Thank God for the atlas, as the highway is backed up with people attempting to go I don't know where, so I end up taking the side roads most of the way. The last thing I want to do is waste our gas idling on a road to nowhere. At one point I flip on the radio, try to figure out where they're all going, but only a couple of stations are broadcasting, and it's just more end-of-the-world stuff, so I turn it off. Maybe it's stupid, but I can't take preachers screaming at me to repent right now. Later, when the guys are awake, will be soon enough to face reality again.

For now I just want to drive.

We're about forty-five minutes out of Albuquerque when I spot a produce stand by the side of the road. Though it's getting late, it's still open, a man and woman sitting behind the rows of fruit and vegetables, a few LED camping lanterns illuminating their goods.

I pull over as soon as I realize what they're selling and back up the van the two hundred or so feet I went past them. Eli wakes up just as I turn the engine off, and he gets out with me, stretches his legs.

I'm starving, and my mouth waters at the sight of all this non-junk food. Every restaurant we've run across today has been closed, and we've been living on granola bars and bags of chips. It's no more than what I deserve for letting two teenage guys pack the supplies, but since I now have a chance to remedy the situation, I'm totally going to do it.

"Get some money," I tell Eli, who reaches into the glove compartment before following me over to the stand.

"I'm so glad you're still open," I say to the woman sitting in back of a large bin of oranges. "We're starving."

"You poor thing," she tells me, reaching over and patting my hand. She's at least seventy, and in her denim overalls and wide-brimmed hat, she looks a lot like those shrunken-apple-faced dolls Emily's mom used to collect. Only with a nicer smile. "What would you like?"

I glance at Eli, who shrugs. But then he hasn't been the least bit bothered by the three family-size bags of Cool Ranch Doritos we've managed to inhale today.

"How much are the oranges?" I ask.

"What do you have to trade?" Her husband speaks up for the first time, eyes narrowed suspiciously.

"Oh no. We don't need to trade. I mean, we have money."
I point to the forty dollars Eli has in his hand.

The old man snorts. "What are we going to do with your money? There's almost nothing to buy out there. Besides, the economy's collapsing and money's going to be useless in a couple of days, anyway. Don't you listen to the radio?"

I want to shrug his words off as the ramblings of a paranoid old guy, but I remember what Theo said after the trip to Walmart, about how I have no idea what goods are going to be in high demand in the near future. This must be what he meant.

"What do you need?" I ask, not sure how to choose stuff to barter from our stockpile. Not sure what we need to keep and what Theo bought for just this purpose. I want to tell Eli to wake Theo up, but they're even more pissed at each other than usual, and the last thing I need is for Eli to know that I trust Theo's judgment more than I do his.

"Henry, these children are hungry!" the woman snaps. "I'm going to feed them."

"And we're going to be hungry soon enough," he answers.

"It's okay, ma'am. We have things to trade. Honest," I tell her.

"You got any batteries?" Henry asks.

"Actually, we do." Eli grins at him. "What kind do you need?"

"Double A. Some Cs and Ds if you have them."

"Sure. No problem." Eli walks to the back of the van, opens the trunk and starts rummaging inside.

"How much will batteries buy us?" I ask.

"As much as you want, darlin'." There's steel in the

woman's voice, and in the look she gives her husband, as she pats my hand. I smile at the sight of her hot-pink nails. They look nice, happy, even with the loose paper-thin skin of her hands. "Without refrigeration, a lot of this food is going to go to waste in a couple of days if we don't trade it."

Henry nods, looking much more relaxed now. "Ginny's right. Help yourself to whatever you like."

I don't want to be greedy—I don't know how many batteries Eli's planning on parting with—so I grab only a few of the paper bags they have on the side. I fill one with plump ripe strawberries, another with peaches, and a third with big bright oranges that make my mouth water just from looking at them. All can be washed without much water, and none of them have to be served with utensils or bowls.

At the end of the table, I grab three bags of pecans (for the protein), a jar of honey, and a couple of thick wedges of cheese that are resting in a barrel of melting ice. It will make the box of crackers in the car much easier to choke down.

Eli comes back with two handfuls of batteries—enough to power three or four flashlights. Henry nods happily, but I feel bad. They aren't enough, not for all the food I got. I know what I want to give them, so I carry a couple of the bags to the trunk, leaving the others for Eli. Once there, I pull out one of the three packs of walkie-talkies Theo bought. They're bright pink and decorated by Barbie, but they'll get the job done.

I add two 9-volt batteries and carry them back to Henry and Ginny. Ginny squeals like a young girl when she sees them, and presses more food on us. Raspberries and plums, grapefruits and figs.

We thank them, wish them luck, then head back to the van. Eli climbs into the driver's seat, and I sit in the passenger seat, peeling an orange. We split it after Eli pulls back onto the road, and then eat a second and a third, laughing and talking about music and movies and school— pretending that it's just a normal day. Pretending that we didn't just step back a thousand years in time, to when bartering for goods was the norm and not the exception.

Theo wakes up about a half hour later, as I'm holding a plum out the window and pouring water over it to wash off the dirt. "Where'd you get the fruit?" he asks, his voice still husky with sleep.

I tell him the story as I pass him a peach, and preen a little under the look of approval in his eyes. I'd worried that he'd be upset about the loss of the walkie-talkies, but I should have known better. He's proved to me over and over again just how generous he is.

Our good moods dissolve around the outskirts of Albuquerque. We're in a fairly nice area of town, judging by the store names at the mall, but you wouldn't know it. As we drive by strip mall after strip mall each one reflects back at us the same experience of human desperation—broken shop windows, shattered bottles and unusable goods strewn over the parking lot. Blood glistening on the sidewalk as our headlights sweep past. The looting's getting worse.

I close my eyes. I don't want to see this—it's too unsettling, too reminiscent of scenes from the news that I never thought could happen here. This is one of the biggest, most bustling cities in New Mexico, and in about forty-eight hours, it's been turned into a ghost town. I wonder where the looters are. Have they moved on to another area of town, or are they, too, all tucked up inside, terrified of the coming apocalypse?

Theo's arm brushes against me, and I open my eyes in time to see him switch on the radio to AM, scanning until he finds a station. The time for burying our heads in the sand is over.

A man's voice comes over the radio, and Theo pulls his hand away, leaves it on this station. The news is even worse than we imagined—yet reflective of what we're seeing. "All over America, the scene is the same. Looting, pillaging, deserted streets whose isolation is broken up only by episodes of brief and intense violence. Communications have not been restored, will *not* be restored, according to a source from the largest telecommunications provider in the country. The network has been decimated, and even if electricity is restored tomorrow—something that is impossible considering the state of the electric grids—it will take months to rebuild things, as they will have to start from the ground up.

"Authorities in all areas are baffled. The Pandora worm has caused catastrophic damage. Irreparable damage. Again, just to clarify the state of emergency we are now in, understand that even if the worm self-destructs tomorrow—and there are no indications that such a thing is even possible— we are months, maybe years, away from getting our infrastructure back where it was two days ago."

"What's the point of playing the stupid game, then?" Eli demands, slamming his hands against the steering wheel in frustration. "If everything's screwed, why are we even bothering? There's nothing left to save."

I put the peach I'm holding back in the bag. I'm not hungry anymore. I'm not anything, really. Not afraid, not hopeful. Even the disbelief has worn away, until there's just this incredible numbness filling up every part of me.

Is this acceptance, then? Or just submission? I don't know. I just know that I'm tired, that there's no more fight in me. I rest my head against the desert-warmed window and wonder if I'm ever going to see my mother again.

"You guys," Theo starts, and I wait for him to tell us it's going to be okay. That we'll find a way to fix this, to beat this. I expect him to outline the next step of the endless plan he has in his head. But he doesn't say any of that. He doesn't say anything, and after a minute I turn to look at him.

His head is down, his forehead resting on the heels of his hands, and I can tell this is it. He's tapped out, finished. He's got nothing left to give himself, let alone us.

Looking at him like this burns through my numbness, bringing panic in its wake. I glance at Eli, realize he's feeling pretty much like I am. We've all contributed on this trip, all pulled our weight, but from the beginning, we've both known that Theo is the leader. The man with the plan.

Now that he doesn't have one, everything seems even worse, even more terrifying. My heart speeds up, and I feel like there's a huge weight on my chest, crushing me. I fumble for the door handle, not caring that the van is in motion. Not caring about anything but getting out.

We're not moving fast, so even as I tumble out of the van, I'm not in any danger. Not that I would notice if I was.

I can't breathe.

I can't breathe.

Ican'tbreathe.

I claw at my tank top, convinced the neckline is strangling me. But it's nowhere near my throat.

Theo's out of the van after me before Eli has even pulled to a stop. He grabs my arms right above my elbows, turns me to face him. "Pandora."

Again, I wait for him to tell me that everything is going to be okay.

Again the reassurance doesn't come.

And in the midst of the panic, the hysteria, a stray thought flits through my mind.

I know what Ayn Rand is talking about now. In *Atlas Shrugged.* I read it last month for AP English and only got a B on my project because I hadn't understood what she was getting at.

But here, now, watching Theo give up, I realize this is it. This is what it feels like when Atlas tires of holding the world on his shoulders, when he gets as confused and lost as the rest of us. He shrugs, and our world, the one we always thought was so safe with him, goes spinning out of control.

Suddenly, Eli's there, forcing me to bend over, to give the blood a chance to rush back to my head. He rubs my shoulders in soothing circles, and as the panic attack, or whatever the hell it was, recedes, I'm embarrassed. Nothing like being the weak link, right? The one everyone else has to worry about and pander to.

I flush with shame as I remember my words to Theo at the gas station. So much for me being able to handle things. What a joke.

When I can breathe again, I straighten slowly. Eli's

standing next to me, his mouth curved down in a worried frown, his usually humor-filled eyes watchful in the shadows cast by the headlights. "You okay, now?" he asks.

"Yeah, fine. Sorry for freaking out."

"No big deal. We're all entitled to a little panic occasionally."

"I think I'm over my quota."

He grins. "Nah, I got you covered."

Reaching for me, he pulls me into his arms and just hugs me for the longest time. Then he skims his mouth over my hair, drops a tender kiss on my temple.

I hug him tightly, then pull back, look for Theo. He's standing about twenty feet away, hands in his pockets, his broad shoulders slumped as he stares into an empty parking lot that looks like a war was fought in it.

I can't leave him like that. Can't leave any of us like this.

"We need to find a hotel room." I pitch my voice louder than usual, so that he'll hear me. "It's late and we're all tired, hungry. Let's find someplace to sleep that does not involve four wheels. We'll take showers and then we'll figure out what we need to do tomorrow. Where we can start looking."

Theo doesn't move, doesn't by so much as a flicker let on that he's heard me. I glance at Eli, realize he's as lost as I am about how to deal with Theo. Not knowing what else to do, I walk over to Theo, reach for his hand.

"Come on, let's get in the van."

"What if I don't want to go?"

"Tough. You're outvoted. I know that's a novel experience for you, but just go with it. No one likes a sore loser."

He smiles, just a little, but allows me to tug him toward

the van. We're about to climb into the back when he speaks again. "I thought I could fix this." His voice is low, so that only I can hear.

"Dude, no one can fix this. It's not a reflection on you."

"Yeah, but what's the end point? If you can't fix things, if you can't win, why bother trying?"

Poor little Harvard-bound boy. He's probably never done anything in his life without a plan and a clear understanding of how to get whatever it is he's going after. No wonder this nightmare has thrown him for such a loop.

"'Brick by brick, my citizens,'" I tell him. "Don't worry so much. We'll figure it out."

He doesn't answer for a long time, and when he does, it's not what I expect. "Julius Caesar ended up getting knifed in the back by his best friend."

"True," I acknowledge. "But since he wasn't the one who said the thing about the bricks anyway, why do you care?"

Theo looks at me. "Are you sure? I thought he was."

"Nope. Hadrian said it."

"You don't have to look so smug."

"Are you kidding me? For the first time ever, I know something you don't. Let me wallow for a minute or ten."

When Theo throws back his head and laughs, I know he's going to be okay.

Now it's just the rest of the world I have to worry about.

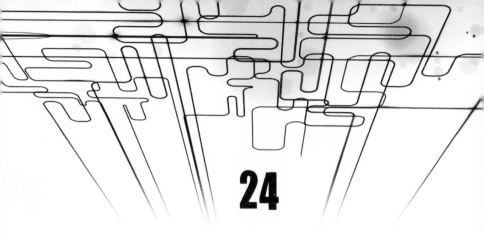

24

WE FIND A CHEAP, and somewhat questionable, motel on the outskirts of town and Eli pulls into the registration area. We could afford better, for a little while anyway, but the last thing we need is to raise questions in a more family-oriented place. I grab my purse—and some of the guys' cash—and go inside before either of them has a chance to say a thing. This is something I *can* do, and there's been enough on this trip that I can't, that I'm determined to take charge here.

I get the room without too much hassle—I'm thrilled that the guy behind the counter is still willing to take cash, though at a much-inflated rate—and we drive around to the back, where the motel map points us.

We all crawl out the front (Theo is completely paranoid about not letting anyone see our supplies) and pile upstairs, loaded down with our backpacks and a couple of bags of food and water. I open the door and reach to switch on the lights. They don't go on, of course, but old habits die hard.

I turn to tell Theo that we need one of the lanterns, but he's already got one in his hand. Eli's carrying the other, so I guess that makes me the only stupid person. Big surprise.

"I get the shower first," I say, trying not to look around the room too closely. The lantern doesn't show much, but what I can see doesn't inspire confidence.

"No problem. I want to bring up a few more things from the car, anyway." Theo empties his backpack on the bed, and it's nice to see him focused again. Back to normal.

I grab some clean clothes from the Walmart bag Theo brought up with him and head into the bathroom with one of the lanterns. The water is lukewarm, but it's still the best shower I've ever had. I wash my hair twice with the hotel shampoo and conditioner, thrilled when the funky dye smell finally comes out, and then just stand under the spray and enjoy the feeling of being clean.

It's only been three days, but I swear, it feels like forever. The only thing that gets me out from under the spray is the knowledge that Eli and Theo must want a shower just as badly.

When I'm done, I wash the clothes I wore today and wring them out before getting dressed in the gray yoga pants and the purple tank top Theo and Eli got me.

It's then that I get the first real glimpse of myself in the mirror, without the cap, since I dyed my hair.

I barely recognize myself.

I reach a hand up, touch the dark brown locks that have fallen into my face. Honestly, it's not bad looking, just different, but right now I'm not sure how much more different I can take. It's hard to imagine that a couple of days ago my biggest problem was my mother forgetting my birthday. Now,

I've unleashed cyber-Armageddon, fled federal custody, faced down men with guns, nearly been caught by attack dogs, and am currently staying in a seedy motel with two guys I barely knew a few days ago, wearing a shirt that is way too skimpy for my taste.

Is it any wonder I'm having problems? I don't think there's much of the old Pandora left to recognize.

Eli knocks on the door. "Hey, Pandora, you okay in there?"

"Yeah, sorry. I'm coming out." I gather my clothes so I can hang them in the closet to dry and then open the door.

Eli's leaning against the doorjamb and he smiles when he sees me. "I knew you'd look good in that shirt." My heart beats a little faster at the look in his eyes, and I can feel a blush creeping up my cheeks.

I don't know what to say. How to act. I've only had one boyfriend before, and he never made me feel anything like the nervousness that comes over me when Eli traces a finger along one of my spaghetti straps.

I take a shaky breath, try to figure out what I want to do. Stand here and flirt with him or make a joke to diffuse the tension? It's not like we don't have other things to worry about right now, and this whole thing, whatever it is, seems like it has the potential to be a huge complication.

"Hey, Pandora," Theo calls from his spot at the table near the door. "Where are those pictures your dad sent you?"

It's the excuse I was looking for, and I cling to it like it's a life raft and I'm drowning. "Here they are," I say, ducking around Eli. I pull the photos out of the front pocket of my backpack and try to hand them to Theo. I don't think I'm up for looking at them right now, though I know we need to if we want to figure out where we're supposed to go now that we're in Albuquerque. Theo doesn't take them, and when I drop them in front of him, he slides them back over to me. At first, I think he's just not getting it, but the way he looks at me, kind of soft but also determined, tells me that he does. It doesn't matter, though, because he's not going to budge.

"Which is the fourth one? From the site."

"I don't know. I wasn't going in order, so I didn't pay much attention."

"You need to figure it out. We have to assume that everything your father did was for a purpose. If we figure out what that reason is, we'll be able to beat the game."

"So what? Who cares if we win if there's nothing left to save?"

I know he wants to argue with me, but I guess I look about as irrational as I feel, because he doesn't say anything else. Just waits patiently as I pull out the photos and start to sort through them one more time.

I go slowly, focused on getting the order right so I don't have to do this ever again.

It hurts to look at them, but I force myself to do it. It's not like Theo has asked that much of me. I can put most of the pictures in the order they came in on the website, but I get stuck when I'm down to two spots—the fourth and seventh. "I don't know which of these is the one we need." I turn the last two photos so he can see them.

Theo looks at the photos for a minute, then asks, "Does it snow in Albuquerque?"

"Sometimes. Not very often, though."

"And probably not this much, right?" He holds up a picture of my father and me building a snowman. We're standing in front of a huge field with a WELCOME TO THE WILLOWS sign in front of it.

"So, we're going to say that this is not the Albuquerque picture." He puts it in the seventh spot, and we both stare at the only photo that's left.

I'm about five, and I'm sitting on my dad's shoulders. We're standing in front of some strange piece of equipment that looks like it belongs in Area 51 rather than the middle of Albuquerque. But the thing is, the longer I stare at it the more I'm certain that I remember the day this picture was taken. When I saw it on the computer, I was struck by how happy my dad and I looked, but now that I'm studying it, I realize it was more than just keeping up appearances for the camera. We *were* happy that day. Very happy.

"This is Albuquerque," I tell Theo, tapping the photo like it doesn't hurt me just to touch it. "We drove up from Austin to visit his friend, Dr. Susan. She's the one taking the picture."

"Dr. Susan? She's a doctor?"

"Not a medical one. She specializes in solar energy. That's a solar cell behind us. It's part of a solar array."

"Do you remember Susan's last name?"

"I don't think I ever knew it. But I remember she was associated with the University of New Mexico. We went to her office there once."

Theo reaches for his backpack, pulls out his laptop, and starts to open it. I can tell the exact second he remembers that there's no point. He puts the computer on the floor and then rests his head in his hands. "You know, we'd be done with this whole scavenger-hunt thing if we had access to Google."

"I think he was counting on us *not* having that access."

"I know, I know. So there has to be another way to figure this out. We just have to think outside the box."

"We can't call the university," I tell him. "And we can't afford to waste gas driving out there in case that's a dead end."

"It's not a dead end, but I agree. That picture wasn't taken on a college campus. So how do we—"

"You could read the name on the equipment," Eli says from behind me. He's dressed in only a towel, and as he braces a hand on the table on either side of me, he smells lightly of oranges. He points at the very bottom of the equipment, to the gray-on-gray lettering I hadn't even noticed but now can't believe I missed.

"Orinoco. But isn't that just the brand name?" I ask.

"No," Theo says. "He's right. You said she was a research scientist. What if this was her baby? What if she works for Orinoco?"

"Are they a New Mexico company?"

"I have no idea. But I know how we can find out," Eli says. He crosses to the nightstand, opens the top drawer, and pulls out a very battered phone book. "It turns out they do still make them."

Within minutes, we're all staring at an address for Orinoco Solar Energy. *Could it be this easy?* I wonder, as I copy down the address. And if it is, what are we supposed to get out of it? I mean, what's the point? I'm confused, but that could just be because I'm exhausted. If I don't close my eyes soon, I'm going to drop where I stand.

Theo goes to take a shower, and Eli and I spread out dinner on the small dining table. We have crackers, the fresh cheese I bought today, honey, the pecans, bottled water, and peaches.

We also have a chocolate bar for dessert. I break it into three equal pieces and divvy them up on paper towels. Then I devour my piece.

Eli laughs and hands me his section. "If you like it that much, enjoy."

I can feel myself blushing as I wonder if he thinks I'm a total pig. "No, it's fine. I've just always liked to eat my dessert first."

"Well, now you can eat mine first, too." He breaks off a chunk, then taps my lips with it. "Open up."

I laugh and let him feed me, closing the chocolate behind my lips. But it feels weird, especially when he runs his thumb over my mouth. I pull away, reach for the water and take a swig.

"Are you thirsty?" I ask, holding the bottle out to him.

"Sure." He reaches for it, and his fingers brush against mine. I think he's going to say something else, but Theo chooses that moment to walk out of the bathroom.

"We need to decide who's sleeping first," he says as he walks up to the table. He's dressed in a T-shirt and athletic shorts that show off his huge biceps and supertoned legs.

"I don't know about you, but I'm going to bed as soon as

we eat," Eli says right before he shoves a whole cheese-and-cracker sandwich in his mouth.

"That's fine. I'll stay awake and keep watch."

"Watch? Over what?" I swear I spend half my time trying to keep up with Theo's thought processes, and I fail every time.

"The van. This obviously isn't a great hotel, and I'm afraid if we don't keep an eye on the van, it won't be there in the morning."

"Are you kidding me? Look around, man." Eli sweeps his arms out wide. "We're practically the only people in this whole place."

"That doesn't mean people aren't trolling." Theo eyes him steadily, and I find myself wondering what he's thinking. Eli's easy to read—he wears his emotions close to the surface. But Theo, he's harder. I never can tell what's going on in that massive brain of his.

"Everything we currently own is in that van. We can't afford to lose it, so we need to take three-hour shifts watching over it."

I want to groan—just the idea of staying up another three hours makes my head throb. But at the same time, I think Theo might be right. Do I really believe anything's going to happen? No, but I figure it's better to be safe than sorry.

"I'll take the first shift," I volunteer, even as my stomach churns. I'm so tired that I'm nauseated, and I'm not sure how I'm going to last another three hours without sleep. I'll have to, though.

"Don't worry about it, Pandora. *I'll* take the first shift. You can do the second, and Eli will do the third." Theo's voice is as calm as always, but there's an underlying steel to it that makes Eli stiffen. I'm afraid he might argue, but in the end he just shrugs.

"Sure, whatever. As long as I get some sleep beforehand."

We finish dinner in silence. There doesn't seem to be much else to say, after all.

As soon as the food is cleared away, Eli stretches out on the bed closest to the door, while I lie down on the other one and pull the covers over me.

The last thing I'm aware of is Theo fiddling with the radio, trying to find out something new. Something more. I fall asleep before he settles on a station.

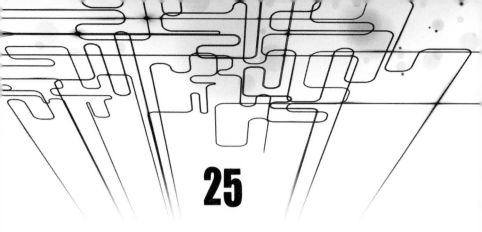

25

DAY FOUR

I WAKE UP SHIVERING, curled into a ball with my arms wrapped around myself. I reach for the covers, but they're not there—which I think is strange, at least until I roll over and realize that Eli is stretched out next to me, and has all the covers wrapped around himself.

I kick him, hard, and when he yelps, he loosens his grip on the blankets long enough for me to grab the covers and pull them back over me. I'm not ready to get up yet and am grateful I don't have to. The sky outside the dusty motel window has barely begun to lighten, which means it's still early. Thank God.

I did my shift from two to five this morning, and nearly froze as I huddled by the window, listening to the radio and messing around with the last couple of levels of Pandora's Box—just in case we missed something—until it was time to wake Eli up.

I stretch out and try to go back to sleep, but I can't.

There's a little voice in the back of my very drowsy brain nagging at me, telling me that something's wrong. I can't quite put my finger on it, though, at least not until Eli rolls over and puts an arm around my waist. His face is close to mine now, and I can hear him snoring softly in my ear.

And that's when it hits me. Eli. In Bed. With Me. His hand shifts, tries to scoot up my stomach to my chest, and I grab his thumb, bend it back.

He howls and yanks his hand back to his side of the bed, but I'm already up, poking at him. "What are you doing? It's only six thirty! You're supposed to be awake!"

"What are you talking about?" He shoves his shaggy blond hair out of his eyes, then stretches.

"It's your turn to take the watch!" I shout at him, and Theo stirs in the other bed, mumbles a protest.

"It's fine." Eli sounds irritated now as he reaches for the covers, pulls them up to his chest.

"But you promised! It's your turn," I repeat. I'm talking to myself. Eli's already asleep.

"Damn it!" I'm furious as I storm over to the window to check the van. It's bad enough that he shirked his duty, but now where am I supposed to sleep? There's no way I'm crawling back into bed with him when he's half-naked, and I'm not getting into bed with Theo, either. No way.

I glance down at the parking lot, then do a double take. Rub my eyes. Am I remembering something wrong? Is the van parked in a different spot than I think it is? I scan the area, but it's empty except for a rusty old Camaro.

Panic makes my heart beat double-time as I walk back

over to the bed and shake Eli awake. "Hey, did you move the van?"

"Forget about the stupid car, Pandora. Come back to bed." He buries his face in a pillow.

"Eli! Listen to me! Did. You. Move. The. Van?"

"What? No." He's annoyed, but also a little worried as he rolls over to look at me. "Why?"

"Because it's gone!"

"Yeah, right, Pandora. I'm not in the mood to be screwed with."

"Well, then I guess you should have stayed up." I turn away to wake Theo.

Eli springs out of bed, then storms over to the window. "This better not be a joke, because it isn't—"

He stops midsentence. Blinks a few times, then rubs his eyes just as I did. Looks again. "It isn't there."

"No shit, Sherlock."

I shake Theo awake. It takes a few seconds, as he's dead to the world, but eventually he opens his eyes. Unlike Eli, he's alert as soon as he sees the look on my face. "What's wrong?"

"The car's gone."

"What?" He shakes his head, like he can't quite make sense of what I'm saying.

"The van? You know, the Odyssey? It's gone. Eli fell asleep and someone stole it."

Again, there seems to be a time lapse between when I speak and when my words register with Theo. But as soon as they do, he's out of bed and standing next to Eli, staring down at the empty parking lot like he's never seen one before in his life.

"What the hell happened?"

Eli shrugs, looks away. "I fell asleep."

"You fell asleep?" Theo's voice is dangerously low now, and I take a step back. I've never heard that tone from him before, and it sets every nerve ending in my body on alert.

"Yeah. I screwed up. Sorry."

Except he doesn't look very sorry, and I can tell that it's getting to Theo. I know it's getting to me. He's ruined everything and he doesn't even seem to care. "What are we going to do?"

I'm asking Theo, but he turns to his stepbrother, an annoyed scowl on his face. "Yeah, Eli, what *are* we going to do?"

"Hey, lay off! I didn't do it on purpose." He turns away, heads back to bed, and Theo snaps. He shoves him, and Eli stumbles. Hits the bed hard.

He comes up pissed, his hands clenched into fists and an ugly look on his face. "Don't you fucking touch me!"

"Or what?" Theo demands. "You think you can take me? You can't even stay awake after six hours of sleep—which was a lot more than Pandora or I got when we did what we were supposed to."

"Yeah, well, we can't all be you, Theo. We're not all early-acceptance Harvard-bound idiots who think we're better than everyone else. So get over it."

"Look, I know you've taken screwing up to a whole new level, Eli, and I can appreciate that. But I'm not your father and this isn't your safe little world where nothing ever touches you. This is the real world, and you didn't just make a mess of your own chances here. You completely screwed Pandora and me as well."

"Like I said. Sorry." Eli's voice is openly mocking now, and I'm afraid Theo is going to beat the crap out of him.

Determined to keep the peace—or at least not let things turn any more violent than they already have—I say, "Come on, guys. This isn't helping. We need to figure out what we're going to do now."

"Why don't you ask Theo? He's the one in charge. Right, bro?" Eli's voice is downright antagonistic now, all the undercurrents between them rising to the surface.

"I have to be." Theo mad dogs him, both staring him down and inviting him to start something. "You're an asshole and a screwup, and I'm sick of it."

Eli's hands curl into fists and I step between them. "That's enough. I mean it. Both of you need to stop."

"Mind your own business, Pandora."

Eli starts to brush around me, and I slam a hand into the center of his chest. "I said, that's enough."

Eli snorts. He tries to move around me again, but the room is small and he accidentally hits me with his shoulder. Hard.

I stumble, catch myself on the dresser, and the next thing I know Theo has Eli up against the wall. "Don't fucking touch her."

"It was an accident, Theo." I tug at his hand, try to get him to let go, but he's about as yielding as an 18-wheeler going ninety miles an hour. "He didn't mean it. It was an accident," I repeat.

"Yeah. Another accident. They happen around you a lot, don't they, Eli?"

"Screw you!"

"Is that the best you've got? You sound like a three-year-old throwing a tantrum." He lets Eli go, storms over to his backpack, and pulls out a pair of jeans.

"Where are you going?" I ask, as he drops his athletic shorts. He's wearing navy-blue boxers that come to the middle of his thighs. I glance away quickly, stare out the window until I hear the zipper on his jeans go up.

"What do you think you're doing?" Eli demands as Theo shoves his feet into his tennis shoes.

"The same thing I always do when you screw up. I'm going to fix it." He slams out of the motel room.

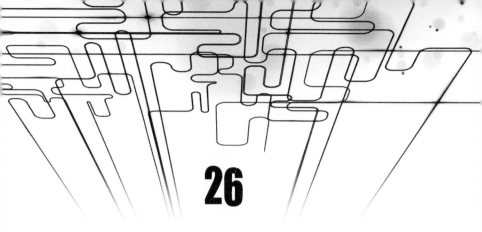

26

I RACE AFTER HIM, but he's walking so fast I have to scramble to keep up. "Wait a minute! Theo! Hold on!"

He ignores me, keeps walking.

I latch on to his elbow, but he shakes me off. "Come on, Theo. Please. Talk to me."

He turns then, and his eyes are such a deep, dark sapphire that the iris and pupil have blended together. It's both beautiful and eerie to look at.

"I don't want to talk right now, Pandora. I'm too busy trying to clean up after your boyfriend."

"He's not my boyfriend." The denial is instinctive.

The look he slants at me says he doesn't believe me—and that he doesn't care one way or the other. It makes my stomach hurt a little, though I don't know why. I stumble back a couple of steps and he just watches me, his face shifting into a blank mask.

"Go back inside, Pandora."

"At least tell me where you're going," I say.

"Where do you think I'm going? I need to steal a car."

"Steal a—can you even do that?"

"You'd better hope so, because otherwise we're stuck in this ridiculous motel while the world crashes down around us."

I know he's right. Even as I'm horrified at the idea of going from book thief to car thief in a little more than twelve hours, I know he's right.

"Give me a second to get some shoes on. I'll come with you."

"I don't need you to do that." His voice is icy, harsh, but something flickers in his eyes, something that tells me he doesn't want to do this alone.

"Yeah, well, *I* need to do it. So just chill out here for a second. I'll be right back."

I slip back down the hall and into the room. Eli's lying on the bed, facing the wall. I don't say anything as I grab my flip-flops and shove them on my feet. They're not the best for running, but better than my Docs when the blisters on my feet have barely begun to heal.

"So, you're taking Theo's side now?"

I stare at Eli's back, mouth agape. I can't believe he even has the nerve to ask, can't believe he thinks there's any side *but* Theo's in this whole thing.

Yes, I'm taking Theo's side, I want to yell, *because you're a self-absorbed idiot.* But that's not going to get us anywhere except in a bigger mess, so I swallow back the rage that is still burning in my throat at his utter and complete carelessness.

"There aren't sides here, Eli. We need a car, so we're going to find one. That's it. We'll be back as soon as we can."

He rolls over, gives me a lost-puppy-dog look that I might have fallen for if I wasn't still so pissed at him. "I'll go with you guys."

Yeah, so then Theo could kill both of us? I don't think so. "We need someone to stay here and watch the stuff we have left." Although, now that I think about it, leaving Eli with that job—again—might not be the best idea we've ever had.

He must see the sudden doubt in my eyes, because he says, "I know I screwed up, Pandora. I'm sorry. I didn't mean for any of this to happen."

If he had just told Theo that, no bravado, no attitude, the last ten minutes would have gone a lot differently. "Look, I've got to go. We'll talk when Theo and I get back."

Eli sits up, looks me square in the eyes, and says, "You need to be careful, Pandora. Watch your back. There's a lot more to Theo than he lets people see."

I don't know how to answer him, am not sure what he means. Especially since Theo doesn't seem like the only one with hidden depths. Finally, I just say, "I'll be fine and we'll be back before you know it."

"Yeah. Right."

I slip out the door, knowing I've been gone more like seven or eight minutes instead of the one I promised Theo. I'm afraid he's gone without me, especially when he's not standing by the stairs where I left him. But then I look down at the parking lot and see him. He's leaning against a light pole, one foot resting on its base, and he looks more like a really tall model doing a layout for *GQ* than he does a teen-ager contemplating the best way to steal a car.

For a second, Eli's warning runs through my mind—that there's more to Theo than he shows to people. I think of all the different things I see lurking in his eyes sometimes, even when he's so calm and in control, and decide Eli might be right. I just don't think it's a bad thing, at least not the way Eli's trying to make it out to be.

I take the steps two at a time but pause at the bottom of the staircase. Theo's watching me as intently as I was just watching him. I wish I could figure out what he sees.

"You ready?" he calls.

"Yeah. Let's go."

Instead of walking farther into Albuquerque, like I thought we would, Theo turns us right when we get to the parking lot, heads out of town. I follow along, even though I'm not sure it's a good idea. Won't we have a better shot at finding a car in the city than we will outside of it?

At the same time, Theo seems to know where he's going, what he's doing. It makes it hard to do anything but trail along in his wake.

We don't speak as we walk, but it's not as awkward as it sounds. Instead, it's almost companionable, like we're two friends out for an early-morning stroll instead of two crimi-nal masterminds bent on breaking the law. Although in my case, I think "mastermind" could be replaced with "bumbling moron" to give a truer version of the situation.

"I'm sorry you have to do this," I tell him.

"I'm sorry I made you open that damn box." He shrugs. "Sorry doesn't get the job done."

"Why are you doing this? You could be at home, safe right now. Why are you here with me?" I ask him the question that's been burning inside me all along.

The look he gives me is inscrutable, but still I feel like I'm missing something big. Something obvious. "Someone has to do it, Pandora. If I can help, if I can try to fix things, why wouldn't I?"

Theo's whole philosophy summed up in less than fifteen words. I can't help feeling ashamed. I want nothing more than to hide from the mess I made, and Theo is running headlong into it, simply because it's the right thing to do.

We're about three miles out of town when we get to what looks like a decent-size ranch. We climb over the gate, and the whole time I'm hoping we don't get shot. After all, everywhere we go these days it seems that people have guns.

Nobody fires on us though, thank God, and we follow the road that leads up to the house, though we're careful not to actually walk along it. Not that the desert gives us much protection, but still. We don't need to paint targets on our chests, either.

When we get closer to the buildings, I realize that the place is pretty run-down. The paint is peeling off the aluminum siding, and more than one window is cracked. But it's obviously a working ranch of some sort; when we peer into one of the barns, we see five horses in stalls.

They're nickering softly, moving restlessly, almost like they know what's going on. Or like they're waiting for their morning meal. I lean over to tell Theo this and see that he's already figured out the same thing. We've got a very short window of opportunity here if we're going to find a car and drive off in it before the ranch owners catch us.

We walk around the barn and past three other buildings before we see four trucks parked between two of the barns. They're working vehicles—big, well used, and capable of handling anything. Each truck also has a five-gallon can of gas in its bed. We've hit the jackpot. I wonder how Theo knew.

"Check those two trucks," Theo says as he opens the door of the one closest to him.

"For what?"

"Keys. Most of the time on ranches, they just leave the keys in the working vehicles."

I do what he asks, searching the glove compartment, the visor, and under the mat for a key. I don't find one in the first truck, and neither does Theo, but we get lucky in the last two, each holding up a key.

"Which one do you want to take?" he asks.

"Does it matter?"

"Not really."

"Then I pick the blue one. It's less noticeable than the red one. Plus it's a little smaller—maybe it'll get better gas mileage."

"Good point." Theo climbs into the cab, inserts the key in the ignition, and cranks it. The engine turns over smoothly.

"Awesome," I say. "It starts." We work quickly, unloading the full gas cans from the other trucks and putting them in the back of ours. *Ours.* I try not to linger on the irony of that word as I climb into the passenger side of the truck.

"Get your seat belt on," says Theo as he puts the truck in drive. "And if anyone comes after us—"

"If anyone comes after us, we give them the truck back!" I tell him.

He grins. "That's not quite what I was going to say—"

"Yeah, well, it's what we're going to do."

"I guess we'd better make sure no one comes after us, then." He opens the window and throws the key for the other truck as far away from the vehicles as he can. And then he's pulling out from behind the barn, driving leisurely so as not to draw attention to ourselves.

We get to the gate and I start to climb out, to pull it open, but Theo reaches up to the visor and pulls down what looks like a garage-door opener. He hits the big center button and the gate swings open.

I settle back, more relaxed than the situation calls for. Theo won't let anything happen to me—strange how I know that now, when only three days ago I worried that he might strangle me. I guess perspective really is everything.

We hit the main road and Theo floors it. The engine rumbles and the truck takes off, responding a lot faster than the Odyssey ever did. I smile, glance over, and realize Theo's doing the same.

"How many laws do you think we've broken since this thing began?" I ask.

"Seventeen. I've been counting."

My mouth drops open. "Seriously?"

"No, not seriously!" he says, laughing. "How anal do you think I am?" Suddenly he doesn't look so amused, and though he's concentrating on the road, I can tell my answer matters to him. His knuckles are white where he clutches the steering wheel.

"Not anal. Just amazingly prepared. I like it."

At first he doesn't respond, but his fingers relax a little and I know it's going to be okay. Still, I'm racking my brain for something to say to fill the silence when Theo finally speaks. His voice is so low I have to strain to hear it.

"My dad was big on being prepared. For anything."

I'm not sure what to say to that, not sure what Theo *wants* me to say. I just know that whatever comes out of my mouth, it can't be the wrong thing or he'll clam up forever. I don't want that to happen, not now that he's finally sharing something about himself.

I settle on the truth. "Kind of like my dad seems to be. Except my dad's psychotic, of course."

Theo's lips twist in the saddest smile I've ever seen. "I don't know. I loved him, but sometimes I thought he was pretty psychotic. He was Special Forces, which meant that when I was young, he was in and out of town a lot, depending on what shape the rest of the world was in. Then the war started and he was gone more than he was around. And when he was around . . . I don't know. He was different. He had a short fuse and a bad temper—everything used to set him off. It got so that my mom and I were walking on eggshells whenever he was home. It didn't matter. The only time he was happy was when he was teaching me something new."

"Like geocaching."

"Yeah. Or how to build a plane. How to skydive. Shoot a gun. Build a fire. It didn't matter. There was always something else to learn."

"Bet you didn't know how much all that was going to come in handy, did you?"

"I didn't have a clue." He shrugs. "I used to hate all his lessons—except the plane. The plane was cool. But I just wanted to do something normal, you know? Play basketball with him. Go to the movies. Hell, my first driving lesson was all about evasive tactics. He wanted me to follow in his footsteps."

"And you don't want to?"

He laughs bitterly. "Not at all. He disappeared somewhere in the Middle East about two and a half years ago. It was a classified mission, so the government couldn't even tell us where he was, just that they were declaring him dead. That there was no chance he could have survived whatever it was that had happened."

"I'm sorry." It's not enough. I know it isn't, but I don't know what else to say.

"I'm not." He shakes his head for a second and looks completely devastated. "I think that's the hardest part. I mean, I miss the dad he *used* to be. The dad I caught glimpses of every once in a while when things were going well. But I don't miss the man he *was* most of the time. I don't miss how afraid my mom looked or how I used to have to get between them to keep him from beating on her when he was lost in whatever black mood grabbed him."

He stops at a red light, keeps his gaze focused on the road in front of us. He looks so tense, so miserable, so *ashamed*, that I can't help it. I reach out, start to stroke my hand down his hair. I mean it to be comforting, but he turns his head at the last second and my hand grazes a nasty bump. He winces.

"I'm sorry." I apologize again, for a lot more than touching his head.

His eyes meet mine, and a shiver works its way down my spine. For a second I wonder what caused it—the look in his sapphire eyes when he glances at me or the knowledge that there's a lot more to Theo than meets the eye.

"No. I just . . . wasn't expecting it."

"Oh." I put my hand back, trace my fingers lightly over the bruise on his high cheekbone, down his strong jaw to the cut on his chin, over the small slices from running through the trees at the farm yesterday. So many different injuries. So many different times he didn't back down, didn't back away, when another guy would have.

"Pandora." His voice is hoarse, but he doesn't move to escape my touch. In fact, he moves toward it, turning his head just a little so that his lips are pressed against my fingertips in the lightest of kisses.

Our eyes lock, at least until the driver behind us leans on his horn. Theo jerks his gaze back to the road—and the light that has obviously been green for a while.

We ride the rest of the way in silence, but my fingers still tingle from where his lips brushed so softly against them. I don't know how I feel about what happened, how I feel about him. And I don't think that's going to change anytime soon. Not when I'm on the run in a stolen truck and the world is about to come crashing down around me.

Theo pulls around the back of the motel, and as we climb

out of the truck I tell him, "I know you're mad at Eli, but we can't afford to fight. Not right now."

His shoulders are tense, his spine so straight that I fear he'll break in half, but eventually Theo nods. "I know. I'll apologize." He says the last like he's choking on the word.

"I don't think you need to go that far. Just don't slam him against any more walls. Sound fair?"

"Sounds fair. Provided he didn't just roll over and go back to sleep."

The first thing I notice when we open the door is that Eli hasn't been sleeping. Everything we brought into the hotel room is packed and resting in a line next to the door, ready to go. Eli has set a few granola bars and some bottles of water on the table for breakfast, and he's sitting on the bed, hunched over the radio like it's his last friend in the world.

"Hey, thanks," I say, gesturing to the food, but he shushes me, his green eyes wide and wild in his very pale face.

We're across the room in the space of a heartbeat, differences forgotten. "What's wrong?" Theo demands.

"I think we just found out what Pandora's dad means by total annihilation. The worm has worked its way into the control systems of every nuclear plant in the world. If someone doesn't find a solution to this in the next couple of days, it's going to be too late."

"Too late?" I echo weakly, my knees turning to Jell-O beneath me.

"To stop the leaks. To shore the plants back up. In seven days, we'll be in the middle of a nuclear holocaust. Game over."

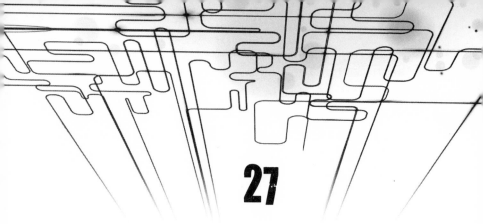

27

FOR LONG SECONDS, what Eli has said is simply too horrible for my brain to comprehend. It can't be possible. It just *can't* be possible. "No one would do that. You'd have to be insane to even contemplate it."

"Well, there *was* Stuxnet," Theo says, sounding like a professor. "It attacked a nuclear power plant."

"*One*," I tell Theo. "We read about it in history last year. It attacked *one* nuclear program, and it didn't even cause that much damage."

"Because the program wasn't fully operational. Not like the places this thing attacked."

"That's the point. Stuxnet didn't come close to doing this."

"No. It just proved this could be done. Which is the problem with cyberwarfare. Once you open the box—excuse the metaphor—you can't ever close it again. Things spiral out of control until we end up exactly where we are right now."

"No offense, but can we talk ethics later?" Eli asks, getting up from the bed and tossing each of us a granola bar. "I think the urgency level on this just shot through the stratosphere, so if you don't mind . . ."

He's right. Suddenly, his falling asleep last night and losing the van doesn't seem so terrible. Not in the grand scheme of things, anyway. Yeah, we're going to be hurt without those supplies, but if nothing else, it's only seven days until the whole world blows up and we no longer have to worry about anything. Especially trying to save it.

We climb into the truck and pull out onto the main streets. I'm driving and I switch on the radio as we try to figure out which way to go. According to the phone book, Orinoco is located on Los Alamos Boulevard, but we don't have a clue where that is. And with no GPS, no MapQuest, nothing, we could be wandering around for hours unless we find a map.

"Pull over here," Eli tells me when we get to a corner with a convenience store.

The place looks like it's been ransacked—shattered windows, broken bottles, ripped-up magazines, and newspapers litter the sidewalk in front of the store. "You don't actually think they're open, do you?" I ask.

"It's worth a shot, even if they aren't."

Of course. What does stealing one more thing matter? I close my eyes for a second, try not to be a baby.

When Eli climbs out of the truck, I go with him. Theo

looks like he's going to protest, but I shoot him a look that basically says to stay out of it. Things are still rough and disjointed with us—someone needs to start patching things up, and I'm smart enough to know it isn't going to be either of the guys.

"Stay behind me," Eli says as we approach the door. As we get closer, I realize it's hanging off-kilter, having been almost ripped off the hinges.

"Why? Are you bulletproof?"

He grins. "I might be."

"Yeah, well, I'll take my chances." I take a deep breath and then push through the door, Eli right at my heels.

I stop dead as soon as I see what a wreck the store really is. It hasn't just been looted. It's been systematically destroyed. Everything that couldn't be stolen has been smashed or ripped, as if stealing wasn't enough for whoever did this. It looks like they wanted to rip the store apart at the seams.

If so, they succeeded.

As I stand there, tears threaten, but I beat them back using sheer will this time. The same will that got me through all those days with my mother, when I wanted to beg for her attention. To plead with her to tell me why she didn't love me, so that I could fix it. Fix me.

A wave of longing rushes over me, so overwhelming, so intense, that I feel it deep inside myself in that place I never even acknowledge exists. I want a do-over. Me, the queen of owning your actions, of moving forward, of never looking back. I want to go back to three days ago, when I was fumbling into my dirty clothes, super late for school.

I want to go back to the Amnesty International meeting at lunch, when I didn't have a clue just how important the rights I was fighting for were suddenly going to be to me.

I want to go back to my conversation with my mother, to the moment I saw the e-mail from my father, to the click of the mouse as I went to that stupid blog.

I just want to go back, to get as far from here—as far from the fugitive me that I've become—as I can get.

But I don't own a time machine, and while this stupid worm can do a lot of things, I don't think it can completely reset the clock, reset me. Even if I'd kind of like it to try.

"Go back to the truck, Pandora." Eli's low, serious voice breaks into my reverie, as does his grip on my elbow as he shoves me behind him.

"Stop it, Eli! I'm not going anywhere. Now you take that side and I'll take this one," I say pointing to the register. "Look for a map and see if there's any stuff left we can use. They probably took everything, but you never know. They might have missed something."

I head for the magazine rack at the front of the store. There's nothing there, though, so I continue on along the front corner. I pocket a few packs of gum that are lying, discarded, on the floor. Grab a couple of cigarette lighters, as well—in case we need to start a fire—then move down the counter, looking for a map.

I'm almost at the end when I see her. A young woman, not much older than I am. She's flat on her back behind the counter, eyes wide open, cheeks stained with tears. And a shotgun-bullet-size hole where her heart used to be.

I scream and Eli comes bounding up the aisle. I scream

and scream and scream. He sees her, too, and pulls me against him, burying my head in his chest. "It's okay, Pandora. It's okay."

How can he say that? How can he even think it? Things are never going to be okay again. The tears are back, and this time I don't have the will to stop them. Everything that's happened, everything we've been through, kind of coalesces inside me. It breaks me open and I cry.

"Let me take you to the truck, Pandora." Eli sounds so subdued, so different from his usual irrepressible self, that it only brings home how fast things are changing.

Theo bursts through the door. "What's wrong? What did you do to her?"

Eli stiffens against me, and I force myself to bring it under control. The last thing we need is another fight, especially with that poor woman lying there, only a few feet away.

"He didn't do anything," I say as I pull away from Eli. I wipe my eyes, then point. "She's dead. The looters killed her. Or somebody did."

Eli's jaw is granite hard as he walks behind the counter, ignoring Theo. "What are you doing?" I ask, watching, horrified, as he steps over her.

"Looking for a weapon."

"Wait a minute. You want a gun? You saw what just happened to her and you still want a gun?"

His green eyes are implacable when they meet mine. "More than ever. It's getting bad. We need to be able to protect ourselves."

He crouches down, and when he stands, there's a gun in his hand. I have no idea what kind—guns aren't my thing—but it's relatively small. It looks like it could be a toy, but the box of bullets in Eli's other hand proves that it isn't.

I turn to Theo, expecting him to protest, but his face is blank again. I'm growing to dread that expression. "Put it in your bag," he tells Eli. Then asks, "Did you find a map?"

"Not yet."

He nods, then starts picking through the discarded papers on the floor. Like we're not in a room with a dead body. Like that woman doesn't even exist.

And that's when it hits me. She doesn't. In this rapidly evolving world, where the only thing you can count on is yourself, she means nothing. And her death means even less.

Still, she meant something to someone, and leaving her lying there like trash hurts me deep inside. I walk over to a door marked EMPLOYEES ONLY and push it open. Inside there are boxes of food the looters were in too big a hurry to look for, I guess. But overlooked cases of beer and chips aren't what I want right now.

On the back shelves I find something that will work, grouped with a bunch of other merchandise that's probably slow moving in a convenience store. I grab one of the packets and open it as I walk back into the main store. "There are supplies in the back," I tell the guys. "You might find something we can use."

Then I flick open the small space blanket, the kind campers use, and walk behind the counter. I close the woman's eyes and slowly drape the blanket over her, murmuring a clumsy prayer I barely remember from my childhood.

"Come on, Pandora, let's get out of here." Eli walks by me, carrying a case of water.

"Did you find a map?"

"Theo did."

I nod, then step away from the girl. Go into the back and grab a second case of water. It's the last one.

Then I walk out the door. I want to look back, but I don't let myself.

Moving forward is the only way to survive.

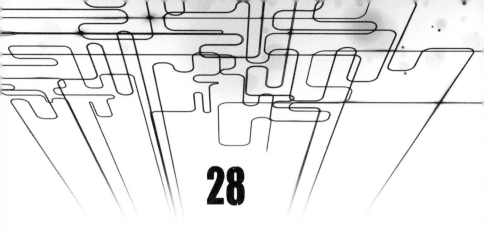

28

WE PULL INTO THE HUGE Orinoco complex at the end of Los Alamos Boulevard a little before eleven. There are a bunch of buildings and parking lots, and behind them, stretching far into the desert, is a huge solar array. It looks so similar to the one in the picture that I know we're in the right spot.

Theo drives around a little and we get a feel for the place. "So, what do you think, Pandora? Where should we start?" he asks.

I wish I knew. But the place is gigantic and, like the aquaculture farm, we don't know what we're looking for. I try to remember more about my visit with my father. Why we were here, what we were doing, where we went, but it's all a blur. I remember Dr. Susan, and I remember the solar arrays, but that's it, really. Except for the large bag of M&M's she gave me from her desk. I ate the whole thing in one sitting and got the worst stomachache ever.

So maybe that's it. Maybe we start with her, since she's what I remember most. "Which of these buildings looks like it would house offices?" I ask. "And have a directory?"

Eli points to the building in the center. It's the biggest, and unlike the others, it's lined with windows. Plus it has a sign in front that says, ORINOCO SOLAR, HARNESSING THE POWER OF THE SUN FOR ALL OF US.

Duh. "Well, then, I guess that's where we're starting."

Theo nods, but doesn't pull the truck up to the door. Instead, he parks it a couple of buildings away and we walk through the empty parking lot, backpacks over our shoulders. If last night taught us anything, it's not to leave the most valuable stuff we have in the car.

My backpack's heavy, as it has my laptop, the atlas, and some water bottles in it, along with my clothes, but I don't complain about the walk. Theo's caution has served us well throughout this whole trip, and I'm not going to start questioning it now.

"How are we going to get in?" I ask, as we approach the front door. "It doesn't look like they're open."

"That's because it's Saturday," Theo comments.

"And here I thought it was because there's no electricity or anything else," Eli says.

I laugh. I can't help it, but really? I point at the solar array. "Does that look like they need electricity? They can probably generate enough power to light up half the state from here."

"So, why aren't they?" Eli asks.

I don't answer because I can't. Why *isn't* this electricity being used to light up parts of the state right now? Why isn't solar energy being used to power a lot more than it is? If it were, we might not be in this situation. It's not like a worm can shut down the sun.

"Because the worm took down the grid," Theo explains as he walks up to the locked front door. "It's not just the power plants that are affected. It's the whole delivery system. So there's no way to get the power out even if there were power to deliver. That's why the nuclear power plants are such a problem."

So strike my previous thoughts. It seems like this worm is omnipotent, after all.

"But what about here?" I ask as something occurs to me. "Would these buildings still have electricity if they're wired directly into the solar array?"

"Probably. Why?"

"Because," I say, just as Eli picks up a giant rock and smashes it through the window on the right side of the door. "If they do, the alarm will probably still be working."

Seconds later, said alarm begins to shriek, lights flashing on and off throughout the whole building.

"Shit." Theo kicks the glass out as fast as he can, then ducks through the window. Eli and I follow him.

After checking the area near the door, he runs behind the welcome desk and starts yanking open cabinets. "What are you looking for?" I ask.

"The control center for the alarm."

I roll my eyes. "What does it look like?"

"This," he says triumphantly, dropping to his knees to dig in a bottom cabinet. He plays around for a minute, and the alarm quiets.

"How did you do that?"

"I told you," Eli says from where he's leaning noncha-lantly on the counter. "He's a boy genius." Again it doesn't sound like a compliment. "So, Pandora." He shifts his atten-tion to me. "We're in. Now what?"

"Now, we find Susan's office." I start rummaging through the drawers until I find a list of employees and extension numbers for the switchboard—the same kind of list I used when I temped at my mom's office last summer. If we're lucky, the extensions here will be like the ones in her build-ing, and the last four digits will reflect the numbers of the people's offices.

I skim the list quickly, come up with three Susans. I write down their phone numbers and say, "We'll have to check all of these, see which is the one I remember."

"How will you know?"

I shrug. "I don't know if I will, but hopefully something will give us a clue as to what we're supposed to be doing."

"Hopefully," Eli mutters beside me. I look at him sharply, but he just shrugs and smiles, his dimple on full display. I shake my head and start down the hall closest to us.

We wander the building for half an hour before finding the first office. But two minutes in and I know it's not the right place—not unless Dr. Susan figured out a way to be in her midtwenties again.

We head back down the hall, passing a series of confer-ence rooms. Each has some pictures on the walls, so I go into the biggest one, hoping to find a photo of Dr. Susan that proves we're not on some kind of wild-goose chase here.

What I find instead shocks me.

The photos are on a wall labeled SOLSTICE BENEFACTORS, and there are two backpacks on the floor under one of the pictures. That picture is the same one I have in my backpack. The one of my father and me in front of the solar array.

Under the photo is a small brass plaque that reads, MITCHELL AND PANDORA WALKER, SOLSTICE BENEFACTORS.

"This is it," I say, my voice cracking. "This is what he wanted me to see."

Theo comes up behind me, rests a hand on my shoulder. I sink back into him, letting him take some of my weight as I try to come to grips with this irrevocable proof that my father really has done this.

"What's in the backpacks?" Theo asks, practical as always. I'm just glad he gave me a second to get a grip before he asked.

"Let's find out."

I pick them up, hand one to him and one to Eli. They're heavier than I expected, which I have to admit piques my curiosity.

The guys pour the contents out on the huge table in the center of the room, and then we sit around sorting through them, looking for I don't know what. Something to jump out at us like the pomegranates and scream, "I'm the code, I'm the code," I suppose.

But nothing does, though it becomes evident within a couple of minutes that my father put these backpacks together to help me do what I need to do. Each has a flashlight, a small first-aid kit—one of which has a full course of antibiotics while the other has a strange little suction thing that Theo says is for snake bites, a box of granola bars, an extra pair of socks, a pocket knife, and a space blanket much like the one I draped over that poor woman at the store. Not to mention that they're solar backpacks, equipped with charging equipment for my MacBook and the guys' iPads.

There are even a couple of bags of M&M's, which make me smile, despite everything.

Each backpack also has two bottles of water, an aluminum water bottle (empty), and some iodine tablets that Theo says are meant to purify water. I'm not sure why we'll need them, as the water is still running, but the fact that my father included them in these survivalist care packages scares the hell out of me. We're only four days in—how much worse are things going to get?

"This doesn't make sense," I say. "If he created this whole game just to watch the world blow up, why is he giving me clues? Why is he trying to help me beat it?"

"Maybe he doesn't really want the world to end," Eli suggests.

"Then he should have thought of that before bringing us to the brink of nuclear holocaust!"

"Whoa, chill out. I'm just trying to say, maybe this whole thing is an attention grab. A way to further an agenda. Stranger things have happened." He stands up, stretches. "Look, I'm going to go see if I can find the employee break room. Maybe there'll be a vending machine and we can get some food. I'm starved."

I watch him go, sauntering out of the room like he has all the time in the world and not six and a half measly days. How does he do that? Stay so calm when all I want to do is scream?

I spring to my feet, hands clenched into fists as the words pour out of me. "I don't want to be here anymore. I don't want to *do* this anymore. I'm not you. I don't want to be a hero! I just want to be normal again."

"Is that what you think? That I want to be a *hero*?" Theo stands up, walks toward me. "Believe me, Pandora, there's not an hour that goes by that I don't wish I was back at home in my room. Even with the lights out it would be better than being in the middle of nowhere, trying to figure out the twists and turns of your father's brilliant but demented mind."

"We're not doing anything, anyway." I sweep my hand across the table, knock some of the stuff to the floor. "No one wants to die in the middle of nowhere, New Mexico. Just go. Just—"

I break off as I realize Theo isn't even listening. He's picking up all the items and shoving them back into the backpacks.

"Oh, don't stop the drama now." He looks over his shoulder. "You were going to say I should save myself, right?"

"You're being an asshole."

"And you're being a baby. Get over yourself. Does this suck? Yes. So what? That doesn't mean we should just give up."

"I didn't say I was going to give up. I said you should get out of here while you still have the chance. I was trying to be *nice*."

"Don't do me any favors." He zips up the backpacks and then comes to stand next to me, his face only inches from mine. "Look, that game says we're going to die in seven days. And maybe you're okay with that. But I'm not. I have shit I want to do with my life, and that does *not* include sitting on my ass while the world blows up around me."

"We can't stop it!"

"Why not? Because there's nothing in the backpacks? Boo-fucking-hoo. We haven't been to Susan's office yet. We haven't been out to the solar array. We haven't even checked the damn picture." He slams his hand against the picture in question for emphasis, and it crashes to the ground, glass shattering.

The loud crack of it echoes in the room, snapping the fury between us until all that's left is the quiet aftermath of the squall.

Theo looks sick. "Pandora, I'm sorry. It's just—"

"I know. You're right. I know." I squat down next to him to help clean up. "I didn't mean to lose it like that."

"You've got the right to a little freak-out," he said, his strong fingers brushing against mine. "Just don't quit. We'll get there. I promise you, Pandora, we'll get there."

I nod, and I'm shocked that somewhere deep inside, I actually believe him. Because if one thing's become abundantly clear in the last few days, it's that Theo doesn't know how to fail.

"Here, throw the glass in this." I reach for a nearby trash can and hold it out to him, but Theo doesn't notice. He's looking at something he picked up from the wreckage.

"What's that?" I ask.

He hands it to me, a triumphant look on his face. "A letter. Addressed to you."

I take it with shaking hands, start to open it. But at that moment, Eli bursts through the door. "A bunch of unmarked black vehicles just pulled up to the front door. We need to move. Now!"

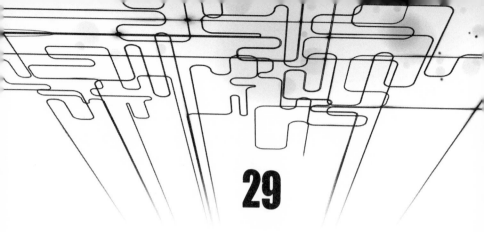

29

BEFORE I EVEN PROCESS Eli's words, Theo's up, grabbing the backpacks and my hand. Then we're running. Down the hall and three flights of stairs. Out the back door.

I start to flee into the parking lot, but Theo holds tight to my hand as he drags me against the building. We race along the perimeter, Theo in front, me in the middle, and Eli in back, until we get to the corner, where Theo stops dead. Flattening himself to the building, he peers around the edge. "Damn! There are four of them at the truck—including that jerk from your house, Pandora."

The information has me reeling, as there's only one "jerk" Theo saw at my house—Mackaray. "That means they're Homeland Security," I tell them. "What are we going to do now?"

"The only thing we can do," Eli says, heading back the way we came.

Theo and I exchange frantic looks, but we follow him. If

he's got a plan to get us out of this, I'm more than willing to go along. It looks like Theo is, as well.

We get to the other edge of the building, and after checking to make sure it's safe, Eli slips around it. "What are you doing?" Theo snarls. "You're getting us closer to them—"

"*Shhh.*"

Eli creeps all the way to the front edge of the building, and Theo and I follow him, even though I'm also beginning to doubt his sanity. We wait, plastered against the building, as eight agents stand around staring at the window we broke earlier. Guns come out, and then most of them are slipping through the same hole we used to get in.

I want to run now, while they're inside, but Theo holds me steady against the building, his hand around my wrist. "What are we waiting for?" I demand, and Eli grins at me. It's a wicked, wild thing, filled with a strange elation I don't understand.

"Grand Theft Auto, anyone? For the second time?" He grabs my free hand and we're running again, straight toward the Homeland Security vehicles instead of away from them.

"Get in!" he yells, yanking open the driver's-side door of the first one.

I don't let myself think as Theo and I pile into the back. Eli's pulling out before we even get the door closed, flooring it as he drives right past the agents investigating our truck.

It's not the brightest move, but it's the only one we've got. Not to mention gutsy as hell. Go, Eli.

Our escape doesn't go unnoticed. "Get down," Eli yells, and Theo shoves me face-first onto the seat, covering me with his body. Shots ring out, and the back windshield, right where I'd been sitting, shatters.

"Shit!" Eli swerves back and forth.

"Hit the gas!" Theo yells.

"I've got the thing floored," Eli shouts back. "Just shut up so I can concentrate."

The next few minutes pass in a blaze of absolute terror. I can't see anything—Theo has me completely covered—but I can hear plenty and that makes everything worse.

Sirens sound as the remaining Homeland Security guys come after us, shots ringing out as they pursue us through the empty business park.

"Where's the road, where's the road?" Eli mumbles to himself as he sends us careening around a corner so fast the SUV takes it on two wheels.

"Up ahead, half a mile," Theo tells him.

"We're not going to make it that far. It's only a matter of time before they hit a tire." He yanks the car to the left around another corner, and Theo loses his balance, pancakes me.

I can't breathe with him crushing my rib cage and my face pressed completely into the seat, and I struggle against him.

"Sorry, Pandora," he says a minute later as he pushes himself up.

"No problem," I answer, before I realize how absurd we sound. Nothing like manners in the middle of a life-or-death crisis.

We hit the main road just as more shots ring out. They hit the side of the car, slamming into the metal.

"How are we going to get out of this?" I whisper to Theo, afraid of distracting Eli.

"I don't know." His hands are clenched, and I know it's hard for him to sit back here with me, leaving our fate in Eli's hands. But Eli's doing a good job, taking turns at break-neck speed, dodging back and forth between the few cars that are on the road.

Homeland Security is still behind us—I can hear their sirens—but they don't seem as close. Eli whips around another corner and hits the brakes, hard, as he strings together every curse word I've ever heard in the most imag-inative way possible. We've hit a solid wall of traffic and people. There's a huge demonstration—or riot, I can't tell—going on. Sitting here, in this car, makes us easy marks.

Theo drags me out before I can even sit up. We're run-ning again, backpacks on, as we weave through a huge crowd of angry people. They're screaming and protesting, throwing things at police officers, and I'm trying to figure out why they're so upset—beyond the obvious, I mean. But when I try to look, Theo barks, "Keep your head down!" So I do, and I realize that he and Eli are slouching deeply, too, trying their best not to stick out in the crowd.

Eli takes the first side street we come to, turning right, and then left again a couple of streets up, so that we're run-ning parallel to the crowd but not actually in it. Hopefully the feds will think we're still out there, trying to get lost in the teeming mass of humanity. They only saw Theo and Eli sitting down in the car—maybe they won't realize just how hard it is for the two of them to blend in.

Eli and Theo are looking down each street we pass, and

then, as if by mutual agreement, we make another quick right. I see why immediately. The whole street consists of apartment building after apartment building, and the curbs are lined with vehicles. "We need another car," Theo tells us.

"Okay." I look around the car-lined street. "Which one?"

"See if you can find one that's unlocked," Theo says. "Easier to keep attention off us if the window isn't smashed in."

"But not too new. The older ones are easier to hot-wire," Eli adds.

"How the hell would you know?" Theo demands.

"I told you, Grand Theft Auto. It's not just a game. It's a way of life." The grin he throws us is cocky and self-deprecating at the same time.

"And here I thought you were obsessed with Pandora's Box before the last couple of days," I comment.

"It's not an either-or situation. GTA's where I learned to drive like that, too."

"I'm impressed."

We're moving while we talk, checking car after car. I lift up on the driver's-side handle of an old blue Chevy Blazer, expecting to find it locked, but this one actually clicks open. "Hey!" I call. "I've found—" But Eli and Theo are already there, pushing me to the side.

"Do you really know how to hot-wire it, Eli?" I demand.

"No, but it can't be that hard, right?" He pops off the panel.

"It isn't." Theo shoulders him out of the way. Bends down and grabs on to two wires. Twists them. The engine roars to life.

The relief I feel is painful, overwhelming, and for a second my legs turn to rubber. Strange, isn't it, how when the fear is rushing through you, your legs are strong and steady. It's only after it's gone, after you realize that everything is somehow going to be all right—or as all right as it can be—that all the fight goes out of you.

"We need to book it," Theo tells us, getting into the driver's seat. I climb in behind him.

"I'm not even going to ask how *you* knew how to hotwire this thing," Eli says, as he settles in the passenger seat next to him. For once, there's no anger in his tone.

I grin. "Boy genius, remember?"

"With a murky criminal past." He snickers, turns back to face the front. "Don't forget to put on your seat belt."

"A little late for that warning, isn't it, Speed Racer?"

"Hey, it worked, didn't it?"

"You did good," Theo tells him. I know it's as close as he can get to an apology for the fight in the hotel room, and a glance out of the corner of my eye tells me Eli realizes the same.

"But we've still got a lot to do before we're home free."

Eli groans. "Same old Theo."

Theo ignores him. "Eli, get the map out and tell me where to go. We need a way out of this mess, and it needs to be side and back roads. We don't want to take the chance of being on the highway, even if we've changed cars. It's too dangerous. And Pandora, get out that letter from your dad. Get to work on figuring out what the code is, and then start on the game. Once we get out of Albuquerque, we need to know which way to go. We can't afford to waste time, or gas."

"How *is* our gas situation?" Eli asks as he unfolds the map.

"Three-quarters of a tank, which is something. It gives us a little breathing room." He makes a sharp left turn, so that we're again running parallel to the demonstration.

I reach into my pocket for the envelope. Pull it out with shaking hands and just stare at it for a minute or two. I know I have to read it, but everything inside me is screaming not to open it. To leave it alone. The last time I read something from my father I'd brought us here.

"Look at it this way, Pandora," Theo says from where he's watching me in the rearview mirror. "We have seven days until the world explodes. How much more could you screw up?"

Amazingly, it's exactly the impetus I need to start reading. So as Eli directs Theo on a path that resembles a slalom race more than it does a coherent route out of town, I unfold the letter and begin to read:

Dear Pandora,

Since you've gotten this far (and congratulations on that, by the way), I figure you must have a lot of questions for me. I know I have a lot for you. Things look complicated now, but if you see this game through, you'll realize that it's all really very simple. That we, the human race, have managed to make so many of our own problems through the years and that unplugging everything is the only way to make it right. I'm just trying to make it right.

Do you remember the day this photo was taken?

*We'd run away from home for a few days to have an
adventure. You were so serious, so earnest, when we
left Austin early in the morning. You hugged your
mother and told her not to worry. We were doing
Walker business, and she wouldn't understand. It
was all I could do not to laugh. Truer words,
Pandora, have never been spoken.*

*I took you to Orinoco to see the solar array, and
you giggled, said it looked like something aliens
would build. You were too young to understand, but
you had a good time anyway. Eating M&M's—except
for the green ones. Those you gave to me because
you said they tasted "weird." I still love green
M&M's. And I love you, Pandora. I can't wait to see
you and can only hope that by the time you find me,
you'll understand just how necessary this game is.*

I know you can do it.

Good luck and I'll see you soon.

Your father

I read the letter twice, getting angrier by the second.
Understand? He wants me to understand what he's done?
Wants me to believe that he loves me? What a joke! Fathers
who love their daughters don't turn them into portents of
destruction. Nor do they pit them against the most dangerous agencies in the United States.

And what does he mean by "see you soon"? Is Theo right?
Are these clues leading me straight to him? Just the thought
infuriates me—if he wanted to see me again, there were a
billion better ways to go about it.

It hits me suddenly, what the code is. Something that both my father and I remember from our first visit to Orinoco.

I whip out my laptop. It opens to Pandora's Box right away—it's not like there's anything else out there, after all—and I waste precious minutes taking my avatar through the motions until I stumble on the level two AR gate Theo had been searching for yesterday.

When the code comes up, I type in "M&M's" and wait for it to open. It doesn't. Damn. I was so sure . . . I glance back at the note and this time I try "Green M&M's." The gate opens and the ten-minute countdown begins.

30

"WHAT'S GOING ON?" Eli says, leaning over the seat to see the game. "Did you get a new power?"

"I don't know. I'm still trying to figure it out." I play with a few buttons, but nothing hits me. "I don't think so."

"You must have. How else are you supposed to deal with all those fumes escaping from the cracks in the earth?"

I'm too busy checking things out to answer. I take a quick run around, try to see what's been going on since I've been here last. There are more players filing in after me than there were last time, though I'm not sure how they got through without the code. Maybe the gates are left open once I plug in the information? I hope so, because that means soon there will be even more people to help us.

Although, to be honest, none of the players seem to be doing so well right now. They're stumbling around, falling down. Some are even lying on the ground, though I don't know if they're supposed to be passed out or dead.

I take a few steps, spin in some circles, but before I can get very far my knees go out from under me. I fall down, and no matter how many buttons I push, I can't get up.

"Come on, Pandora! Get back on your feet," Eli says from where he's watching in the front seat. "You've only got eight minutes."

"I'm trying! It's not as easy as you think."

"Let her play, Eli. You need to focus on the map," Theo barks.

I glance up, see a huge group of people huddled together in the center of the road about a hundred yards ahead of us.

"Turn right at the corner. It'll get us out of this mess."

Theo does as Eli says, then slams on the brakes so hard that I fear whiplash as I jerk against my seat belt. When my brain stops rattling in my head, I peer out the front windshield. There's a huge group of people blocking the street. They're carrying bats and metal pipes, makeshift weapons that they're using to bash in store windows and car windshields.

"Shit, I'm sorry!" squawks Eli.

"Get out of here, Theo!" I yell.

Theo throws the car in reverse, starts backing out the way we came, but it's too late. The crowd from the main street is pouring onto this one, blocking us in as they loot and destroy.

"What do we do?" Eli asks. He's trying not to show it, but I can tell he's afraid. Then again, so am I.

Theo crawls forward with the car, hoping, I think, to intimidate people into getting out of the way. But another look proves that's not going to happen. All he'll do is get them angrier, and the last thing we want is for them to turn that fury and fear on us.

Conscious of the time limit ticking away on my laptop, I shove it in my backpack anyway. "We need to ditch the car."

"What?" Eli goggles. "Are you crazy? They'll rip us apart out there."

"Not if we get out now, before they reach the car." I toss both Theo and Eli their backpacks.

"She's right," Theo says, even as he casts an uneasy glance behind us.

The mob's getting closer. Another minute and they'll be on us. "Let's go!" I say, grabbing my backpack, throwing open the door, and plunging into the mass confusion.

Eli and Theo are right behind me—I can tell because they're both swearing as they follow my headlong flight away from the car and through the throngs of seething humanity. It's a dangerous move, especially with the game's time limit running out, but staying in that car is even more dangerous.

I'm jostled and bumped with every step I take, but it isn't too bad. Isn't nearly as bad as it could be. When I reach the corner, I look back. People are already on the Blazer, beating in its windshield and side windows while others rip out the radio.

"Don't stop!" Theo tells me, shoving me forward with a firm hand on my lower back.

I turn the corner into more chaos, start wrestling my way through it. As I do, I'm conscious of every second that passes. If I don't find a spot to play the game now, there's no way I'll be able to complete the task. No way we'll be able to advance.

Looking around, I make another executive decision and duck through the shattered window of an already-looted store. From the looks of it, it was a women's boutique, but there's not enough merchandise left for me to be sure. Just a few broken bottles of bath salts and some ripped blouses and sweaters.

"What are we doing in here?" Eli demands, but I don't waste time answering him. I just duck behind the counter and pull out my laptop. Two minutes and fifty-eight seconds left. I am so totally screwed.

Not sure what else to do, I systematically press Ctrl plus every key on the keyboard. I finally hit paydirt when I land on *K*. I start to glow again, but this time it's not the helpful, vibrant red from the last level. It's bright yellow and it starts in the center of my being. A burning, pulsating heat that grows and grows until it all but encompasses me.

"What do I do? What do I do?" I'm back to pressing every key, hoping for some clue as to what's happening. Am I going to implode? Spontaneously combust? Turn Supernova and suck everything and everyone around me into the sixteen-pronged force field that is growing around me with every second that passes? As the Vergina Sun, a symbol of the twelve gods of Olympus, forms behind me, that last idea seems more and more likely.

Eli and Theo are leaning over my shoulder, eyes wide as they watch me amass more and more energy, more and more fire, on the screen. If I don't do something with it soon, I'm going to explode. There's no way I can hold all this.

I glance at the countdown timer. Two minutes and three seconds.

A noise sounds at the door, glass crunching under boots, and Eli and Theo throw themselves on the floor behind the counter. If it's more looters, we don't want to be caught here with our solar backpacks and laptops. If it's the cops, we don't want to be caught here at all. And if Homeland Security has somehow managed to catch up with us . . . Well, it doesn't even bear thinking about.

I hit the Mute button on my computer, try to keep playing even as I'm afraid to breathe. The guys are sitting up against the wall, weapon-like shards of glass clutched in their hands as they wait for whoever's at the doorway either to make a move or to head somewhere else.

On-screen, time's passing at what feels like warp speed, and I still don't know what to do. People are IMing me, but I don't have time to read, don't even have time to look as I search desperately for a way out of this mess.

Whoever's at the door of the store decides not to move on, their footsteps coming closer to the high counter we're hiding behind. The countdown hits 1:00 and I know this is it. I either try to do something or bail out of the game right now. Following my instincts, I run across the rocky, ripped-up desert, leaping over small cracks and fissures until I get to the huge fracture that so much of the noxious gas is pouring out of.

This is fracking at its worst—Big Oil polluting the dirt

we grow things in and the groundwater we drink by inject-ing chemicals into the earth to release natural gas to the surface. The only problem is it releases all these other tox-ins as well, more evil into a world already saturated.

Knowing this is my last hope, I jump straight into the fracture. As I fall, I pray I'm doing the right thing, that I won't die like all the others who fell through the earth dur-ing the giant attack.

Long, excruciating seconds pass as I fall and fall and fall. Longer, more excruciating seconds crawl by as who-ever's invaded our space pokes around, looking for some-thing. *Merchandise to barter?* I wonder. *Or three teenage fugitives on the run from every government agency in the country?*

Suddenly, my laptop screen lights up, the entire thing turning supernova bright. I throw myself over it, try to cover it as my avatar slowly floats out of the fissure, my entire body alight with the power of the sun. Next to me, growing larger with every ray that shines over him, is a young man clutching a bow and arrow and a harp. Apollo, god of the sun.

He's glowing as brightly as I am, and as I watch through the gaps in my fingers, the noxious odors disappear, baked away by the sheer, unconcentrated power of the sun that I have somehow managed to harness. I think of Orinoco, of its huge solar array, and wonder if what my father is saying here is possible. Can we really—

A huge hand slams down on the counter above me, and I jump, terror rushing through me as I look up and into the eyes of one of New Mexico's finest.

"Drop the glass and stand up, hands in the air," he says to us, gun drawn and leveled straight at Theo's chest. We obey, making sure to keep our hands where he can see them as he shifts the gun back and forth between the three of us.

"What are you doing in here?" he demands. "This is private property."

Figuring I'm the least threatening of the three of us, which isn't saying much as I'm about three inches taller than the officer is, I take it upon myself to answer, sticking as close to the truth as I can manage. "We were driving and got caught up in the mess outside. When they stopped our car and started pounding on it, we got out and ran. We figured this was as good a place to hide as any until they moved on."

He doesn't know whether to believe me or not. I can see it in the way he's looking at me, weighing my words. "Let me see some ID. One at a time and very slowly, please." He nods at me. "You first."

Oh shit, is all I can think. We're sunk. Completely and totally finished. Major communications failure or not, it's hard to imagine that he doesn't know my name when Homeland Security is currently combing these streets looking for me. It occurs to me that he could be here right now because he's been notified to be on the lookout for us.

"It's in my bag." I point to where my backpack lies drunkenly on its side. "Can I get it?"

His gun dances back and forth across Theo and Eli—a threat if ever I've seen one—before coming to rest on me. "Go ahead. But don't do anything stupid."

It's way too late for that warning. I bend down, pick up my backpack. Fumble with it for a few seconds to buy myself some time—for what, I don't have a clue. "Hurry up!" he tells me, and I know this is it. It really is done.

I reach for my wallet just as the walkie-talkie on his belt screams to life. I don't understand the code that comes through it, but the words that follow are easily distinguishable. "Where are you, Crewshank? I've cleared my stores and am heading toward yours."

As the words register with me, everything seems to slow down. I can hear Crewshank's breathing, even as the pounding of my own heart slams in my ears. Backup is coming. Another police officer. Our chances of escaping just dwindled even more.

Before I even know I'm going to do it, I swing my heavy backpack out as far as I can, slamming it into Officer Crewshank's face at the same time I dive back down behind the counter.

His gun goes off as he falls, the bullet flying into the wall directly behind where my head just was.

"Jesus Christ!" Eli yells as I scoop up my laptop and leap toward the back of the store. I slam through the shop's back door, my two partners in crime hot on my heels. I've just added assault of a police officer to our list of offenses.

"I'm sorry!" I tell them as we careen around a corner, this time searching *for* the angry mob to get lost in. "I didn't know what else to do."

"You did fine," Theo says, though his face is completely white. He's as shaken up by what I just did as I am.

"I *assaulted* a *cop*!"

"Yeah. I'm trying to forget that part."

"Good luck with that. By now, every cop in the vicinity is looking for us."

Eli grabs my elbow, yanks me around another corner and into another shop. "Change your shirt," he tells me as he rummages in his backpack. "The brighter the better." Seconds later, he takes out his red hoodie, pulls it over his head.

I glance at Theo, who's already following Eli's directions. Soon, he's wearing an orange polo shirt and a black baseball cap. I yank on the purple hoodie they bought me the other day at Walmart, and then we're slipping out the back and into the alley behind the store.

I figure we're going to make a run for it again, but sitting right there, next to the door, is a black BMW SUV. The driver's window is smashed in, the radio's missing, and the driver is passed out on the steering wheel, blood trickling down the side of his face.

Eli looks at Theo, Theo looks at me, and I stare at the ground. I know it's the best way, know it's what we need to do, but I don't think I can do it. I really don't think I can steal this car right out from under an injured man, even if it means we'll be saved.

"We need to get him help," I tell them. "We can't just leave him here to die."

"He's going to be fine. He's got a bump on his head. We need to get out of here." Eli's already opened one of the back doors and tossed his backpack inside. Then he heads around to the driver's side. "Give me a hand, Theo."

"Theo, no!" I tell him. "We're not doing this."

For the first time since I met him, he looks truly con-flicted. "We have to, Pandora. We've got to keep moving so we can beat the game."

"Screw the game! We are not just abandoning someone who's hurt. Otherwise, what are we trying to do here? Who are we trying to save?"

"Ourselves!" Eli runs a hand through his hair in frustra-tion. "You're going to get us all killed. We need to move. Now."

"So go. I'm not stopping you."

"Damn it, Pandora! You're wrong here." He grabs hold of my arm, yanks me out of the way before reaching in to pull the driver out.

I see red—at his words and at the hand that is still locked around my bicep.

"That's enough!" Theo steps into the fray, his voice low and final as he pries Eli's hand from my arm and pushes him away from the car. "You need to chill the hell out."

"Yeah, she does—"

"I was talking to you." He points in the direction we came from when fleeing Homeland Security. "We passed a hospital about eight blocks that way. We can drop him off there."

The fight leaves me as relief abruptly overwhelms me. "Thank you," I whisper.

"Don't." He shakes his head. "You're right. What's the point of saving the world if we aren't willing to save the people in it?"

He slides into the driver's seat, moving the man to

the passenger seat as he does. I climb in the back with Eli, doing my best to ignore the way he's glaring at me.

The next few minutes pass in tense silence as Theo negotiates around the crowd. We have to go about twelve blocks in the wrong direction to avoid them, but it's worth it. The whole time Eli and I slump down in the back so that if we pass any cops, they won't see three of us traveling together.

When we get to the hospital, Theo and Eli pull the guy out of the car and carry him inside. I hop out and run for the parking lot, hoping to find another car to take. Besides having a broken window, the SUV is almost out of gas.

I find one—an old Ford Explorer—and hot-wire it the same way I saw Theo do. The engine roars to life, and I pull it around to the front of the ER so I can transfer the backpacks from the BMW to the Explorer.

Seconds later, the guys are back and buckled into the front seats. Eli's still annoyed with me, but I don't actually give a damn. I've done the wrong thing for the right reason over and over again since this disaster began. It feels good to do the right thing for a change. Now if only doing the right thing doesn't end up getting us caught or killed . . .

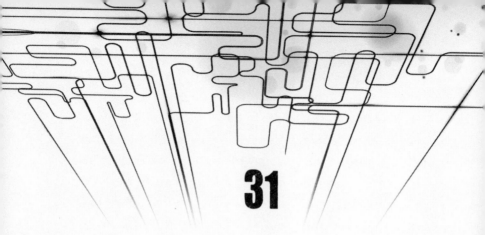

31

AS THEO DRIVES THROUGH THE WINDING STREETS of Albuquerque, I log back on to Pandora's Box, praying that whatever it is I did at the end of level two was enough to bump me up. It turns out it was, because when I start looking around I realize I'm no longer in the middle of the West Texas desert.

"I'm in," I tell them as I begin exploring.

Eli reaches for his iPad, logs in, and races into level three to meet me.

"Where are we?" he asks once he catches up.

"I'm not sure."

I'm in the middle of a town square somewhere, standing next to a large fountain. I turn in a circle, look around. There are trees everywhere and huge buildings, all Spanish in flavor but each with a distinct character.

A couple of them look familiar, and I run up to them, look closer. Smile. "I'm in Balboa Park."

"Where?" Eli asks.

"San Diego. It's a huge park, with museums, the Old Globe Theatre, an amphitheater for outdoor concerts. My dad and I used to love . . ." My voice breaks. I clear my throat, try again. I'm not going to get upset over something that was but never will be again. "We used to love to come here. When I was young, he was working on some superimportant project at a think tank here, and my mom and I would visit him every month or so."

"What kind of project?" Theo asks intently.

"I don't know. I just remember it drove my mother nuts when he talked about it, especially since he became so critical of her day job, which in those days was as counsel for Anderson Natural Gas."

Theo doesn't say anything else, but I see that the name registers. Just as I can see him thinking, filing all the bits and pieces away.

"So, where did you like to go?" Eli asks.

"Everywhere. We spent a lot of time at the Reuben H. Fleet, though. It's a science museum for kids." I fumble for the pictures, pull them out. Search for one that jogs my memory of Balboa Park. I find it in the one of my parents and me standing in front of some kind of a decorative white arch, connected to a fancy gazebo.

My dad is holding me with one arm—I'm about five or six here—and his other is wrapped around my mom. He and I are smiling hugely, but my mom just looks like she wants to get away. I don't remember that from this trip. I wonder how I missed it. Wonder if my dad missed it, too, or if this was the beginning of the end and I just didn't realize it.

"I know where I need to go," I tell the guys as I take off running toward the amphitheater. It's a hike from where I started, so I keep my finger on the arrow key, making my avatar run as fast as possible, jumping over, spinning around, or fighting any obstacles that pop up in the way.

It's close a couple of times—there are more NPCs to get through in this level, and some of them, like the Eryines, or Furies, are tough enough that Theo pulls the car over and hurtles into level three to help me for a few minutes. By the time he pulls back onto the road, I'm feeling pretty good about myself—especially as I approach the amphitheater. There's nothing here I can't handle. At least until a huge, meaty fist comes out of nowhere and latches on to my hair, pulling me right off my feet and dangling me high off the ground. I look up and up and up, right into the large center eye of a Cyclops.

"Oh, shit," I say as he brings a club around, poised to strike me. "I think I'm screwed."

"Not yet you aren't." Eli races toward me.

The club comes right at me, and I twist and turn, try every key I can to avoid the hit. It doesn't work, and he hits me hard enough to rip some of the hair off my head, to send me spinning across the hard concrete ground.

I land with a *thud*, and it's obvious I'm hurt. I'm limping and holding the side that still hasn't recovered from the giants' attack. Plus I have the mother of black eyes.

I don't have time to think about it, though, as the Cyclops is coming after me again, his club hitting the ground inches from where I am. I scramble backward, crablike. I scoot under a bench from the amphitheater and roll over, start to crawl from one to the next, trying to lose him.

He smashes at all of them, shattering one stone bench after another. But he's always a second late, so that I'm not crushed beneath the rubble. I am, however, victim to flying stone pieces. Soon blood is dripping off me.

Other players get in the way, try to bring him down, but they end up being crushed beneath his powerful club. Old and young, male and female, rich and poor. People who won't get another chance. My stomach hurts as a young girl meets a particularly gory end.

My shot at saving the world could be over as easily as hers. One wrong move and I'm gone.

My father really is insane. The fate of the world hanging on his teenage daughter and a video game. If I fail here, I let everyone down.

The Cyclops's club slams into my back, knocks me to the ground. He lifts it again, starts to bring it down. But it doesn't connect. Eli is there, blocking it, his huge strength pitted against the Cyclops.

"Run, Pandora!"

I do, ashamed of myself for leaving him, but this is too important. I have to get through this, have to find the next city coordinates.

Behind me, Eli and the Cyclops are locked in battle, the sounds terrible to hear. I glance back. Eli's huge and strong, but he's only a giant by reality's standards. Here, in the game, the Cyclops towers above him—in height and muscle mass. He doesn't stand a chance against him, not for long.

"Eli!" I scream as the club descends. "Look out!"

At that moment, Theo jerks the car to the right and drives halfway down a small alley before pulling over and turning it off.

"What are you doing?" I ask.

"Trying to be invisible. There are caravans of military trucks out there." He reaches for his backpack.

"Caravans?" Eli and I echo at the same time, the game forgotten for long, crucial seconds.

"Yes. And soldiers with guns and riot gear. I think the National Guard's been called in to restore order."

We're silent as we try to absorb what that means for us. How are we going to dodge the authorities and avoid popping up on the National Guard's radar, too? And, since we're attempting to figure out impossible problems, I add one more dilemma to the list. How are we going to get out of this alive?

As the question echoes in my head, I'm so mad, I'm shaking. How could my father do this to us?

The Cyclops roars, in duplicate and high definition, from both Eli's and my computer screens. The noise startles us and we jump. But it drags our attention back to the game, where it needs to be right now.

"Just stay out of sight," Theo says furiously, and we all slump down, trying to make the car appear empty. With my height, it's hard for me, but I figure it's impossible for Eli and Theo. "Get back here," I tell Eli as I throw myself into the cargo hold of the Explorer.

He crawls under the bench seats and stretches out in an awkward bent-in-half manner. It looks uncomfortable, but

I figure cramped is better than dead. Theo kind of drapes himself across the backseat, and he looks even more squeezed than Eli.

Then we play the game.

I don't know where to begin looking for the coordinates. This place is huge, and half the hiding places have already been destroyed by Rampaging Cyclops Guy. I can only hope the numbers weren't under any of those benches.

I remember playing on the huge pipe organ at the front of the amphitheater and run to it, checking in and around it, but there's nothing there. I check the stone podiums, jump up onstage and check out the actual pipes the music comes from. Nothing.

In the background, Eli and Theo are taking on the Cyclops. Theo has managed to scale his giant muscles and currently has his hands wrapped around the monster's throat as Eli beats and pokes at his legs with a huge stick he's found in the rubble.

As I watch them, I notice the ornate archway a little bit up the hill from the amphitheater. It leads to a gazebo—the same gazebo my family and I were standing in front of in the picture. I hightail it up the hill, through the arch, and into the gazebo. Look up at the ceiling, like the rotunda, but there's nothing there.

I was wrong.

Behind me, the Cyclops falls with a huge roar and Theo is crushed underneath him. I run to help and as I do, I see the uneven stones on the path up here. One seems to be sticking out a little more than the rest.

I glance up. Eli has managed to get the Cyclops off Theo

and is currently clubbing it in the head—so things seem like they're under control, or at least as under control as any of this can be. I drop to my knees and start to dig.

It takes a couple of minutes, but I finally manage to pry the stone out. Turn it over. And right there, written in glowing green, are these coordinates: N 38°50'2", W 104°49'14".

"I've got them!" I shout. "Give me the atlas."

Eli tosses me my backpack, and it lands with a *thud* on the pile of laundry at my feet. For the first time, I look around the cargo area, where I'm lying.

There's a big laundry basket with neatly folded clothes in it. A red backpack. A black guitar case. A ratty pair of tennis shoes that are obviously the source of the disgusting smell I've been trying to ignore since I crawled back here.

Whose car is this? I wonder. *A college kid who came home to do laundry only to have the world blow up around him? Or a man stuck in one of the hospital rooms because his plan for getting out of town went somehow awry?*

The guilt is nearly suffocating. How many lives are we ruining as we run from one section of town to another, taking things that don't belong to us?

I don't realize I've asked the question out loud until Theo says, "How many people are we going to save if we pull this off? Get your head back in the game, Pandora."

I know he's right, but I've just about had it with his brand of tough love. I shoot him a nasty look even as I flip open the atlas.

It takes me a few seconds—I still don't have the hang of

this book yet—but I finally find the coordinates a little north of where we currently are. "We're going to Colorado Springs."

"What's in Colorado Springs?" Eli asks.

"The air force," Theo throws out.

"My dad's not real big on military rank and file. What's there besides the air force?"

"It looks like we're going to find out."

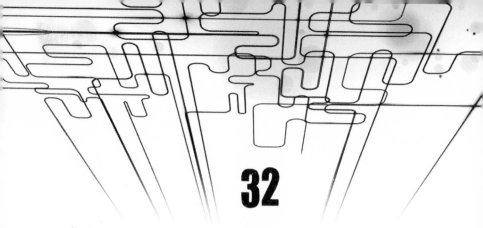

32

SIX HOURS LATER, we're closing in on the New Mexico–Colorado border—this time in a gray Chevy Malibu. The Explorer ran out of gas close to Santa Fe, and we ended up having to steal yet another car because every gas station we ran across was either dry or unable to pump the gas that they did have.

We've been listening to the radio forever, though it hasn't been broadcasting much of anything new in the last few hours, just going over and over the same grim news we already know.

The cooling towers at the nuclear power plants are under the worm's control, and though government hackers are working around the clock, so far they can't find a way in. The cores keep getting hotter and hotter as the electricity generated has nowhere to go because of the grid shutdowns, and within days we'll be dealing with leaks that, if unchecked, will have catastrophic effects.

Civil unrest has turned to anarchy, while transportation everywhere has ground to a halt—no planes, trains, buses, or boats are operating.

And the president has been evacuated to a nondisclosed location.

Theo reaches over and turns off the radio. "I can't take it anymore."

I understand what he's saying. The bad news, coming in bits and pieces as news agencies raid museums to communicate with such antiquated devices as Morse telegraphs, has gotten to all of us. The earlier jubilation of finding the next coordinates has worn off, and now all I can think about is how tired I am. And how futile playing my father's game really is.

The car in front of me hits its brakes, slows to a crawl. I do the same, impatience eating at me. We left the main road behind in favor of back roads a long time ago because it was congested, filled with people trying to evacuate to God knows where. But now the back roads are just as crowded, filled with people who just want to be somewhere else. Their comfort zone has failed them—the place they feel safest—so they're looking for someplace better, someplace safer.

I want to tell them that there is no such place.

That this is it.

That things are only going to get worse, not better.

I don't think anyone would believe me. They couldn't, because then that would mean this is for real. That this *is* the point of no return, just like the game promises.

It's crazy, really. I thought we would have lasted longer,

that the veneer of civility we wear would have taken longer than this to erode.

I read once in history class that all civilizations, all people, are just nine meals from total anarchy. I'd thought it was crazy at the time, had argued with my teacher about the absurdity of it, but my father has proven me wrong. The wholesale breakdown of everything we know has sent all of us plunging over the edge of civilization and into a yawning void, where there are no rules except survival.

I can't help thinking about what happened earlier. About how Eli was ready to leave that man. How for a fleeting second, so was I. It makes me queasy to think of what we're becoming. Sure, we're working together now, but if things get really bad, will it be each of us for him- or herself? Will Eli abandon Theo and me as easily as he was going to abandon that man?

Will I?

The thought echoes inside me until I shut off my brain, refusing to go there right now. I'll lose my mind if I keep thinking of all the what-ifs that are laid out in front of us.

We inch along in traffic for what feels like hours but is really more like fifteen or twenty minutes. I'm antsy as hell, my internal radar screaming that we're missing something, but I don't know what it is.

"How far are we from the Colorado border?" I ask. I'm starving, but I don't want to eat any of our small stash of food. Not yet. Who knows when we'll find more?

"The sign we passed a few minutes ago said five miles," Theo says. He doesn't turn from looking out the window.

Eli's in the backseat, asleep, after finding the level-three AR gate in Pandora's Box, so we can plug the code in when we find it. "Five miles? So why this holdup, all of a sudden? It doesn't make sense." More concerned than I want to admit, I concentrate on drumming my hands in a complicated rhythm on the steering wheel in an effort to get rid of the restless energy building inside me.

Theo grins.

"What?" I demand.

"You're playing my favorite song." He drums along on the dashboard.

"You like the Chili Peppers?" I ask, amazed.

"Why do you look so surprised?"

"Oh, I don't know. Maybe it's all the Ralph Lauren polo shirts you wear, Harvard boy."

He snorts. "Yeah, well, we can't all look good in Social Distortion tank tops. And going to Harvard does *not* preclude a love of good music."

"Like you even know who Social D is."

"Excuse me. I've got all of their albums, thank you very much."

"Oh, yeah? How many are there?"

"Nine, including the two live albums. Just because I don't wear my music preference on T-shirts like you and Eli doesn't mean I'm all about chamber orchestras, you know."

We grin at each other for a second, and it's the first time I can remember being happy since this thing began. Then Theo's eyes darken, turn more intense, and things get awkward. Suddenly, sitting here with him in the quiet—dusk falling around us—feels strange. There's power in this silence, and I feel everything inside me, all my thoughts and hopes and fears, straining toward him.

It's wrong, the last thing I need to be thinking about when my feelings for Eli are so unsettled. He tried to talk to me before he fell asleep, wanted to put his arms around me. But I can't forget how he grabbed on to me, how he told me to shut up and tried to force me to do something I knew was wrong.

"So, how long do you think it's going to take us to cross?" I ask, desperate to fill up the silence.

Theo doesn't answer right away, and I get the feeling that he's waiting for me to look at him. But I can't. I won't.

Finally he says, "Seeing as how we've been in the same place for five minutes, it could be a while."

For whatever reason—my subconscious working overtime or my brain finally puzzling things out—at that moment, the answer becomes clear to me. The strange delay, the long line of cars that started too close to the border, the feeling that I'm missing something that's been plaguing me since we first slowed down.

"They're doing border checks!"

"What?" Theo looks at me like I'm crazy.

"How much do you want to bet that's what this is? They've put up a roadblock at the border."

"Colorado?" Eli asks, proving that he isn't asleep in the back, after all. Now I'm more glad than ever that I looked away earlier, before Theo could say anything.

"Homeland Security." Theo's voice is grim. "They're looking for us."

"How do they know what we're doing?" I ask. "I mean, how did they even know to look for us at Orinoco?"

"I think that was accidental," Theo says. "They probably traced the game from you to your father—no offense, Pandora, you just don't have the vibe of a computer mastermind."

"And somehow I'm totally okay with that."

"According to the wall we saw, your father is a big investor in Orinoco and probably other places as well. It stands to reason that they're checking him out, trying to find him."

"And when they found us there, it was like hitting the jackpot. More proof that I'm in cahoots with him."

"Cahoots?" I can hear the smile in Eli's voice.

"What? It's a word."

"Not a very good one."

"Whatever. I don't think my vocabulary choices are the point right now, do you?"

"We need to figure out a way to get out of this," Eli says, calmly packing up his backpack and mine.

"Should I leave the road?" I start to turn the wheel, more than ready to make a run for it. What's one more Homeland Security chase in the grand scheme of things, after all?

"No! Don't do that!" Eli and Theo answer at the same time.

"You'll draw too much attention," Theo continues. "If they see you head out into the desert, they'll know something is up."

"What if I hide in the trunk while the two of you cross over?"

I think it's a good idea, but Theo shakes his head as he reaches into his backpack, pulls out the CB radio he's been toting around for two days now. He tunes it into a frequency that has some chatter, then says, "Hey, I'm on back road forty-six looking to cross into Colorado. Anyone out there right now looking to do the same?"

The CB crackles emptily for a minute, two. As Theo gets ready to try again, someone says, "I just crossed. It's a mess. Government types are everywhere, all over the road and fanning into the desert. They're looking for something big."

All three of us meet eyes in the rearview mirror.

"Oh yeah?" Theo continues. "They got dogs out there? My wife is terrified of dogs."

"Oh yeah, man," someone else chimes in. "They got dogs and heat-seeking technology. And they're going through every car like the answer to this disaster is inside it. Took them fifteen minutes to clear my family."

"Thanks. Guess I'll settle in for a long wait." Theo turns off the radio, then says, "Trunk is definitely out."

"Yeah, I got that. If we turn around, we can try a back road into Oklahoma and then go up to Colorado from there," Eli suggests.

I shake my head. "If they're being thorough, they'll have all the roads out of New Mexico covered. And even if they don't, we have nowhere near enough gas for that. And we can't keep stealing cars—eventually we'll get caught."

"So, what are we going to do, then? Anybody got an idea?" Eli asks.

I don't say anything, because my ideas pretty much end with "Run for our lives!" I guess Theo feels the same way, because he doesn't speak, either. We crawl forward a little more, and I steer around a car that has run out of gas.

Its owners are pushing it the last few feet onto the shoulder. And that's when it hits me. I drive a little farther, then pull over and shut off the engine.

"What are you doing?" Theo asks.

"We just ran out of gas."

"But we had half a tank," Eli counters.

Theo catches on right away. "Nice, Pandora. I like it." Then, to Eli, "Make sure we've got all the important stuff in the backpacks. And drink some water. We're walking from here."

Though it pains me, I put on the pair of heavy socks from my father, and then step into my Docs. They hurt my blisters with every step I take, but this is the desert, and there is no way I'm traipsing around it at night in nothing but a pair of flip-flops. Blisters are one thing. Snake bites and scorpion stings are something else entirely.

It takes only a few minutes for us to clean out the car—we've packed up so many times that we're pretty much experts by now—and then we're walking. But instead of keeping close to the road, like most of the people who have started forward on foot when their cars ran out of gas, we strike out into the desert.

Four miles doesn't seem like that long a walk. We run that much in PE a couple of times a week, not to mention having done much longer hikes since this thing began just a few days ago. But we're tired now, and hungry. Breakfast, such as it was, was a long time ago, and the granola bars we ate for lunch were burned up almost as soon as we finished them.

Every step takes more effort than I've got, and when I

allow myself to scan the long stretch of desert in front of us, crossing it seems like an insurmountable task. So I don't let myself check. Instead, I look at the ground a little bit in front of my feet and tell myself to go just a few more steps. Again and again and again.

We've been walking maybe half an hour or so when Theo reaches into my bag, yanks out the two packs of M&M's. "You need to eat," he tells me, opening one of the bags and shoving it into my hand. "The sugar will give you something to burn, at least for a little while."

He tosses the other pack to Eli, who catches it on the fly.

"So do you," I say, pouring out a handful of candy and then passing the bag to him.

"I'm fine."

I snort. "Who's being a martyr now? Eat the stupid candy. It's not much farther to Colorado, right?"

"Two miles. Maybe a little less."

"Cool. Will we even be able to recognize when we pass?"

"I've been thinking about that. If we keep up this pace for another hour or so, it should guarantee that we're a couple of miles in. Then we can head back to the road. We'll have missed the roadblock, and hopefully we'll be far enough away that no one will notice us."

"What do we do after we get to the road? We don't have a car. We have money, but I'm not sure how much good it's going to do us."

"We'll think of something."

"Speak for yourself. I am *completely* out of ideas."

"That's 'cause your last one was so good." Eli winks at me.

"Oh, yeah. Right. This is a fabulous idea."

"Better than going to jail as cyberterrorists."

I shrug. "At least it would only be for six days."

Theo laughs. "Wow, from despair to cynicism. You've come a long way in eight hours."

"What can I say? Nothing lasts forever. Obviously."

"You're a real laugh riot today," Eli says.

I look down my nose at him. "Sarcasm is *so* unbecoming."

"So's fatalism. So get over it already, will you?" He points at some nebulous area in front of us. "Bet I can beat you to that cactus."

"We're in the desert. There are eight million cacti out here. You're going to have to be more specific."

"That huge forked one way up ahead. You see it, over—"

I'm off and running before he finishes the sentence. Am I cheating? Absolutely. Do I feel bad about it? Not at all. But I figure if I'm going up against the two of them, it's only fair that I get some kind of advantage.

I hear them pounding the sand behind me. They're getting closer, so I put on an extra burst of speed and cross the finish line a split second before Theo. Eli finishes about a second later.

"You are *such* a cheater," Eli tells me breathlessly, then tugs at one of the locks of hair that have fallen across my eye. "I'm going to remember to watch my back around you."

"And why is that?"

"Because you're dangerous," Theo says, opening a water bottle and handing it to me, along with yet another granola bar. This one's apple-cinnamon flavor. Lucky me.

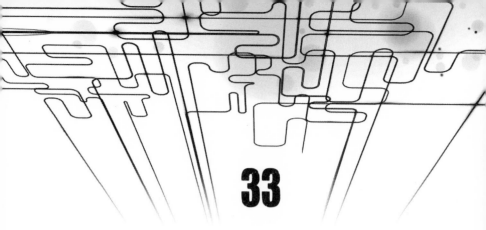

33

A FEW HOURS LATER we make it to a small apartment complex on the outskirts of Trinidad, Colorado. We're dirty and exhausted and dying of thirst. But at least we're back in civilization. If I had to spend much more time in the desert, I would have lost it.

The first thing I do is lean against a car, pull off my boots, and slide into my flip-flops. My feet are a bleeding mess, and I'm totally miserable. It hurts to breathe.

"You all right?" Theo asks me, crouching down to get a better look, his flashlight aimed at my heels.

"I'm fine," I say, shrugging off his concern. "So, what's next?"

They both just look at me. As if there's any doubt about what we're going to do now.

"Okay, then. Let me be more specific." I turn toward the parking lot and open my arms wide. "What kind of car do you want this time?"

• • •

We end up in a forest-green Bronco with 170,000 miles, Oklahoma license plates, and an almost-full tank of gas. It also has a fairly detailed map of Colorado Springs in its center console.

Eli and Theo sit in the back looking at the map, trying to figure out where the best bet for farmland is in the area. So far, they aren't having much luck.

"I guess we could ask somebody," I say, stopping at a major intersection and looking both ways. I swear, of all the things we've lost, I miss traffic lights the most. This stopping at every corner is more obnoxious than I can say.

Not as obnoxious, of course, as having another accident would be, so I stop again two hundred feet later and wait as the huge truck to my left starts through the intersection.

Only, it's not a regular truck. It's a military one, and there are armed soldiers on every side of it. *National Guard?* I wonder. *Or air force?*

I'm concentrating on Eli and Theo's conversation in the back, so after my initial thought, I don't pay much attention to the truck one way or another. Until it stops in the middle of the street and two soldiers with very large guns come straight toward us.

"Theo?"

"Yeah?" He's distracted and not looking, I can tell.

"Theo!" I say again, this time making sure my voice reflects my urgency. But by then it's too late—one of the men is knocking on my window. I roll it down slowly as I search desperately for some explanation as to how little old fugitive me has ended up in Colorado Springs.

Except he doesn't ask for any ID as he shines a flashlight in my face. He just asks, "Where are you coming from tonight?"

I start to say New Mexico, but at the last second remember the Oklahoma license plates we're sporting. "Tulsa," I tell him. Behind me, Eli and Theo are hyperalert. I can feel them willing me not to screw up.

"You know there's a curfew here, don't you? It goes into effect as soon as the sun goes down." He shines a light in the backseat, his mouth growing grim when he takes in Eli and Theo.

"I didn't, no. We just got into town, and we're coming from St. Mark's." I name a hospital I saw a couple of blocks earlier.

"What happened?" His eyes jerk back to mine.

He's got a country accent, small-town Alabama, I think, and now that I get a better look at him, I realize he's not much older than I am. Figuring it can't hurt, I lay on the country pretty thick myself. "My dad got snake bitten a little ways out of town. Rattler. We dropped him and Mom at the hospital, and my brothers and I are going to try to find a hotel room nearby."

Behind me, Eli chokes at the brother comment, but the guy doesn't hear him. Thank God.

"There's not much open around here right now," he tells me. "Your best bet might be to spend the night in the hospital waiting room."

"If you think that's best, then that's what we'll do." I flutter my eyes at him a little, feeling like an idiot, but it seems to work because he smiles at me. That or he really does buy the country-girl act. "But my dad's college roommate has a farm outside of the city. We could go there, if you think it's safe. It's where we were headed when Dad got hurt."

"Where's it located?"

My brain tries to freeze as panic sets in, but I force myself to think through it. "On Willow Road," I improvise. "It's called Willow Farms."

"Oh, I know that place!" The other soldier speaks up for the first time. "It's the biggest co-op in town. But it's not on Willow Road. It's off of East Cooper."

"Oh, right. Sorry. I'm messed up, worrying about Dad." I blink fast, then bravely—and unsuccessfully—attempt to battle back tears. "Do you know, is East Cooper close enough that we can make it tonight? Or should we just go back to the hospital and sleep in the waiting room? We'll do whatever you think is best."

I swear, his chest actually puffs up a little at that. Both of theirs do, and it takes all my willpower not to laugh.

"Well, it's about twenty minutes from here on the side streets." He turns and points back the way we came. "But you're going the wrong way. You need to head that way, make a left on Bradley and then a right on Hillside. Follow Hillside a few miles and you'll run into Cooper. Make a right and then just follow it all the way."

"Thank you so much."

The first guy nods. "But you need to be careful." He pulls out a sheet of paper, scribbles something on it. "If anyone else stops you, show them this. But don't go joyriding around the city. I'm writing that you're going to East Cooper. That's as far as you'll be allowed. Understand?"

"Yes. Of course. We really appreciate it."

"Good luck." His eyes soften just a little. "And I hope your dad's okay."

"Thank you. Thanks so much. And you stay safe, too. Okay?"

He nods, completely professional again, as he slaps a piece of bright-yellow duct tape across the hood of my car. "This should keep you safe for tonight. Now make a U-turn and I'll cover you."

I nod, wait for them to step away from the car. Then I roll up the window with a wave and whip the Bronco around.

"Holy crap," Eli says. "What the hell was *that*?"

"Thanks for jumping in, by the way," I say, shooting a dirty look behind me. "Did you at least get the directions?"

"We did," said Theo, and I can hear laughter in his voice. "And why should we have stepped in? You were doing fine by yourself, playing the damsel in distress."

"I thought it was more femme fatale, myself," Eli comments. "All that eye batting, I was afraid you were going to take off under your own power."

"Yeah, well, at least we're not on our way to a military jail. That's something." I glance at the paper, realize the soldier's given us his version of a hall pass, which is weird and not nearly as comforting as it should be. I mean, why is it even necessary?

"But what are they doing off base?" Eli asks. "Those weren't National Guard guys."

"No," I agree. "They were wearing air force uniforms."

"There must be more," Theo tells him. "Or they wouldn't have been worried about us making it to the farm."

Even before he's done speaking, I realize how true his words are. I brake abruptly and watch as a tank—a *tank!*—rolls down the street. It's followed by a truck very similar to the one we just saw, but this truck doesn't stop. The passengers shine flashlights toward us, but the yellow tape seems to satisfy them. I wonder what would have happened if it didn't. Could I have sweet-talked another soldier, or would our number have been up this time?

"Turn left here," Theo tells me, and I do, glad one of us can still think. My brain is working overtime at the realization that our government has turned the military on its own citizens. How bad does the situation have to be for them to roll tanks down the center of the road like it's an everyday occurrence?

I turn onto East Cooper and it's dark, empty. I flip on my brights and keep driving for what feels like forever. Thirty miles and a couple of gallons of gas later, we make it to the end of the road and a sign that is lit up by what I think are solar-powered lights. It reads, WELCOME TO THE WILLOWS and is the same sign that's in the picture of my dad and me. I shudder in relief.

But I no sooner stop the car than three men with guns walk out of the shadows. One gestures for me to roll down the window.

"Pandora." Theo's voice, rife with warning, comes from the backseat.

"I know." But it's not like we have any other choice—if

they're part of the farm, then we have to talk to them. And if they're not . . . I shake my head. I'm not even going to think about that possibility right now.

I crack my window.

"You need to turn this car around and go back the way you came, miss," one of them tells me. He's old and looks tired, but his grip on his gun never falters. "We're not open to the public right now."

"Please," I tell him. "We've come so far to get here. We don't want anything from you, just . . ." What? What do we want?

The second guy steps in front of the car, looks at the plates. "You're from Oklahoma?"

"Actually, we're from Texas."

"What are you doing here?"

I don't know what to say to him that won't sound completely absurd. In the end, I go with a small truth and hope it's enough. "My father sent me."

"And who is your father?"

"Mitchell Walker."

I wait for a flicker of recognition to pass over their faces, but at first nothing happens. Then the third man moves toward the car, leans down to peer in the window. I turn on the overhead light so he can see our faces.

"Are you Pandora?" he asks. "Mitch's girl?"

I've never heard anyone refer to my father as Mitch before, but I'm not about to let that stop me. "Yes, sir."

He studies me for a second. I'm not sure what he's looking for, what attitude I need to project, but he must be satisfied because he nods and turns to the other two. "Let them in."

He gestures for me to put the window down more and I do, despite Theo's warning growl from the backseat. "Follow this road for about a mile, then turn right. You'll see a house at the end of the trail. I'll radio to Jean, tell her to be expecting you."

"Thank you."

He shrugs. "Jean would skin me alive if I left Mitch's little girl out here in the middle of this mess."

And just that easily, we're in.

The men step back, open the gate for us, and we drive slowly through.

"Am I the only one who thinks this is bizarre?" Eli asks a couple of minutes later as we cruise along the well-lit road. "I mean, your dad is a cyberterrorist, and yet these people act like he's their best friend."

"I'm going to go out on a limb here and say they don't yet know he's trying to destroy the world."

A woman is waiting on the porch when we pull up to the house. I don't recognize her, but she rushes down the steps before I can even yank the keys from the ignition. She pulls my door open and then I'm surrounded by her, yanked out of the car and into a vanilla-scented hug that goes on and on.

At first, I look frantically at Eli, who is now standing behind her, looking bemused. It's no different from how I feel. But eventually the calming scent of her seeps past my defenses, and I find myself relaxing despite myself. It's been so long since a grown woman has hugged me this way— maybe forever—and though I didn't know it, it's exactly what I need after everything we've been through.

I close my eyes, burrow a little closer as she pats my

back and makes soothing noises. Eventually she pulls away, but she seems as reluctant to let go as I am to have her do so. "I know you don't remember me, Pandora, but you were such a delightful child. I loved every second of the month you and Mitch stayed here and hoped I'd get to see you again. Though," she says with a sad smile, "not exactly under these circumstances."

I'm reeling from her revelation. If my father and I were here for a month when I was a kid, where was my mother? Why hadn't she come along? And why didn't I know that they were separated or whatever?

The whole thing seems odd, and I feel the tension creeping back like it had never left. Why is this woman so happy to see me? What does she want from me? I can barely get myself through the day right now, let alone find a way to give her whatever she needs.

I step back, gesture to Eli and Theo. "These are my friends." I introduce them and she practically beams.

"So nice to meet you boys. Get your bags from the car and come on into the house. You must be exhausted—from what the radio says, it's crazy out there."

"It's been a long day, ma'am," Theo tells her as he pulls our backpacks from the car, hands them to me and Eli.

"I can only imagine. This Pandora's Box thing, it's foolish."

"Foolish?" I echo. It seems like a huge understatement.

"Your father is a great man, Pandora, but this . . ." She shakes her head. "It's absolute craziness what he's done."

"Does everyone know?" I ask, wondering if we'll be safe here. Jean seems to be taking this in stride (which makes me think my father isn't the only crazy one), but I can't see others being so understanding of my presence. And since I'm trying to stop the madness, I don't relish being murdered in my sleep for the crime of being Mitchell Walker's daughter.

"Of course not. I didn't even know for sure until you showed up. It's just, I know Mitchell." She shakes her head, walks back up to the porch. "We don't need to talk about this now. There will be plenty of time tomorrow. Let's get you fed and bathed. We'll talk after you've slept."

I want to talk now—there's no time for niceties. But as we follow Jean into the kitchen, which is warm and homey and delicious smelling, it becomes obvious that she has her own agenda and nothing I do is going to budge her from it. For now, that agenda means that Theo, Eli, and I do nothing more strenuous than lift a fork.

Within minutes, we're seated around the kitchen table eating plates of reheated vegetables and cheese lasagna. There's bread, a quickly assembled salad, and glasses of cold homemade lemonade. We try for manners, but after a few bites we fall on the food like it's been a year since we've had our last decent meal instead of just a couple of days. We don't talk beyond a quickly murmured thank-you, and Jean doesn't press us. She just watches us with sad, knowing eyes, making sure to keep our glasses and our plates full.

When we're finally stuffed—which takes a lot longer for Theo and Eli than it does for me—she offers us homemade peach cobbler. I decline, but the guys somehow make room for it.

I settle back and watch them eat dessert with abandon,

all the time conscious of Jean's eyes on us. I don't know what to say to her, don't know how to ask her why I'm here. The farm is huge, with seemingly endless acres of land. I have no idea where to begin looking for the code I need to unlock the next powers.

I need that code, have to find it, have to keep going before it's too late. It's so easy to relax at this table, to enjoy delicious food in a room that is neither too hot nor too cold, but I can't forget that we're the exception tonight. That outside this house, men are standing guard with guns in an effort to keep their land safe from others—from people who don't have the luxury of ice-cold lemonade and steaming-hot lasagna. People who are suffering because my father thinks they're expendable.

I shove away from the table so fast that my chair legs scrape against the warm wood of the floor. "Thank you for dinner, Jean. I appreciate it."

Theo and Eli look at me in surprise, but their mouths are too stuffed with cobbler to say anything.

"You're dead on your feet, you poor thing," Jean says. "Let me show you to your room." She turns back to Eli and Theo. "Help yourself to more cobbler—I'll be back to check on you in a few minutes."

We walk down the halls, and her slippers make a soft, swishing sound against the wood. I could get used to that sound, to what it feels like to be looked at as more than a bargaining tool. I expect her to ask me things as we walk, expect to ask her a few things. But instead, we make the trip in silence, like both of us are too afraid to speak what's on our minds. I know I am.

She leads me to a room done in shades of aqua and yellow. There's a huge bed in the middle of the room, covered in what looks to be a handmade quilt, and fresh flowers on the dresser—as if she'd been expecting me all along.

"The bathroom is through here," Jean says, leading me to an open door. "There's shampoo and soap. Let me know if you need anything else."

"That's great." I put my backpack on the dresser. "Thanks."

"You're welcome." Her smile is soft. "I'll see you in the morning, for breakfast."

"What time?"

"Whatever time you get up, honey. You look like you could sleep the clock around."

I probably could, but that's not going to happen. Not for a while, anyway.

Jean starts to leave, but at the last second she pauses at the door. "You're a lot like your father, you know. The way you look, the way you talk. The way you stepped up and are doing what needs to be done with this game."

"What do you know about Pandora's Box?"

Her expression grows shuttered. "Same thing everybody does, I expect." She closes the door behind her, and though I need a shower desperately, I don't move for the longest time.

Like your father? The words echo in my head, make my skin crawl.

Is it true? I wonder. *And if it is, what am I really doing here? Stopping Armageddon or falling right into his trap?* When, ten minutes later, I finally head into the shower, I still don't have the answer. Even worse, I don't know if I ever will.

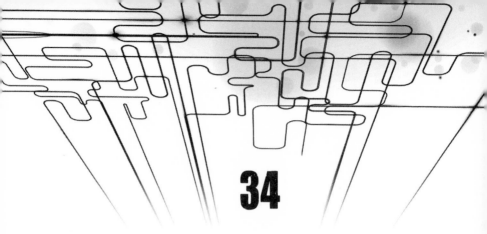

34

DAY FIVE

I AWAKEN EARLY, heart racing, blood pumping, a scream lodged in the back of my throat. The closet light I left burning went out sometime in the middle of the night, and I am all alone in an unfamiliar room. In the dark.

The same old tightness rises inside me, and I sit up quickly, groping for the large lamp I remember seeing on my nightstand. I finally find it, cool glass beneath my burning fingertips. I fumble for the switch, knowing all along that it won't go on. That I'm stuck here, in the dark, on my own.

Click. The switch turns once. Nothing.

Click. I turn it again. Dim, golden light fills the room, and has my too-wide pupils blinking at the sensory assault. Yet even as I struggle to see, I breathe a sigh of relief. Not completely in the dark. Not yet.

The old-fashioned windup clock on the dresser reads five fifteen. I've slept only four hours, but it's going to have to be enough. I brush my teeth, wash my face, slip on a pair of jeans over the underwear I slept in. I add a blue cotton blouse—my last clean shirt—and then, because I'm cold, slide the purple hoodie over my head.

Seven minutes have passed. Not enough time. I think about staying in the room, messing with Pandora's Box or washing my dirty clothes in the sink. But I'm not in the mood, not now. I can't breathe in here. I want to be outside, where I can feel the earth beneath my toes and the crisp, cool morning air in my lungs.

I grab a flashlight from my backpack and make my way slowly down the hall and out the front door. It will be dawn soon. Already I can see the beginning tendrils of morning snaking their way across the inky darkness of the sky.

I sit on the porch and wait for the light.

Dawn finally arrives, with a burst of reds and pinks and golds as it streaks triumphantly across the sky. It lights up the world around me, chases away the last of the dark, and I realize that though the farm has hundreds, thousands, of acres of land to harvest, Jean has planted a personal garden in a heated greenhouse not too far from the front door.

I walk to it, smiling at the neatly labeled plants. Lettuce, broccoli, carrots, tomatoes, squash, strawberry, watermelon, just to name a few. She has almost everything out here, growing in rich, beautiful soil. My fingers itch to bury themselves in the earth, and I refuse to deny them, deny myself, this simple pleasure.

So in the midst of chaos and fear and indecision, in the midst of the darkest dawn of my life, I drop to my knees and begin to harvest.

I pick ruby-red strawberries, bursting with sweetness

and size. Shrug out of my hoodie and create a makeshift basket for them with the sweatshirt. Then I move on to the tomatoes and green peppers and finally the blackberry bushes lining the edges of the greenhouse.

"You like to garden." Jean's soft voice comes from nowhere, but instead of startling me, it just makes me smile.

"I love it. I grow a bunch of herbs and vegetables back home." A flash of sadness as I think of my own flourishing garden and wonder if it's going to go to waste or if Homeland Security is going to ransack it like they did everything else, just to be mean.

"The last time you were here you picked apples. Your dad balanced you on his shoulders and you brought in four or five bushels, one right after the other. He kept trying to talk you down, to get you to stop, but you were having so much fun he wouldn't force the issue."

The memory creeps into my mind. Slow and sticky like spilled syrup, it works its way into my synapses until I can't believe that I ever forgot it. We were out here, alone save for Jean and her son, Matthias, and my dad took me down to the apple orchard.

"Tell me about my father," I say impulsively, carrying my bounty back to the house and into Jean's kitchen.

She sighs and pours each of us a cup of coffee. For a long time it's quiet between us, and I finally decide she isn't going to answer. But then she does.

"Being with your father was like harnessing lightning. Thrilling, fun, but more dangerous than anyone caught in his orbit likes to imagine."

I think back to my mother, to her making me swear to

stay away from my father. Was that her experience, too? Was being married to him like trying to hold on to a lightning bolt? And if it was, how come I never noticed her struggles? I remember her being the interloper, but maybe I was too young to understand anything more.

"I first met him when I was the same age you are now. We were at school together, at UC Berkeley, and he was leading a protest against nuclear armament. There was chaos all around him, students protesting, campus police trying to keep things in line, other students trying to push through the demonstration so they could get to class.

"And there was your father. Right in the middle of it all. Completely cool, totally in charge, and having a fantastic time. I was hooked, from that moment on. I'd never thought much about the arms race—I mean, beyond what everyone else did—but I walked right up to your dad and told him I wanted to join the cause."

She shrugs, smiles a little shyly. "We were inseparable after that. For years."

Even after he and my mom got married? I want to ask. I think back on those times here, with Jean and my father, and know that yes, even then, they were together. I don't understand any of this, but I want to. I really do. Something tells me it's a key to figuring out everything else that's going on.

Even with all of that to process, there's another question that begs to be asked. "Protest against nuclear arms?" Bitterness is in my mouth now. It coats my tongue, and when I laugh, it's not a happy sound. "Tell me, please, how a man who once protested nuclear weapons went from that to creating a worm that breaks down nuclear-cooling towers? A worm that guarantees to eradicate the planet? It doesn't make any sense!"

"He won't go through with it." Jean's voice sounds certain, but her hands are trembling when she reaches for the coffeepot.

The desire to believe her is a fire inside me, burning me with the need to see my father as something other than a villain. Something more than a spoiled little boy who decided to break everything because he couldn't have his way.

"He already has. We've got six days left. I'm dancing to his tune, we all are, and yet the countdown keeps ticking. Technology as we know it has all but disappeared, and the nuclear-cooling towers aren't functioning properly. It's just a matter of time before this all gets away from him."

"You don't know that. Mitch isn't the kind of person—"

"He's exactly that kind of person! Can't you see? Or are you so isolated on this farm that you don't understand what's going on?" I get up, walk to the window that looks out over acres and acres of food, and I think about that convenience store, emptied of supplies, its clerk murdered.

"People are already dying. Right now, as we speak. They're dying, Jean. And more are going to, even if he is bluffing about the nuclear thing—and I don't think he is. Hospitals can't run forever on their generators. Think about the people on life support. Don't tell me he didn't think about them. And if he didn't, then he's even more of a monster than I already believe he is."

"Pandora." Her blue eyes are horror stricken and watery, tears slowly sliding down her cheeks. "He's not a monster.

Whatever you say, whatever he's done, I won't believe that of him. The Mitch I know—"

"What? Tell me. Help me understand."

"Is that why you're here? To understand?"

"I'm here because it's where he put me. I'm playing the game, trying to stop him, and he brought me here."

"Which just proves he doesn't want to succeed! He would never involve you if it meant you might get hurt."

I stare at her in disbelief, as I think of everything I've done in the last few days. Stolen cars, fled federal custody, been in a high-speed car chase with Homeland Security, faced down men with guns, assaulted a cop, walked through miles of desert with very little water. Any one of those things could have ended badly for me, for Theo and Eli.

Would my father have even cared? Or are we all just pawns in this crazy game he's created? I shudder as I think of my own strategy regarding pawns when I'm playing chess. I *always* sacrifice them for the greater good of the game. Why should I think my father's strategy is any different?

I start to say as much to Jean, but she looks wrecked, and I've never been one to kick a person when she's down. Instead, I walk to the sink and rinse out my cup. "Can I help you make breakfast?" I ask. "We probably need to get on the road soon."

Jean wants to argue, I can see it in her eyes. But she must see something in mine that changes her mind, because all she does is shake her head. "Go wake up the boys. They're in the room next to yours. And get your dirty clothes so I can wash them. We'll have breakfast and then I'll pack some food for you, get you some gasoline, and you can be on your way."

"You have gasoline?" I ask, surprised. "Here?"

"We have a lot of machines for harvesting. They don't run on air, though it'd certainly be nice if they did."

I nod my understanding. "You don't have to do this, you know. I appreciate it, but you may need the supplies."

Her look is surprisingly fierce, and seems out of place on her warm, kind face. "You're Mitch's daughter. If he didn't send you here to stay, then I guarantee he sent you so I could do exactly this." She holds my gaze for long seconds, as if she's trying to tell me something I can't quite understand. Then she shoos me out of the kitchen, turns toward the sink. "Hurry up and get your clothes. I'll put on a load of laundry right away."

I nod even though she can't see me and walk slowly down the hall to my room. It's even prettier in daylight than it was at night. Sunlight reflects off the crystal knobs on the bedposts, sending rainbow prisms spinning across the floor and bed.

I empty my bag, pull out my dirty clothes. Start to head next door. At the last second, I open up my laptop, stare at the AR gate waiting for the right code to let me level up. I pause for a second, then type in J. E. A. N.

35

THE GAME BEEPS and I'm back in Balboa Park, in front of the entrance to the San Diego Aerospace Museum. A bunch of players cross through the open AR gate with me, and we stand there, staring at the circular white building, trying to figure out what we're supposed to do now.

Part of me wants to walk away forever. To smash my laptop into a million pieces so I never have to play this game again. I can't do it now, but I promise myself that once I find my father I'm never logging in to Pandora's Box again.

I walk into the museum. Inside it's one big hangar, with a bunch of planes on display, ranging from some of the first airplanes up to some of the most modern fighter jets. I look around for a minute, try to figure out what I'm supposed to do.

One of the planes is glowing, so I walk toward it. It's a small, two-seater plane like they use for crop dusting in old cartoons, and I have no idea what to do with it.

Just then CarlyMoon IMs me, and instead of ignoring the message as I usually do, I click on it:

PStar, I know how to fly a plane. In case you need some help or something.

I write her back:

    I'm not sure what I need yet, but thanks.

We chat for a minute or so, then:

It's interesting the way this game is set up, isn't it? How, no matter what shape the Internet is in, you can still log in wherever you are and then get transported to real places around the globe. Like I'm in Boston, yet I can connect to SD because that's where your avatar is. You pull us with you.
    I'm sorry. I don't mean to.
No, it's cool. Are you in all these places in real life? Like, are you in SD right now?

Her questions set off alarm bells inside me. I close our chat, but that doesn't seem good enough. Or safe enough. If my instincts are right, and CarlyMoon is a federal agent, can she trace us through the game? Can she find out where I am?

I slam my computer shut just as there's a knock on my door.

"I'm coming, Jean," I call, scooping up my dirty clothes. But when I open the door, Jean's not on the other side. It's Eli.

"Hey, Pandora." He smiles lazily, his green eyes still a little unfocused from sleep, though he smells of mint toothpaste. "I'm supposed to tell you breakfast is ready."

"Great." I grab my backpack and follow him out into the hall, where we run into Theo, fresh from a shower.

"I found the code," I blurt out. "To the AR gate. It's Jean. She and my dad . . ." I trail off.

"Did you finish the level?"

"No. I ran into a player who freaked me out." I tell them what happened, and they both look as concerned as I feel.

"I don't think they can trace us here, not with none of the com lines working," Theo says as we settle at the table. "But I'd stay away from anyone who's playing with us."

"I agree," Eli says. "It's impossible to tell who they really are."

"How long do we have before the time limit runs out?" Theo asks, pulling out his tablet.

Oh, crap. I'd been so caught up in worrying about Carly-Moon that I let the time limit get away from me. "Probably not long." I log on to the game and the guys do the same, entering the AR code so they drop down right next to me. As one, we stare at the glowing airplane.

"We need to fly that baby?"

"I think so." The clock reads 5:34.

"Then let's do it." Eli hops in the back. "You can sit on my lap, Pandora."

Theo climbs into the front, starts up the plane, and I clamber into the back. As soon as the plane starts to move forward, the walls of the museum disappear, and we're rolling through the fields of Balboa Park.

"You really know how to fly this thing?" I ask Theo.

"*This* thing? Not exactly, but hopefully it's not much different from my plane."

We bounce our way across the grass to a huge parking lot that is, thankfully, devoid of cars. Theo hits the throttle, or whatever that thing is called, and the plane starts coasting faster and faster. Within seconds, we're airborne.

"Now what?" I ask, and though the timer is quickly winding down, it's nice to be able to concentrate on the game for once instead of having to flee for our lives.

"I have no idea." Theo does a loop-de-loop that has my avatar clutching on to Eli. As Theo straightens up, he flies higher than he had been, and lightning crackles across the sky.

"Is that a good thing or a bad thing?" Eli leans over to get a better look at the clouds we're flying through.

"I have no idea," Theo repeats as he does another spin and more lightning crackles, followed by the *boom* of thunder.

We soar over the scorched croplands outside of San Diego, and the higher we go, the more thunder and lightning there is. And then, as Theo executes a complicated sequence of twists and turns, it finally begins to rain.

As it does, the fields below us start to grow.

Instead of dusting the plants with chemicals, as the plane was originally intended, we're bringing them water and the chance to flourish.

Huge expanses of field stretch before us, and the timer is quickly ticking away. 1:21. "Can we get them all done in time?" I demand, as Theo pushes the plane to go faster.

"We'd better," Eli answers.

We soar over the last field just as the countdown ends. This time, a man with a full beard appears on the screen, dressed in a white robe and clutching a lightning bolt in one hand. Zeus, king of the gods and weather, has appeared as we level up.

We're feeling good, at least until we move on to level four, and end up in the middle of what looks like a war zone. Streets messed up and houses in all states of disrepair.

Eli takes one look and puts down his iPad. "Glad that's done. I'm starving."

"Me, too," Theo agrees, and I nod, as I can't talk around the food I've already shoveled into my mouth. Jean is an amazing cook and she's gone all out—fresh fruit salad, homemade cinnamon rolls, cheese-and-vegetable omelets, hash browns, coffee with cream. It's a far cry from my regular morning bowl of Crunch Berries.

When we're done and I've carried my plate to the sink, I wash my hands and then reach for the pictures my father sent me. I lay them out, until I'm looking at the next photos. Neither are in front of something recognizable, not like a solar array with Orinoco's name on it or a "Welcome to" sign. But still, Theo has no trouble identifying what my father and I are standing in front of in picture five. I'm an infant, wrapped in a lavender blanket with rosebuds all over it, and he's holding me up for the camera, a look of pride, excitement, and love in his eyes.

For a moment, I wonder who is taking the picture—Jean or my mom. Whoever it is, it's obvious my dad is crazy about her.

"That's Jackson Square," Theo tells me, pointing to the huge church behind us. "That's the St. Louis Cathedral, in New Orleans."

"New Orleans?" I ask, surprised. I didn't even know I'd been to the Big Easy. But it makes sense. In the game, that war zone we were in was probably just post-Katrina New Orleans.

"What are you guys talking about?" Jean asks, leaning in to see the pictures. From the way her eyes soften at the sight of the New Orleans photo, I suspect she is the one who held that camera long ago.

"I remember this day," Jean tells us. "It was so cold the pipes had frozen at the hotel—one of those rare early winter days that New Orleans doesn't quite know what to do with."

"What were you doing with him?" I ask. It comes out more accusatorily than I would like, but Jean doesn't take offense. Or at least, it doesn't seem as if she does.

"We were in town for a convention, and your dad brought you and your mom along. He thought you'd have fun. But your mom worked most of the time, with conference calls or whatever, so he usually ended up carrying you around with him from meeting."

Now that, I *can* believe. My mom's been wrapped up in work for as long as I can remember. I just didn't realize it had started back when I was only a baby. It's strange, after all these years without him, to think of my dad as the primary caregiver when I was young. I'm not sure how I feel about that.

"You don't happen to know where this picture was taken, do you, Jean?" Theo asks smoothly, sliding the picture of my dad and six-year-old me across the table to her. We're kneeling in front of a huge field of corn, wearing jeans and matching red T-shirts. My dad is facing the camera, and the front of his shirt reads, "Try a tankful." I'm kneeling away from the camera, my long red hair divided into two pigtails, and the back of my shirt proclaiming, "You'll be thankful."

"Somewhere that makes ethanol," she tells us. "That slogan is about a million years old and that's what it refers to. 'The Fuel of the Future.'"

So, that's where we'll be going next. Some state that grows a lot of corn and produces a lot of ethanol. I reach for my laptop again. Might as well play the game and find out where. It's nice here at Willow Farms, but as I open up my computer, the counter reads, "Total annihilation in 6 days." It's not like I've got so much time to waste here.

We start to run down the torn-up streets, turning right and left and right again, looking for a way to get to Jackson Square, but we can't do it. Everything narrows, hems us in, keeps us in this desolate stretch of New Orleans until we're simply going in circles, spinning around ourselves.

"What is going *on*?" Eli demands, frustrated. "Why can't we move?"

I slow my pace to little more than a crawl, look around the neighborhood we've been pacing for what feels like forever. And that's when the truth hits me. "We have to do the task first."

"What's the task?" Theo asks, sounding as annoyed as Eli.

I point toward one of the dilapidated houses, where a huge pile of building supplies sits in the front yard, waiting to be used. "We need to build," I say simply.

"What? Like Habitat for Humanity?" Eli runs over to check what we have to work with.

"That's one of your father's favorite charities," Jean says. "He's spent two weeks working with them every year for as long as I've known him."

I turn to her. "Where is my father, Jean? If anyone knows, I figure it would be you."

She shakes her head sadly. "I wish I did, Pandora. But he disappeared off the face of the earth two and a half years ago, and I haven't heard from him since."

"What happened two and a half years ago?"

She looks uncomfortable, like she's got secrets to spill but doesn't know if she should. I start to press her, but Theo looks up from where he's knocking a hole in the wall of the existing house. "Your father walked away from a lucrative job at the number-one think tank in America."

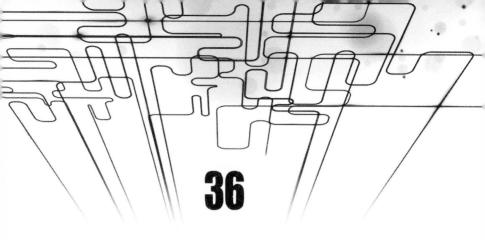

36

AS THEO'S REVELATION SINKS IN, I stare at him for long seconds, mouth agape. In some dim corner of my mind, I realize Eli is doing the same.

"How do you know that?" I demand. "What game are you playing?"

He looks at me coolly. "The same one you are. But I've been thinking about this whole thing for days now, trying to put the pieces together. The Balboa Park fight helped me get my thoughts together a little more clearly, and then, being here, listening to Jean, made another big part of the puzzle slide into place."

I glance between him and Jean. She smiles sadly at me, then gets up to refill our coffee cups.

"Will somebody *please* tell me what is going on? Because I don't understand anything!"

"Yes, big brother, do tell." Eli's all smooth sarcasm, but I can tell he's as pissed as I am that Theo's been hiding something this huge from us.

Theo doesn't flinch under our scrutiny. "All along I've been wondering what the game has to do with this. From a programming perspective, it's a million times more complicated to do what your father's done than it is to just launch a simple worm. I mean, the worm is complex and all—so complex that it had to be uploaded in twelve pieces, something I've never even heard of before.

"But at the same time, why use the game? Why spend all that extra effort hacking into it, changing it to fit his and Pandora's relationship, using it to actually upload the worm and destroy the world as we know it? From an efficiency standpoint, it just doesn't make sense. You're talking about months, probably years, of extra work that didn't need to happen."

"How else was I supposed to follow the clues? I mean, he wanted to send me on a scavenger hunt, so he used Pandora's Box." Bewildered, I look between Theo and Eli.

"Yeah, and there are a *million* easier ways to create a scavenger hunt than to mess with an existing game's matrix. Unless—"

"Unless you already know that matrix intimately!" Eli crows. "You really are a genius, man."

"He may be, but obviously I'm not, because I don't have a clue what you're talking about!"

Theo sighs, and I can tell he's trying to bring his explanation down a level or five. "I've always been as interested in the makers of the games I play as I am in the games themselves. The makers of Pandora's Box, Coronado Programs, aren't big game makers. They're definitely the new kids on the block, so when they came up with this epic game that captured the attention of pretty much every gamer in the world, I wanted to know who they were. So I dug."

"And?" I ask, still baffled. "What did you learn? What are they?"

"A San Diego–based think tank that specializes in solutions to major global environmental crises."

"And they make video games?"

"They never have before. That's the thing. But about three and a half years ago, if I remember correctly, they ran into a major cash-flow problem. The whole green movement exploded, and cash that used to be exclusively theirs started being earmarked for all kinds of different projects at different companies."

"So they became video-game designers? That doesn't make any sense."

"No, what they became were backstabbing bastards." Jean speaks up for the first time, her voice passion filled. "Your father . . . your father worked for them for years, warned them of what was coming if things didn't change."

"Coming? For what?"

"For the earth. For the environment."

"Nobody listened?"

"Oh, they listened. But in the end, they sold him out. Not because he was wrong, but because he was right. In politics, being too right about a subject is almost as bad as not having a clue about it. At least that's what we learned from Coronado Programs. That benign misinformation is actually the best bet in most cases."

A feeling of dread comes over me, one that tells me I'm not going to like what I hear next. I want to run from the room, to cover my ears and sing at the top of my lungs like I did as a child when I didn't want to hear something. But it's too late for that. Too much is resting on us figuring this thing out.

"So what happened?"

Theo sits back, gestures for Jean to continue. She shakes her head, presses her lips together, but in the end she does as he asks. "Your father spent five years, at the behest—and expense—of ten major governments, working on a worst-case scenario for where we, as a planet, were heading. They wanted to know, from a scientific perspective, what Earth was going to look like in fifty, seventy-five, one hundred years. They wanted a ranked list of what the offenders were and how things could be changed to eliminate the worst of the problems.

"Your dad headed up the project, was involved in every aspect of it. But when he was finally finished, when he presented it to them, it frightened them so much—and pointed fingers at the biggest of the big campaign contributors—that they buried it. Buried *him*. He went from top dog at Coronado to working on projects that didn't matter and no one else wanted."

"And then they took that virtual worst-case scenario— the most brilliant of its kind—and turned it into Pandora's Box," Theo concludes. "The culmination of all your father's work and research became an apocalyptic MMO that is one of the largest economies in the world and an incredible drain on the environment.

"I remember reading about it, about how he quit after staging a huge fit that succeeded only in putting the nails in his coffin," Theo said. "For a man like him, it had to be a slap in the face, a nightmare of epic proportions."

"It was. I've never seen Mitch like that. So angry, so hurt, so determined to make them pay for what they'd done—to him, to his team, to everyone in the world who would suffer because the people who could do something about his predictions were too blind and too afraid to try."

"He was able to hack Pandora's Box so easily because he designed it?" I ask.

"Pretty much." Theo nods.

"And now he's done what they tried to tell him couldn't happen. He's created his own worst-case scenario, using all of us—all of our lives—as research subjects." The horror of it rips through me, claws at me until I can barely think. "We're all just collateral damage to him."

A few hours later, Jean sends us off in one of the Willow Farms trucks, on a back road in Colorado on the way to Hugoton, Kansas. The truck is filled up and loaded with enough extra gas to get us through the five-hour drive. We finally found the coordinates, N 37°10'31" and W 101°20'59", but only after we built three houses (one for each of us) and battled with Oceanus, the Greek Titan in charge of the world's water systems. He called forth the Mississippi and nearly drowned us—I'm still not certain how we survived, especially since he almost got me in his huge pincer claws more than once. There's another task for us to complete, but we won't be able to do it until we get to an ethanol plant in Hugoton, Kansas, and find the code word.

"Hey, Pandora, can I have an apple?" Eli asks from the driver's seat.

I roll my eyes, but he can't see me as I'm stretched out in the back. Still, I hand him the fruit. Jean fed us again before we left, as well as filling up half the backseat with extra food. I'm so stuffed I can't imagine eating again until tomorrow, but Eli and Theo don't have that problem. Makes me wonder just how hungry they must have been in New Mexico, when even I was starving.

I close my eyes, overwhelmed once again by what they've sacrificed to help me on this terrible quest. I know Theo says he's doing it for himself, but I saw through that argument even as he was making it. He rescued me, came with me, because he's the kind of guy who does that. The kind of guy who stands up when no one else wants to.

As for Eli, I still haven't decided if he's just along for the ride or if he really wants to save the world. I don't suppose it matters, as the end result is the same. The two of them are in this with me. I'm so grateful I don't have to do it alone.

"When we get to Hugoton, how are we going to find the right ethanol plant?" I ask.

Eli's too busy slamming on the brakes to answer.

Despite my seat belt, I nearly roll into the seat in front of me. "What's going on?"

"Cars are backed up heading into town," Theo answers.

"I can see that."

Both Eli and Theo grow more alert, which makes me nervous. "What's wrong?" I ask, poking my head up.

"Stay down, Pandora." Theo reaches a hand back and actually shoves my head down to the seat.

I stay down.

"Homeland Security?" I whisper, afraid to even say the words out loud in case it conjures them up. They're the bogeyman in this new story of my life.

"I think Homeland Security would be an improvement," is Eli's cryptic reply as he hits the locks.

"What do you want to do?" he asks Theo.

"About what?" I demand.

"I'm not sure. We could try to turn around, but you need to get into the other lane—"

"Damn it, I'm here, too, you know. Tell me what's going on!" I sit up to look for myself, and both Eli and Theo curse. This time it's Eli who shoves me down, and he's nowhere near as gentle about it as Theo was.

"There's a motorcycle gang outside, okay?" Theo tells me in a furious whisper. "They're working their way down the cars, robbing people. The last thing we need them to do is catch sight of you."

"Why? What's wrong with me?"

He and Eli exchange another look, and I'm beginning to feel stupid, not to mention left out of the good old boys' club they've got going on in the front seat. Nice that they've gone from hating each other to being bonded together in silence against me.

A woman's scream splits the air around us. Theo stiffens even more, and I can sense Eli's growing alarm as Theo reaches for the door handle.

"Stay in the car, man!" Eli says from between clenched

teeth, his hand grabbing on to Theo's biceps like he plans to physically hold him in place.

"Goddamnit, Eli, they're going to rape that woman!"

"And if you get out of this car, they'll kill you and me and then rape and kill Pandora. Do *not* draw attention to us." Eli glances at me in the rearview mirror. "Can you find a blanket back there, Pandora? Cover yourself up?"

"Are you serious? They're really—"

Another scream splits the air, more high-pitched and terrified than the last. "We have to help them, Theo. We can't let them do this—"

"They're already doing it, Pandora. There's ten of them and they're armed. Judging by the way they're working their way through the line, they've got this down to a science."

The car next to us pulls out of line and starts to make a U-turn over the center divider. But the road is just as packed going in the other direction—more proof that no one knows where to go in the middle of this nightmare, only that they don't want to be where they are.

The next thing I know, two motorcycles zoom past us, zipping between the rows of cars. They stop when they get to the car that made a break for it. I peer through the side window and watch as one of them smashes the window in with a baseball bat. Then they're yanking the driver out.

She's young and pretty, and I can hear her baby scream-ing from the backseat even through the rolled-up windows of our truck. Eli shifts uncomfortably, and Theo's hands clench the dashboard so hard that I'm afraid he's going to rip it off.

Eli glances to the right, tries to look past the cars in

front of us. "The next turnoff isn't that far up, right? Can we drive on the grass and get off there?"

"If we could, wouldn't other people be doing that?" Despite his words, Theo risks putting down his window and sticking his head out to try to see around the cars. When he turns back to us, his face is even more grim. "There's a lot more of them. They've got all the avenues of escape shut down in every direction I can see."

Even so, more people are starting to make a run for it. The car two spots in front of us tries to pull out of line, but gets its tires shot for the attempt.

"We've got to do something. We can't just sit here!" I whisper loudly.

The mother screams again, and I'm out of the car before I can think twice about it. But then, so is Theo. Even as I do it, I know it's a bad move, know we're probably going to end up getting hurt, but I can't just sit here and do nothing while those bastards hurt whoever they want.

"Stop it," I yell, charging across the highway toward them. Maybe if we're lucky, more people will step up. They can't stand against all of us. "Leave her alone."

The two men turn to glare at me, and I freeze under their stares. I can't help it. I've never seen such dead eyes in my entire life. There will be no reasoning with them, no talking them out of leaving her alone. I don't even have a weapon.

Their gazes rake me from top to bottom, and I feel the chill all the way down my spine. Eli was right. They're not going to be content to just hurt me. Still, I won't back down, won't show fear. Like with any wild animal, that's the kiss of death.

I know Theo's right next to me. I can feel the warmth radiating from his body. Behind us, Eli is rummaging in the car for something—I don't know what.

"Don't worry, darlin'," one of them says in a mockery of a southern drawl that makes my skin crawl. "There'll be plenty left for you when we're done with her."

He comes closer, and Theo grows even tenser, though I didn't know that was possible. He thrusts me behind him, stands up to his full height of six foot eight inches, and just watches, his face as blank and intimidating as ever. I know he's scared, can feel the fine tremor shaking him, but he doesn't back down an inch.

"Isn't robbing her enough?" Theo asks. "Get what you need and move on."

The second man points a pistol at Theo, cocks it. A scream wells up inside me, an apology for putting us in this situation. Already the other men have finished whatever they were doing up ahead, and are coming toward us. We need to get back in the car before they reach us, but it's already too late. I know it is.

There's no way they're going to let us just walk out of here.

"Why don't you get back in the car, son? You don't want to tangle with us." This from the man with the gun.

"I'm already tangling with you and you need to let that woman go."

"What I need is to let Mike here shoot your oversized ass."

An older man fumbles out of the car behind us. "Leave those kids alone!" he shouts.

"Really, Grandpa? Are you going to stop us?"

Two more men get out of their cars and join us. "You've got what you wanted. Now leave us alone," the first one says.

The two bikers exchange a look, like they know things are getting out of hand. Eli's behind me now, and he grabs my shoulder, tries to shove me back toward the truck. "Get in, Pandora."

Believe me, I want to. But standing here, watching these assholes figure out that things aren't going to be as easy as they expected them to be, makes me understand the power of numbers. And the power of speaking up. I'm not going to hide until they turn around and leave that woman, and these people, alone.

"Look, I'm going to give you one more chance," the biker with the gun growls. "And then someone's going to die." He waves the gun around, pointing it at all of us in turn before focusing it on me. "My friends are almost here. Get back in your cars and you won't be hurt."

I know he's right, can hear the other members of his gang running the last few feet toward us, cursing. I don't look, though. I can't. I'm spellbound as I stare down the barrel of the gun pointed right at my chest.

"Leave us alone!" someone else yells. And I can see it in the way the gun shifts, feel it in the hate emanating from the man pointing it at me. I'm about to die.

I start to drop to the ground at the same time Theo broadsides me, knocking me halfway to hell and back. I hit the ground hard, Theo on top of me, just as four shots ring out.

Theo goes limp on top of me at the third shot, and I

shove him out of the way, see that he's bleeding from his arm. "Oh my God! He shot you!"

I turn to Eli for help, but he's standing there, gun in his hand and face slack with shock. I look around wildly and realize what's happened. Two of those shots weren't from the bikers. They were from Eli. To save Theo, he's shot them both. One in the head and the other in the chest.

Horror, terror, revulsion, relief, shock all tear through me at the same time. I look around, realize every single person here is as freaked out as I am. I also realize the other bikers will reach us in seconds. All hell breaks loose as the growing crowd surges to meet them, ready for battle now that first blood has been drawn.

The chaos is the best chance we've got to escape, as I have a feeling the biker gang is not going to take the murder of two of its members very well.

"Can you stand?" I ask Theo.

"Yeah, sure." But he's pale, and looks like he's going into shock.

"Eli, can you help me?" I call urgently. He doesn't move, doesn't even acknowledge that I'm speaking to him. Just stares at the two men on the ground—one dead and one dying—in absolute horror.

I climb to my feet, then help Theo up and to the truck. "Get in the back," I tell him as I grab Eli. "We have to go."

He doesn't answer, so I shake him a little. "Eli, get in the truck!"

Still no response. I slap him across the face, hard. "Get in the fucking truck!" I shove him with all my strength.

It's enough to get his attention. He drops the gun and

though he moves slowly, like he's in a dream—or more accurately, a nightmare—Eli finally heads toward the truck. I think about picking up the gun but can't bring myself to do it. Instead, I follow Eli as he climbs in the driver's side, then scoots over as I shove against his shoulder and get behind the wheel.

"What are you going to do?" Theo demands from the backseat.

"Get the hell out of here. What do you think I'm going to do?"

I twist the steering wheel all the way to the right and hit the gas, just as one of the bikers reaches for the door handle. We scream onto the shoulder, taking out the bumper of the car in front of us. And then we're flying down the pavement, and I'm twisting and turning the wheel to avoid obstacles. Thank God it's a wide sidewalk.

I try to take the first right, but it's blocked off by men with motorcycles and guns, so I keep my foot on the gas and blaze straight ahead. This bottleneck has to end somewhere.

Shots ring out behind me, but they don't seem to hit anything vital and I'm not stopping to check. I plow ahead into town and onto a narrow sidewalk. I dodge a fire hydrant and mow down a small white picket fence and a bunch of patio tables and chairs that obviously belong to a sidewalk café.

Theo curses, but other than that keeps his mouth shut.

"Put pressure on the wound," I snarl. "You have to stop the bleeding."

"It's just my arm. I don't think it's bad."

"You got shot! That's pretty much the definition of bad, you moron!"

Up ahead, I can see freedom. Open, unrestricted road. But there's a huge line of motorcycles and men with guns between me and it. I glance in the rearview mirror—two motorcycles are closing in fast. They get a little distracted by the café debris, but I can't outrun them forever.

"Hold on!" I yell.

"What are you going to do?" Theo demands, sitting up. "No, Pandora. Don't!"

It's too late. I'm committed now. "Get out of the way, get out of the way, get out of the way," I murmur as I press the gas pedal all the way to the floor.

Two of the men level their guns at the truck. I grab Eli by the hair, shove him down. Duck low over the steering wheel and keep on driving, right through the makeshift barricade of men and machines.

37

THE CRUNCH OF METAL hitting metal rings through the cab, followed by the sickening *thud* of bodies that means they weren't fast enough to get out of the way—or were too stupid to believe that I would go through with it.

The truck shudders and bucks, but it's big and tough and going close to ninety miles an hour when it hits them. In the end, we make it through. I glance in the rearview mirror, see three or four men lying in the road. They're moving, but that's all I can say about them. I yank my gaze away, shove the horror down deep inside me. I can't think about them, about what I've done, and still function. Not now. Eli and Theo are depending on me.

I take the first right way too fast, make an immediate left, followed by another right. I don't know if they're still following us or not, but my gut instinct says they are and we need to hide. Otherwise, we're dead.

I drive about a quarter of a mile down what I think is a

main street in this small town, then make two quick lefts. "Where are you going?" Theo yells, hanging on to the back of the seat for all he's worth.

"I have no idea. Look for someplace we can hide."

I roll down the window, listen hard as I drive. From a couple of streets over, I can hear the roar of half a dozen motorcycles. I was right. They're looking for us, and they're nowhere near far enough away to make me comfortable.

I scan the streets even as I make another hairpin turn, going right this time. We're on a suburban street and there are lots of houses with garages, but I don't know if they're still occupied or if the owners have evacuated like so many of the people in this area. Don't know if I have the time to figure out how to open the doors, anyway.

Damn it, there's nowhere to go.

I take another right, for a second heading back in the direction we've just come from, looking for something, someplace, where we might have a chance . . .

A three-level parking garage looms large on the left, and I swing into it at the last second. I race past the ticket booth and around corner after corner, climbing higher and higher. I narrowly miss plowing into a group of cars parked right on the corner of the second floor.

I correct, keep driving until I get to the top. Part of me is terrified that I'm doing the exact wrong thing—if they follow us, we're trapped up here. But at the same time, we're trapped down there. There's a lot of them on very-easy-to-maneuver motorcycles that go a lot faster than this truck. It's only a matter of time before they catch us if we stay on the streets.

The only good thing about this is that the garage is attached to a building. I'm hoping I can get the guys inside and settled so that I can check out Theo's wound. Maybe find a blanket and something sugary for Eli to drink, as he's giving every indication that he's in shock.

Not that I blame him. I'm barely holding on after playing bumper cars with the bikers, all of whom were at least alive when I last saw them. I can't imagine what it would feel like to actually have shot someone. Killed him.

I careen to a stop outside the glass door leading to the third floor of the building. I get out and try to pull the door open, but it's locked. Whoever was in charge of security here took their job seriously before heading off for parts unknown.

I hear the roar of motorcycles down below and know I don't have much time. I rush to the back of the truck, pull out the jack Jean made sure to include in case we got a flat tire. Then race back to the door. I slam the jack into it and the whole thing shudders, sending vibrations up my arms to my shoulders, but it doesn't shatter.

Theo crawls out of the truck. "Let me help."

I glance at him, bloody, pale, swaying where he stands. "Yeah, right. I'd rather you don't die right here, okay?"

There's a small, narrow window to the right of the door. It's not much, but if I suck my stomach in really tightly, I just might make it through. I pull back the jack and hit the window with every ounce of strength I have.

It shatters easily, and I nearly go flying through it under the power of my hit. I stop myself, barely, but manage to slice my arm open on one of the pieces of broken glass. Terrific.

Theo leaps forward. "Pandora, are you all right?"

I roll my eyes at him. "I think I'll live. You're the one I'm worried about."

I rip off my shirt to do as Theo did a few days ago, knock out the glass, and squeeze my arm through the tiny window. It's a close fit, but I make it. I reach the other side of the door, flip the lock, and then swing it open.

"Get inside," I tell him. "See if you can find a room with a couch or something."

I go to the truck, open the door, and yank on Eli. "Look, I know you're freaked out. I would be, too. But I need some help here. Theo's hurt and those guys are coming after us. We have to hide."

It takes a few seconds, but Eli's blurry gaze finally focuses on me. "Can you get the backpacks?" I ask him. "Carry them inside?"

He shakes his head, as if waking from a nightmare. "Yeah, of course." He leans into the back, scoops up all the backpacks and a couple of the food bags.

I breathe a sigh of relief. "Follow Theo. See if you guys can find a room with a sink or something. We have to clean him up."

"Where are you going?"

"To park the truck. The broken window's bad enough. We don't need to put our location up in lights."

"I'll go with you."

"Go with Theo! He's the one who was shot."

The reminder seems to galvanize him, and he takes off down the hallway after his stepbrother. I watch until he catches up—it doesn't take long. Theo's moving slowly and listing to one side.

I glance in the back of the truck. Most of the seat is bright red. It must be worse than he's let on—he's lost a lot of blood.

"Damn, damn, damn." I hop back into the truck, put it in gear, and drive it down to the second level. I saw an SUV there with a cover over it. I park a couple of spaces down from the Suburban, rip the cover off it, and rush around our truck, tucking it under the canvas. I don't know if it will work, if it will fool them, but it's worth a try.

I'm just pulling the last corner down around the truck when I hear the motorcycles zooming up the ramp. I take off running as fast as I can, racing for the stairwell, hoping to get inside before they reach me.

The door is locked. Panic, complete and all-encompassing, races through me, takes me over, and I run like I've never run before. I make it onto the third-floor ramp just as the motorcycles zoom to the second level. Much as I hate to admit it, I'm really regretting not picking that gun back up.

I hear them shouting at each other as they look for the truck. Shit. We're screwed. I race toward the open door, see splotches of Theo's blood on the ground. I grab my shirt off the floor and wipe up every drop that I can see. Then I race inside, lock the door, and go flying down the dark hallway looking for Theo and Eli.

Eli grabs me as I pass the third doorway. "Hey, what's your rush?"

"They're here. We need to move."

We both look at Theo, who is stretched out on the conference table and looking like he can't go anywhere. He struggles to his feet, his breathing more labored than it was a little while ago, and I can see the puddle of blood on the table.

"Go," I tell Eli. "Get moving."

I grab my backpack from him, yank out my hoodie, and mop up the blood. Realize I'm bleeding as well and tie the ridiculous purple tank top around my wound. Then I'm chasing after them, checking each room for somewhere to hide.

Please don't let them decide to come in here. Please don't let them find us.

A gunshot rings out, followed immediately by the shattering of glass. They found the broken window and obviously managed to find a way through the door I couldn't open.

I give Theo my hoodie, make him press it to his wound so he doesn't leak any blood on the carpet and leave a trail that leads them right to us. We run faster, but I can tell Theo doesn't have much more fight left in him. I slam open a door that reads, DONALD MASTERTON, PRESIDENT, and yank them inside, shutting the door quietly behind us. It's not great, but it will have to do. Eli and Theo don't argue— they're too busy checking the room for weapons.

I go to the next doorway, find an executive bathroom with a walk-in closet to the left of the door. I drag Theo inside, hiss at Eli to follow us. As soon as he's in, I check the carpet for blood. There's a spot, on the right side, and I drag one of the big armchairs over to cover it.

Then I duck in the bathroom, and close the door. Lock it.

Eli has a wicked-sharp letter opener clutched in one hand and a large bottle of scotch in the other. "You're planning on getting drunk?" I whisper incredulously.

He rolls his eyes and dumps the scotch down the sink.

Then he goes into the closet, drops the backpacks on the floor, and slams the bottle as hard as he can against one of the back clothes racks. The bottom half of the bottle shatters jaggedly, and he hands what's left to me. It's not much against a group of angry bikers, but it's something, and I'm grateful to him for thinking of it.

Theo collapses toward the front of the closet—away from the broken glass—and I go to him. I tug him over to the left side, so that he's hidden behind the door if it opens. I check the bathroom floor for blood—nothing this time— and then close the closet door, locking it.

There are no windows in the closet, unlike the bathroom and office, so it's pitch-black in here except for the tiny strip of light that shines through the crack at the bottom of the door. The dark seeps inside me, terrifies me on a whole new level, and it's all I can do not to scream. Not to rip the door open as the excess adrenaline in my system ratchets the terror even higher.

I can't breathe in here, can't think. The walls feel like they're closing in, and my heart is pounding so hard and fast the beats are blurring one into the next.

Don't freak out, Pandora, I tell myself. *Don't lose it. Not yet.*

I don't, but it's hard. Harder than I ever would have imagined. I swallow the scream still swelling in my throat, but it's back seconds later, and harder to hold in.

Cold sweat rolls down my back. I move toward the back of the closet, my hand hovering over my backpack. If I can just turn on a flashlight, just get a little beam of light, I'll be okay. I swear I will.

Just the thought of having light at my fingertips calms me down a little, even though I don't unzip the pack. We can't risk a light in here, can't risk doing anything to attract attention. I just need to suck it up a little while longer and they'll be gone. This whole thing will be over. Just a little longer.

It becomes my mantra.

I scoot back up to Theo, put a hand on his knee. "You okay?" I whisper, almost soundlessly.

"Yeah." He doesn't sound okay, though.

"Here, let me put some pressure on your wound." I shift toward his shoulders, feel the warm stickiness of his blood beneath me on the ground. I don't know how much more he can lose and still be okay. Already, he's weaker than I've ever imagined he could be. I press the hoodie hard against the wound and he grunts softly. I shush him and keep the pressure steady. It's too dark to see if the bleeding is stopping, but at least it doesn't seem quite as bad anymore.

"Are you okay, Eli?"

"Yeah, fine." He sounds defensive and a little angry that I'm even asking, so I don't push the issue. If we live through the next half hour, then I'll worry about his psychological issues.

The door to the office crashes open.

38

"NOT IN HERE," someone calls, and I hold my breath. Sense Eli and Theo doing the same. Is it really going to be that easy? Are they not even going to check . . .

Heavy footsteps cross the room, and the bathroom door rattles. "It's locked."

"Check it out, anyway. They could be hiding in there."

Something hits the locked door handle once, twice, and then I hear the door open. I forget my fear of the dark in my dread of what is on the other side of the closet door.

Theo sits up silently, all trace of weakness gone as he slips the bottle out of my hand. Eli doesn't move, but I know he's ready, too. Not that I think we have much of a chance, but still . . .

"It's just a bathroom," the first man says.

"Empty?"

"Yeah."

"Then let's move it. I want to kill those little bastards myself."

The next thing I hear is their boots moving away, followed by the crash of the office door against the wall. Eli starts to stand up, but Theo and I both hold on to him. I shake my head vehemently. I know he can't see me, but I pray he gets the message. They're right next door—any sound, any movement, can still give us away.

We wait more than half an hour, each minute feeling like an eternity, until it seems safe to move a little. I scoot as quietly as possible over to my backpack. Pull out the flashlight and turn it on. Relief swamps me as the thin beam of light pierces the darkness.

"Let me see your wound," I whisper to Theo.

He shifts to make it easier for me to see. I unwrap the hoodie from his heavily muscled bicep and check out the damage. The bleeding has finally eased to a sullen ooze, but the hoodie is soaked. I don't know how much blood he's lost, but it seems like an awful lot.

"Is the bullet still in there?" Eli asks quietly, moving to sit on Theo's other side.

"No," Theo answers.

"How do you know?" I demand.

"I checked it out in the car. I've got a hole on both sides of my arm—I think that means it passed right through."

The description makes me queasy. "We're going to have to find you a doctor. Maybe this town has a hospital?"

"A hospital?" Theo asks incredulously. "Are you frickin' kidding me? One, you injured a bunch of those bikers, so if there is a hospital, they're probably going to be there. Two, they know that I've been shot, so again, even if they're not at the hospital for themselves, they're probably going to be there for me."

"Well, what do you suggest, then? You need a doctor."

"What I need is for you to clean out the wound. There's a couple of antibiotic shots in one of the first-aid kits your dad gave us, as well as a full course of antibiotics. I'll take it and I'll be fine."

"Clean out the wound? This isn't a dog bite. I can't just squirt some peroxide on it and hope for the best!"

"I don't think we have a choice." Eli glances at the door. "Do you think it's safe to open up?"

"I have absolutely no idea."

"All right, then. We'll give it a try." He unlocks the door and opens it, inch by inch. We've been in the dark so long that even the slow exposure to light makes us squint, struggle to see. I rub my eyes, listen intently, but I don't hear anything, thank God.

"Here, let me help you up," I say to Theo as I climb to my feet, extending my hand to him.

Eli snorts, elbows me gently out of the way. "Let me do it." A look passes between him and Theo, one I don't understand and haven't seen before. It makes me a little nervous, but things must be okay because Theo grabs on to Eli's hand with his good one and allows his stepbrother to pull him to his feet.

Out in the bathroom, his wound looks a million times worse. "We need to find a doctor," I say again, determined to talk sense into him.

"Yeah, well, we need a lot of things. I think a well-stocked first-aid kit is about as good as we're going to get. Besides, your arm is in almost as bad shape as mine."

My triceps throbs at the reminder, and I turn toward the mirror, wanting to see what it looks like. I blanch when I get my first glimpse of myself. With everything happening so quickly, I totally forgot that I was wearing a pair of jeans and a see-through bra. Nothing else.

"Oh my God!" My hands go in front of strategic places on my body, and Eli and Theo both laugh. I dive back into the closet for my backpack.

"We've already seen it, Pandora," Eli calls. "And do you really want to mess up another one of your shirts before you get yourself cleaned up?"

"Yes. Yes, I do."

I grab one of the tank tops they got me, slide it over my head. "Okay, let's try this again."

While I check out my arm—not great, but not terrible, either—I have Eli get the desk chair out of the other room and roll it into the bathroom for Theo to sit on. Then I brace myself to deal with Theo's wound, something I really don't want to do.

I open both first-aid kits, lay them out on the bathroom counter. Rummage through to see what's there, even though I already know. Then I rummage through again.

"Procrastinating's not going to get you anywhere," Theo says, amused.

Sure it will—it will keep me away from the huge hole in his arm, which is more than enough for me.

But then I look at Theo, really look at him. I notice the

pain bracketing his mouth and eyes, see how pale his skin is. I can't put this off any longer,

Reaching into the small linen closet in the corner, I pull out a handful of thick navy-blue towels. I wrap one around my arm and then spread another over Theo. "I'm going to have to wash this out. Or you'll get an infection."

The eyes staring at me are tired, but there's a grim amusement lurking in the back of them. "That's what I've been telling you all along."

There are two shots of lidocaine in the first-aid kit, and I use them both on Theo. I don't know if it's enough or too much, but he's a big guy, and I want him to feel as little as possible. It will help both of us.

"Are you numb?" I ask, poking at his arm.

"Not really, but go ahead."

"I swear, have neither of you ever had stitches?" Eli demands, exasperated. "You need to give it a few minutes to kick in."

"Oh. Well, in that case . . ." I lay out everything I'm going to need. As I do, I see that there's a problem, namely that there's no bandage big enough to fit the wound.

Eli notices, too. "I'll go look around and see what I can find," he volunteers.

"What if those guys are still out there?" I ask fiercely. "No way!"

"We haven't heard anything in a while, remember? And anyway, I'll be careful."

I start to protest more, to tell him all the reasons it's a bad idea to leave this office, but Theo latches onto my arm with his good hand. He doesn't say anything, but his steady look tells me to let Eli go.

Then he's gone, slipping out of the bathroom and out of the office in a few long strides.

The door closes behind him and I turn on Theo. "Why did you let him leave?"

"He needs a few minutes alone," Theo tells me. "Couldn't you tell? He's not handling the fact that he shot those two men very well. Give him a chance to walk it off."

"Walk it off?" I ask in astonishment.

"You know what I mean. He doesn't want to fall apart in front of us."

"Oh." There's nothing I can really say to that, so I concentrate on getting things ready to clean Theo's wound. I open some gauze pads, find the antibiotic shot he was telling me about—penicillin, it says.

Lidocaine, penicillin. These are controlled substances not found in your average first-aid kit. How did my dad get access to them? And how did he know we would need them?

But that's a whole different question, with an answer I don't want to dwell on too deeply. At least not right now. So I focus on Theo instead. I put on a pair of gloves and poke at the wound again.

"Do you feel that?"

His eyes are closed, his head resting back against the chair. "Feel what?" he asks.

That's exactly what I want to hear and definitely the best I can hope for. I wet a hand towel and then liberally douse it with soap. Then I rip the arm of Theo's shirt away.

His eyes pop open. "You know, Pandora, if you wanted

to rip my clothes off, all you had to do was ask. You didn't have to wait until I got shot."

His grin is a little goofy, and I wonder if it's possible for a local anesthetic to make you stoned as well as numb. Then I shake it off—probably not, but if it does, more power to him. It'll make things easier for both of us. Maybe we should have given him some of that scotch instead of dumping it all.

I lean forward and start to clean the jagged hole that runs through his bicep. He winces, but doesn't make a sound, and I figure if he can be this stoic about the whole thing, then so can I.

Even if it kills me.

The wound looks awful, and as I clean it, it starts to bleed again. It's angry and oozing and I'm scared I'm making it worse. By now, Theo is clutching the arm of the chair so hard that he's gouged holes in the leather.

"I'm almost done," I tell him.

"It's fine," he answers. I glance at him—his eyes are closed again, and sweat is dripping down his face.

I want to hurry this part up, but I don't want to miss anything that could lead to an infection later. After what feels like forever, I reach for a bottle of water and rinse the wound thoroughly to get rid of all the soap. Then I douse it in hydrogen peroxide, wincing as Theo growls low in his throat.

"Do you need more lidocaine?" I ask.

"*Is* there more?"

"No."

"Then why bother asking? Just get it done, okay?"

"Yeah. Sure." And then I douse his arm with iodine.

I only thought he was pale before. Theo turns whiter than I knew a human being could, his skin chalky and sick looking. Plus, it seems like he's going to throw up. I rush for the small trash can under the sink, thrust it at him.

He gives me a what-the-hell look, and I take it away again as he swallows convulsively, trying not to get sick.

"I'm sorry," I tell him. "I'm really sorry."

He shakes his head. "Next time, warn me, okay?"

"I thought it'd be better if you didn't know what was coming."

"Obviously not." He runs his good hand through his hair. "Are we done?"

"I don't know. I mean, do I need to do anything else?"

Please let him say no, please let him say no. I'm not sure how much more of this I can take—and I'm not even the one who's injured.

But the wound is bleeding again, pretty steadily, and I know what's coming before Theo even opens his mouth. "I think you're going to have to stitch it. Do you know how to sew?"

A million answers run through my head, and all of them start with variations of "Hell, no!" But I figure why waste my energy on protesting when it's abundantly clear that he does need stitches. And that there's no one else around to do them.

But that doesn't mean I have to be gracious about it.

I rummage through the first-aid supplies until I find the suture kit. The needle is long and supersharp and pretty much scares the crap out of me. There are also three different kinds of thread, or sutures, or whatever you call them, all different widths. I don't have a clue which one to use.

In the end, I decide on the middle one—it looks pretty multipurpose—but my hands are shaking so badly that it takes me three or seven tries before I'm able to thread the needle.

I don't want to do this. I don't want to do this. I *really* don't want to do this. I took a sewing class last year with Emily, who talked me into it because she said it would help with the costumes for the school plays. Sliding a needle through fabric is a far cry from doing it to human flesh.

But Theo's waiting, his whole body tense, and it's not fair to torture him just because I can't work up the nerve to do what needs to be done. *Just finish it*, I tell myself. *And then you can fall apart later.*

When I'm ready, I look at Theo, who is very determinedly not looking at me or the instrument of torture in my hand. "Are you ready?" I ask.

He laughs and it sounds rusty. "No. But do it, anyway."

I squeeze his hand and he latches onto me, his big fingers squeezing mine tightly for the space of one heartbeat, two. And then he's pulling away, taking a deep breath. "I'm okay."

The next fifteen minutes are among the most excruciating of my life. I hate every single stitch, have to brace myself for the little "pop" of the needle every time it slides through Theo's flesh. And it slides through a lot of times.

He's a great patient, doesn't move, doesn't say a word to distract me, but still. By the time I'm finished, I'm a nervous wreck. Shaky, sweaty, scared to death.

When the last stitch is done on the second side, I knot the thread quickly and then drop the needle onto the counter. I'll clean it up later. All I know right now is that if I never have to touch that thing again it will be too soon.

"How're you feeling?" I ask Theo, crouching down in front of him.

His smile is weak. "I've been better."

"I bet." I strip off the gloves, then fumble two Advil out of a package, as well as the first of the antibiotic pills. "You need to take these."

He nods, and I hand him a bottle of water from his backpack.

I wash my hands as he takes the medicine. When he's done, Theo hands me the empty water bottle. I set it aside to refill, then look at him, really look at him for the first time since this whole thing began.

"We need to get you cleaned up." I glance at the glass shower stall in the corner. "Get the blood rinsed off you."

"You have no idea how good that sounds." He pushes to his feet, sways unsteadily for a second, then seems to get it together.

"Do you, umm . . ." I look everywhere but at him. "Do you need help?"

He grins. It's weak, but it's definitely a grin. "I think I've got it."

Oh, thank God. Stitching him up was one thing, but dealing with a completely naked Theo is something else entirely.

I quickly finish cleaning up, then yank a pair of jeans out of Theo's backpack, lay them next to the largest towel I can find on the edge of the counter closest to the shower. I don't include a shirt because I'm afraid getting into one will strain his stitches.

"I'm going out there." I point to the office. "See about getting something for you to eat."

"Okay."

I nod, start to leave, but he grabs my hand with his good one, stops me in my tracks. "Thank you."

I go to brush it off—I'm the one who got him shot, after all—but when I turn back to him there's an intensity in his eyes that I can't ignore. That I don't want to ignore. "I'm just glad you're okay." I have a difficult time getting my tongue around the words.

Theo must understand, though, because he reaches up, strokes the back of his hand over my cheek. My breath catches in my throat, and I turn my face a little, press my cheek more firmly into his touch. It feels good, right, the spark that's been there between us from the very beginning building to a full conflagration. To something more.

I lift my hand, cover his so that our fingers tangle together. He squeezes just enough to let me know he's as affected by this moment as I am. I smile, then, and he smiles back, a lopsided grin that has no trace of his usual coldness. And when his thumb brushes over my lips, once, twice, it's all I can do not to close the small distance between us.

I want to feel his body against mine, want to know— really know—that he's safe. That he's going to be okay. I actually take a step forward before reason kicks in and I stumble back. He's been shot, for God's sake. Now is not the time to be thinking about anything but helping him heal.

"Try not to get your arm wet." My voice is huskier than usual, and though I clear my throat, it doesn't change. "And call me if you, umm, need anything."

He laughs. Here I am, doing my best Florence Nightingale impression when all I really want to do is curl up against him and make him promise me that everything is going to be okay, and he has the gall to laugh. I pick up the backpacks and flounce into the other room, closing the bathroom door firmly behind me.

It doesn't matter. I can still hear him laughing.

While he showers, I clean the gash on my own arm. It's not as deep as I originally thought, so after I douse it with peroxide and iodine—which, I might add, gives me a whole new sympathy for Theo—I bandage it up and hope for the best. Nothing else to do right now.

I glance at the huge ticking clock on the wall. It's close to five thirty. This whole terrifying, mind-numbing experience only took about three hours. It's hard to imagine as it feels like several lifetimes have passed since we left the farm earlier.

Theo comes out of the bathroom dressed in jeans and an old Aerosmith T-shirt. It's from their *Pump* album, the one with the two trucks on the cover, and I stare at him for a second, shocked. If there was one person in the world— besides my mother—who I'd guess would never wear that T-shirt, it would be Theo. Looking at him in it makes me wonder what else I'm wrong about in regard to him.

I guess I stare at the shirt longer than I think, because he finally asks, "Is something wrong?"

"You didn't hurt your arm getting into that?" I seize on the excuse.

He holds up the arm in question. "I'm good."

"Still, you need to lie down for a while," I tell him, gesturing toward the couch.

"I'm fine. I just want some water. I'm thirsty."

"That's because of the blood loss." I walk him to the couch, and when he stands over it, like he's going to argue, I give him just a little push. The fact that he topples onto the couch and doesn't immediately get back up tells me more than anything else can about how he's doing.

"Here, drink this." I hand him a bottle of water. "And then you need to eat."

I reach for an apple to hand to him, but at that moment, the office door slams open. We both jump, thinking it's the bikers coming back for a second look, but it's only Eli. And his arms are loaded with medical supplies.

"There's a doctor's office on the second floor. I got bandages and a bunch of other stuff we might be able to use." He deposits the supplies on the desk, then opens a big plastic bag that he's been carrying. "And I brought dinner à la vending machine. It's not great, but it's something." He pulls out a few sandwiches, some yogurt, a couple of bananas.

I reach for a roast beef sandwich and hand it to Theo. "You need protein after all that blood loss. It will help replenish the iron you lost."

"Since when are you a nurse?"

"Since you made me perform surgery on you." I shudder. "I'm going to have nightmares for the next six months."

He flashes a grin that looks tired but real. "Careful, Pandora, a guy could get the wrong idea with all this babying."

Eli slams a bottle of Coke down on the table harder than necessary. "I only brought enough for dinner, but I figure we can raid it again before we leave."

"That sounds really good, thanks." I smile at him.

"Did you see anyone?" Theo asks, levering himself into a sitting position so he can eat.

"No one. I didn't hear anything, either, even when I peeked into the parking lot. I think they're gone."

My entire body relaxes, and I bite into my sandwich—turkey and cheese—with a lot more relish than the sad, soggy thing deserves.

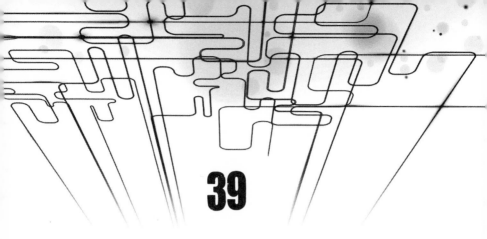

39

AN HOUR LATER and we're back on the road again (big surprise), heading toward Hugoton, Kansas, and this time we're in a Toyota minivan. The guys were exceptionally disappointed with my choice, but it's not like there was so much to work with in the parking garage. And besides, there's not much in the world more nondescript than a silver minivan. I swear, half of America drives one.

I really wished we'd had more time to stick around the office building. I know it was just a holding pattern—we weren't going anywhere or doing anything—but Theo needs more rest. He's stretched out in the back right now, arm bandaged and high on the painkillers Eli found in the doctor's office. He's dozing, but when I glance in the rearview mirror at him, I can tell he's uncomfortable. Not that it's a hard guess—he *was* shot, after all.

Eli's driving and I'm sitting next to him, trying to sleep, since I'm next at the wheel. It isn't working. Every time I close my eyes, the last few days play in my head until I feel like screaming. Like crying. How did I go from being a seventeen-year-old girl worried about my calculus grade to a cold-blooded almost-murderer?

My stomach twists and turns, and I shift uncomfortably in my seat. If I feel this bad, how is Eli feeling?

I glance at him out of the corner of my eye. His mouth is grim, his fingers tight on the steering wheel, and I think he looks a little green. "You okay?" I ask.

"Yeah, why?" He doesn't look at me, keeps his attention firmly on the road.

"I don't think Theo or I ever thanked you for—"

"Don't!"

I freeze. "I'm sorry," I say in the most soothing voice I can muster.

"Jesus, don't apologize, either. Just don't thank me."

"You saved our lives."

His grip on the wheel tightens even more—I can tell by the way his knuckles drain of color. "I don't want to talk about it. I'd do it again, but that doesn't mean I want to dwell on what I did. I just want to forget it."

Me, too. I start to tell him I don't think it will be as easy as it sounds, but he chooses that second to glance over at me, and his eyes are so tormented that I don't say anything. I just reach for him, squeeze his shoulder.

He shrugs me off, but before I can be embarrassed or hurt, he takes his right hand off the wheel and grabs on to mine like it's a lifeline, squeezing so hard that I have to work not to wince. Eventually his grip eases a little, but he doesn't let go. We drive like that for a long time, holding hands for comfort and watching the road in front of us as we chase it down, one mile at a time.

Eventually I flip on the radio. We haven't listened to it at all today, and while I don't really want to know what's going on, I figure we need to. We listen to the only station we can find for a while before the panicked voice of a radio commentator fills the car. "We've just received some . . ." His voice breaks. "Just received some devastating news here, for Europe and the whole world. The Dungeness Nuclear Power Stations in Kent, England, have suffered a mass breach. Nuclear radiation began leaking yesterday at a higher rate than expected, and early this morning an explosion rocked the plant, releasing a never-before-seen amount of nuclear radiation into the atmosphere. A mushroom cloud the size of which we've only imagined in sci-fi movies hovers over England.

"Mass death is being reported, though no one has been able to give a numerical estimate yet. Those who did not die outright are suffering burns and radiation poisoning at such a high level that death is imminent.

"Again, for those of you just tuning in, the Dungeness Nuclear Power Stations in Kent, England, have suffered the worst nuclear accident in history. While they are the first since Pandora's Box was opened four days ago, they surely will not be the last. Already, low levels of radiation are leaking from plants all over the world as their cooling systems fail, and it is only a matter of time until they all meet the same fate as the Dungeness Station.

"The Pandora's Box countdown says six days until total annihilation, but many of the world's experts believe that is an optimistic number. As nuclear power plants continue to hemorrhage at an alarming rate, we may only be looking at three or four days before the catastrophic, the unthinkable, happens."

Eli slams his hand against the steering wheel hard enough to leave bruises. I lean forward, switch off the radio, and we drive the rest of the way in silence. There really isn't anything else to say.

"We're here," Theo says as we drive past a sign that reads, WELCOME TO HUGOTON, NATURAL GAS CAPITAL, and another one, a little farther down the road, that reads, I ♥ HUGOTON, POPULATION 3,955.

"Oh, joy." Sorry if I sound bitter, but really, it's hard to get excited about this. Because while Jean may have convinced Theo and Eli that we're looking for an ethanol factory, I'm more than a little afraid that what we're actually looking for is a cornfield.

Every other picture has been of the exact area we need to visit—why should this one be any different? Of course, judging by the number of cornfields we've already driven by, finding the right one could be the biggest challenge yet.

Things go dim all of a sudden, and I look out the window just in time to see a huge storm cloud, dark gray and ominous looking, slide in front of the sun. Off in the distance—over one of the ubiquitous cornfields—lightning sizzles across the sky. About ten seconds later a huge rumble of thunder rolls through the air above us, shaking the ground with its intensity.

Of course. Because the only thing worse than looking for a specific cornfield in Kansas is looking for a specific cornfield in Kansas in the middle of a thunderstorm. I look at the guys in the front seat, try to see if they're thinking the same thing I am. Eli looks blissfully unconcerned, while Theo is driving with the same grim focus he always has.

He turns at—you guessed it—Main Street, and as we drive through the streets of Hugoton, I'm struck by how different it is from Colorado Springs. Not just in size, but in atmosphere.

Here, there are no tanks in the street, no men in military trucks, and there doesn't appear to have been any looting—at least not in the area we're in.

There are people in the streets here, talking to each other while the occasional car drives by. It's a tiny town, certainly the smallest we've had as a destination so far, though we've driven through towns smaller than this on the back roads in both New Mexico and Colorado.

"I guess we could just ask someone," Eli suggests. "It's not like there are so many plants around here that no one will know what we're talking about."

"What about cornfields?" I ask, still annoyed about the crazy task in front of us. "Should we ask them where to find this one?" I wave the picture around.

Theo and Eli ignore me, which only makes me feel more like a little girl throwing a tantrum. Closing my eyes, I practice some deep yoga breathing and try to calm down. It doesn't work, but I bite my tongue to keep from saying anything obnoxious as Theo pulls up to two old men sitting on a wooden bench in front of a mercantile-type store.

I'm astonished to realize that it's still open, and there are still goods on the shelves. Not a lot, but some. And while there's no electricity, it's still in good shape, unlike everywhere else we've been. I can't help wondering why that is.

Is it because everyone knows everyone else, and it's a lot harder to destroy the property of people you work with or have had dinner with? Or is it just that small towns operate on a completely different system of chaos and disorder than large cities do?

I start to lean forward, to ask the men if they've had any problems around here at all, but after giving Theo directions—he was right, there's only one ethanol plant in town—one tells him, "Going out there is just a waste of your time. That plant is closed up tighter than a drum."

"Yeah," the other one says, a serious look on his weathered face. "And there's a storm brewing. Looks like a nasty one. There's not much left open in town, but you're welcome to come to my house and sit out the storm, if you'd like."

His generosity and trust in the face of everything going on humble me. Make me feel even more churlish and childish. And do what Eli and Theo haven't been able to do—convince me that we really have a chance to win this. My father may no longer see the good in the world, may think that setting us back to zero is the only way to fix things, but that doesn't mean I have to agree with him.

"Thanks," Theo tells him. "We appreciate the offer, but we're in kind of a hurry."

"Yeah, but do you know how to drive in a storm like this?" the first man asks.

"We'll be careful," Eli promises. "Thanks again for your help."

Still, once we pull away from the curb, Theo starts driving pretty fast. "I want to beat the storm out to the ethanol plant if we can. That way, instead of wasting the time sitting around waiting for the storm to end, we can be inside, trying to figure out what we're supposed to find."

We ride the twelve or so miles to the ethanol plant in silence. Theo's concentrating on driving, Eli's lost in thought, and, as for me, I just keep glancing out the back window at the storm that's chasing us. For most of the drive, Theo's done a good job of keeping ahead of it, but in the last couple of minutes it's started closing in fast.

I turn back around, peer out through the sudden darkness at the huge buildings and tanks looming to the right of us. We're almost there, the turnoff to the plant only a few hundred yards ahead. I point it out to Theo as a lightning bolt splits the sky in front of us. It's followed, only a second later, by a huge clap of thunder.

"Hurry," I tell him. "We can't get caught out here in this."

"I know." His voice is grim, his eyes narrowed in concentration.

"What's the big deal?" Eli asks. "It's just some rain—"

He breaks off as something slams hard against our windshield.

"What was that?" he demands, while Theo makes the sharp turn as fast as he can and speeds down the lane toward shelter.

As he drives, the loud bang is followed by a bunch of

other hits against the roof of the car, one right after another, like machine-gun fire.

"It's hail," I tell him as Theo slows down the van considerably.

"Maybe we should have taken the old guy up on his offer," Eli says uneasily, and I realize that, as a California boy, he might never have seen hail.

Before I can answer, more hail hits us, slamming into the windshield, the hood of the van, the roof, the tailgate. From what I can see—which, admittedly, isn't much—it's the size of golf balls. Maybe even bigger.

"Shit." Theo hits the brakes, and the van slips and slides across the muddy road before finally coming to a stop.

"What are you doing?" Eli demands. "We're sitting ducks like this."

Theo is too busy turning the wheel and creeping forward, angling the van directly into the hailstorm to answer him, so I say, "Yeah, well, getting hit by hail when we're stationary is a lot better than getting hit by it while we're moving."

"The faster the car is going, the more impact the hail is going to make," Theo adds.

"You guys should get back here." I scoot to the far right of the backseat, trying to give them more room. "I don't think that windshield is going to make it."

Seconds later, three hailstones the size of baseballs hit the windshield, one right after the other. The last one actually craters the windshield, making a tangerine-size hole in it. Eli jumps and scrambles into the back. Theo quickly follows, and we sit out the storm huddled together as best we can.

Outside, the wind picks up, slamming hail and debris hard against the driver's side of the van. Rocking us back and forth. Another hailstone slams through the windshield, making another large hole for rain and cold air to flow through. I glance at Eli, and he's paler than I've ever seen him. Not that I blame him. I've been in dozens of hailstorms, and this is making me crazy-nervous. I can only imagine what he's feeling right now.

Eventually, the air cools enough that the hail stops. I breathe a sigh of relief, even though the storm is showing no sign of abating. But I can handle rain. It's the hail that makes me nervous. All my life I've heard horror stories of people dying from getting hit in the head by hailstones. Jules always tells me they're just urban myths, but I've seen enough stories about it on the news to know it's possible.

"Is it done?" Eli asks. In answer, lightning arcs across the sky, thunder following almost simultaneously.

"Not quite," Theo mutters, even as he climbs back in the front seat to get a better look at the world around us.

"The hail is over," I tell Eli.

"But the storm's just getting started." Theo points at the sky to the left of us, where new bolts of lightning are ripping through the clouds every second or so. Thunder has become a continuous, never-ending rumble that shakes the truck and the ground all around us.

I look on in horror, knowing what Theo is going to say even before he gives voice to his thoughts. "We can't," I tell him.

"We have to," he says, trying to start the van. "Eli's right. We're sitting ducks out here."

"I thought the hail was done," Eli says.

"It is. But the lightning's just beginning." The engine won't catch, making a high-pitched whiny noise every time Theo tries to turn over the ignition. It wasn't in the best shape to begin with, and the storm must have damaged something.

Theo says as much, and Eli responds with, "Who cares? We'll wait for the storm to blow past, and then we'll search the plant. Surely they have some kind of truck we can take."

Theo's hands clench around the steering wheel, while the nerves jangling through my system coalesce into a cold ball of fear in the pit of my stomach. "We're not going to be able to wait. We've got to get out of here," he tells us.

"Are you nuts?" Eli demands. "It's lightning out there."

Theo glances at me. "You know I'm right."

I nod because I can't speak. All the saliva in my mouth has suddenly dried up. Still, I reach for my boots and slide my feet into them, ignoring the pain from the blisters on my heels. The boots are rubber soled, which gives me a better shot at surviving this latest twist.

"I *don't* know you're right!" Eli shakes his head in disbelief as another flash of lightning slams into the ground a few yards from us.

"This van is the only metal thing out here," I tell him. "It's going to get hit by lightning."

"*We'll* get hit if we go out there. Besides, I thought the tires made the car safe."

"Maybe so, but I'm not willing to take that risk. Especially with those holes." Theo points to the destroyed windshield. "If the storm gets worse, the last place we want to be is in a truck that doesn't work and can't block out the elements or flying debris."

"I'm not going out there—"

"Yes, you are." Theo's tone leaves no room for disagreement. He points to the closest building. "That's where we're going. You ready, Pandora?"

No. Not even close. But as lightning electrifies the sky around us, I know we're out of time. "Let's go."

I slip my backpack over my shoulders, grab the door handle, slide it open. "In case lightning struck the van or the ground near us, when you jump out make sure you land on both feet," I tell Eli. He nods, grim faced. I give him a reassuring smile that I'm far from feeling, and then I jump.

The frigid rain hits me, followed immediately by the sharp slap of the wind that nearly knocks me to the ground. But then Theo and Eli are there, on either side of me, grabbing my elbows and bolstering me up. "Let's go!" Theo shouts.

Bent low, we take off running, dodging around or leaping over debris every few steps. I look at the ground, fighting the wind and doing my best not to trip as I trust Theo to guide us in the right direction. Putting one foot in front of the other is hard enough right now without having to worry about direction, too.

Still, with the wind pushing powerfully against us, it seems to take forever to get where we're going. I'm exhausted, terrified, barely able to catch my breath in the electrified air all around us.

I stumble, go down onto one knee.

Get back up.

Run a few more feet.

Stumble again.

This time I hit the ground hard. Before I can push myself up, Theo lifts me against him, throws me over his shoulder in a fireman's carry, and takes off even faster toward the building.

I don't fight him, though my face flames with embarrassment as his breathing grows heavier. I'm not overweight, but at almost six feet tall, I'm not a hundred pounds, either.

We finally make it to the building, just as lightning explodes around us. I hear a loud *pop*, see the van light up for a second. Theo and Eli don't notice as they're busy trying to find a way inside, but my heart nearly stops. We could have been in there.

Before I can wrap my mind around what I've just seen, Theo slides me to the ground. He tries the door right in front of us while Eli tries one about fifteen yards away. Neither one opens. At that moment, lightning hits the ground a few feet from us.

"Screw this," I hear Theo mutter, and then he kicks the door as hard as he can. Eli runs over, joins him. A few seconds later, the door rips away from its hinges. We're in.

We rush across the room, not stopping until we get to the center, well away from the open door. Then we collapse on the floor in a heap. We watch the storm raging through the windows that line the right side of the room.

I don't know how long we sit there. Long enough for my heart to stop racing and my clothes to grow clammy. More than long enough for my body to start registering the new aches and pains that falling twice has given me.

I stretch a little, groan as my muscles protest.

Theo looks at me with a frown. "Are you okay?"

"Just peachy." I smile a little to soften the sarcasm of my answer.

He clears his throat. "I guess trying to beat the storm out here wasn't such a good idea, after all."

Eli and I just sit and stare at him in amazement. And then we start to laugh.

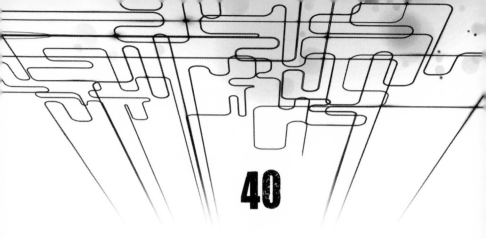

40

IT TAKES ME LONGER TO STOP laughing than it does Eli. When I finally wind down, he and Theo are staring at me with bemused expressions on their faces. I want to reassure them that our mad dash through the storm isn't the thing that's finally pushed me around the bend, but since I can still feel a bubble of hysteria deep inside me, I'm not sure it's the truth.

"So?" I ask when I catch my breath. "Any bright ideas?"

Eli shakes his head. Theo says, "Not a one."

"That's what I was afraid of." I push to my feet. "I guess we should probably start looking for the clue. Whatever it is."

"We don't know that it's in this building," Eli says as he, too, stands.

"Yeah, but we don't know that it isn't, either." I pull my flashlight out of my backpack. It's dark outside, and any small amount of light cast by the moon and stars has pretty much been obliterated by the storm clouds.

I shine the light around, try to figure out what kind of building we're in.

This room is huge and cavernous, with large stainless-steel tables running the length of the back wall, covered in chemistry supplies. There are a number of what look like lab stations set up in the center of the room—that's what Eli, Theo, and I had been leaning against when we first got in here—and a chemical shower in the front corner. I know what it is because it looks just like the one in my AP Chem classroom.

When I shine the light up, I realize I can't see the ceiling. The second and third floors are built so that they ring the edges of the building and look down on this central lab. I'm not sure what's up there, but I do know one thing. This is a huge building with a million places to search. And it's just one of the buildings at this plant. If we don't get lucky here, God only knows how long we're going to be at this.

With the way things have been going, I think our only hope is to keep moving. Staying around here for too long is just asking for trouble.

Theo comes up behind me, places his hands on my shoulders and starts to rub exactly where it hurts. I almost ask him how he knows, but I'm afraid he'll stop—and the absence of pain feels so good that I want it to go on forever.

"You want to search down here?" he asks softly. "Eli can take the second floor, and I'll do the third."

"The faster we get started, the faster we'll be done," Eli says, coming to stand next to us.

"Sure." Reluctantly, I pull away from Theo. "I just wish I knew what we were looking for."

"You can't remember anything about this place?" Theo asks.

"Nothing."

"Piece of cake," Eli tells me with a wink.

"Yeah. Right."

I move away from him, start looking over the stainless-steel tables against the wall. As I look, I hear Eli and Theo head toward the metal stairs in the corner. They start to climb, and I bend down, look under the tables. Nothing. Big surprise.

As I get to the end of the wall, the noise from the storm suddenly seems much louder. There's also a banging sound I can't identify, at least not until I turn the corner and see a dull slice of light. It's incongruous here, where the only light should be coming from our flashlights. The banging is getting louder, though, so I follow it—and the odd beam of light. That's when I realize it's a weak flashlight, pointing at a wide-open back door. The door is banging against the wall, and I rush to close it. As I do, I can't help wondering who the flashlight belongs to. The not knowing makes me nervous. Still, I keep going until I stumble over some debris from the storm. I nearly fall, but slap my hand against the wall to steady myself. As I do, I look down and realize what I've tripped over. It's the thing that's holding the door open. Not debris, but a human hand.

I'm too tired, too inoculated to horror, to stage a full-blown, center-stage meltdown. I do, however, turn my head and call for the guys. Just because I can cope doesn't mean I have to do so on my own, after all.

Eli comes running, Theo at his heels, and together the

three of us pull the man inside. He's dressed in a blue T-shirt with the words "Liquid Gold" on it and a pair of jeans, steel-toed boots on his feet. And he's dead. Not injured, not unconscious like I first thought, but dead. We're too late to do any good, which seems to be the story of our lives lately.

Still, we can't just leave him here to rot, can't pretend he doesn't exist. The guys carry him into an empty room down the hall, and I find a blanket, drape it over him the same way I did the woman in the convenience store yesterday morning.

They say everything gets easier if you do it enough, but as I stand over this man, I don't think I'll ever get used to dealing with death. I hope I won't, because if I do, I'm afraid that's when I'll lose the last kernel of hope I carry inside me. When I'll let the evil win.

I can't stand it anymore, so I turn. Walk away. Try to focus on what I was doing before I saw him. But I can't. There's something about that man. Something about—

I run to where Eli dropped our backpacks earlier, rip mine open, and pull out my laptop. I look back at where the man lies under the blanket, and I know what the code words are. I remember standing there, in that cornfield, staring at the ear of corn in my father's hand and listening as he spoke about ethanol and biomass and the future.

I type in the words on the man's shirt—"liquid gold"— which is how my father always referred to ethanol. The game beeps, and I'm back in Louisiana, standing in front of an oil-drenched Gulf of Mexico.

Theo and Eli see what I'm doing and come running. "Did you—"

"Yes."

"Awesome," Eli crows, picking me up and swinging me around. "That's my girl."

Theo's more subdued, but his grin looks just as real. When he smiles at me like this, it feels like I've won the lottery—it's so different from the cold, blank face I used to get from him, and sometimes still do.

"So where are you now?" he asks.

"The Gulf. I think we're supposed to clean up the mess from the latest oil spill."

"Really?" Theo cocks an eyebrow. "And how are we supposed to do that when the experts haven't been able to figure out how?"

"I have no idea." The guys settle down next to me with their iPads, and together we race to beat the ten-minute time limit. I press a bunch of buttons, trying to figure out what my new power is. Eli and Theo are doing the same, but nothing happens. At least not until a shimmery gold glow appears in the distance.

We have to get to it—I'm not sure how I know this, but I do. And I'm not the only one. A couple of the other players who followed us through the AR gate have noticed the glow as well and rush toward it, dodging around various obstacles the game has laid in our path.

I get tripped up attempting to scale the edges of a bridge that spans the mouth of the Mississippi and plummet into the disgusting oil-and-pollutant-rich water below. Eli and Theo try to catch me, but they're too far away.

"Keep going," I tell them as I search for a way out of the filthy river. It isn't easy. Ships keep cruising by, churning up the river and knocking me into currents that try to pull me deeper and deeper underwater. I struggle back to the surface time and again, but I'm getting weaker. I can feel it, even before I see that my life and power points are spiraling downward.

"Are you out?" Theo demands as he continues to hurtle through obstacles.

"No. Damn it."

"I'm coming back for you."

"Don't." Already the glow in the distance is diminishing. "You need to get to that glow quickly."

Above us there's another huge crack of lightning, followed almost immediately by a loud rumble of thunder. Seconds later, a deafening screech rips through the air.

"What *is* that?" I ask.

"I'll go check." Eli leaps to his feet.

"We only have four minutes left to beat this level! We don't have time for this."

"It's not going to do us any good to level up if we end up dying for real," Theo tells me as he follows his brother.

He's barely done speaking before another series of high-pitched shrieks nearly rupture my eardrums. I duck my head and cover my ears, even as I start gathering up my stuff. I finally recognize the sound—a heavy-duty battery-operated fire alarm is going off. Which can only mean the lightning has finally gotten lucky and hit something flammable.

I run to the window behind Eli and watch as the world lights up all around us, fire streaking along the ground as it follows what I can only assume is an ethanol trail. One of the big tanks must have gotten damaged and this fire—beautiful, hypnotizing, terrifying—is the result.

"We've got to go!" Eli shouts, shoving his iPad beneath his shirt.

"Isn't it safer to stay in here?" I scream above the alarm.

"The fire's already in here," Theo yells. "Why do you think the alarm's going off." He, too, protects his iPad under his shirt, and, numbly, I do the same to my laptop. Then we grab our backpacks and rush for the open door, flying through the central laboratory, and back out into the night. There is lightning outside, but somehow risking a lightning strike sounds better than sealing ourselves in a building and burning alive.

The cold air strikes my face as we run. It stings, but not as badly as earlier. The rain has let up some, which might be good for us but is doing nothing to stop the fire, which is growing in strength as it zips straight toward the leaking ethanol tank. "It's going to blow!" I scream.

But Theo and Eli are already ahead of me on the realization front. They run for the closest shelter they can find, the walkway under a flight of outside stairs, and drag me in their wake. It's far from ideal, but it's better than nothing when, seconds later, the huge ethanol tank explodes.

Theo throws himself over me as debris rains down. Most of what comes this way hits the stairs above us, thank God, but some falls through the gaps between the steps, while other debris flies in from the side, propelled straight out by the power of the blast.

In the middle of it all, curled into a ball for protection, Eli pulls out his iPad and once again starts to play.

"What are you doing?" I yell at him. "Cover your head!"

"There's not much time left. Only a couple of minutes."

"Damn." Theo and I move so that we're partially shielding him as well. A searing piece of metal falls through a crack in the stairs and lands on my leg, burning me through my jeans. As I jerk around like crazy, trying to knock it off, I wonder how many burns Theo's sustained while covering me.

"I'm sorry," I tell him, even as I pull out my own laptop and try to play. For all I know, my avatar could be dead, considering it was stranded in the middle of the Mississippi when we made our mad dash under the stairs.

I'm not dead, though. Another player whom I don't recognize—Darkness191—has pulled me to safety. My avatar lies gasping on the edge of the river, while his stands over me. I want to thank him, but it will have to wait until I'm in a safer place.

Eli makes it to the glow on the other side of the river, which I now realize is at least half of the Greek pantheon. Poseidon reaches out, touches him on the head, and Eli begins to turn green. Not a glowy green, like has happened to me, but kind of a sick green that sweeps over him from his feet to his head.

He plays with a few keys, and a steady stream of green comes from his fingertips in a strange wavy line. When I zoom in, I see it seems to contain a bunch of microorganisms.

"What are you doing?" I ask as other players crowd around to watch him.

"I have no idea," Eli says, except as he presses more

buttons the microorganisms grow, change shape, become other, larger organisms.

As he continues to produce more and more, each a little different from the one that came before it, the first organisms launch themselves onto the oil spill and begin to eat. The countdown continues: 14, 13, 12, 11, . . . Eli produces more and more organisms, launching them into the water faster and faster. They gobble up the oil spill, but it's not fast enough. There's no way the life that Eli's created is going to be enough. No way it can get through everything in time.

Theo must reach the same conclusion, because he rolls off me—the debris has stopped falling—and launches himself into the game. With six seconds to go, his avatar holds his hands out and sets fire to all of the remaining oil spill.

The last of it disappears just as the clock hits zero. Which is a good thing, because at that moment another huge explosion rocks the ethanol plant.

41

I START TO DUCK AND COVER AGAIN, but Eli yells, "We have to go!"

I want to argue with him, but the world around us is one giant inferno. There's fire surrounding us on nearly every side, huge walls of flames that are spreading in a wide circle that is closing in rapidly from both directions.

"Come on!" Eli yells again, tugging Theo and me to our feet. I glance at Theo, whose face is completely white, and I know he's in bad shape. There are numerous holes in his T-shirt from where burning debris got him, and his bullet wound has started to bleed again.

When he takes a step forward, he sways a little. "He's not going to make it," I tell Eli, wrapping my arm around Theo's waist to brace him. When I touch him, I realize he's burning up. Despite my best efforts, infection has set in from one of his wounds and he has a raging fever.

Anything else? I want to scream to fate, to the universe. To my father. Is there any other obstacle you want to give us right about now? Because, seriously, this doesn't seem like enough. We need more.

"Here!" Eli shoves his iPad into his backpack and tosses it to me. "Take this." And then he bends down, puts a shoulder into Theo's midriff. Theo crumples over him, and Eli stands up slowly, staggering under his stepbrother's massive weight, even in the fireman's carry he's got him in.

I whip off my hoodie and slam it down over Eli's face to block the worst of the fumes, before doing the same for myself with my shirt. Then I scoop up the other backpacks, and we're running straight for the small hole in the flames. Correction—I'm running and Eli's staggering, and the hole is closing so fast that I'm terrified we're not going to make it in time. Of course, the rain has stopped, so any help it might have given us is long over.

"Come on!" I yell at Eli, wrapping my hand around his free arm and trying to drag him. It's like trying to move a mountain, especially when most of my strength is taken up by carrying three of the heaviest backpacks in creation.

By the time we get to the circle of flames, the opening we'd been aiming for has shrunk to the width of one human body. I shove Eli through in front of me, run through behind him. As I do, one of the backpacks catches on fire and the flames sweep all the way up the strap.

I drop it before the flames can do much damage to my bare skin, kick it along the ground until the fire is out, then scoop it up and keep running, despite the heat of the strap against my hand. There's fire everywhere, the smoke so thick I can barely see, and it's only getting worse. We need to find a way out of this hell. Now.

"Where do we go?" I scream at Eli. The fire has me lost, turned around.

"Over there." He points at a black truck, then dissolves in a fit of coughing so hard I'm afraid he's going to collapse a lung.

I take the lead then, heading in the direction he pointed, though I'm coughing so hard that running is almost impossible. Finally, I see it looming in front of us.

"Almost there," I tell Eli.

He nods, too out of breath to speak.

We stumble up to it, and Eli rasps, "I think the key's in my pocket. I found it on the guy."

I shudder a little at the image of Eli searching a dead man's pockets, but since it's about to save our lives, I can't be picky.

After opening the truck, I run around to the driver's side and climb in so I can help Eli maneuver Theo into the middle of the bench seat. As soon as he and Eli are both in, I start the engine and take off.

It's like the fire is chasing us, and in the end I hold my breath and pray Hollywood knows what it's doing as I imitate the movies and drive straight through a big patch of flames. The truck doesn't blow up or catch fire, which pretty much constitutes a miracle in my book, but I'm too busy driving and coughing to give thanks.

"How is he?" I demand of Eli, who's in even worse shape than I am. But Theo's not coughing much and it worries me. He inhaled as much smoke as Eli and I did.

"I'm okay," Theo rasps. Relief fills me. At least he's coherent enough to track the conversation.

I gesture to the backpacks. "Eli, get Theo some Advil and his antibiotic. They're in the front pocket of his backpack." I wish I could give him some of the painkillers from earlier, but I need Theo alert for a while.

Eli does as I instruct, and Theo downs them in a couple of swallows. Even that seems to be too much effort for him, and his head falls listlessly onto my shoulder.

"Hang on, Theo. I'll find somewhere for us to get you help." I don't know where, since most of the area has been abandoned, but it makes me feel better to say it.

At least until I go around a curve and see proof of why it's a terrible idea to taunt the universe about matters of bad luck, even worse to ask what else can happen, as I did a little while ago. Because it turns out I only thought we were in bad shape before.

"Look out!" Eli screams, even as I slam on my brakes in an effort to avoid plowing into the two black cars with darkly tinted windows that have put themselves directly in my path.

Men and women with guns pile out.

I start to throw the truck in reverse, but it's too late. Another two cars have pulled behind us, blocking us in.

Homeland Security has finally found us.

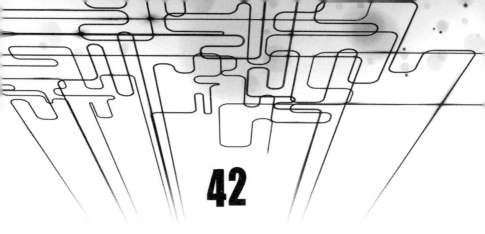

42

EXCEPT AS I GET A CLOSER LOOK at the agents surrounding our car, guns raised, I realize they're not being
led by Mackaray at all, but by Lessing. These people are FBI.
I don't know why, but somehow that makes me feel a little
better. Ridiculous, I know, but based on that late-night visit
to my house, if I had to choose an agent to be in charge of
me, Lessing would definitely be the one.

Still, that doesn't make getting out of the truck any
easier, especially when they grab Eli and Theo and immediately handcuff them.

"What are you doing?" I demand. "Where are you taking
my friends?"

"You aren't in a position to be asking questions, Ms.
Walker," says Lessing. "That's my job."

There's a hard edge to her voice that wasn't there when
I first met her in Austin. Oh, she wasn't easy on me then,
but now she looks like there's not much—if anything—that's

going to stand in the way of her doing her job. Certainly nothing as pesky or pissant as the United States Constitution.

Of course, with her blaming me for 104 nuclear power plants getting ready to blow up in America alone (it's amazing the trivia Theo knows), I can understand why she might not be interested in playing nice.

"He's sick," I say, pointing to Theo. "He's been shot." I'm coughing so hard I can barely understand myself, so I repeat the words. They need to get Theo some help.

"Let's go," she says to me, grabbing my arm and shoving me into the back of her SUV. I don't like that she's separated me from Theo and Eli, don't like that I can't know what's going on with them. Right away, my imagination conjures up the worst, most disgusting prison available. With Theo as sick as he is, he can't even put up a fight.

The idea torments me, and even as I tell myself to be quiet, not to give her any information, I beg, "Please. Tell me what you're doing with them."

"You ought to be more concerned about what we're going to do with you. *They* helped a fugitive flee custody, but you, Pandora, *are* a fugitive in the worst case of cyberterrorism ever committed."

"It wasn't their fault. Please, don't hurt them." Even as the words leave my mouth, I know how stupid they are. I have just given her everything she needs to take me apart. But I can't bring myself to care. Theo and Eli have done nothing wrong—they don't deserve to suffer just because they were concerned enough to help me try to save the world.

Sure enough, Lessing narrows her eyes. "If you want to

keep them safe, you need to give me something in exchange. Tell me how to stop this worm."

"I *can't*! Don't you think if I knew how, I would have stopped it by now?"

"I don't know." She settles back against the seat and looks at me. "When I met you at your house, I thought you were just some dumb kid. An unwitting pawn in this whole thing. But now . . . I've chased you halfway across the country, Pandora. You can't tell me it's just dumb luck that's kept you from being caught before now. Which begs the question: Who's helping you?"

Her words hit home, echoing my thoughts about how my father has used me. Somehow they hurt even more coming from her, though the look on her face says she isn't trying to be malicious. Which just makes it worse.

"Two boys I go to high school with. You just took them away."

"You're telling me they designed Pandora's Box?"

"No! Of course not. They just helped me . . ." I shut up, afraid of making it worse for Theo and Eli.

Lessing looks like she's going to press the point, but something changes her mind, because she looks toward the ethanol plant. That it's on fire is evident, even from this distance.

"Tell me about what happened over there."

"The storm swept through, damaged the tanks, caused a leak. Then lightning ignited the fuel, and the whole place blew up."

"What were you doing there?"

I shrug. "I don't think you'll believe me if I tell you."

"Pandora, in five days the world as we know it will

cease to exist, which is something I never thought I'd see in my lifetime. So, if you want to tell me something far-fetched, now is the time to do it." She holds out her arms, inviting me to trust her. But I don't know if I can. I don't know if the truth will make things better or worse for me. And, more important, for Theo and Eli.

When I don't immediately say anything, the momentary softness fades from her demeanor. "Okay, then, tell me about your father."

"I barely know him."

"If that's true, why are you the one running around out here, fleeing federal custody? Nearly getting blown up."

I don't know how much to say. If I admit that I know my father is responsible, will that make me look more or less guilty? I need to figure out how to play this, how to make her understand. Quickly, because if I don't find out what the next clue is, no one will.

Closing my eyes, hoping that I'm doing the right thing, I finally say, "My father sent me a birthday e-mail. The worm was a link. I uploaded it without knowing it."

"Twelve times?"

"Yeah. It was attached to pictures of the two of us. I clicked on them and . . . you know the rest."

"Why didn't you tell me this when I was at your house? Why did you run?"

"Agent Mackaray was threatening to throw me in a deep, dark hole. What would you have done?"

"Trusted the other officers there not to let that happen," she says, brows arched.

"I didn't have the luxury of trusting you."

"Yes, well, now I don't have the luxury of trusting you."

I have nothing to say to that, and for a long time, neither does she.

I'm just beginning to think the impasse between us is going to last forever when she says, "Give me something, Pandora. Something you can prove. Where have you been the last five days. What have you been doing?"

"You mean you really don't know? How did you find me here if . . ." I break off when I realize she hasn't traced me here. Her running into us was just more bad luck on our part. Like Mackaray in New Mexico, she was just covering the places my father was known to support. "Pure dumb luck, huh?" I tell her.

"There's a little more to it than that. The gentlemen you asked directions from were worried. They reported three teenagers alone at the ethanol plant. We did the math, and here you are."

That she shares something impresses me, and I tell her, "I've been playing the game. It's the only way to save the world."

"Are we back to that? We've had gamers around the world working on Pandora's Box since the worm uploaded, even had some make contact and try to assist you, and nothing's happened."

I think about CarlyMoon and her offer of help. It seems I'd been right to be suspicious. The thought depresses me more. Finally, determined to stay focused on the issue at hand, I ask, "Are they using the AR gates?" She looks startled. "Because if they're not, then they aren't going any-where. That's the key to the game. Drive evil out of the world with the techniques of the future. You have to com-plete the tasks if you want to level up."

"We've been leveling up. I've seen your father's rabid environmental agenda."

"His agenda actually makes sense, if you think about it." Am I seriously sitting here defending him? After everything that's happened? After everything he's done? "It's the way he's gone about it that's all wrong."

"He's set us back a hundred years, Pandora. Where's the money going to come from to fix everything he's broken?"

"Maybe we shouldn't fix it. Maybe we should make new stuff. Better stuff."

"And who's going to pay for that?"

I don't answer. I can't and she knows it. She presses her advantage. "This whole game is nothing but a pipe dream, Pandora. One that's going to become a nightmare very soon."

"It already is. Do you really think Theo, Eli, and I are having fun doing this? We're playing because we're the only ones who really have a chance of winning."

I wait for her to say something, but for a long time, she just studies me. And when she speaks, it's not exactly what I want to hear. "Don't bullshit me, Pandora."

"I'm not. I'm telling you the truth. We've been following the AR gates around for days—including the clues my father has left out in the real world. The only way to beat the game is to follow the virtual clues and the real clues all the way to the end."

"Really? And what are some of these real clues?"

"They're code words. From my life. From my time with my father."

"You said you barely knew your father."

"That's true. But he was around until I was seven, and I have memories from before that. For me, beating Pandora's Box is about going back and tracing that relationship. All the clues have had very special meanings to us, things that no one else will get."

Long seconds tick by as she studies me. Finally she says, "I can't decide if you're the world's best liar or if you really believe the absurdities you're spouting."

"Look, believe me, don't believe me. I don't care. But the fact of the matter is we both know that total annihilation isn't nearly as far-fetched as some people think. And from my perspective, Theo, Eli, and I are the only ones standing in the way of utter destruction."

"I thought you said the clues were for you." She pounces on this like a hungry cat on a cornered mouse. "But now you're saying Eli and Theo have been helping you."

"The game is complicated. They play with me. And in case you haven't noticed, it's a little dangerous out there. They've protected me as we searched for the clues."

"They protected you right out of governmental custody."

I don't answer, because really, what can I say? Theo and Eli did do exactly that.

"If you want me to believe all this, you need to give me something. What's the AR code to the first level?"

"Pomegranate," I tell her instantly. Believe me, this is not a secret I enjoy carrying around. If the government wants to help, I'm all for it—as long as it doesn't mean locking Eli, Theo, and me away in a dank room somewhere for the rest of our very short lives.

"Are you trying to be funny?" she demands.

"No. Try it. Have someone plug in the code and see what happens."

She seems like she wants to protest, like she's afraid I'll make her look like a moron. I don't push her—I have a feeling if I do, she'll completely shut down.

In the end, I think she decides that living is more important than looking like a fool, because she radios the code in to someone.

"Now what do we do?" I ask after a couple of minutes of silence.

"Now, we wait. If you're lying to me, you're going to be a very unhappy young woman."

A few minutes later, Lessing's radio crackles and she steps outside the car. She's only gone a few seconds before she yanks the door open and says, "Fine. You've got my attention. Tell me what you're looking for now."

"I have to play the next level of the game first."

She nods, grudgingly. "Fine." She calls for my backpack on her radio.

"I need Eli and Theo."

"Don't push it."

"I'm not. We work best together."

She studies me, then says reluctantly, "All right."

"They're fine?"

"They're alive and kicking."

I stare at her through narrowed eyes. "That's not the same as being fine."

"Yeah, well, it's the best you're going to get. Okay?"

"Okay." I mimic her bitchy tone and headshake. "Let's do this, then."

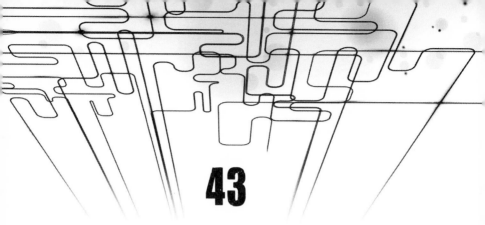

43

THEY DRIVE ME TO A MOTEL two towns over from the ethanol factory before they actually give me my laptop . . . or let me see Theo and Eli again. When they walk into the room Lessing has commandeered for me to play in, it's pretty obvious my friends have been messed with. Theo's old scrapes are bleeding again, plus he's got a number of new ones. And Eli is walking with a distinct limp.

"What did they do to you?" I demand as I rush toward them.

"Nothing," Theo says, with a look that tells me he'll explain later. At least he's more coherent than he was, the cloudy fever light gone from his eyes. Nice to know they got him medical treatment before they beat the hell out of him.

"So, you ready to play the game?" Theo continues softly. His way of telling me to cool it in front of Lessing and her crowd. Not that I need the reminder—I'm well aware that our every move is being watched, and that makes it difficult for me to think. I try to remember what it felt like to stand out here with my father, try to remember what we talked about. Any inside jokes we might have had, but nothing comes to me.

I hate this. Hate the helplessness of it, the fact that we are completely at their mercy.

"Hey." Theo reaches for my arm, pulls me toward him. That little *zing* of electricity shoots through me at the contact, but then it's drowned in the fountain of anxiety brimming inside me. "Pretend they're not here, Pandora."

"You make it sound so easy. Look at what they've done to you."

"We're fine," Eli assures me.

"No, you're not. And the last thing I want to do is help them when they've spent the last hour hurting you."

"So don't think of it as helping them. Think of it as getting us one step closer to your dad. We can't get there without this clue."

I know he's right, but it's hard to listen when blood is running down his face and darkening the bandage around his arm. I turn to Lessing, glare at her with every ounce of anger I have inside me. When she simply stares back blandly, it only increases my ire.

"Just ignore her," Eli suggests, handing me my computer before logging in to Pandora's Box himself.

"Where are we?" Theo asks after we drop into the game.

"Seattle, I think." I fumble for the seventh picture. "This picture was taken at Pike Place Market—I recognize the Public Market Center sign."

In the photo, I'm about five and I'm standing underneath

the iconic sign, arms up and a huge grin on my face. My shirt is hot pink, with white writing that reads, "Save Puget Sound." My dad is right behind me, dressed in wrinkled khaki shorts and a navy-blue T-shirt that proclaims, "Your Trash Doesn't Know How to Swim."

"Is there any environmental issue your father *doesn't* stand for?" Eli asks incredulously.

"He seems okay with nuclear holocaust. But that could be a new thing."

I turn to the game. We're in front of the Space Needle right now, but that's obviously not where we need to be. I'm not really sure which way Pike Place Market is from here, so I just take off running.

We end up making a few wrong turns—and seeing more dead virtual bodies than I've ever had any desire to, but eventually we make it to Pike Place. We enter at First Avenue and Pine Street, and then follow Pine until we get to Pike Place, which is the main drag of the market.

I'm not sure where I should look for the latitude coordinates—near the sign from the picture or somewhere inside here. We decide to split up, Eli and Theo looking in the market while I head for the sign. But I've gone only a few feet on Pike Place when I'm broadsided by the ugliest, scariest multiarmed, multiheaded giant I could possibly imagine.

If my Greek mythology is up to snuff, this is one of the three Hecatonchires, giants with one hundred arms and fifty heads. I don't know anything more about them—like what their weaknesses are—and I sure as hell don't know how to fight them. As the thing flings rocks at me, one right after the other, I duck behind the building and try to figure a way out of this.

I dodge the stones flying at me by weaving in and out of marketplace stalls. I round the corner and whip up Virginia Street and then down First Avenue again. Another giant jumps out at me, and suddenly I find myself sandwiched between two, both of whom look delighted at the prospect of ripping me limb from limb.

I punch one of them as hard as I can in a few of his one hundred eyes and then take off running while he's still howling. I almost make it to safety, probably would have, if the third giant didn't grab me and lift me clean off the ground.

I'm dangling about twenty feet in the air now, and it looks like I'm headed straight for his huge, slimy-toothed mouth. I shudder with disgust. Dying is one thing. Being eaten alive by a Hecatonchire is quite another, and one I don't have any desire to experience, even on a virtual plane.

Not that I have much choice in the matter. I have no idea how to get away from this guy, especially since his brothers are right behind him, backing him up. In the end, I use the only power I have that no one else does—that strange radiation I discovered way back in Zilker Park.

I start to glow from the inside out, and when I put my hands on the giant arm holding me, he screams and lets go. I start to fall, and the other arms try to catch me, but my whole body is glowing red-hot now, and every time I come into contact with him, the giant howls.

The only thing that saves me from hitting the ground hard enough to break every bone in my body is that at the last second I grab on to the lowest of the Hecatonchire's arms. He screams and shakes me off, but it's enough to break my fall. I land with a *thump* instead of a *crash*, and then I take off running again.

I take the first right onto what I think will be Stewart Street, but suddenly there are all kinds of new twists and turns within the marketplace. My father has turned Pike Place into a labyrinth, with three giants instead of a minotaur chasing me down. Of course, it's early yet and he could have that in store for me as well.

I slip into one of the farmers' markets, then drop to my hands and knees and start to crawl between the stalls. I know this isn't exactly a stellar expression of bravery on my part, but I figure living long enough to fight another day is more important, at least until Theo and Eli can get to me. They're on their way—surely I can hold on a little longer . . .

Except that the giants follow me into the market. They're way too big for the place, and each step they take squishes another booth. I duck into the flower stall, squeeze myself into a ball behind the sunflowers, and try to come up with a plan good enough to bring down three giants. Unfortunately, nothing comes to mind.

Glancing around, I realize there's a coil of rope under the table next to me. I don't know if it will work, but I figure it's worth a try, so I grab the rope and tie one end around the concrete pole I'm leaning against. Then I take hold of the other end and start to crawl through the booth and straight across the aisle to the fish market, making sure not to allow any slack on the line.

Within seconds, one of the giants comes running by. He

trips on the rope and falls flat, hitting the ground hard enough that everything bounces. He's groaning and trying to get to his feet when I grab the biggest knife the fish market has and leap onto his back, burying the blade right between his shoulders.

He screams in pain and rage, and then I'm plunging the knife in again. I think it hits his heart this time because the bellows stop, and all of his heads and arms collapse, lifeless, on the ground.

One down and two to go.

One of the other two giants is coming now, lured by the sound of his brother's agony. I don't think he'll fall for the rope-across-the-path trick, so instead I throw one end of the rope over a high ceiling beam that is just waiting to be used. I fasten the other end into a loose loop. I set it next to his brother's body and do my best to disguise it. Then I wait, breath held, to see if he will really be stupid enough to fall into my haphazard trap. Turns out he is, and more yells fill the marketplace as he is yanked off his feet.

"What is it with my father and these monsters?" I demand of the guys. "Has he raided every Greek myth in the damn world to make this game? Would it be so much to ask to get some normal people to fight?" I barely dodge razor-sharp claws in my face.

"Normal people aren't direct representations of Gaia," Theo says.

"The mother of the Titans?" I ask, confused. "What does she have to do with anything?"

"Mother Earth," he corrects me. "Don't you get it? Every creature we've fought has been an offspring of Gaia. Your dad has us set up in an adversarial relationship with the earth, one in which she's not only holding her own in most cases but also usually kicking our asses."

His words strike me hard. Is that what we've become in my father's eyes? Adversaries to the earth? I think back to the car ride to Hugoton, to how I was thinking that he had made us incredibly vulnerable, given us no way to protect ourselves.

Is that how he views the earth, then? How he sees Gaia? As this sentient being with no ability to protect herself from the whims and destructions of mankind, save the natural disasters that seem to dominate world news programs today?

If so, I see his point.

But how can he think that's enough to justify what he's done? That it's enough to account for the mass death that we've seen or that's yet to come? There has to be a better way. I don't know what it is, but I know that it must exist. Because this—I look around at the world of the game—this is so not okay.

Theo's avatar arrives at the market just in time to see the giant dangling upside down, his hundred hands already working to get himself out of the trap. Theo grabs the same knife I had earlier and uses it to split the giant open from chest to belly button.

Two down, one to go. And if I have my way, the boys can take care of that one. I have a bunch of numbers to find—six, to be exact.

I say as much to Theo and Eli and they agree, so I go running in the opposite direction from where I last saw the giant. Who knows if the coordinates are over here or not, but I'm good with assuming that they are. Of course, if it will get me out of here, I'm also good with assuming the coordinates are in Siberia.

I head out to the huge market sign. As I round the corner, I glance back and see Eli and Theo in the process of wrapping the rope around the third giant. He falls to his knees. Now that I know they have him under control, I run outside, circling the sign again and again. I look up at it. Nothing. Look at it from the back, the front, both sides. Still nothing.

I'm about to give up and go look somewhere else when one last idea occurs to me. I scale the sign, slipping twice on my way up and skinning my arms on the sharp edges of the *M*. But when I finally make it to the top I see the numbers, set on top of the word MARKET: N 41°10'18", W 105°51'48".

I shoot a look at Theo and Eli in reality, wait for them to join me before pointing out the numbers to them. None of us says them out loud and none of us writes them down, because I know once we give the government what they want, they're going to take everything. Seize control of the game and, more important, of us. And I don't care what Lessing said back there about cooperation, I know very well that the second we're no longer valuable to her, the three of us will get a one-way ticket to solitary confinement. And the world won't get a second chance.

Working with the FBI must be what it feels like to get in bed with the devil. Which is crazy, because if you had asked me three hours ago, I would have told you that I was already in hell, dancing to my father's tune. Suddenly

Dante's Inferno is making a lot more sense to me—there is more than one layer in hell, and the deeper I get into this thing, the farther down I spiral.

But good intentions will only get me so far, and when Lessing crosses to me, I know my time is up.

"You've found it," she says, and it is in no way a question. "What do we need to do?"

I fumble for a lie, but Theo jumps in. "We need to find a way to get to Arizona," he tells her.

For a second, I panic. Wonder how Theo could so misread what I'm thinking. I want to hide things from her, not invite her along for the journey.

"In the game?" Lessing asks incredulously.

"No. In real life."

"How do you know?" she asks.

He gestures to the name emblazoned across the wall we're standing in front of. Phoenix Designs.

And that's when I know. Really know. We're going to do it again. I'm not sure how, I'm not sure when, but we're going to escape from the FBI.

44

DAY SIX

THE NEXT MORNING, as we head out of Kansas, I wonder for the millionth time if Theo actually knows what he's doing. They haven't let the three of us be alone together since they first picked us up, but at least we have our backpacks again and we're all riding in the back of the same SUV. We can't talk much, but I take comfort in the fact that Eli and Theo are both where I can see them.

I did get a chance to look at the atlas. The coordinates we found, if I remember them correctly, are nowhere near Arizona. They lead to a spot in the middle of the wilderness outside of Cheyenne, Wyoming. That's the next stop on this crazy-ass tour. But figuring out where to go isn't the hard part. Finding a way to get there is.

Suddenly, the driver stomps on the brakes. Tires squeal and we spin out for a second before he manages to correct himself. I breathe a sigh of relief—the last thing we need is to be in another accident—but then someone slams into the back bumper of our car. Seconds later, another car swerves in front of us and hits its brakes. We bang into its front bumper.

We're stopped, totally caged in.

Lessing and the other driver both pull out guns, but a shotgun blast rips through the front windshield before they can so much as aim. The driver jerks, slams back against the seat in front of me, and then slumps over the steering wheel.

"Shit! Get down, Pandora." Theo throws himself over me as another shot slams into the car.

I don't bother answering, not that I can as my face is smashed into the upholstery and Theo is on top of my rib cage, both of which prevent me from drawing enough air to so much as utter a syllable.

Lessing fires off three shots from the front seat, and then I hear another shot, followed by a gurgling sound that sends chills through every part of my body. I've never heard a noise like that before and hope I never do again.

"What now?" Eli shouts.

Theo raises his head a little, looks around. I'm not sure what he sees, but suddenly he shoves the door open and climbs out of the car, yanking me with him. Eli slides after us and then we run. A few bullets fly past us, and I'm convinced we're going to be shot in the back. But no more gunshots follow the initial few, and a quick look back tells me that we're the last thing on our attackers' minds. They were never after us, weren't even after Lessing and the other agents, though it looks like they've managed to kill all of the ones in our convoy of five cars.

They want the gasoline *in* the cars.

I slow down a little as I watch a man squat next to one of the cars and place a jerrican under where the gas tank is. Then he sticks a knife into the tank, and I see gas start to drain into the can. It must not take long because in less than a minute, he's up again and headed toward the next car.

There are other men milling around, guns in hand, but they, too, seem much more interested in the gas than in us. Still, Theo tugs on my wrist, hard, obviously displeased with the fact that I'm not keeping up.

We don't stop until we get to a copse of trees pretty far from the road. Theo yanks me behind one of the large trunks, and I bend over, bracing my hands on my knees as I suck air into my starving lungs. We watch as they finish with the last of the cars, and then they all pile into the trucks that bracketed our SUV and are gone.

"So, that's where we've been screwing up," Eli cracks. "We've been stealing cars when we should have been stealing gasoline." His voice shakes a little, and when I look at him, he's staring back at the road. At the dead agents.

I want to scream. I wanted a way to get out of this latest mess, but I never wanted this. Not even when I realized what they had done to Theo and Eli while Lessing was interrogating me.

I look at Theo, who—for the first time—seems a little uncertain, like he's not quite sure what we're supposed to do now. Which means *I* have to know. And crying isn't going to solve anything.

The next stop on this tour is Wyoming, so that's where we're going. Even if it kills me.

"We need to go back to the cars," I tell them.

"They took the gas," Eli answers.

"Yeah, but they didn't open the doors, which means they didn't take our stuff." I'm not sure why they didn't, but I'm not going to look a gift horse in the mouth. Not now.

The walk back to the car seems a lot longer than our race away from it was. Once we get there, we scoop up our things from the cargo area where the agents put it, being careful not to look inside the car. "Where are we again?" I ask Theo.

"On Route Fifty-Six." He pulls out the atlas, which is looking kind of raggedy after everything it's been through, and flips to the road we're on while I rummage in the back of the cargo area for extra supplies—water, food, flashlights, whatever we can find.

"So?" I ask. "Which way is Wyoming?"

Theo looks at his compass, then points to the right. "About five hundred miles that way."

"Then I guess we'd better get started."

We've been walking for miles when we finally come across a farmhouse. But when we knock on the front door, there's no one home. Again. I swear, it's like *The Vanishing* around here.

"Check the garage," Eli says as he walks around the house to see if someone's in the backyard. "Maybe there's a car or something."

I go with Theo to check things out, but there's nothing there save a tool bench and a couple of bicycles. I'm about to suggest them as a mode of transportation when we hear

Eli shouting. We take off running. Or, to be more exact, Theo does. I do the best I can with my sore, bleeding heels, which isn't great. More of a hop, limp, shuffle, really.

When I finally catch up to them, they're standing in front of the barn, mouths agape as they stare inside. I approach slowly, not sure what to expect. A crazed farmer with a gun? A survivalist camp bent on killing all of us? The biker gang from Colorado back to get revenge?

Another week, in another life, those thoughts would have been absurd. But here, now, after the last few days, anything seems possible. At least until I look into the barn and realize it's not a barn at all. It's a hangar. An airplane hangar.

I turn to the guys, baffled by the excitement I see on their faces—at least until I remember that Theo built an airplane.

"Can you—"

"Yes." His voice never wavers.

"Are you sure?"

"Yes."

"Because if you aren't, we can find another way. This really isn't the only option." Except it is, and I think all three of us know it by now. But neither of them is contradicting me, neither is telling me to rethink my comments, which means that they think I have reason to be concerned.

"How many times have you flown before?" I demand as Theo walks toward the small airplane, running his hand smoothly over its side.

"Enough to know how to get us out of this mess."

"Okay." I'm willing to concede the point. "But is it

enough to land the plane? From what I hear, taking off is the easy part."

"I can do it." His voice is resolute, his eyes steady on mine when he continues. "You're just going to have to trust me."

I nod. I've trusted him all along. Why should now be any different?

Theo climbs up on the airplane, pops open the pilot's-side door, slips inside, and starts looking for something. I don't know what it is until there's a loud beeping sound and then the plane powers up.

"What are you doing?" I demand, scrambling into the seat next to him. "Are you ready to go already?"

He laughs. "I've got to check out the controls," he tells me as he messes with a few switches in the front, then goes over every gauge on the plane.

"Does it have enough fuel?" Eli asks him.

"I think so. It should get us to Wyoming, but I don't think it will get us much farther than the five hundred miles."

I nod, resigned to our fate—at least for the next little while. "Do you need any help?" I ask, though I have no idea what I'd look for if he says yes.

In response, Theo smirks at me. I choose to take that as a no.

So as he does his thing, I settle into the plane's small backseat. In theory, there is enough room for four people, but that's only if they're normal size. With Eli's and Theo's long legs and my own height issues, we're lucky to cram three of us in here. I hope Theo knows the weight limit of this thing . . .

Eli and I talk uneasily as Theo finishes up his flight check, and then we're ready to go. I think about all of the things that normally go into a flight—the ground support, air traffic controllers, the little guys with the orange sticks in their hands—and wonder how the hell we're ever going to get into the air alive.

Theo doesn't have the same doubts, though. He flips a few more switches, presses a couple of buttons, and then we're inching our way out onto the tarmac (though it's really more of a wide sidewalk).

"Ready?" Theo asks, after we've cleared the large barn doors.

"If I have to be," I respond.

"You bet!" Eli crows. I glance at him and he actually looks excited. His green eyes have that daredevil glow they get just about every time we do something dangerous. For a brief moment, I wonder what I look like in times like this. Probably like I'm going to throw up.

And then it's too late to worry or freak out. Way too late to change plans as we're cruising down the runway at an alarmingly fast rate.

I clutch my armrests and close my eyes as the plane rattles and growls its way along before pulling away from the ground, lifting off. Into the air.

It's an amazingly smooth takeoff. Maybe Theo knows what he's doing, after all.

I start to settle back in my seat, start to breathe a little bit, when something suddenly occurs to me. "Hey! How do you know where we're going? And if there will be a place to land when we get there?" The panic is back.

"I plotted the coordinates and already found our course," Theo answers soothingly. "As for the rest, I guess we'll figure it out when we get there."

Which is so not the reassurance I'm looking for. Overwhelmed, I lean my head back against the seat and close my eyes.

Somehow I make it through the next hour and a half without losing my mind, though I'm honest enough to admit that it's a close one. I remember hearing once that prolonged exposure to violence makes it easier to accept, more commonplace—that you go into a kind of amnesiac fugue. If so, there must be something wrong with me, because every day of this just makes me feel worse.

"Okay, I'm going to need your help." Theo's voice jolts me out of my reverie, and I flail upright, looking around wildly.

"What's wrong?"

"We have to find someplace to land this thing."

"We're there already?"

"As close as we're going to get, since the coordinates are actually in the middle of nowhere." He points to the wide expanse of forest below us.

"Are you sure you did this right?" Eli demands. "Shouldn't we be in a city or something?"

"No. Remember the atlas?" I say. Earlier, when we'd had access to an SUV, all that wide-open space had looked fascinating. Now it was just terrifying.

"There's the road," Eli says, pointing to what I suppose roughly qualifies as a road.

"That's not going to cut it," I tell him. "You can't land a plane on a dirt road. We'll all *die*."

"Yeah, but it connects up to something bigger. Look."

I do and realize he's correct. Theo must, too, because suddenly we take a sharp right to align ourselves with the road.

"Are you ready?" Theo asks.

"Are *you*?" Eli demands. "I don't think we're the ones you should be worrying about right now."

I tend to agree. Nervous, freezing, freaking out but doing my best to hold it together, I place a hand on Theo's shoulder, rub a little. Try to lend him whatever moral support I can.

He reaches up, clutches at my fingers for a second, and for the first time I realize he's as nervous as I am. So how does he do this? How does he just plow through every obstacle, even when he's worried? I feel like my fear is crippling me, making me useless, and he just steps up to the plate again and again and again.

I look over at Eli and realize he's watching our exchange. I think about pulling my hand away, but I can't. The last thing I want to do is hurt Eli, but Theo needs me, too, and as long as he does, I can't make myself let go of him.

Then Theo takes a deep breath, straightens his shoulders. When he looks back at me, the nervousness is gone and in its place is the familiar resolve that tells me everything is going to be okay. Theo won't let it be any other way.

We drop altitude fast, moving lower and lower until we're about level with the treetops. Then even that's too high, and we're moving lower, lower, lower . . . The wheels touch down and Theo slams on the brakes, hard.

It's a bumpy road, definitely not your average runway, and we skip and jump across it as he does his best to get us stopped. It takes a little longer than I expect—I guess small, private airplanes don't have the same braking systems as 747s. But eventually we roll to a stop. Impulsively, I lean over and hug both Theo and Eli. "We're alive!"

I'm out of the plane before Theo even takes off his seat belt, stretching my legs and considering kissing the ground for good measure. Eli clambers after me, picking me up and swinging me around as he laughs and laughs.

"I can't believe you did it, bro!" he tells Theo. "I mean, I know you're a wonder and all, but still. You flew the frickin' plane!" There's no trace of animosity in his voice, just pure joy. Despite everything, I'm shocked at how far we've come.

Theo's shoulders are a little slumped, relief written in every exhausted line on his face. "Yeah. I've never actually done that before."

"What?"

Eli and I both turn to him, slack jawed with astonishment. "I thought you and your dad built an airplane," I say.

"We did. But he always flew it. Obviously, he taught me what to do, but I've never actually soloed before."

"Well, then, you did even better than expected," I tell him, but my heart is beating triple time. I can't imagine how terrified he must have been.

He nods, starts gathering our backpacks out of the plane. "We'd better get going."

I shoulder my bag, nod. "Which way does your compass say?"

He looks at his watch. "That way."

We haven't been walking very long when we see a building in the distance. I start to walk faster, driven by an urgency I don't quite understand. Suddenly Theo and Eli are the ones struggling to keep up with me.

The closer we get, the easier it is to tell that we're going to a house, not a business. There's smoke curling out of the chimney, and a small woodpile sitting to the right of the front door.

And there's a man standing on the porch, watching us approach. As I get my first good look at him, everything inside me goes still.

Because the man I'm looking at isn't some stranger, like I first supposed.

He's my father.

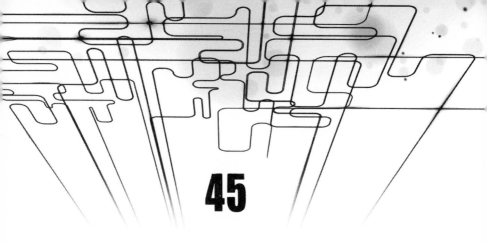

45

AS THE REALIZATION SLAMS through me, my feet stop moving of their own accord.

"Pandora?" Theo asks, reaching for me. I clamp on to his hand, weave my fingers tightly through his, and wait for the shock to stop ricocheting through me. It takes longer than I expect.

"What's wrong?" he asks.

Before I can answer, my father starts down the steps. "Pandora?" he calls as soon as he's close enough to really see my face.

Theo stiffens. He's figured it out, too.

"Are you all right? You look awful." My father runs up to me, reaches a hand out as if to touch me. I can't stop myself from physically recoiling.

"How could you?" I whisper, horror and anger and fear roiling around inside me until I think I'm going to explode. "You sick bastard! How the hell could you do this?" I'm screaming now. I can't help it. Now that I'm here, in front of him, I can't hold it in any longer.

"Oh, sweetheart, I'm sorry." He glances at Eli and Theo. "Who are you?"

"Pandora's friends." Theo's eyes are narrowed, his tone more unfriendly than usual.

"They saved my life, *a lot*, these last few days." I throw the words at him, a definite challenge.

His shoulders slump. "Come on into the house. We need to get the three of you cleaned up."

"What we need is for you to turn off this damn game."

"It's not that simple, Pandora."

"Sure it is. You upload the kill code and then we can get the hell out of here."

"Come inside." His tone is firmer now. "We'll talk."

When none of us make a move forward, he sighs. Then he turns around and walks back up the stairs and into the house. He leaves the door open, the choice up to us.

I'm pissed that he's still calling all the shots, but standing out here isn't going to do anyone any good. The guys must reach the same conclusion because we start forward as one.

As we cross the threshold, I'm a little shocked by how comfortable his log cabin is. It's warm and cozy, despite the chill in the air. There's electricity, the smell of coffee percolating. It's a far cry from the Unabomber cabin I was imagining.

"The bathroom's down the hall to the left," he says from the kitchen, where he's cutting thick slabs of bread to assemble sandwiches.

"This isn't a social visit, Mitchell." I can't bring myself to call him Dad. Not now, after everything that's happened.

He lays the serrated knife he's using on the counter, turns to me. "I know. I just thought you'd be more comfortable after you clean up."

"That's what we've been doing for the last five days. Cleaning up the mess you started." My voice breaks and I stop, try to pull myself together. I hate that I showed him even that small weakness. "Why would you do this?"

"Because I've tried everything else. This was the only way."

"Killing people? Destroying the world?" I gesture to myself, to Theo and Eli, both of whom look like they've been to hell and back. "This isn't a game. These are people's lives you're messing with."

"Do you think I like seeing you like this?" he counters, reaching for the coffeepot and filling four mugs. As he pours, I realize his hands are shaking. What does he have to be nervous about?

"I don't know what to think. What kind of man does this? What kind of father?"

Something in his eyes softens. "I'm sorry, Pandora. I didn't know what else to do. I've tried every way there is to get people's attention. Nothing else has worked."

"This isn't working, either. How can you not see that? People are terrified. They're dying in the streets."

"People die in the streets all the time—from famine, disease, war. This is no different, except that now it's here, where you can see it."

"That's your defense? A lot of the world's in bad shape,

so why not bring the whole thing to the brink of nuclear annihilation?"

He slams two mugs down on the table so hard that I think they're going to break. "Let's get one thing straight. The politicians brought us to this point, not me. With their lobbyists and campaign money and agendas that have nothing to do with their constituents or solving real problems. They've been warned, the world over, again and again and again, that they couldn't continue to do what they're doing. There are consequences to their actions."

"Death isn't a consequence! This isn't a game. These are people's *lives*."

"I know that," he replies fiercely. "Believe me, I know. They've been monkeying around with people's lives for decades. Filling the earth with chemicals, poisoning our land, our water, our food, the very air that we breathe, because turning their backs on the issues gives them a better chance of being reelected, and being reelected brings them more power and money. And you stand there and accuse me of murder?"

"How is what you've done any better? Have you been listening to the radio? It really is the end of the world out there. A nuclear power plant in England has already blown up. There's anarchy in every major city in the country, in the world." I take a step back, gesture to myself. "Look at us! Do you know how close I've come to dying these last few days? How many different times and different ways I've nearly been killed?"

"I can't stand the idea of your being hurt, Pandora." He

slumps down at the table, looking years older than he did when we first saw him. "I never wanted that."

"Never wanted? *You* did this. *You* created this worm, *you* sent it to me so I could set it loose. Don't tell me you didn't want exactly this to happen."

"I wanted you to see, to understand. I wanted a better life for you than the one you have now. A life where cancer isn't an everyday thing, where you have the chance to be happy and healthy and whole."

"Do I look happy? Do I look healthy? I know I'm not whole, not after everything I've seen and done these last few days to get here. None of us are." Theo reaches out, rubs a hand between my shoulder blades, and it's all I can do not to crumple right here. "There are some lines you can't cross. Some things you can't come back from."

"That's exactly my point!" He shoves back from the table, begins to pace. "We're at a crossroads. Not just you and me, but this entire planet. It's reached crisis stage. We can either go on the way we have and kill this planet once and for all, or we can start over and do things right this time."

"Do things right? Poisoning the planet with nuclear radiation is doing things *right*?"

He waves his hand. "That was never going to happen. I wouldn't have let it. Besides, I knew you'd make it in time."

"But I didn't, Mitchell. All those people died in England, and I couldn't do anything to stop it. The earth will be poisoned there for decades."

"That was a mistake. It shouldn't have happened. If they'd taken better precautions—"

"Are you listening to yourself? 'It shouldn't have happened. That wouldn't have happened. It's the politicians' fault.'" The words burst out of me. "Well, it is happening. And what about you? What are you responsible for? You can't really think you're innocent in all those people's deaths?"

"I know my sins very well, Pandora. I know the evils I've unleashed."

"Then stop them!" I plead with him. "Turn off the game before things get any worse."

"I can't do that."

"You mean you *won't* do it."

"I mean I *can't*. I'm not a monster. After what happened in England, I tried to stop it. But it's too late. It's taken on a mind of its own."

"What does that mean exactly?" Theo jumps into the conversation for the first time.

"It means that the fail-safes I built in aren't working. The back door I was planning on using to shut it all down has been corrupted." He pauses, takes a deep, shuddering breath. "I'm locked out of my own matrix."

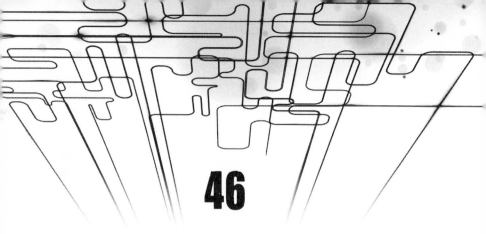

46

I'VE IMAGINED THIS CONFRONTATION countless times in the last few days, thought about it from every angle and every possible outcome. But I'm not prepared for those words. Not prepared for the idea that my father *wants* to stop things, but can't.

"Can I see what you've done?" Theo asks.

"Who are you exactly?" my father asks.

"He's my friend."

My father studies him for a minute, then shrugs. He crosses the room, pushes a button that slides the entire paneled wall to the side, and reveals a computer system that looks like it belongs in NASA instead of a log cabin in the middle of Wyoming.

Despite everything, Theo's eyes light up at the sight of it. Eli and I smile at each other—boy genius is very definitely in his element.

Theo sits down in my father's chair, his hands flying

across the keyboard. All kinds of code scrawls across the screen, lines and lines of symbols that I have no hope of understanding. My father stands behind him, watching the screen as intently as Theo. Every once in a while one or the other throws out a comment, but it might as well be Greek to Eli and me.

Long hours pass and Theo doesn't move from the chair, his fingers flying faster and faster over the computer keys. I feed him, take a shower, explore my father's cabin and the world directly outside it. Feed Theo some more. Watch him and my father work. Play tic-tac-toe with Eli. Take a walk.

I finally fall asleep around midnight. I'm sitting in one of the recliners in front of the fireplace, and everything that's happened these last few days catches up with me. If you'd told me a week ago that I'd be able to sleep with the threat of imminent nuclear annihilation hanging over my head, I would have called you a liar. But sitting here, knowing that the fate of the world is no longer in my father's hands—it's in Theo's—makes it so much easier to believe that things are going to be okay. When my eyes start to close, I let them.

I wake up a few hours later to see Theo stoking the fire. "Did you do it? Did you find a way in?"

"Not yet." His voice is grim as he drops down beside me.

"You'll do it." I scoot forward and press a hand to Theo's cheek. He looks so tired, so worn down, yet so much like a warrior, with his bruised face and battered body. Not to mention the bad-ass gleam in his eyes that tells me he's determined to run this thing down. It's hard for me to imagine I once thought he was crazy.

He closes his eyes at the first touch of my fingers. He

doesn't move away, so I trace one of the many cuts that still decorate his dark-angel face. He pulls in a sharp breath and I yank my hand away. "I'm sorry. Does it still hurt?"

"No."

"Oh." I put my hand back, lightly brush my fingers over the bruise on his high cheekbone, then move down his strong jaw to the cut on his chin, and over the small slices from falling debris that decorate his cheek. So many different injuries. So many different times he didn't back down when an average guy would have.

I pause at his full lower lip, then sweep my finger over the scrape there, toying with it. He looks at me again, and this time his eyes are so dark that I can't distinguish his pupil from his iris.

I know I'm playing with fire right now, know I should take my hand away just as I know that I'm not going to. I can't help myself, don't want to help myself. For days I've sat by and watched while Theo stayed cool and calm and in control, no matter what happened. I've watched him get beat up for me, shot for me, seen him do things that only someone incredibly brave or incredibly stupid would do, again and again and again.

It's hard to forget all of that, hard to think that it didn't mean something to him. Because it meant something to me, means something to me still as he continues to battle to save the world. I've never kissed Theo, but sitting here, touching him as dawn streaks across the sky, feels a million times more intimate than anything I've ever done before.

Then Theo stands up abruptly, pulls me outside. My dad and Eli are asleep, but I understand his need for privacy. I feel the same way. Out here, as red and purple and orange make their way across the early morning sky, I don't want to think about everything that's waiting for us, all the responsibility we still have to carry. I just want Theo to kiss me.

It's cold out, the wind harsh, but I barely feel it as Theo presses me back against the house. His arms come around me and he holds me to him, his chin resting on the top of my hair. "This isn't the right time," he tells me.

"I know."

"Everything's messed up, confused."

"It is."

He smiles against my hair. "You don't care, do you?"

"Not really. Not anymore."

"I really like you, Pandora. I don't want to make a mistake with you."

"Life's full of mistakes, Theo. And if you don't kiss me now, when are you going to? We're almost out of time."

"I won't let us run out of time."

I think about everything we've been through, everything he still has to do to end this nightmare. "Promise?" I ask.

He doesn't answer. Instead he puts a finger under my chin, tilts my face up until I'm looking him in the eye. Then he lowers his mouth to mine. And I was right. I've never, ever felt anything like it.

It's fireworks after a baseball game, a cool dip in the pool on a sweltering, summer day. Front-row seats at a kick-ass concert.

It's the sweetest melody I've ever heard, playing in my head over and over. I don't ever want it to end.

I press myself against him, wrap my arms around him, and tangle my fingers in the cool silkiness of his too-long hair. The hair that should have been a tip-off about who he really was all along.

His arms harden around me, his hands clenching at my back as his lips move gently against mine. His tongue comes out, traces my lower lip, and I gasp at the sweetness of it.

Theo laughs a little, and then he's kissing me, really kissing me, his tongue sliding against mine as rockets—forget the fireworks—launch all around us.

I laugh, too, even as I draw him deeper. He tastes like spicy cinnamon and smooth, sweet caramel. He tastes like hope, which I need more now than I ever have before.

We're both breathing hard and he starts to pull away, but I stand on my tiptoes, yank his mouth back to mine. I'm not giving this up—not giving *him* up—at least, not yet. I want to hold him to me a little longer, to take his light inside me until it burns so brightly that nothing diminishes it, not even this nightmare we're both locked into.

It's Theo's turn to gasp, and then he's kissing me everywhere—his lips traveling over my cheek to the ticklish spot behind my ear.

Down my neck to the hollow of my throat.

Across my eyes to my temples and back over my jaw to my lips again.

I don't know how long we stand there, kissing and touching and murmuring to each other, but when he finally pulls away, his lips are swollen and the dazzling colors of the morning sky have faded to blue.

"We need to go in," he whispers.

"I know." I fight the urge to beg for just a little more time.

"You know, no matter what happens, we're going to have to call someone. Your dad—"

"I know."

"I'm sorry."

"He made his choices. He deserves to go to jail. No matter how good his agenda was, no matter how much he wanted to help, this isn't the way."

Theo nods, then leans down and kisses me one more time. I cling to him, cling to this one perfect moment before letting him go. He takes my hand and we walk back inside.

Eli's sitting on the couch, reading. He looks up with a smile that quickly clouds over when he sees my fingers twined with Theo's. He doesn't say anything, though. For long seconds, none of us do. We just stand there, absorbing this newest shock wave to rip through our world. It's so much less, yet so much more, than the ones that have come before it.

Finally, Theo walks over to the computer and starts to work. I head into the kitchen to find something for breakfast, and Eli . . . Eli heads outside without another word.

I follow him, the cabin door slamming behind me like a gunshot. I expect Eli to be sitting on the porch, but he's not there. Instead, he's halfway across the meadow, running like the demons of hell are after him.

I don't stop to think, don't try to figure out what I want to say. I just take off after him. He's faster than I am, though. Has more stamina, especially after everything we've been through the last few days. I finally get a stitch in my side and have to pause as I struggle for breath.

I expect him to keep going, but a few seconds later, he circles back. Drops onto the ground at my feet. And smiles up at me—that same charming grin I used to see before I got to know the real him. It hurts a little to see it now, to realize he's using it as a form of self-protection—against me.

I sit down beside him, but don't touch him. For a long time, I don't say anything and neither does he. We just sit there, staring out at the horizon. Finally, he comments, "You and Theo, huh?"

I nod. "Pretty much."

"You know he's a mess, right? His dad's death really screwed him up."

"Yeah, because the two of us are such pictures of mental health."

He laughs, drapes an arm over my shoulder. "It was worth a shot."

"Give me a break. If things were normal, you'd be so blinded by your harem that you wouldn't even know I existed."

"Sure I would." He reaches over and plays with a strand of my still-brown hair. "None of my harem had purple hair, after all."

"Well, there is that."

"Anyway, normal is highly overrated."

"I don't know." I lay my head on his shoulder, watch as a flock of birds takes off, flying in some preordained formation as they fill the sky. In no way disrupted by the nightmare that has all of mankind in its grip. "I kind of miss normal."

He sighs. "Me, too."

We sit there for a while, quiet but content—or as close as we can get to content with the fate of the world hanging in the balance. At least until Eli's stomach growls and shatters our hard-won peace.

"Come on, let's go." I leap to my feet, extend my hand to help him up. "I'll make you some eggs." It's a peace offering, and we both know it.

He stares at me for a second, his crazy green eyes lit up with emotions neither of us wants to explore. Then he asks, "Scrambled?"

"Uh, yeah. It's the only kind I know how to make."

He grabs my hand, lets me drag him to his feet. "Race ya." This time, he's the one who takes off without saying go.

I follow, laughing, as the sun beats down on me. Maybe everything is going to be all right, after all.

Half an hour later, I'm in the middle of cooking Eli's eggs when my father's computer lets out one long, high-pitched *beep*. Theo shouts in triumph, and seconds later my dad slams out of his room. His bare feet slap against the concrete floor as he runs down the hall. Even Eli gets up from his spot on the couch.

"Dude, you're in?" he asks incredulously.

"I'm in."

"Awesome!" I run over to see what he's done, but stop when I see a gun in my father's hand. A gun that's pointed directly at the center of Theo's chest.

"Mitchell! What are you doing?"

"I never thought he'd manage it." He shakes his head, bemused. "You're almost as good as I am, kid. I'm impressed."

Theo doesn't move, doesn't so much as blink. He just stares my father down even as his life flashes before my eyes.

Ignoring Eli's warning shout, I shove between them. It's my turn to face my father. "Really? You said you wanted to end this thing."

"I do. Just not yet. One more day and we can turn the game off. If we do it now, it will ruin everything." The hand holding the gun shakes violently, but he keeps it aimed straight at me.

Which is where I want it. Better me than Theo. From the way he's snarling behind me, I know Theo disagrees. But I don't care. I'm betting on the fact that my dad won't shoot me. And if I'm wrong, then it's still better me than either Theo or Eli.

"You've already ruined everything," I tell him. "You're just too stupid to realize it."

"By tomorrow, the water plants will go out. Shipments will have been disrupted long enough for gas to be a problem, even for the government. Generators will fail, and things will grind to a halt. Forever. It will be beautiful."

"You're insane!" I back up so my body is covering as much of Theo's as possible.

"I'm a visionary. You'll see."

"You're a madman."

"I'm also your father. And I'm ordering you to move aside."

"After Theo stops the worm."

"That's not an option." He lifts the barrel of the gun, points it straight at my head. "Step away from the computer, Theo."

"Theo, don't . . ."

But it's too late. He's already stepping back.

"Good. Now, Pandora, sit down. We're going to fix whatever your boyfriend messed with."

I know I should do what he says. Know that defying him will do nothing, as he can fix it himself anytime he wants. But I won't do it. There's no way I'll sit in his chair and help him destroy the world. He already used me for that once.

My father sees the refusal in my eyes, and his face falls. The gun wavers, and I brace myself for the feel of a bullet ripping through me. But he doesn't shoot. Even when I'm sure that he will, he doesn't. Instead, I hear the soft *snick* of the gun uncocking. And then it hits the ground. Hard.

"Pandora, please. We can change everything," he pleads.

"You already have." I bend over, pick up the gun, then turn and walk out the door. Back toward a world turned upside down and an airplane that is almost out of fuel. It won't get us far, but it will get me away from him. Away from here.

Eli and Theo are behind me as we walk away from my father and all of his empty promises. None of us speak. There isn't anything to say.

When we get back to the plane, I walk straight to the radio at the front, turn it on. Send out a call for help.

"What are you doing?" Eli demands. "You're going to get us caught."

I ignore him, send out another call. I'm doing what I should have done the second I realized where we were. Who we were with.

For long seconds the radio waves are empty, and I'm about to try again when a voice crackles back at me. "This is Sergeant Michael Butler from the Wyoming Police Department. What kind of assistance are you in need of?"

I freeze for a second, try to find my voice even as my heart races. I didn't let myself hope that someone would really answer. Finally, I take a deep breath and say, "My name is Pandora Walker. My father, Mitchell Walker, is responsible for the Pandora's Box worm. I've found him, here in Wyoming." Under Eli's stunned gaze, I give them our GPS coordinates.

The police officer has a lot of questions, but I don't answer them. Don't say anything else at all as I reach over and flip the radio to Off. I know the day is coming when I'll have to give the government a full explanation of everything that has happened. But that day, God willing, isn't today. Not when there's still so much at stake.

I turn to say as much to Theo, to tell him and Eli that we have to go, but he's not standing behind me like I expected him to be. Instead, he's scrunched into the passenger seat, my laptop on his lap.

"What are you doing?" I demand.

He looks at me then, for the first time since we left my father's house. Theo's eyes are fierce, and the smile on his face is even fiercer. He holds up a USB drive.

"What is that?" I ask, trying to grab it.

He holds it out of my reach. "The game matrix."

I feel my legs go weak beneath me. "You stole it from him?"

"Damn right, I did!" He slides it into one of the empty drives on his laptop. "And now we'll see if I'm half as clever as I think I am."

The next few minutes pass in tense, horrifying silence as Eli and I watch Theo's fingers fly across the keyboard. I shudder, fight fatigue and fear as he tries to work his magic. I refuse to get my hopes up—the disappointment might kill me if it turns out there's nothing he can do—but I can't help it. Hope is a fragile feather right below the surface of my consciousness. A stiff breeze will blow it away, but until then—until then—it trembles and shakes in the sharp, prevailing winds of fear and disillusionment.

Finally, when my nerves are frayed and I'm convinced I'll die if Theo doesn't say something, he shoves the laptop away from him.

"Well?" demands Eli. "What did you do?"

"See for yourself," Theo says.

I turn the computer to face me, watch as the walls of Pandora's Box start crumbling on the screen. "You stopped the game?" I whisper.

"I did more than that," Theo answers as words and numbers begin scrawling across the screen. "I destroyed it. But before I did that, I traced it into every nuclear power plant it's touched and dug out the program that took control of the centrifuges. It's over."

He points at the screen, which now reads:

Total annihilation in 1, 2, 3, 4, 5, 6, 7, 8, 9, 10 days . . .

"Does that mean what I think it does?" Eli asks, reaching out to trace the numbers on the screen.

Before any of us can answer, the present that started it all takes over the screen. Except this time, instead of opening, it rewraps itself. There's something inside and I strain to see it. Nearly cry out when I can finally read the word: "Hope."

Theo's given it back to the world.

The box grows bigger and bigger until it explodes, little shards of hope raining down over the whole screen—the whole world—like confetti.

"Time to start all over," Theo says.

"With the game?" Eli asks incredulously.

"With the world," I tell him. Then I throw my arms around Theo and hug him as hard as I can. "You did it."

"We did it." He kisses me, hard, then throws back his head and laughs. Soon Eli and I join him. We stand there for a long time, looking out over the fields that surround my father's house as we contemplate the idea that our imminent deaths are no longer guaranteed. We might very well live long, productive lives.

They won't be the lives we had once planned for ourselves, but in this place, at this moment, that doesn't matter. Nothing does except that we—like so many others—will have the chance to live, after all.

"So," Eli eventually says. "What do we do now?"

The words carry with them endless possibilities and challenges. For a moment, I'm paralyzed by how much everything has changed and how very much there is left to do. But then I remember his response when I asked that same question only a few days ago.

I gather up my backpack, hand the guys theirs as well. Because if there is one thing this wild nightmare of a ride has taught me, it's that there is no going back.

Not in the game.

Not in our lives.

Not in anything.

We can only push forward into the new reality set before us. Push forward and hope like crazy that we're doing the right thing. Because in this world, there are no guarantees.

"What do we do now?" I repeat Eli's question. "What else?" I say. "We walk."

As the distant sound of a police helicopter breaks the stillness all around us, I hop down out of the plane. Wait as Theo and Eli do the same. Then, together, we set off in the opposite direction from my father's little house of horrors.

It's a brave new world out here, and I, for one, can't wait to be a part of it.

ACKNOWLEDGMENTS

With any book an author writes, there are many people to whom she owes thanks. But with this book, the number of people to whom I owe gratitude surely stretches into the hundreds. This book really did take a village to write and edit and name and design, and I am thankful to each and every person who helped me along the way.

First of all, I need to thank the wonderful and amazing team at Walker Books for Young Readers: Emily Easton, Stacy Cantor Abrams, Laura Whitaker, Donna Mark, Regina Roff, and Patricia McHugh. I know this book has been a major undertaking, and I can't begin to express how thrilled and grateful I am with the final product. Thank you, thank you, thank you from the bottom of my heart.

I also need to thank my dear friends and the other two-thirds of Ivy Adams, Shellee Roberts and Emily McKay, who put up with texts, e-mails, and phone calls at all hours of the day and night while I was trying to work out all the twists and turns of this story. I truly believe this book would never have been written without the two of you, and I appreciate you more than I can ever say.

A huge thank-you goes out to Sherry Thomas, who clipped Stuxnet articles for me, brought me cake, and gave me the swift kick in the butt I so desperately needed to finish the last few chapters of this book. Though I changed it to an airplane in this version, I still call dibs on the Hot Air Balloon idea.

I also owe my husband, intrepid electrical engineer that he is, a huge debt of gratitude. Thank you, honey, for patiently answering the thousands upon thousands of questions I peppered you with while writing this book. I can't imagine how tired you grew of hearing, "What do you think of . . ." and "Just tell me if this is possible . . ." I couldn't have written *Doomed* without you.

Thank you, the brilliant Skye White, who patiently brainstormed with me at the very inception of this book and who first thought up the idea of using an MMO; I owe you more than I can say. Thank you so much.

I also have to thank my ARWA chapter mates Ana Farrish and Jackie Hinson, who answered a million gaming questions for me, no matter how minute, impractical, or just plain stupid they were. You're the best!

As for my wonderful, wonderful, wonderful agent, Emily Sylvan Kim, who has stuck with me through four pseudonyms, twenty-six books, and countless ideas, I don't even know what to say. Thanks for being my biggest cheerleader and confidante (and also the voice of reason when I need it most). And thank you, thank you, thank you for saying those ten fateful words that changed everything: "What if Pandora opened an attachment instead of a box?" I can't imagine making this journey with anyone but you.

To my three terrific sons, who put up with the worst summer on record when I was writing *Doomed* and *Tempest Unleashed* back-to-back, thank you so much for being such amazing kids. I really got lucky with the three of you.

And finally, I want to give a huge shout-out to my fans, who have waited and waited for this book to finally hit the shelves. Thank you so, so much for your support and unflagging enthusiasm. You truly make this job a joy for me.